MASTERCLASS

MASTERCLASS

MORRIS WEST

St. Martin's Press
New York

For
my new grand-daughters
Siobhan and Natascha Louise

MASTERCLASS. Copyright © 1988 by Companià Financiera Perlina SA.
All rights reserved. Printed in the United States of America. No part of
this book may be used or reproduced in any manner whatsoever
without written permission except in the case of brief quotations
embodied in critical articles or reviews. For information, address
St. Martin's Press, 175 Fifth Avenue, New York, N.Y. 10010.

Library of Congress Cataloging-in-Publication Data

West, Morris L.
    Masterclass / Morris West.
        p.   cm.
    ISBN 0-312-05895-0
    I. Title.
    PR9619.3.W4M37 1991
    823—dc20   90-28090
                                                                    CIP

First published in Great Britain by Century Hutchinson Ltd.

First U.S. Edition
10 9 8 7 6 5 4 3 2 1

The study of the beautiful is a duel in which the artist cries out in terror before he is vanquished.

Baudelaire, *An Artist's Confession*

People always confuse the man and the artist because chance has united them in the same body.

Jules Renard, *Journal*

AUTHOR'S NOTE
I have been buying and living with pictures for
more years than I care to remember.

This book translates the experience of those
years into a fiction whose personages exist
only on the printed page.

M.L.W.

ONE

At thirty-five, Maxwell Mather counted himself a fortunate man. His health was excellent. His body was trim, his looks still unravaged. His bank balance was comfortably in credit. A prolonged sojourn with folk richer than himself had taught him frugality and given him a certain skill in the management of money. He had a modest reputation as a scholar, both in the study of ancient manuscripts and in the history of European painting. He had a generous patroness who lodged him in discreet luxury in an antique tower which was a dependency of her villa. He had an occupation which taxed him not at all: custodian and conservator of the Palombini archive; thousands of books, folios and bundles of yellowing files, stored tier on tier in the cavernous vaults which had once been the stables and the armoury of the household guard.

In the beginning the place had been called 'Torre Merlata', because it was built as a watch-tower with battlements and embrasures for bowmen and cannoneers. Over the centuries the words had been shortened and softened to 'Tor Merla' – Blackbird Tower.

The name was apt, because there was a big chestnut tree in the courtyard where singing birds nested – safe from the cold mountain winds, sheltered from the parching heats of Tuscan summer. In the mornings Pia Palombini would ride up in the electric inclinator from the villa below and settle herself on a chaise-longue in a sunny angle, whence she could watch him while he worked and share the tales recorded in the frayed yellow pages – the lawsuits and lecheries, cabals and conspiracies of the high families of Florence, the Palombini among them.

In the evening he would dine at the villa, in the vaulted refectory where the pine logs blazed in the great fireplace under the carved escutcheon of the Palombini . . . 'on a ground azure, a

1

cross gules, quartered with doves volant'. Afterwards, when the servants were dismissed, they would make love in the big *letto matrimonio* with its brocaded drapes and golden tassels and its long history of passionate encounters. Sometimes, without warning, Pia would tire of the pastoral rhythm of their days and whirl him away to Venice, to Paris, to London or Madrid, to shop extravagantly and entertain lavishly.

It was an agreeable existence, which Mather accepted without guilt and without question. He was good-tempered and good-looking, potent in bed, a well-mannered escort, an intelligent talker, an acceptable guest at any party. He fitted perfectly into the historic role of *damigello* – the squire, the scholar in residence, who earned his keep and kept his place, and posed no threat to the heirs because milady might love him but would never marry him.

Then one fine spring day Pia, who had been feeling poorly, went to consult her physician in Florence. He sent her to Milan immediately for extended clinical tests. The verdict was unanimous: motor neurone disease, a wasting and atrophying malady of the nervous system. There was no cure. The prognosis was emphatically negative. All that was in doubt was whether the end would be swift or slow in coming.

Either way the progress of the disease would be inexorable: a wasting of muscles and tissue, a steady failure of the nervous system, an increasing risk that the patient might suffocate or choke to death.

When Pia told Mather the news, she asked him bluntly whether he wanted to stay or go. He said he would stay. When she asked him why, he managed the most graceful lie of his life and told her that he loved her. She kissed him, burst into tears and hurried from the room.

That night he had a macabre dream in which he lay shackled to a corpse in the old four-poster bed. When he woke, sweating and terrified, his first impulse was to pack his bags and flee. Then he knew that he could never live with the shame of such a desertion. Indolence and self-interest added strength to the conviction. He was living in a hot-house. Why step out into the winter cold? Pia was lavish in her demonstrations of gratitude.

2

It was not too hard to offer her the simple decencies of tenderness and compassion.

At mealtimes he sat next to her, instant to help if she had a choking fit, dropped a fork or became breathless. As the spasms became more frequent and the wasting more apparent, he would bathe and dress her, walk her in her wheelchair, read to her until she dozed off by the fireside. The women of the household, who at first had called him milady's lapdog, now gossiped his praises. Even Matteo the major-domo, crusty and ill-tempered, began calling him 'professore' and telling his cronies in the wine-shop that this was a man of heart and honour.

Pia herself responded with the desperate affection of a woman seeing her beauty ravaged, her passion numbed, her life reduced to borrowed months. She gave Mather expensive gifts: a Tompion watch which had belonged to her English grandfather, a signet ring of the sixteenth century with the arms of the Palombini engraved on an emerald, a set of cufflinks and dress-studs made by Buccellati. Each gift was accompanied by a note in her once-bold hand which now was becoming shaky and uncertain: 'To my dearest Max, my scholar in residence whose home-place is my heart . . . Pia.' 'To Max, through whom I will continue to live and love . . . Pia.' The notes were all dated by feasts – Ferragosto, Easter, Pia's name day, his own birthday. He kept the notes, squirrelling them away with other mementoes. Of the gifts themselves he protested to Pia.

'They're too many – and too precious! They put me in a false position. Look. You pay me generously. But I do work. I'm not a kept man; I don't want to be. When I came here the Palombini archive was a shameful mess. Now it's beginning to look respectable. Given time, I can make it something the family can be proud of. It's one way I can pay back some of the debt I owe you . . . You're not angry with me, are you?'

Angry? How could she be angry? All he had done was provoke her to new expressions of attachment. There were days when she could not bear to have him out of her sight. There were nights when she begged him to take her to bed – not for sex but for simple comfort, like an ailing child. Then when he held her in his arms she would become petulant and tearful because he was not stirred as he used to be.

3

At weekends, mercifully, he was free. Pia's family came visiting – uncles, aunts, cousins, nephews, nieces, in-laws of every degree. They came to pay respect, show solicitude and make sure their names, deeds and kinship were remembered in her will. They had disapproved of Pia's scandalous follies, but now that the sexual association with Mather was clearly ended they were prepared to accept him as a family retainer, like a physician or a confessor. They approved the geography of the thing, whereby she kept to the villa and he was relegated to celibacy and solitude in the Tor Merla.

In fact, his weekends were neither celibate nor solitary. He had acquired a girl-friend in Florence, Anne-Marie Loredon, a leggy blonde from New York – daughter of a senior auctioneer at Christie's – who was studying in Italy under an endowment from the Belle Arti. She was lodged, expensively for a student, in a roof-top apartment behind the Pergola Theatre. They had met over drinks at Harry's Bar, found each other agreeable, spent a night together, found that agreeable too and – presto! – struck a bargain. Mather would install himself as weekend lodger and pay his bill with wine, food and scholarly instruction in the arts. The sex, they both agreed, was a bonus – no strings, no price-tag, no questions.

The arrangement worked well; they were a pair of acknowl-edged egotists openly using each other. At the end of her studies Anne-Marie would become a dealer and an auctioneer like her father. For the present, she had a good-looking escort and an entry into the folk world of Florence – the old craft families of sculptors, brassfounders, workers in stone, wood and leather, the painters, engravers and potters.

Mather for his part was offered safe sex, a base in the city, a message centre and a legitimate identity amongst his peers. With Anne-Marie he could shrug off the griefs of the Palombini house-hold; with the Florentines he could present himself as a working scholar, librarian and archivist to a noble family. This identity would soon become vitally important to him. His patroness was dying; he would be forced to find a new place in the academic world.

So he chose his Florentine friends carefully. First among them was the Custodian of Autographs at the National Library, a

4

white-haired savant who looked like Toscanini. To him, Mather paid special deference. Every Saturday he would bring an item or two from the Palombini collection and discuss its significance and its value with the old man, who had an affectionate regard for his younger disciple.

In the arts, his closest friend was Niccoló Tolentino, a small, gnomish man with a hump on his spine and a wonderful limpid smile. He was Neapolitan-born and had served a youthful apprenticeship to a fashionable artist who lived in Sorrento. Now he was the senior restorer at the Pitti and reputed to be one of the great copyists and restorers in the business. To him Mather brought one panel of a badly defaced triptych of the Dormition of the Virgin and asked him to restore it as a birthday gift for Pia. The little man turned in a beautiful imitation of Duccio – all gold leaf and heavenly blue. Mather was delighted and paid him instantly in cash. Tolentino responded by inviting him to dinner and regaling him with hair-raising stories of fakes and forgeries and the shadowy millionaires of Greece and Brazil and Switzerland who commissioned the theft of masterpieces and their illegal export.

Meanwhile, with Anne-Marie, he paid court to the senior scholars and connoisseurs of the town. They made assiduous rounds of the galleries. Mather let it be known that he was working on a small monograph: 'Domestic Economics in Florence at the Beginning of the Sixteenth Century'. This would be based on one of the less spectacular items in the Palombini archive – a set of account books kept by the steward of the villa from 1500 to 1510. These recorded sales and purchases of every conceivable item: wine, oil, cloth, cordage, tallow, livestock, furnishings, harness and ornaments for the horses. They were also the volumes which he displayed most frequently to the Custodian of Autographs, seeking his interpretation of archaic names and unfamiliar abbreviations. The nature of the task he had set himself matched perfectly with the image of the comfortable well-subsidised scholar, content to paddle quietly down a never-ending stream of historic trifles.

His liberty ended at eight o'clock on Sunday evening. Pia would be waiting for him, tired and fretful after the siege of relatives. He would share supper with her – tea and English-style sandwiches. She would expect a chatty little account of his weekend adventures and encounters, which had to be reasonably accurate because, in her more desperate moments, she was quite capable of checking the details through informants in the city. A family which had carried the gonfalon of the Medici was still a name to conjure with in Florence.

She knew that he lodged with Anne-Marie Loredon; she didn't like the idea, but accepted the fiction that Anne-Marie's father was an old friend and Mather had no sexual interest in the girl, nor she in him. Pia would not believe that he lived a sexless life, so he told her that he took his pleasures in a well-known and exclusive house of appointment, where the sex was clean but a whole world away from the passionate and selfless love he bore for Pia Palombini. Since there was no rival to shame her, she shrugged this off as a necessary indulgence. Sometimes she made him share the fun by telling her scabrous little stories of bordello life and practice. She would keep him talking until nearly midnight and then he would carry her to bed, settle her amongst the pillows and walk wearily to the tower, black and menacing against the night sky.

Once inside there was no need to lie any more. He was alone with what he was – a half-good scholar, a lazy, venal man working out his bond service to a dying lover and wondering how the hell he was going to organise the rest of his life.

Meantime, day by painful day, Pia Palombini declined towards death. She was still lucid, but the choking spasms and respiratory blocks were becoming more frequent. She was losing weight rapidly and when he took her in his arms she was fragile as a Dresden doll. Mather now insisted that the family arrange for her to be attended by a day and a night nurse and for her physician to make a daily visit. He hated to see her suffer, hated more to see her humiliated by her illness. He dredged up comfort for her from the most unlikely corners of his nature. When she pleaded with him to end her misery, he was tempted to it more strongly than he would ever have thought possible. He even went so far as to raise the question with her physician, who fixed him with a shrewd but sympathetic eye and warned him, 'This is not Holland, Mr Mather; we have much more Christianity and much less compassion in our law. So put any thought of mercy killing out of your mind. It would release her; it would put you and me in prison. Lend her your love a little longer. One day soon she will simply stop breathing.'

Which was exactly how it happened: one cold winter evening, while the night nurse was knitting at the fireside and he was seated on the settee cradling Pia in his arms, she reached up a tiny clawed hand to touch his cheek. Then, as if the effort were too much, she gave a small sigh of weariness, turned her face to his breast and died. He carried her upstairs, watched the nurse settle her decently in the bed, called the doctor and the family and the parish priest and then sat by the dying fire, lonelier than he had ever felt in his life. He had escaped her at last, as he had so long wished to do. The real irony was that she had escaped him. She had been the focus of his life for so long that now there was nowhere to look except inwards at the fragmented image of himself.

At the funeral he tried to spare the family embarrassment by joining the group of villa staff; but when the coffin had been carried into the vault and the bronze doors were closed and locked, he found himself weeping uncontrollably. Then he felt a protecting arm clasped around his shoulders and heard old Matteo's voice crooning a litany of comfort.

'There now, *professore!* You must be happy for her. She has no more pain. She is beautiful again. She wants you to remember her like that.'

All of which was easy to believe. What he could not understand was the black desolation inside himself. When he had told her months before that he loved her, it was with the conventional reservation that had always attached itself to their relationship. They were in love, they were acknowledged lovers, they were everything else in the dictionary of the act. But love itself was experienced only in agony, in terrible wrenching at the heart-strings.

Back at the villa, he paid ritual respect to all the members of the family and then, as soon as decency permitted, returned to Tor Merla, poured himself a large brandy and sat in the court-yard, watching the small chill wind stirring the first autumn leaves. There, an hour later, he was visited by Claudio Palombini, the nephew who was the nominated executor of Pia's will. He

7

was a cool-eyed, handsome Florentine who doled out words as carefully as if they were golden florins. He handed Mather a copy of Pia's will – a holograph document in the Italian style.

Then he announced gravely, 'It seems, Mr Mather, that you have more need of sympathy than my aunt's family.'

'I feel . . . ' Max Mather pieced out the phrases very slowly, 'I feel as though I am locked in the vault and Pia has flown away.'

Claudio poured himself a brandy and perched on the edge of the rustic table. He offered a formal apology.

'I confess, Mr Mather, that I have come reluctantly to admire you. You made my Aunt Pia very happy. You nursed her with a devotion few husbands would have displayed. We are all most grateful to you.'

Mather digested the compliment in silence and then told him coolly, 'You owe me no thanks. I loved your aunt. I shall miss her very much.'

'You know that she has made provision for you in her will?'

'I was not aware of it.'

'You receive two years' salary, you keep the automobile and any personal gifts. You have your choice of a memento from the archive material on which you have been working. The bequest is reasonable, I believe.'

'It's more than reasonable.' Mather's tone was brusque. 'I have been generously paid; I expected no other rewards.'

'It would please me – and help me greatly – if you would consider staying here to continue your work on the archive.'

'Thank you, but no. Without Pia the tower would be intolerably lonely. But if you were prepared to entertain a suggestion?'

'Of course.'

Mather led his visitor into the tower and displayed to him, like a museum guide, the stacks of books and manuscripts and folios ranged about the old vaulted chambers. He said, 'Unless you see it with your own eyes, you cannot understand how much work is involved in an archive of this dimension.'

He picked up a bundle of paper tied with rotting tape, blew the dust off it and handed it to Palombini.

'This, for instance. The first document dates it at 1650. I daren't open the whole package, because most of it will fall apart. There may be valuable things in it, there may not. What it needs is skilled conservation, in the right conditions . . . What I'm trying to say is that the archive is historically important, but it needs work – constant and expensive work. Even if I stayed, I could not cope with it alone. The classification itself is an enormous task. The conservation is another thing altogether – a job for experts. Why not hand the whole thing over to the National Library? It would be a princely gesture and, at the same time, relieve the family of a heavy financial burden and a big cultural responsibility.'

Palombini pondered the thought for a few minutes, then nodded a vigorous agreement.

'Good, very good! Who knows? There may be some fiscal advantage for the estate as well as a gain to the Province.'

'I can easily establish the fiscal position,' said Mather. 'The Custodian of Autographs is a friend of mine.'

'Would you be willing to stay on long enough to set the arrangements in train? There would be no problem if you wanted to have a friend stay with you. You see, there's another service I need.'

'Which is?'

'A professional catalogue and a valuation of the art works in the villa. Could you provide that?'

'Arrange it . . . but not provide it. I would advise you to bring in Niccoló Tolentino from the Pitti.'

'I would accept your recommendation, of course. But these are two most important steps in the settlement of the estate; I would feel very happy if I could entrust them to you.'

'I'll give you six weeks,' said Max Mather. 'After that, I must be gone. I have a whole life to rebuild.'

'Thank you.'

'There's a price,' Mather added. 'Double my present salary and the cost of my transfer back to the United States. The legacy to remain untouched and paid before my departure.'

'Done.' Palombini was suddenly cheerful. 'You are a good trader. I like that. I regret we didn't get to know each other sooner.'

'One of life's ironies,' said Mather with a humourless grin. 'One has hardly touched hands when it is time to leave the party. You'll be keeping the same staff at the villa?'

9

'For the present, yes. Why do you ask?'

'If you don't mind, I'll move into the city and drive out here each day. If I stay here at night, I think I shall go mad.'

'I know how you feel.' Claudio Palombini was suddenly sombre. 'It's an old and bloody land. The vines grow out of the mouths of dead men.'

That same evening Mather drove into Florence and booked into a small *pensione*. He did not call Anne-Marie. Their pact specified that his room be available only at weekends; mid-week there might be other visitors and he was in no mood for unfamiliar company or embarrassing situations.

He telephoned the Custodian of Autographs to tell him of his impending departure and the donation of the Palombini archive. The old man mourned solicitously with his friend for Pia's death, but was clearly delighted at the thought of acquiring the archive for his institution. He promised to discuss the matter with his directorate and examine the tax advantages to the donor. He warned that this process would take time – as did all official acts – but he would do his best to expedite the matter.

Mather then telephoned Niccoló Tolentino, who immediately offered to divert him from his troubles with supper at the Gallodoro.

It was Tolentino's favourite watering-hole – a big cellar whose whitewashed walls and vaulted ceiling were covered with drawings by Florentine artists. Over the kitchen door was the great golden image of a strutting cock from which the place took its name. Niccoló Tolentino, who had painted it, sat always in the place of honour – a corner table, where an elevated chair and a footstool were provided so that none of commoner breed could look down on the little man who was, in the estimation of his peers, also a great one. When Mather arrived he was already ensconced with a glass of *punt e mes*, a dish of pistachios and his sketch-block and pencil set before him.

Their encounter was emotional as always. 'Eh, Max!' 'Eh, Nicki!' A long embrace, then more exclamatory phrases which ceased only when Mather's drink was set in front of him. The meal was already decided, the wine decanted – a princely vintage whose maker had endowed the painter with a private cellar. The old man raised his glass in a toast.

'To your lady, Max. *Requiescat.'*

'May she rest peacefully,' echoed Mather.

They drank deeply. The old man set down his glass and talked gently and casually.

'The old ways are still the wise ones. After a death, you eat and drink and remember the good things and try to laugh again. Grief profits no one, least of all the departed, who are quit of it for ever. You are hurting, eh?'

'More than I thought I would, Nicki – much more.'

Tolentino gave him a swift shrewd glance and asked an odd question. 'Have you ever been in gaol, Max?'

'Not yet.' Mather laughed in spite of himself. 'Why do you ask?'

'They say the hardest time of the sentence is the day when they shove you out into the street again . . . You were tied to your Pia for a long time. She is released; you have still to accept your own manumission. You will make a new life, with a new woman; not tomorrow or next week, but soon it will be time to begin looking. Be glad you are not like me, when looking is all you can do! Tell me: this girl you visit in Florence . . . the one who wants to be a dealer, an auctioneer?'

'Anne-Marie Loredon? What about her?'

'That's my question to you, Max. What about her? I know you play house at weekends. You visit the studios and galleries together. Clearly, you don't hate each other.'

'We're good friends. She likes my cooking. She thinks I'm a good tutor.'

'And what do you think about her, Max?'

'I think she has a career on her mind and I don't figure in the career plan. Now let's change the subject. Are you free to accept private commissions?'

'Of course. Like every State employee in Italy, I live by them. What do you have in mind?'

'Claudio Palombini wants the pictures in the villa catalogued and valued. I suggested you were the best man to do it.'

'And what did he say?'

'I should go ahead and arrange it.'

11

Niccoló Tolentino gaped at him in total disbelief, then he burst into high cackling laughter that turned the head of every diner in the place. He laughed until the tears ran down his face and Mather feared he might be having a fit. When he recovered, he called for more wine and announced between new gusts of merriment, 'That, my friend . . . that's the funniest joke I've heard in years. You mean Claudio didn't know who I was?'

'He didn't seem to.'

'Oh, little brother Max, I made that collection what it is today. I know every piece of junk that's in it and the few good pieces that hide in the shadows!'

'You're not proud of it, surely?'

'In a way I am. Did your lady Pia never tell you the story of Luca Palombini – the one they called *l'ingannatore* – the double-dealer?'

'No. Never.'

'Then . . . let's keep it, like proper gentlemen, for the pears and the cheese. The food here is too good to spoil with talk.'

The food lived up to the promise, but the story told by Niccoló Tolentino was by far the best item on the menu.

'During the Fascist time and right up until the end of the European war, the head of the Palombini clan was a doughty old pirate whom the locals called "*Luca l'ingannatore* – Luca the Swindler".' Niccoló Tolentino wagged a cautionary finger. 'Don't be put off by the name. He was not only the perfect mirror of his time; he was the perfect archetype of the Florentine merchant prince. Put him in any century and he would have been the same high man. The Fuggers would have lent him money. Cosimo – and the magnificent Lorenzo himself – would have honoured him. The French, the Romans and the Venetians would have made bargains with him – but always counted their fingers after each handshake. He was ruthless in the pursuit of his ambitions, yet he had a singular charm and always the cool nerve of the gambler.

'For Luca, the marketplace was the natural habitat of the human animal. Every man and woman, every beast, fruit and vegetable had a price. Every price was negotiable and Luca dealt

12

in the past, the present and the future. Art – which meant sale-able art – belonged to the past; its value was in its rarity, in the fact that it was patinated, proven durable and listed in the catalogues like the contents of the Uffizi or the Vatican Museum. According to Luca, it was the tourists who made the market in antiquities – the new-rich globe-trotters, the steel barons and oil kings who were being stuffed with a late and suspect education by Duveen and Berenson and their like.

'However, unlike natural products, art was a one-time growth. You couldn't seed it. You could, however, imitate and replicate it. So Luca hired a certain talented young Neapolitan – that was me in those far-off days; I was young, clever and cheap – to copy every major work in the Palombini collection. Then, using the same transports which carried his wines, his fruits, his silks and leather goods across Europe, he began shipping out some of the original master works to safe repositories in Switzerland. He also shipped some of my copies at the same time, calculating – like a good trader – that if the buyer didn't know the difference between a silk purse and a sow's ear, he'd get exactly what he thought he was paying for.

'Who knew what was going on? Who cared in those palmy Fascist days when the Mediterranean was "Mare Nostrum", our trains ran on time, Calabrian peasants were colonising Eritrea and Hitler had just annexed Austria? Luca knew. Luca cared. Luca had solid holdings in neutral Switzerland, in Portugal and Brazil and Argentina. A Perugino or a Caravaggio was a more bankable commodity in Rio or New York than it was in its home-land. But Luca's villa and the apartments he furnished for his mistresses looked no different because Niccoló Tolentino, the little hunchback from Naples, was a splendid painter, a genius at reproduction. . . .

'But, my dear Max,' Tolentino interrupted the flow of his story to emphasise a point, 'I was not, and never have been, a forger. I never palmed off a copy as the work of a master. When Luca traded off my copies to the Nazis for big money, for protection, I didn't care; I hated the bastards anyway. But he was the dealer, not I. I want you to remember that, because it is a matter of honour with me.'

13

'I'll remember it, Nicki,' Mather reassured him, 'but I can't wait to hear the rest of the story.'

'The night's too short to give you all of it, Max. But here's how it goes. On the outbreak of war in 1939, Luca shipped his wife and two infant sons to Switzerland in the care of his bankers and the directors of his Geneva affiliate. Then he set himself up at the villa with a succession of lively girl-friends. When the war began to go badly, he made accommodations with everyone: the Fascists, the Germans, the Church, the partisans, the Communist underground, Allied agents who popped up all over Tuscany and the Romagna like moles in a lawn. When the Mussolini regime collapsed and the Germans were fighting their long, bloody retreat up the peninsula, Luca Palombini took out an extra insurance policy.

'In three days, with the help of a partisan group, he stripped the villa of its remaining valuables and walled them up in the vaults of the Tor Merla. The new stonework was covered with stucco; the stucco was soiled and aged with mud. The partisans were paid off handsomely with money and the use of the tower as a refuge and a food dump for their groups. When the Germans came in strength, the partisans moved out. The Wehrmacht troops turned the tower into an observation post, while their officers dined in spartan discomfort at the villa with Luca Palombini and his latest girl-friend, Camilla Dandolo – a coloratura from La Scala whose body was much better than her voice.

'After the cease-fire, Luca reopened the vaults and set about trading off most of the remaining genuine art works for hard currency to rebuild the family fortunes. The villa walls were hung with my copies of the great works and with third-rate originals that weren't worth selling, but the Palombini enterprises at home and abroad were flush with capital.

'Then Luca summoned his family from Switzerland; but before they arrived he died – in the middle of a love duet with the soprano. Luca's wife made a big brouhaha, claiming that many important items were missing – though she was vague about what they were. She swore roundly that the bitch from La Scala had robbed her husband before riding him to death. Then, obviously on the advice of kinfolk, she fell silent. Luca the Double-Dealer had done well by his heirs. If he'd had to make pay-offs along the way – Boh! Florence had always been a traders' town. So . . . *sta' zitta Madonna*! Cut your losses and count your blessings and keep a still tongue in your head!

'And that's the end of it, Max. Except it's not the end. Here we sit, all these decades afterwards, and you're inviting me back to appraise the dregs of Luca's collection and be paid for doing it. *C'é una pazzia*, it's crazy!'

'A question, Nicki.'

'Ask it, my dear Max.'

'If the collection was as you describe it – a mixture of good and bad, of original and fake – why did Luca take so much trouble to hide it in Tor Merla?'

The little man chuckled and spread his hands in a series of eloquent gestures.

'Already, you see, you have forgotten his name: Luca the Swindler, the Double-Dealer. With him, nothing was ever the way it looked. The mere fact of walling the stuff up in the vault created a value for it. It *had* to be precious. If it was betrayed or discovered, he wasn't losing too much. But if, as happened, it survived and was brought triumphantly to light again – then every item, even my copies became *ipso facto* a masterpiece. That's how he financed his family's post-war empire at home and abroad. . . . '

'So . . . will you do the job, Nicki?'

'For you and for Palombini's money, of course I'll do it. Now, if you'll promise to see me safely to bed, we'll have another brandy.'

Next morning, early, Mather returned to Tor Merla, hung-over but purged of his devils. Claudio Palombini was still at the villa. He was happy to know that the archive would probably be taken off his hands and that tax advantages were possible. He charged Mather to begin the negotiations with the National Library and to supervise Tolentino's valuation of the art works. He handed over a cheque for six weeks' salary, told Mather that his legacy would be paid within thirty days and then left for Switzerland.

Mather pottered about the archive for an hour, noting what had to be done to set it in passable order for inspection by the

15

directorate of the National Library. He needed trestle tables and shelving to get the stacks of documents off the floor before they were all eaten by cockroaches and paper-worms. He was aware, though he had not mentioned it to Palombini, that the Library – short of staff and storage space – might well balk at the unwieldy mass of documents still to be examined.

He called up the villa and asked Matteo to have the carpenter start work the following morning; then, because the day was bright and the courtyard warm, he made himself coffee and settled down under the chestnut tree with his own reference books and the unfinished text of the monograph.

He was working through the account book for the year 1505 when he stumbled on an unusual entry for the month of October. On the eighth day of that month it was noted that a sum of 80 florins was paid to Master Raffaello, painter from Urbino, on account of two portraits – the one of Donna Delfina Palombini, wife of the *Gonfaloniere* Andrea Palombini; the other of their daughter, the Maiden Beata. In addition, there was payment of 60 florins for five cartoons for a *pala*, an altar-piece, for the chapel of San Gabriele on the confines of the villa. The note added that these sums were in full payment – signifying that the commissions had been executed and the works delivered.

The entry fascinated him. It was the kind of boiler-plate provenance that art dealers and historians begged heaven to provide. But he could not remember any reference to Palombini portraits or cartoons in the *catalogue raisonné* of Raffaello works. He cast through the volumes on his own bookshelves, found a Passavant and a Carli. Neither made any reference to the portraits or to the altar-piece. So – another of those mysteries beloved by scholars and browsers – had the works survived the centuries? If so, where were they now?

Yet another line of inquiry: were there records of other art purchases in the old account books? His coffee grew cold while he worked carefully through the antique script and the puzzling abbreviations. He was only half-way through January 1506 when Matteo, the major-domo, came up from the villa with Luigi the carpenter to measure for the shelving and trestles he needed.

These were practical country matters which demanded his full and respectful attention for half an hour. He was required to offer coffee and a tot of grappa. He must listen to a lament from Luigi the *falegname* that it was unfair to ask for good carpentry in a hurry. Mather understood what was required of him. He knew that there was no way to fight the Apennine wind; you turned your back to it, muffled your ears and waited until its fury was spent. He put a marker into the account book, packed away his notes and devoted himself body, soul and breeches to the questions of shelving, trestle tables and the choice between dressed and undressed timber. If he would accept undressed timber, the work could be done tomorrow. If he wanted craftsman work, he would have to wait another two weeks. Just as he was about to scream surrender the telephone rang. Anne-Marie was on the line; she too had a complaint to make.

'Max, I've just heard the news of your bereavement. You must be feeling awful. Why didn't you call me?'

'If you want the truth, I was too embarrassed.'

'About what? We're friends, aren't we? What are friends for if you can't share grief-time with them? Nicki Tolentino told me you're sleeping in town – what's wrong with my place?'

'Nothing. Except I only have weekend visiting rights, remember?'

'Nonsense! You'll come to me tonight. If it makes you feel any better, you buy the food and cook it. We have to talk anyway, Max; I've got a proposition to discuss with you. Shall we say seven-thirty?'

'I'll be there.'

As he hung up he felt a sudden surge of gratitude and relief. A grieving man was almost as vulnerable as a man in love. Each – for a different reason – was scared of making himself look foolish.

At the same moment he realised that Matteo and Luigi the *falegname* were still waiting for his answer – and for a second glass of grappa. As he poured the fiery liquor he announced firmly, 'Use whatever timber you've got. I simply want space to stack files and books off the floor. We're not building an apartment for the pope.'

'But we have our pride.' Luigi was suddenly eloquent. 'When the gentlemen come from the Library, we cannot bring them into a pigsty! To your good health, *professore*'.

*

17

That night Mather made a princely meal for Anne-Marie. The ceremonies of preparation made intimate conversation difficult, but she was content to wait until the meal was done and they sat close and quiet, watching the yellow moon climb over the campaniles. Then she began, patiently, to coax him into talk.

'What happens to your job now, Max?'

'I've agreed to stay on for six weeks, to arrange the hand-over of the archive and the valuation of the art collection. After that, who knows? I never realised until now how much I depended on Pia, how far I counted on the permanence of our relationship.'

'You never told me much about the kind of relationship it was.'

'I never questioned it myself; I took everything at face value . . . until the end, when Pia became absolutely dependent on me. I fed her, bathed her, dressed her, carried her from place to place like an ailing child. Quite literally, she died in my arms.'

'You must have loved her very much.'

'I must have.' Mather gave her a small embarrassed grin. 'Are you surprised?'

'A little. You have to be pretty tough to offer that kind of support. Frankly, I never saw you as that kind of man. The rest of it made perfect sense – wealthy widow, handsome scholar, an alliance of interest and convenience.'

'Whatever it was, it's over . . . *finita la commedia*! But enough of me . . . tell me about your plans.'

'I go home, I look for gallery premises and begin putting together a stable of artists and clients. My father's lending me enough money to make a start.'

'Good for you!'

'I wondered, Max, if you'd be interested in working for me?'

He considered the proposition for a long moment, then shook his head.

'Working *for* you, no. Working *with* you on some basis that would leave me a free agent – yes, possibly. Could we leave it open for discussion until I get to New York?'

'Of course. But tell me frankly: why wouldn't you consider working for me?'

'Because,' said Mather flatly, 'I've had a bellyful of patronage. I've lived on it all my life – endowments, grants, fellowships and funds supplied by wealthy ladies like Pia. I don't feel so badly

18

about her because I was able to repay some of the debt I owed her, but from here on, my love, I fly solo. If I fall out of the sky, too bad. That may not sound very important to you, but to me it's life or death. Academically I'm sound, though I was always too lazy to attempt brilliance. But now or never, I have to test myself and the metal I'm made of.'

'I'll drink to that, Max. I'll be interested to see how you test out. Now tell me something.'

'What?'

'How much did you tell Pia about me?'

'Not much. She knew I lodged here at weekends, that I was tutoring you in art history and appreciation – beyond that, nothing.'

'And she believed that was all?'

'She chose to believe so.'

'You can't have had very much sex during her illness.'

'We didn't. She accepted that I was getting it elsewhere, but so long as I didn't present her with a visible identifiable rival, she didn't make an issue of it.'

'I'm not sure I'd be as complaisant.'

'You would – if you didn't want to lose a good cook! Not to mention a trouble-free bed-mate.'

'That sounds more like the Max I used to know.'

'That one? Well, lately he comes and he goes. I'm never sure whether he's there or not.'

'Let's find out, shall we?' suggested Anne-Marie. 'It's a shame to waste that moon.'

They slept late the next morning, so it was midday before Mather returned to Tor Merla. Luigi the *falegname* had kept his word. The shelves were finished. The frame of the table was completed. There was a note to say that he was looking for material for the top; he would be back later. His tool-box was lying unlocked on the floor.

Mather's first task was to set the files in order on the shelves. It was a hot and dusty job that gave him an attack of hay fever. When it was done he discovered that the files had been resting not on the stone floor of the chamber, but on a wooden pallet like those used by carriers for stacking bricks or packages of a standard size. Closer inspection revealed that it was not a pallet but a slatted box about three feet long, two feet wide and six inches deep, packed with straw matting.

It was idle curiosity more than hope of any discovery that urged him to prise open the slats and unfold the matting. Inside was a large thick envelope of heavy canvas, sewn with a sail-stitch and sealed airtight and watertight with brown beeswax. His heart seemed to miss a beat and for a moment he trembled and gasped for breath. Then he closed and locked the entrance door, carefully repacked the straw mats in the box, nailed back the slats and carried the canvas envelope to his bedroom at the top of the tower.

He drew the shutters so that the light inside the chamber was dimmed. Then, using a razor-blade, he peeled back the wax along one edge of the envelope and began, very carefully, to unpick the heavy stitching which had been done with cobbler's twine. He was the complete professional now, working slowly and rhythmically. Whatever was inside the package was precious. The packer had taken great care to shield it from air and damp; it would be an unmentionable horror to damage it by incautious handling. His exploring fingers first felt two rigid objects wrapped in velvet, then beneath the velvet something else wrapped in silk.

Carefully he drew out the velvet-covered objects – two panels of aged wood: two portraits, one of a woman, the other of a child; head, shoulders and bust against a background of Tuscan hills and summer sky. They had obviously been cleaned before they were packed, because there was no evidence of retouching. Both subjects wore the square bodice of the period; painted into the buttons of the one and the embroidery of the other was the signature 'RAFFAELLO URBINAS FEC'.

Mather felt suddenly dizzy. He dropped to his knees by the bedside, propped the pictures against a pillow and knelt for a long time staring at them like a monk in adoration. But he was not praying. His brain was racing like a buzz-saw. The damned things *had* to be right. They looked right, they felt right . . . the draughtsmanship, the brush-strokes . . . the palette. His eyes

20

blurred, he closed them and bowed his head down to the counterpane.

The dizziness passed. He drew out the rest of the treasure – the cartoons, faded by the centuries but still legible, still vibrant from the master-touch. The first was the design for the whole altar-piece, the Entry of Christ into Jerusalem riding upon an ass, with the people waving palm fronds like banners and shouting hosannas. The rest were studies of the separate elements – the animals, the figures, the architecture. All the personages save the Christ were depicted in the Florentine costume of the period and matched to a background of rural Tuscany. The men waving palms were the young Palombini males, courtiers to the Medici. The women were their consorts.

Once again, everything looked right. The objects matched the description in the old account book. The paper looked and felt right. The draughtsmanship seemed characteristic of the young Master. They had been packed with great care but stored in a hurry in a wartime emergency, where they had lain buried under a pile of paper for forty years. The only man who could have been aware of their loss was dead. The only man in the world who knew of their existence was Max Mather. And by legacy from a dead lover, he could lay valid claim to own them.

Italian law differed from Anglo-Saxon law in one important particular: it laid more emphasis on the form of the document than on its intent. And the form of Pia's bequest to him was very clear. First, it was a holograph document. The testator had written it herself; it was, by the strongest presumption, a total expression of her wishes. Second, the Italian phrasing was specific: ' . . . *la sua propria scelta d'un oggetto ricordo dal archivio* . . . his own choice of a memento from the archive.'

The other heirs – provided they knew – would obviously dispute his title. They would claim, not without reason, that a package of old master art works worth tens of millions of dollars was hardly an '*oggetto ricordo*'. The Belle Arti would obviously intervene and impound the works pending a court settlement, which could take years. And even then they could forbid the export of national treasures.

So simple common sense prescribed that he begin immediately to protect his title to the master works and – as soon as possible

21

– get them out of Italy and into a safe-deposit in Switzerland. However, even as he was doing that he must have a care that the perfect provenance of the works was neither damaged nor destroyed.

They had been commissioned from Raffaello by and for the Palombini family. There, in the authentic account books of the period, was the record of the transaction in October 1505. They had obviously remained in the possession of the family right up to the present day, but while Luca the Double-Dealer had been running the estate they had found their way into the archive and remained buried for more than forty years under piles of dusty paper.

. . . Comes now Max Mather, rummaging in the archive for a memento of his own choice – a legacy left to him by Pia Palombini. He stumbles upon a curious canvas envelope which is clearly part of the archive. The fantasy takes him that this should be his memento – a surprise packet. He does not open it immediately, therefore he remains ignorant of its contents. It is only when he is on neutral ground that he discovers the art works and connects them with the entry in the family account books.

Even then, he has no certainty that the works are the originals. He is aware that Luca the Swindler caused copies of many master works to be made. So these pieces must be checked by experts. Until they have been declared authentic, there is no ground for dispute. In all of this no blame or suspicion attaches to Mather. He has acted with perfect propriety. If at any later stage his title to the works is challenged, it can be only on civil and not on criminal grounds.

All in all it seemed an excellent legal position. Max might have private doubts about its morality, but he could hardly be expected to make them public and brand himself a greedy or a venal man. After all, the Palombini played rough-and-tumble games too. They had only one rule: let the other fellow watch out. It was not beyond the bounds of possibility that they would be willing to make a deal to get the pictures back. That would be another situation to contemplate if ever the game got too rough.

Conscience thus having been momentarily lulled to rest, the next move was to shift the works out of Italy. A moment's calculation convinced Mather that he should do it immediately.

22

He could drive to Milan in two and a half hours to take the last flight to Zurich, visit his bank in the morning, leave the pictures in a safe-deposit and then fly back in the afternoon. After that, he could sleep soundly and plan calmly for a prosperous future.

He laid the pictures and the cartoons on the desk-top one by one and took a series of flashlight photographs in colour. Then, with infinite care, he rewrapped them and replaced them in the canvas envelope. Clumsily he restitched the canvas, melted the wax with a cigarette lighter and resealed the package completely. He found that it would fit snugly inside the hanging carrier he used for his suits and still leave room for a jacket and trousers. These and a change of shirt and underwear were all he needed for the overnight trip. He checked his wallet – money, passport, credit cards, traveller's cheques. With Pia in the old days he had formed the habit of being always ready to move at a moment's notice.

He hefted the hanging bag over his shoulder and walked downstairs. On the way out he passed Luigi and his assistant, a spindly youth from the village. Mather thanked them for the work already done and handed them half a bottle of grappa to encourage them to finish it by the next day. He was almost out of the door when the telephone rang. The Custodian of Autographs was on the line; he was very excited.

'Max, my friend, great and important news! Our director is most interested to acquire the archive. He would like to inspect it with me on Tuesday next at ten in the morning.'

'Good. I'll be here to welcome you both.'

'And you can tell Signor Claudio Palombini that there are tax advantages for the donor. These are described in a letter which will be posted to you today.'

'That's most helpful. Anything else? I'm rushing to catch a plane.'

'Even so, you must hear this last piece of news. If the archive is accepted in the Library, I may well be named curator and you will most certainly be inscribed in our golden book of benefactors!'

'I am very touched, my friend. I only regret that I must leave so quickly, but I'll call you as soon as I get back. Meantime, Tuesday at ten a.m. I'll put out the red carpet. *A presto! Ciao!*'

He slammed down the receiver and hurried out to the garage. Three minutes later he was on the road and heading for the entrance to the autostrada.

The final weeks of Mather's bond service to the Palombini passed slowly. The transfer of the archive to the National Library involved him in endless discussions with the director and exasperating phone calls to Palombini. The Library was short of storage space and conservation facilities. For the present the documents would have to remain at Tor Merla. Then came the questions of security, insurance, custodial responsibility and who would foot the bill. The tax benefits to Palombini were less than he had hoped; his lawyers recommended approaches to other institutions. Thus and thus, until Mather wished them all to hell and himself to some tropical retreat.

Niccoló Tolentino was easier to cope with. He padded round the chambers and corridors of the villa with a notepad, measuring canvases, making notes, offering only the briefest of comments on what he was doing. His manner was so brusque that Mather felt it necessary to ask whether he had offended the little man.

Tolentino frowned in puzzlement. 'Offended! How could you possibly offend me? We're friends . . . If you ask why I am irritable, I am always like this when I work. I have to be alone; I cannot distract myself with questions and comments. Later, we discuss things.'

Then it was time for Anne-Marie to leave Florence. Mather staged a big farewell party for her at the Gallodoro. All her friends came – scholars, artisans, painters, sculptors, gallery folk – and the crowd did not disperse until two in the morning. Afterwards Mather walked her home through the sleeping city – an odd nostalgic pilgrimage that, for both of them, marked the end of one life and the beginning of another.

'That was a wonderful end to a pretty wonderful time,' Anne-Marie told him. 'Thank you, Max!'

'It was my thanks to you for letting me share the good times.'

'We'll have more in New York.'

'I'm sure. How do you feel about going back?'

'Glad – but scared too. I just hope I'm good enough to survive among the hucksters.'

'You are. Don't doubt it. Don't let fear undermine your convictions about yourself. Here you've lived with the best, you've drunk in the tradition with your morning coffee. You're not guessing now. You *know*! Be strong in the knowledge.'

'I hear, maestro. I won't let you down. And what are your plans?'

'I'm going to Switzerland first. I have business to do in Zurich. Then I'll give myself a holiday in the snow. I'll probably do a circuit of the resorts, meet old friends, make some new ones . . . which I need. I expect to be back in New York about the end of January.'

'And you will think about our working together?'

'I'm already mulling over some ideas. I'm sure we can work something out. What stage are you at now?'

'Interesting things are happening. A realtor has offered me the lease of gallery space in SoHo. It belongs to a man called Ed Bayard; he's a lawyer who acts for the Art Dealers' Association of America. His wife was an artist who died in tragic circumstances some time ago and he himself is a well-known collector. Who knows, I might get myself a landlord and a client in one stroke.'

'It sounds promising.'

'It is . . . but what about you? What do you really want to do, Max?'

'Professionally or personally?'

'Either . . . both.'

'I've told you already. I'm sick of dependence. I must take control of my own life. To do that I've got to make money – big money if I can. How do I do it? I'm not creative. I'm not like an artist or a writer whose money is in his head; I have to trade on what I've got in terms of knowledge and experience. That's why I'm going to Switzerland, to get some legal and financial advice on where to start.'

'Will you stay in Europe?'

'That's an option I'm considering. I'm a polyglot, I'm comfortable on either side of the duck-pond. Why do you ask?'

'Because if you were here and I were in New York, we could

really set up some good deals together – exchange of artists, buying and selling in both directions, import and export of exhibitions. Think about it, Max. Promise me you'll think about it very carefully?'

'I promise.'

'I wonder if you know how much I'm going to miss you?'

He stopped, tilted up her face to the moon and kissed her lightly on the lips.

'Sure you'll miss me. I'll miss you. But let's be honest, my sweet. The mourning won't last long in Manhattan – you'll be knee-deep in eligible males and up to your eyeballs in new ambitions. But you and I will always be friends, because we know how to spell the words and we've never needed a dictionary to tell us what they meant. That's maybe less than we need to make us the world's greatest lovers, but it's more than a lot of others find in a lifetime. So let's hurry home before the cold gets to us and we lose the nice warm glow of the party!'

Max's own exit from Florence was much less ceremonious. He initialled the final draft of donation of the archive and sent it by courier to Switzerland for Palombini's signature. Then he took delivery of Tolentino's inventory and valuation of the art works to lodge with the attorneys for the estate. When he remarked on the number of works which carried the notations 'attributed to', 'school of', 'copy by unknown hand', 'copy, possibly contemporary', Tolentino offered a bland explanation.

'It's the best I could do, Max, seeing that old Luca paid me to protect his interests in the first place. The notations I've made will set red lights flashing in any reputable auction house. After that, it's up to the buyer to draw his own conclusions.'

'I understand, Nicki. It wasn't my business to ask anyway. You're the expert. It's your document. But one thing interests me: did you miss many old friends from the collection?'

'Quite a few, Max; but if you want me to name them, I won't. Remember there are at least two versions of each one in existence: the original and my copy. It would be a dangerous folly to speculate where each may be now and how it was acquired by the present owner.'

26

Mather laughed. 'Aren't you exaggerating a little?'

'Not at all.' The little man was very emphatic. 'Suppose, as often happens, the owner of a great piece of art pledges it to his bank for a loan. Suppose, by an incautious word, you or I suggest that it may be a forgery. The bank calls in its loan. The borrower's credit is destroyed or at least damaged. . . . Suppose a more extreme case. The buyer has paid a lot of money for a dud, so he goes out and shoots the man who sold it to him. . . . But who could make the final judgment between the original and the copy? A small cadre of experts, using modern laboratory techniques – and, of course, I myself. My private cipher is painted into every copy I make.'

'May I know what it is?'

'You may not. It's a personal mark which only I can identify.'

'Forgive me, Nicki. Forget I asked.'

'I'll forget and forgive – provided you get those damned lawyers to pay me promptly.'

'I'm going in to collect my legacy from them today. I'll try to have them write your cheque at the same time.'

'You're a good man, Max. We're going to miss you.'

It was pleasant to hear, but in his heart of hearts he knew the truth that every foreigner in Italy learns sooner or later: family comes first, friends of the blood and heart come next and foreign friends are a disposable luxury, because they subsist outside the intricate web of rights and duties and debts and credits which holds the society together. So . . . an embrace, a farewell, an exchange of gifts – a pencil sketch from Tolentino, an eighteenth-century edition of Petrarch from Mather – and the ceremony was over.

At the lawyers' office it was all brusque politeness. Yes, without question the Tolentino cheque would be in the evening's mail. Here for you, Mr Mather, is a dollar draft for the amount of the legacy, for which we should like a receipt. We understand you will vacate Tor Merla in the morning and hand the keys to Matteo, the major-domo.

'There is nothing else you need from me?'

'Nothing else, Mr Mather, except to thank you on behalf of the family for the services you have rendered and to wish you good fortune for the future.'

'Thank you, gentlemen – and good-day.'

He could hardly believe his good fortune. No one had bothered to ask him to specify whatever memento he had taken from the archive or to sign a receipt for it. He was half-way back to the villa before he worked out the very Latin logic of the omission. To all intents and purposes the archive had passed from the family to the State and it was up to the State to mind its own business. The family was no longer interested; the Palombini had been schooled for centuries to the maxim that whatever didn't earn a florin – man, woman or olive tree – was not worth a second thought.

Which meant that Max Mather was legally in possession of two putative Raffaello portraits and a complete set of cartoons, all with an impeccable provenance. The only shadow that hung over the portraits was the possibility that they were copies made by Niccoló Tolentino.

As he drove through the gathering dusk towards the dark hump of the Tor Merla, Max Mather burst into laughter. Now there was spice to the game and, with luck and careful planning, there would be a fortune at the end of it.

TWO

On the first anniversary of his wife's death Edmund Justin Bayard, attorney-at-law, had an appointment at the Frick Collection on Fifth Avenue.

The distance was not great: ten blocks uptown from his Park Avenue apartment, two blocks crosstown on Seventieth Street. The time-span was much greater: twelve months of reclusive existence, a bleak desert of days during which he had functioned like a machine—precise, predictable, in perfect passionless rhythm.

However, on that clear winter day the machine turned into a man suddenly eager for the sight, sound and touch of his fellows. The pilgrimage to the Frick was his compromise with whatever hostile deity ruled the random universe.

A chamber group from the Juilliard was playing Mozart's Concerto for Clarinet in A major. The small formal music matched his mood of elegy. Madeleine had loved this place and all its elegant certainties.

'It's so settled,' she would say in that quiet emphatic way of hers. 'It's a flash-frozen dinner party. You could come back this year or next and pick up at any course on the menu.'

In point of fact the whole place was a splendid anachronism: an Italianate villa perched arrogantly on a prime patch of New York real estate, with interiors designed by an Edwardian Englishman, a collection of pictures, sculpture, furniture and ornaments that reflected not the princely lifestyle of its founder but the tastes of the great Duveeen, art pedlar extraordinary. Henry Clay Frick, whose bust graced the entrance hall, had made his fortune from coal and steel in Pittsburgh. He had been shot and stabbed as an enemy of the people, yet survived to become their posthumous benefactor with parks, hospitals, educational endowments and this collection of master works.

29

With a silent salute to the sleek marble image, Bayard walked swiftly through the South Hall and into the Living Hall which for Madeleine had always been the heartland of the collection. It was as if she were beside him now. A painter in her own right, she was as obsessed as the Dutch with interiors and composed little verbal improvisations to fix their quality in her vision.

'I can imagine what it must have been like sitting in this room on a winter evening with the fire blazing, coffee and brandy served, the servants retired. And there's Henry Clay Frick himself with St Jerome staring down at him from above the mantel and the two mortal rivals, Thomas More and Thomas Cromwell, facing each other across the blaze. There are two Titians looking over his shoulder: Aretino who died laughing at a bawdy joke and a young man in a red cap dreaming a young man's dreams, while Bellini's St Francis looks heavenward in ecstasy. There's not a sound from outside because of the snow; and since the people are so quiet they must be content. Mr Frick is so full of goodwill and philanthropy he can forgive even the anarchist who tried to kill him. . . . '

For Madeleine there had been no time for absolution. She had been stabbed to death in her own warehouse studio in SoHo. It was a senseless, bloody crime, committed – the police seemed to believe – by an addict desperate for a fix. Neither the assassin nor the weapon he used had ever been found.

The memory of that day had brought Bayard to the edge of madness many times, but today he could contemplate it with a strange detachment, like an illustration in a history book far outside the context of his personal life. The drama had gone out of it – played and replayed to extinction. He had been too long absent from the workaday world. It was time to set about the business of living again.

'Mr Bayard? Mr Edmund Bayard?'

He swung round to face the questioner. At first glance she bore an odd resemblance to the Whistler portrait of Lady Meux in the Oval Room. He answered brusquely, 'Yes, I'm Bayard.'

'Anne-Marie Loredon. You were kind enough to suggest we might meet here.'

'Hugh Loredon's girl – of course! I haven't seen him in a long time.' He gave a small deprecating shrug. 'I've dropped out of things since my wife died. Today is the anniversary of her death.'

'It's kind of you to see me.'

For the first time he smiled and the smile made him look ten years younger. 'Not at all; I'm very glad of your company. Shall we do the tour?'

By the time they reached the Oval Room he was relaxed enough to stand her against the portrait of Valerie, Lady Meux, to see if there really was a resemblance.

Anne-Marie protested. 'She's much prettier than I am.'

'I wasn't thinking of pretty,' said Bayard with a grin. 'She was a wild one, as I think you could be. She came from nowhere, married a beer baron and raised happy hell wherever she went. I'm told she once appeared at a county fox-hunt riding an elephant.'

'And you think I could do that?'

'You might,' said Bayard judiciously. 'I think you just might.'

'And you can read all that in the portrait?'

'Not really, I'm just showing off my rag-bag of useless information.' The smile disappeared and he drew her back to stand beside him while they studied the painting. 'I'm not sure how much is left of what Whistler really put there. Some of his materials were unstable and some of his techniques were questionable. Time hasn't dealt kindly with all his pictures. Look at the Montesquiou, for instance — ' He broke off, suddenly embarrassed by his own pedantry.

Anne-Marie prompted him. 'Go on, please. I'm really interested.'

He shrugged and declined. 'My wife was the painter; I'm just a collector. She lent me her eyes and her intuitions. We built our collection together.'

'I'd love to see it.'

'You shall, I promise. Let's leave Whistler and go talk to some of the big boys in the West Gallery. You can tell me as we walk what you need from me.'

'It's very simple. You own a studio building in SoHo.'

31

'How do you know that?'

'The realtor with whom I'm dealing told me. I'd like to lease the place from you.'

'For what purpose?'

'To set up a gallery of my own.'

'That's an ambitious project.'

'I'm ready for it, I think. I've spent all my postgraduate life in the art business; I trained with Sotheby's, I worked at Agnew's and the Marlborough and took summer courses sponsored by the Belle Arti in Rome and Florence. I'm still a novice, but I figure I'm more qualified than a lot of people with brass nameplates on Fifty-Seventh Street. Wouldn't you agree?'

'I don't have enough information to offer an opinion.'

His tone was dry and detached. When she looked up in some surprise, she caught a glimpse of the other Edmund Bayard: the cool-eyed attorney, third on the partners' list of a prestigious mercantile practice, whose opinions commanded high fees and deep respect.

Anne-Marie challenged him: 'You're hedging, counsellor. Why shouldn't I make a good dealer?'

'No reason at all. I was just pointing out that an education in the fine arts is only the first step, just as a law degree is only a beginning in my profession. There's a fiduciary element in both, you see. You're the matchmaker between buyer and seller. Both have to trust you. "Let the buyer beware" is a bad motto in the art business. There have been too many fakes, too many phoney attributions and too many hucksters peddling sows' ears as silk purses. They've inflated the prices and debased the currency.'

'That's quite a speech, Mr Bayard. Do you care so much?'

'I have to care. Your father must have told you that our firm represents the Art Dealers' Association of America. We have to go at least part way to keeping them honest.'

'I'm impressed'.

'No need to be. Let's talk about this gallery of yours – I'm sure you realise that it takes quite a time to build a client list and the kind of reputation that gets you serious notice from the press and the big buyers.'

'My father has promised to help me. He's putting up some cash to secure a lease on gallery premises.'

He gave her a swift sidelong glance. 'Has your father looked at the premises?'

'No. This is my business. He won't meddle in it. Money will be tight, but what the hell? I'll be doing what I want and having fun.'

Bayard nodded approval. 'That's the key to it – having fun. So long as you enjoy what you do, the odds are that you'll be good at it. I'm afraid there's been very little fun in my life since my wife was killed.'

'I heard about that while I was in Italy. I grieve for you.'

'Don't distress yourself. It's history now. I mentioned it because I find it hard to be in company under false pretences.'

She stared at him in surprise. 'What a strange thing to say.'

'I don't know how else to put it. I seem to have lost the knack of polite communication.'

'You've been living alone all this time?'

'Alone? No. Solitary? Yes. I have a Filipino couple who keep house for me. I'm busy at the office during the day; I go to theatres, to concerts, to exhibitions. I pass the time of day with people, but I shy away from companionship. It's something of a sleepwalker's existence.'

'By choice?'

'Of course not!' He was suddenly vehement. 'You have to understand – a crime like this is a curse laid on the survivor. I stayed out of society because I felt like a leper with a bell around my neck, obliged to declare myself unclean.'

'As you've just done with me.'

'Yes.'

'Then you've paid me a compliment. I thank you for it.'

'What are you doing for the rest of the day?'

'There's not much of it left. I'm open to suggestions.'

'Come back to my place; I'll show you my collection and Madeleine's as well. We can discuss the question of the lease and have an early dinner at Le Cirque. What do you say?'

'I'd like that very much.'

As they strolled down Madison, he asked the ritual question. 'Are you married?'

'No.'

'Committed to anyone?'

'No. I'm busy and happy. While I'm building a career, I prefer to stay mobile.'

He turned into an old but still fashionable apartment block, steered her through the foyer past the curious eyes of the doorman and into the penthouse elevator.

She had expected something heavy and old-fashioned: oak panelling perhaps, period certainly, a middle-aged clutter of expensive possessions, a bachelor fussiness. Instead there was light and uncluttered space and minimal furniture designed for casual comfort. All non-structural walls had been breached, so that one space flowed into another without losing its own particular contour, its own area of privacy. Books, pictures, sculptures were dispersed to match the rhythm of the space and the light, so that they could be enjoyed at will and contemplated at leisure. Anne-Marie made no secret of her surprise.

'This is extraordinary – quite different from anything I expected. Who designed it?'

'Madeleine. She had wonderful ideas about living space. She used to say, "Walls and doors don't create privacy. Once you solve the problem of heating and cooling large areas – and you can – why break them up into cubbyholes?" I didn't really believe her at the beginning, but I let her do what she wanted. This is the result. The only change I've made is to turn the dining room into a gallery for her pictures. It's a huge room, as you'll see – and I don't give dinner parties anymore. I'm saving that viewing until last.'

For a moment Madeleine, twelve months dead, was a palpable presence in the room. Anne-Marie felt a sudden prickle of fear; the dead should stay buried and let the living be about their own lives. She asked with careful detachment, 'Where did Madeleine exhibit?'

'She never held an exhibition; she sold privately through Lebrun. However, I've often thought of arranging a posthumous show. There are about fifty works in all. I'll be interested in your opinion after you've seen them. . . . Anyway, let's do the five-dollar tour first.'

'You lead, I follow.'

Feeling a sudden need to re-establish a physical contact that would exclude the ghost, she held out her hand so that he had to clasp it and lead her on a circuit of his domain.

'Our joint collection starts here. This canvas is by Annibale Caracci, one of three brothers painting in Emilia in the last half of the sixteenth century and into the seventeenth. As you probably know, a whole collection of Caracci works was sold for peanuts in London in 1947. I stumbled on this one in an antique dealer's in Devon. . . . This next one is Madeleine's find, an early version of Milton Avery's "Seagrasses and Blue Sea". All the American pieces are her choice. I'm responsible for the foreigners.'

'How do you explain that? Did either of you reserve a right of comment on the other's choice? Which had the final say on money?'

Bayard gave her a swift appraising glance and then smiled.

'Now I know you'll make a good dealer. First you have to know who makes the decisions on matters of taste, then who signs the cheques.'

'It's a reasonable question, isn't it?'

'Of course. And I'll try to answer it for you. Madeleine's whole vision as an artist was of urban America. No matter how much she travelled, Manhattan was still the home-place of her mind. She was interested in history, but only in so far as it embellished or explained the present. Nevertheless, she had great care for artists and craftsmen who were trying to express other aspects of the continent. She corresponded with them; she travelled the country to meet them; she bought their works and helped them to find markets. Above all, she had respect. It was a very special relationship into which I never wanted to intrude. I was, I am, a different animal.'

'I'd be interested' – Anne-Marie was deliberately provocative – 'to know what kind of animal you really are.'

'Why don't you look at the pictures instead of at me?' His chiding was only half a joke. 'This is a Klimt which was knocked down to me on a slow day at Sotheby's.'

'It's a beauty; I love that hectic seductive flush on his women. . . . You have an eye for quality.'

'I know, but my pocket isn't deep enough to afford this quality anymore. Look at this . . . a sketch for what later became Ingres' portrait of Madame Rivière. I picked it up ten years ago for two thousand dollars. I was twenty-five when I first started buying pictures. I'm fifty now. The price of art has inflated far beyond even the most inflated currencies. So the cinquecento is out of my range, the Impressionists are as inaccessible as Mars. . . .'

'It seems to me you've done very well. This is an important and very valuable collection. What started you off?'

He mused over the question a moment. 'I guess it was because I realised early how vulnerable I was.'

'Vulnerable? That's an odd thing to say.'

'Look, I'm a lawyer, a desk-bound man. I could easily become brain-bound too. So I've always had to find myself other regions to live in—a distant time, an exotic place, even an imaginary family.'

'That sounds rather dangerous.'

'It is, because it can lead to total divorcement from reality, which is what nearly happened to me this last year. But my father had taught me another way of using imagination. He was a worshipper of ancestors, a believer in continuities. He taught me how to read history in an art gallery through costume and architecture and the details of daily life. He himself was a physician and he led me through the history of the healing arts from Aesculapius to the Arunta tribe of Australia. He used to say: "Yesterday, today and tomorrow are all one in the river of time. There and here are the same country, because they co-exist in the one mind."'

'Wise man. I would like to have known him.'

'I loved him. It is my greatest regret that Madeleine and I were never successful in giving him a grandson before he died.'

It was as if a barrage had broken and all the memories dammed up behind it came flooding out in a foam and flurry of talk. The pictures on the walls took on a glow of new life as each one was invested with an aura of personal memory.

'This is a pencil sketch of my French grandmother, done by Tissot while he was painting in London. She was a beautiful woman, much courted in her youth; though by the time I knew her she was a very formidable old lady and not at all proud of her gauche grandson. I think the truth was that she didn't like children at all. They reminded her of her age. Tissot really knew how to paint women, didn't he? Look at the lift of the head and the subtle curve of the lips. He had much more subtlety than the pundits gave him credit for. His paintings were always highly finished. One can linger over them for a long time.'

'You admire that, don't you? The finished look?'

'It's not the look.' He was eager to explain himself. 'It's the talent, the craftsmanship to execute whatever one chooses – an instant of bravura or a painstaking texture that glows for centuries. Take a look at this little beauty. At first glance you'd swear it was a Monet. It's actually by a Japanese, Seiki Kusoda, painted about 1912. It was given to me by a client in Kyoto for whom we'd just set up an American affiliate. The client was an ineresting man in his own right; his father had been a maker of wood-blocks for children's colour books and had passed on the craft to his son, who channelled it into one of the best offset printing houses in Japan. Actually he offered to do the illustrated catalogue if ever I set up an exhibition of Madeleine's work.'

Suddenly a surge of unease took hold of her. The collection was making the same impression as the man – it was somehow diffuse, unresolved, a rag-bag of valuable items with no coherence. Abruptly she told him, 'There's too much here for me to take in at one viewing. I'd like to break off and look at Madeleine's work.'

'Of course. I've been very thoughtless; I'm afraid I'm a rather boring guide.'

'You're not boring. It's just that you're not aware of the emotional impact you create in the midst of a collection that reflects so much of your life. If I'm to enjoy your wife's work, I need to concentrate my attention on that.'

'We could leave it for another day if you wish.'

'No. I'd prefer to do it now.'

'Then would you indulge me? I want you to view the pictures alone.'

She was instantly uneasy. 'Why?'

'I can't see Madeleine's pictures any more – only a single brutal image of violence. I want you to look at her work with a critical eye, a dealer's eye. Ask yourself whether you could honestly back it as an entrepreneur in the market. Give me your best judgment. Good or bad, I won't mind – just so it be honest.'

Intuition told her that this was a dangerous moment upon which might hang the whole outcome of their business dealings. Consciously or unconsciously he was testing her, weighing her against some private scale of whose norms she knew nothing. She hesitated, groping for the right words, then asked him the flat question, 'What hangs on my answer?'

Bayard's response was curt and precise. 'Each of us has revealed a private interest. Yours is to set up a dealership and a gallery. Mine is a posthumous exhibition of Madeleine's work. I'm trying to determine whether those interests can be served together, or whether they should be kept apart.'

'No.' She was suddenly angry. 'No, no, no! Already you've put me in an impossible position. You know I want the gallery. I know you can give or withhold the lease. If I say I don't like the work, I offend you mortally. If I tell you I like it, I'm compromised by a self-serving decision. . . . I think we'd best call it a day.'

For a long moment he stared at her and there was no message she could read in his cold eyes or the stony mask in which they were set. Finally, he said, 'Now that you've managed to insult us both, why not leave a tidy situation? Look at Madeleine's pictures, but keep your opinion to yourself.'

'You're manipulating me.'

'To what end?'

'I don't know. I just feel as though I'm opening that last fatal door in Bluebeard's castle.'

He threw back his head and laughed. 'After you've discovered Bluebeard's secret, he'll be waiting to serve you a drink and buy you dinner.'

He opened the door, switched on the lights and stepped back to let her pass into the dining room.

The moment the door closed upon her, Anne-Marie was overcome with panic. She shut her eyes and leaned back against the panels, shouting silently to command her screaming nerves.

'What the hell did you expect? You're supposed to be negotiating a lease – instead you let yourself in for cocktails with a middle-aged widower who looks like Cary Grant, talks like a character out of Henry James, has a lurid family history and an emotional hang-up as well. He's got at least six million dollars in assorted art hanging on his walls and he shoves you into this great white chamber because he wants – he says – an independent appraisal of his dead wife's talent. Well, go on. Give it to him. The sooner it's done, the sooner you'll be out of this crazy cuckoo-land. . . . '

Finally she opened her eyes and tried to focus on the pictures that streamed along the walls like the banners of an ancient army.

Once again the sheer mass of the work daunted and confused her. It needed a long, slow promenade to give her any focus at all. First and foremost, Madeleine Bayard was a traditionalist, in style and education. Her draughtsmanship was impeccable. Her brush-strokes were totally controlled. The harmonies of her palette were in classic mode. At first sight, everything on the canvas was so sedulously executed that the viewer was unprepared for the shock of the dominant theme.

Every one of the pictures was a Manhattan interior: an uptown penthouse, a Harlem tenement, a store, a subway, a covered walkway, a shanty built of packing-cases, the cabin of a tug-boat on the river. At first glance each interior framed an episode of urban life, beautifully rendered but conveying in some fashion instability and unease. Then it became clear that all the characters were imprisoned in their own milieu and were thrusting desperately to break out of it. They were drawn – as the viewer was drawn – irresistibly towards a fragment of the outside world: a geranium in a window-box; a long perspective of city canyons, with only a hint of sky and water at the end; a solitary gull, wheeling over a seaway. There was one stunning piece that looked like a Dormition of the Virgin in which a bag-lady, frozen to death in the archway of a church, gazed placid and unseeing at a little girl walking down a snowbound street.

In spite of the sombre settings, the whole thrust of the painter's emotion was outward and upward to the American dream: a hope still visible, a heaven still dreamed of, a liberty not yet beyond hand's reach.

Madeleine Bayard must have felt herself imprisoned, otherwise she could never have painted so poignantly the frustration of the shut-in soul. But where or by what had she been bound? By marriage to Bayard? By the restriction of urban life, the concrete skyline, the light diluted by smog, the surging humans who clogged the streets of Manhattan? Whatever it was, a crazed assassin had released her from it. Now her husband was in bondage to her memory and, by some strange inverted logic, was using her life-work to set himself free. Which led to another mute self-inquisition for Anne-Marie.

'What do you say when you walk out of this room? "Thanks for letting me see your wife's work, Mr Bayard. Very impressive. Now, if you don't mind, I'll skip dinner and go home and wash my hair. . . . " You know you can't do that. It's an insult to your own intelligence. You're staring at the kind of talent that pops up once in a quarter of a century. It can't, it mustn't, be left to moulder in this mausoleum. And don't overdo the altruism either, my girl. You smell money – big money – and a reputation to be made overnight. So you go out there like the daughter of a good auctioneer and hustle what you've got and even what you haven't. If Edmund Justin Bayard wants to be hustled, you've got it made. If he doesn't, at least you'll know where a couple of caches of art treasures are buried – and that's worth a hefty finder's fee any day of the week.'

It was a scene easy to stage in solitude and dumb-show, but not half so easy to play with a very complex actor in the lead. So she lingered a while, contemplating the haunting image of the bag-lady wrapped in her frozen draperies under the Norman arch of a fashionable church. The longer she looked at it, the more it seemed like a master work, with the superb sculpture of the waxen features, the cast-off clothing subtly transmuted into cerecloth, the artful management of grey stone and winter light and the innocence of a solitary child.

Suddenly she felt another small shiver of fear. The woman who had painted this picture was too formidable to have as an enemy, even in death. She had to be placated, praised, turned into a friend and ally. What better way than to become her posthumous patron, the knowing and compassionate soul who made her genius known to the world?

She took a deep breath, strode to the door and walked into the lounge to confront Edmund Bayard.

His greeting was studiously banal. 'What will you drink?'

'What are you having?'

'A vodka martini.'

'That will do fine, thank you.'

'I've rung Le Cirque. They can't fit us in for dinner until nine.'

'That makes it very late. Why don't we just enjoy our drinks?'

'Just as you like.' If he was displeased, he gave no sign of it. 'Olive or twist?'

'An olive, please. Let me say it straight and plain: I am bowled over by your wife's pictures. She was, she remains, a big talent. The next question is what you want to do about it. In short, is it your intention to hold the collection intact or to break it up and sell it?'

'To maintain it myself would make no sense. I'd have to find a home for it with an institution. The institution would have to create a posthumous reputation and then spend a lot of money to mount travelling exhibitions. If I were a trustee of such a body I'd decline gracefully in favour of better-known collections. No . . . ' – he was suddenly tense and emphatic – 'I loved my wife. She's dead, but her pictures keep her alive. I have to get them out of my house – and her ghost out of my bed.'

It was a cry of pure desperation, but Anne-Marie would not respond to it. She told him calmly, 'So you pick the canvases you want to keep and put the rest up for sale. If you do that, I'd like first offer to mount the selling exhibition. Before you do anything, however, there's another decision you have to make.'

'Which is?'

'Once those works go on show, the whole story of your wife's murder will hit the headlines again. Can you face that?'

'It seems I have little choice. Perhaps a final public confrontation with the past would be the remedy that would work for me.'

'How much would you endure to make it work?'

'I don't understand.'

'An exhibition as well publicised as this one would make Madeleine's murder as much a part of art history as Van Gogh's ear.'

'That's pretty cold-blooded.'

'It's the truth. You can accept it or not, as you choose. It's your life that's at stake.'

'And what's at stake for you?'

'My career – this exhibition could give it a flying start. But before we get to that, there are still more questions.'

'Go ahead.'

'You told me your wife used to sell through Lebrun. Is there any contract or even any courtesy that binds you to him?'

'None. He has a small, very exclusive gallery from which he moves Impressionists and post-Impressionists out of deceased estates and into the market. His transactions for Madeleine were done as a personal favour and on a picture by picture basis. He wouldn't know what to do with Madeleine's collection. He knows it exists but he hasn't even asked to see it.'

'Fine. Now, about your wife's studio . . . '

'It's an old warehouse on West Broadway. Madeleine used the top two floors; the first floor was empty. We were going to redevelop the whole building. When she died I put in a caretaker and tried to forget about the place.'

'I've seen it. I'm sure it can be turned into a gallery. I'm asking you to give me a decent lease at a reasonable rent with an option to buy. I'll do it up and stage the exhibition where Madeleine created the works. I'll call it "Liberation", because that's what the pictures are about.'

He stared at her in total disbelief. 'That's macabre!'

She moved instantly to the attack. 'Macabre? My God, what could be more macabre than that mausoleum next door, a room you can't bear to enter? But that's your business . . . I think I'd like another drink.'

'Are you always as brutal as this?'

'Only when I'm threatened.'

'And I threaten you?'

'Yes.'

'How, for God's sake?'

'I think you manipulate people. You're trying to manipulate me.'

'That's the second time you've used that word; I begin to find it offensive.'

'Then give me another. It was you who talked about ground

42

rules and mutual interest. It was you who asked for a dealer's judgment on your wife's pictures. I've given it to you. I've made an open bid to represent them in the market. I've offered to take a lease on a property that is presently earning nothing for you. I think it's up to you to respond.'

'It seems to me,' said Bayard deliberately, 'that what you're asking me to do is take your talent on trust and endow you with a gallery and an opening exhibition.'

'Not so.' There was an edge of anger in her voice. 'As far as the gallery's concerned, I'll pay a fair price for a lease. As for my dealing talents, you gamble on them as you would do with any candidate. With me the risk's better because I'm educated, eager and hungry. . . . Think about it, counsellor.'

'I will, Miss Loredon.' His taut features relaxed into a grin. 'And don't get angry with me. Lawyers are cautious brutes. Which prompts my next question. Let's presume you've got a gallery and you've arranged an opening exhibition. Where do you go from there? How do you find artists for future shows?'

'Travel and correspondence and telephone. I can tell you now what talent is offering in Taos or Toronto or Cleveland. I'm very good at records and cross-indexing and I have correspondents in London, Paris, Florence and Sydney, Australia. I'm not worried about continuity as such, but continuity in high talent is another matter. Anyway, that's my risk, not yours.'

'It would be if we were partners.'

She took a few moments to digest the idea, then rejected it emphatically.

'I have to tell you frankly – I would not consider such an arrangement.'

'If I made it a condition of our deal?'

'The answer would still be no. Think a moment. This has always been a bitchy business. With today's astronomical auction prices, it can be downright lethal. If there's the slightest rumour of patronage or pay-off between you and me, the exhibition will be still-born; Madeleine's reputation as an artist will be destroyed and my career will be dead from day one. Besides, we both know the rules of the game. You're fragile and I'm building a personal career. Let's not complicate our lives.'

'I would like very much to have your friendship.'

43

'I would value yours. I simply do not want to complicate a business situation.'

'Which seems to be more important to you than anything else?'

'Just at this moment, it is. I've worked hard for a long time to prepare myself for a break. From where I sit now it looks like a big red apple right on top of the fruit bowl. I only have to reach out and take it.'

'What happens,' asked Bayard deliberately, 'if I suddenly snatch it away – no lease, no exhibition?'

'Then I'll know you're a cruel destructive man and I'll want nothing more to do with you. Let's not play games, Mr Bayard – put up or shut up. Do we have a deal?'

It seemed an age before he answered.

'We have a deal,' he told her.

THREE

There was a cold wind and pelting rain as Max Mather drove into Switzerland via the railhead frontier town of Chiasso. The Italians waved him out and the Swiss let him in with a minimum of fuss. He should have been dog-tired, but the adrenalin was pumping at full pressure. He drove straight through to Zurich, checked into the Baur au Lac and slept till noon the next day.

His first call after lunch was to a camera shop to have his photographs of the Raffaello pieces developed and printed in two sets of enlargements.

Next he paid a visit to the Consul-General for Panama, an urbane and elegant gentleman in his mid-forties. Fluent in Spanish, English, French, German and Italian, his expositions were eloquent and admirably clear. He explained to Mather that for a down payment and an annual fee he could acquire, ready made, a legal company registered in Panama, a set of Panamanian directors, a book full of bearer shares which constituted his legal title to the company, a minute book and a document of procuration which would enable him or any other person to act on behalf of the company.

He could choose the company name from an existing list or he could invent one himself – this latter choice would, however, involve an administrative delay. So Mather chose a title from the list – Artifax SPA. As to the functions of the company, it could do whatever he wanted it to do, from oil drilling to making women's underwear. He paid the Consulate in cash and headed straight to the Union Bank of Switzerland on Bahnhofstrasse. There, having displayed the documents of registration and the bearer shares, he opened an account for the company with the dollar draft from the Palombini bequest. This done, he rented in the name of the company a large safe-deposit box in which he lodged the pictures, the cartoons and the foundation documents of Artifax SPA.

Now he had two identities, one personal and the other corporate. The corporate one was an almost perfect mask, since the true ownership of the company was vested not necessarily in the purchaser but in the holder of the bearer shares. One identity could therefore be completely divorced from the other. To complete the divorcement, he took himself off to a lawyer recommended with careful reluctance by the bank.

'It is not a thing we usually do, Mr Mather, but in your case – a new client, a stranger in our city – we bend the rules a little. The man is very reputable. His name is Alois Liepert.'

Liepert was a trim forty-year-old with an agreeable smile, a firm handshake and an excellent command of Oxford English. He also had a woman colleague whom he introduced as Dr Gisela Mundt, former lecturer in jurisprudence at the University of Zurich. She seemed to be in her early thirties, had an infectious laugh, wore expensive tailored clothes and was fluent in French, Italian, English, High German and her native Schweizerdeutsch.

Mather presented his introduction from the Union Bank. Alois Liepert agreed – subject to a retainer of five thousand Swiss francs – to act as attorney for Max Mather, while Gisela Mundt would act as procurator for Artifax SPA under a limited delegation of powers. Thus, in the space of fifteen minutes, a fiction had been created whereby Artifax SPA enjoyed an independent legal existence while its ownership was cloaked in almost impenetrable secrecy and its assets – possibly worth tens of millions of dollars – were locked in a bank vault on the Bahnhofstrasse.

Gisela Mundt gave a happy laugh and said, 'Now you own us, Mr Mather. How do you wish to dispose of our services?'

'First,' said Mather, 'I should like to know how legal privilege works in Switzerland.'

'Between lawyer and client, it is absolute.'

'Between Swiss lawyer and foreign client?'

'Equally so,' replied Alios Liepert. 'We are a neutral country, a safety-valve for the world. Secrecy is our most valuable asset. Without it, I doubt we could survive.'

'In that case,' Mather announced deliberately, 'I wish to make a deposition which you will notarise and keep in a safe-deposit. I wish to make it in as formal a fashion as possible so that you, as my attorneys, may be able to respond in good faith to any questions which may arise in future about me or my affairs. You may make whatever inquiries you wish to verify my statements, but once you have verified them I shall hold you most rigidly to advise and act in my best interests. You will keep me always well within the law and you will neither propose nor permit me to drift into risky or ill-defined areas. Do I make myself clear?'

'You do,' said Dr Mundt. 'We should incorporate the statement you have just made into a formal briefing instruction which you will sign later. Now if you'd like to begin dictating . . . the machine is running.'

'My name is Maxwell Mather. I am an American citizen. My passport number is 9378567. I am unmarried. By profession, I am an academic. I hold a doctorate in palaeography from Princeton University and a master's degree in the History of European Art. For the past four years I have been employed as archivist to the Palombini family at their villa called Tor Merla, near Florence. I was also, during the whole of this period, the acknowledged lover of the Signora Pia Palombini, mistress of the estate and head of the family. Some six weeks ago she died after a long fight against motor neurone disease, during most of which I nursed her night and day. Her legacies to me, recorded in her holograph will – of which I tender a copy with this deposition – were as follows: two years' salary paid in US dollars, all the personal gifts she had made me, the automobile which she had bought for my use and a memento of my own choosing from the archive on which I had been working. The family raised no objection to these legacies. The executor of the estate, Claudio Palombini, was lavish in his praise for my care of his aunt. On my advice, he dedicated the archive to the National Library in Florence and he asked me to stay on to complete the negotiations for the transfer. We parted amicably and with mutual respect. It is my intention to set up business in Europe and America as a dealer and consultant in the fine arts. I am adequately supplied with funds and I look to you, Dr Liepert and you, Dr Mundt, for such legal counsel as I may need from time to time. End of deposition.'

'That's admirably clear.' Liepert sounded puzzled.

'But what is not clear,' said Gisela Mundt tartly, 'is what prompted you to make such a vacuous statement.'

'Because,' said Mather blandly, 'the gift I chose from the archive was a canvas envelope sewn with cobbler's thread and sealed with beeswax. It had been lying buried under a pile of papers ever since I had begun work on the archive . . . I am the only person in the world who knows of the existence of the envelope or its contents.'

'Which are, precisely . . . ?' It was Liepert's question.

'Which may be – I repeat *may* be – two Raffaello portraits on wood and a complete set of cartoons for an altar-piece. The provenance of all the pieces goes back to 1505.'

'So,' said Gisela quietly, 'you could be a very rich man. Did no one ask you what it was you had chosen as a memento from the archive?'

'No one. Neither the attorneys for the estate nor Claudio Palombini himself, with whom I was in regular contact.'

'Didn't that seem strange to you?'

'It did. Then on reflection I realised that they had no further interest in the archive; it was already being passed to the Library. The family was no longer concerned with it.'

Liepert and Mundt looked at each other, then he turned to Mather and asked:

'Is it your intention to retain this legacy?'

'It is.'

'Would you be prepared to litigate about it?'

'Yes.'

'Where are the pictures now?'

'In a safe-deposit here in Zurich.'

'How did you get them out of Italy?'

'I carried them out, quite legally.'

'It is illegal to export historic works of value without a permit,' Gisela pointed out.

'I am aware of the law, Dr Mundt. I submit – and can prove – that there exists at this moment a very grave doubt as to the authenticity of the works and that therefore no infraction has been committed.'

'What is the doubt that hangs over the pieces, Mr Mather?'
Once again it was Gisela Mundt who was pursuing him.

He told her at length and in detail of his encounters with
Niccoló Tolentino and the copies he had executed for Luca Palombini the Swindler. At the end of his narrative he made a gesture
of appeal.

'So tell me, either of you, do I have right on my side or not?'

'Given that everything you have told us is true,' said Alois
Liepert deliberately, 'then without a doubt you have the law on
your side.'

'Whether you have right on your side . . . ' Gisela Mundt
smiled disarmingly as she spoke. 'That's another question which
you have to answer yourself. We deal only with the law; so you
could say, Mr Mather, that you're a very lucky man. You could
be worth a mint of money and you've just hired two of the best
advocates in Zurich to make sure you keep it.'

'In which case,' said Mather happily, 'I'll call in tomorrow to
sign the statement. Here's a copy of the will, which is registered
at the Anagrafe in Florence. I'll also deposit with you tomorrow
the negatives and a set of photographs of the art works. I suggest
we complete your education by a private viewing in the strong-
room of the Union Bank. If it's convenient, we can do that
immediately after I sign the deposition.'

'And after that,' Gisela asked, 'how do you wish us to
proceed?'

'By masterly inactivity,' said Mather agreeably. 'Do nothing
until you have instructions from me. I'm going to give myself a
month's holiday. After that, we'll see. . . . Thank you both for
your courtesy. Until tomorrow.'

When he had left, Liepert and Mundt looked at each other;
Mundt asked the first question: 'Well, what do you think of him,
Alois?'

'I think he's telling the truth. What's your notion?'

Gisela looked thoughtful. 'He interests me. I'd read him as an
academic who's never taken a risk in his life. He's a house-
martin, always nesting under the shelter of the eaves. Now he's
free and flying with the falcons. He's enjoying it. I just hope he
doesn't get torn to pieces!'

*

Max Mather arrived in New York trim and tanned after a month on the ski slopes. He booked into a serviced apartment on the upper East side, laid out his books and papers, made enough telephone calls to plug himself back into the Manhattan circuits and began to plot the next stage of his campaign, which was to prepare at long range a buyers' market for the treasures which he believed he held. He himself would not be involved in the sale. That would be negotiated by Artifax SPA. However, he could with perfect propriety and safety prime the public interest with some scholarly revelations and speculations. He had learned a great deal about the art market from Niccoló Tolentino, the dealers and connoisseurs of Florence and his own travels with Pia.

Another and equally important part of the exercise was to enable him to proceed without challenge to his ownership, or civil litigation which would inhibit a sale of the pieces.

The whole operation appealed to his sense of humour. He was acting out a fantasy that wasn't a fantasy any more but a *fantasquerie*, a fly-away whim like that of a gambler playing with the house's money, win, lose or draw.

His opening gambit was a lunch with Harmon Seldes, editor-in-chief of *Belvedere* magazine; one of the recognised Brahmins of the art world. Seldes had been a hard fish to hook. He cultivated a reputation for elegance, aloofness and Olympian authority. In the end, however, Mather's well-practised charm – and the fact that he, too, had graduated from Princeton – carried the day and the luncheon was arranged.

Seldes understood patronage and preferment. Something of a snob himself, he was intrigued by the notion of a private archivist to a noble family. An indefatigable fund-raiser, he was impressed by the fact that Mather had stage-managed the donation of the Palombini archive to a public institution. He was curious to know why Mather had sought him out. With careful modesty Mather explained.

'I'm doing a study on "Domestic Economics in Florence" in the early sixteenth century, working from a set of account books of the period. I have them on loan from the Palombini archive.'

'It sounds interesting.' Seldes was polite but non-committal.

'A lot of it is drudgery, but at the end I think I'll have something valuable. However, that's not the reason I wanted to see you. The fact is that I've stumbled on something quite curious and I don't know where to go with it – or if, indeed, I should go anywhere. I thought that with your long experience and all your connections in the arts, you might be willing to advise me.'

'This curious something – what is it precisely?'

'Two Raphael portraits and five cartoons for an altar-piece – none of which appears in the *catalogue raisonné*.'

Seldes gaped at him.

'You mean you've seen these things? They've been offered to you? You've authenticated them? What?'

'I can prove they were painted and paid for. I can give you the date – October 1505. What happened to them after that is still obscure. But I'd like to show you the evidence I've got. It's not something I can cart around easily, so I wondered if after lunch you'd be willing to stroll round to my apartment. It's only a couple of blocks from here.'

'Of course, of course. This is an important piece of news. It could cause quite a flutter in our little world.'

'That's what's been bothering me.' Mather made a small, dubious protest. 'I'm not sure that sort of publicity is wise. From my own point of view, I know I couldn't cope with it and I would hate to embarrass the Palombini family, who have been very good to me. I guess that was the real point of my coming to you. You would know how to handle such a matter in a muted and – how shall I say? – academic fashion.'

'Naturally. I couldn't agree more.' The words were casual but Seldes' eyes betrayed eagerness and a hint of greed. 'The first question is, what one would be expected to handle: a simple research project or a worldwide investigation into missing master works – presuming, of course, that they have survived the ravages of time. The second question is, what you personally hope to get out of it.'

'I?' Mather's laughter was happy and boyish. 'God knows! At most a footnote in history, a credit mark for a scholar's work. At least the fun of a treasure hunt.'

'That encourages me.' Seldes nodded ponderous approval. 'Nothing taints a project so badly as hope of personal gain. Look, it's not impossible that one could fund a certain amount of

51

research. I could commission a piece for the magazine; I could
without difficulty find a sponsor for a year's work in Florence.
The answer to the puzzle is probably in the archive itself, which
you tell me is only partly codified. Would you be able to under-
take that research?'

'I could; I have privileged access both to the family and to the
Library. On the other hand, there's a very real inhibition.' He
hesitated just long enough to convey a hint of emotion. 'Pia
Palombini and I were very much in love. I nursed her during her
last illness. I couldn't face the villa or the city without her. So
you must count me out.'

'Forgive me.' It was hard to know whether Seldes was offering
compassion or expressing relief. 'I understand, of course. But
you could offer guidance and help to another researcher?'

'Yes.'

'In that case, I might even plan the project myself – write the
introductory piece, set the direction of the inquiries as it were.'

'Would you really?' Mather was the perfect wide-eyed innocent. 'That's the last thing I expected.'

'But first I'll have to authenticate your material, verify the
sources.'

'Let's do it now; I'll get the check.'

Two hours later Harmon Seldes was huddled in an armchair in
Max Mather's apartment with a brandy in his hand, reading the
latest item in the chain of evidence – a recent letter to Mather
from the Custodian of Autographs:

Dear Colleague, dear friend,

I miss you. We all miss you. Now that the charming Miss
Loredon has also left us, we are doubly bereft. In the city of
flowers we need friends to share our springtime.

You will be happy to know that the transfer of the Palombini
archive to our custody is now complete, and that I have been
named curator of the collection. For this honour, which also
reflects itself in my pension arrangements, I am deeply in your
debt.

We had a big ceremony to celebrate the occasion. Palombini was there, also our director, the mayor, the senior members of the *Comune*, officials from the Belle Arti. Kind things were said about you. Your name is inscribed in our golden book of benefactors.

You have done me another favour as well. At that happy, tipsy farewell party for Miss Loredon, you suggested I research the life and times of Luca Palombini. I didn't take the idea too seriously at the time. Like most scholars I am more at home in the safe and distant past. Besides, I have my own unhappy memories of wartime and I was not eager to revive them. It was a period of moral confusions and divided loyalties and most of us were left with some tally of private guilt. However, the notion took hold of me and finally I became enthralled by it.

I know our friend Nicki told you some things about Luca. You expressed a special interest in the women in his life. Of all of them – and my list is long but incomplete – his wife was perhaps the least interesting. She was well-born, convent-educated, had lived all her life in an envelope of unquestioned certainties. Luca paid her the respect due to the matron of the household; he cherished her and her children and arranged the rest of his life to suit himself. In that, of course, he was every bit as conventional as his wife.

To his mistresses he was generous but never lavish. He bought them jewels, clothed them in high fashion, lodged them in comfort. He was, by report, an energetic lover. He was also a tyrant who would tolerate neither scenes nor gossip; the smallest hint that the woman was telling bedroom secrets meant an instant end to the affair.

The opera singer Camilla Dandolo seems to have been a special case. Her voice was mediocre; she was never a *diva*. However, she was beautiful and intelligent and Luca Palombini made full use of her talents. I get the impression that she was at various times agent, courier and a personage of trust in his political life. This would account for the respect in which she is still held by senior male members of the Palombini family; it also explains why they were unwilling to involve her in quarrels or litigation with Luca's wife. It is clear that he made good provision for her. He bought her a piece of land in the Romagna; he endowed her with blocks of shares in various *enti*. It is not clear, however, whether he gave her any family property of substantial value. You will note, dear colleague, that I have been a busy and very happy voyeur.

After Luca's death Camilla Dandolo returned to Milan. She was no longer in demand as a singer, but the authorities at La Scala were happy to let her sit out her contract. She sang in benefit performances, coached young performers, behaved in exemplary fashion.

Then, surprisingly, she married – this was in November 1947. The bridegroom was one Franz Christian Eberhardt, a Brazilian national resident in Rio de Janeiro. I enclose for your edification the extract from the records of the *Ufficio Anagrafe* in Milan. According to a press report, the couple went first to Lisbon for a honeymoon and then took ship to Rio.

There is, however, a piece of unconfirmed gossip which my twisted old mind tells me could be true. The gossip is that Franz Eberhardt was one of those Nazi officers who fled south to Italy and then, with the help of old friends in church and state, escaped finally to the South Americas. . . .

And there, my dear young colleague, the history ends, as do all our Italian histories, with a hint of melodrama. Now, what have you to tell me? Does the work go well? I am fascinated by the draft material on your thesis that you have sent me. You ask about an old chapel within the grounds of the Palombini villa. I made some inquiries about this and discovered that there did exist as late as the mid-seventeenth century a votive chapel dedicated to St Gabriele. However, it was the scene of the particularly brutal rape and murder of a peasant girl from the estate. The building was deconsecrated and razed to the ground; the timber and the stones were used in barns and outbuildings attached to the villa. The peasants say the site is still haunted by a veiled maiden who waits for unwary lads to lure to destruction.

This I find is one of the fascinations of our profession: turn a dusty page and a whole history is displayed before you. But I grow lyrical – and when that happens, my wife tells me I become a bore.

Write again soon. I am intrigued by your tales of wild doings on the snow-fields. I am even more intrigued by your dedication to energetic sports like downhill racing. These are unlikely talents in a scholar. Or does that very sentiment display my ignorance? After all, the British always put a premium on sporting prowess and the Russians turned it into a political tool. Our prowess is in the bed or on the battlefield. *Eheu fugaces!* Either way, I am getting too old to play games.

Affectionate salutations,

Guido Valente
(Custodian of Autographs and now Curator of the Palombini Archive)

Seldes folded the letter carefully and handed it back to Mather. When he spoke there was a new respect in his tone.

'You seem to have a talent for friendship.'

'Guido Valente is very special: a Renaissance man to his fingertips.'

'May I ask, Max – you don't mind if I call you Max, do you? You must call me Harmon.'

'Thank you.'

'May I ask, Max, whether you have shared this information about the Raphaels with the Palombini family or with your friend Valente? This letter would seem to indicate that you have.'

'On the contrary. For very good reasons I have refrained from doing so.'

Seldes shot him a quick appraising look and said carefully, 'Perhaps I was misled by the reference to the chapel of St Gabriele in both the letter and the account books.'

'You were.' Mather was blunt. 'The chapel and the references to Luca Palombini belong in the context of my exchanges with Pia during the last months of her life. She suffered from a wasting illness called motor neurone disease; she slept fitfully and always in fear that a choking spasm would take her during the dark hours. I used to sit with her and encourage her to talk and to tell me stories about her relatives and their tribal memories. By the very circumstances of their telling the tales were disjointed and fragmentary. Lately I've been trying to recall them and set

55

them down. I . . . it doesn't make the pain go away, but it seems to make it more bearable.'

'I understand that,' said Seldes mildly. 'I don't mean to offend you, but may I know why you have not chosen to discuss the Raphaels with the Palombini family? After all, they were the original owners.'

'Two reasons.' Mather's answer was prompt but edgy. 'First, I came upon the reference only after Pia's death. Second, Pia had made me aware of certain disputes within the family about Luca's administration of family assets during the Fascist period and the German occupation. Obviously he was buying survival and betting on all the numbers. I never asked for details, Pia never volunteered them. We were lovers, but I was still the outsider. However, after she died the family became very respectful and caring. That relationship is very important to me. I want to keep it intact. So I keep a still tongue in my head about family matters. I confess in the privacy of this room that I've often wondered whether Luca used these and other lost works in a deal with the Germans, possibly with Goering's art agents who were active in Italy at that time. But, as you know, the Italians don't take kindly to that kind of inquiry from a stranger.'

'So they know nothing of this passage in the account books?'

'Correct. However, before anything is published here I would feel obliged to inform them of the situation and at least invite their cooperation in any inquiries.'

'My sentiments exactly.' Seldes was obviously satisfied. 'If you'd offer me another small brandy – then I must go.'

He held out his glass and made no protest when Mather poured him a generous measure. 'Max, let's get down to cases. I'd like to publish a few extracts from your thesis in the *Belvedere*. We pay well. It will probably help you when you go looking for a publisher. From my point of view it would set a proper academic tone for a research project. What do you say?'

'I'd be delighted. I would of course need your guidance in the selection of suitable passages.'

'For that I'd give you one of our senior editors. Do you have any objection to working with a woman?'

Mather was quick to see the barb under the lure. He grinned. 'On the contrary, I'm very fond of women.'

'Good.' Seldes seemed relieved. 'Which brings me to my next point. If one is to do this thing properly, give it the right cachet, one needs a prime sponsor. After seeing all your material, knowing that there is much much more to be examined, I'm sure I could persuade the directors of *Belvedere* to back the project. How would you feel about that?'

'I'd feel very flattered.'

'Would you consider joining us on a retainer basis with the title, say, of "Contributing Editor"?'

'Well . . . if you think I'd be up to it?'

'My dear Max,' Seldes was suddenly expansive, 'you're a scholar of distinction. Your experience, although limited, is special. It has its own category of values. I'd be grateful if you would share them with me. I might even try to arrange my schedule so as to include a trip to Florence in late May or early June. If you were unable to come with me, you could perhaps arrange the introductions?'

Mather was hard put to restrain his joy. Seldes' greed was clear to see. He wanted the credit of discovery and smelt big gains for himself afterwards. So be it, then. He was a power in the business. Where he went, money followed—gallery money, private money, trust money. No matter where he turned, he would never, could never, find the pictures, but every move he made would add to their ultimate market value.

But Seldes knew that too and he was likely to prove a persistent inquisitor, full of dangerous surprises. He asked now, 'This Miss Loredon mentioned in the letter; is she any relation to Hugh Loredon, the Christies man?'

'His daughter. She was working in Florence under the auspices of the Belle Arti. She's a clever girl.'

'Good-looking, I take it?'

'Very.'

'Hugh was a handsome devil, too, in his day.'

'I've never met him.'

'You should. He knows nothing about art, but everything in the world about selling it. By the way'—he was off on another tangent—'we haven't talked about the Palombini collection itself. You must know it very well?'

'Reasonably well; I superintended the cataloguing done for the estate by Niccoló Tolentino. I have to tell you that apart from a few good pieces the greater part of it is junk – copies and low-grade originals. One thing I can affirm: there are no Raphaels. We know they had them at one time. So when did they let them go and to whom? Anyway, if and when you go to Florence I'll arrange for you to visit the villa and be shown the collection. I'll also have you meet Tolentino, Guido Valente and a couple of other interesting folk in Florence.'

'Generous of you, Max. Most generous. I have of course my own long-time friends in Florence. But yes, I'd love to meet your people.' Seldes' Olympian laurels were slipping a little. 'About the job. Call me on Monday. We'll fix a time to chat and meet some of my bright people. If you'll allow me, I'll take a copy of your manuscript so that I can get an editorial reading before we meet. As for the Raphaels, that's thee and me only until we have the whole thing in focus. *Capisce?*'

Mather ushered him out and watched him pace down the sidewalk towards Lexington. A pompous ass he might be, but he was bright. In a few brisk moves he had put himself in control of the investigation and all the publicity attached to it, and therefore of any profit which might grow out of it. Which was exactly what Max had planned. Harmon Seldes and his magazine provided yet another patent of legitimacy. They distanced him by long strides from the pictures themselves; they made him a humble scholar overshadowed by a greater one. Amen. So be it. Seldes would always be an unsafe friend who could turn into a dangerous enemy overnight; but pray God he wasn't mugged or hit by a taxi. For this moment, anyway, he was worth a lot of money to Maxwell Mather.

With which happy thought bubbling in his brain, Mather picked up the telephone, called Anne-Marie Loredon and invited her to drinks and dinner at Gino's. Her protest rattled the receiver.

'Max, you're a monster. You haven't offered me a meal since you arrived and now the best you can suggest is Gino's.'

'What could possibly be better? I love the old joint – zebras and all. I'm embraced when I go in, I get a free Sambucca before I leave. The wine's honest. The food's good. And we can both brush up our Italian. By the way, I had a letter from Guido Valente. He misses you. They all miss you in Florence.'

'I've missed them, too.'

'Did you miss me?'

'Not too much. I've been busy—and I've struck it lucky. I'll tell you about it over the drinks.'

'I've got news for you, too. I'll keep mine for the pasta. Love you.'

'You don't at all, but it's nice to hear you say it. Seven-thirty okay?'

'Seven-thirty it is. *Ciao, bambina.*'

As he set down the telephone and began tidying his desk and washing glasses, he was caught up in a wave of unbidden memories—of the 'Blackbird Tower'; of Pia Palombini, frail and fearful, clinging to him for comfort; of Niccoló Tolentino, the humpbacked one with the luminous eyes and the magical hands. There were memories of Anne-Marie too, of waking at dawn in her apartment to the sound of Angelus bells and wondering, if only for a moment, where and when all the innocence of things had gone.

The sudden onrush of memory gave a special touch of emotion to his meeting with Anne-Marie. They embraced warmly. They perched themselves at the bar for two cocktails apiece, then settled at a table under a whole wall full of rampant zebras. They ordered pasta, vitello alla Toscana and a bottle of Barolo. While they waited, Anne-Marie continued the breathless recital of her news.

'So the upshot of it is, I have the gallery. I'm opening with the exhibition of Madeleine Bayard's pictures. Bayard himself has appointed me to deal for him—buying and selling. His collection is very valuable, but it's a hodgepodge lot that needs weeding and refocusing. Beyond that I haven't been able to plan anything. Bayard's driven a hard bargain. He's given me a five-year lease with a three-year renewal option, but he insists I take the whole building. Now I have to rent off the two top floors to pay for it. That leaves me more stretched than I wanted to be.'

'Would you think of sub-leasing two floors to me?'

'What would you do with them?'

'Convert one into an apartment for myself. Set up the other as a studio and lecture hall. I have the notion of inviting Nicki Tolentino to New York to give a series of lectures and master classes. If that works, I'll invite other experts.'

Anne-Marie ruminated for a long moment, then she demanded, 'Would you share Nicki with me?'

'Share him how?'

'We split costs and receipts – but I run him under the auspices of the gallery. It would be a marvellous draw card – establish us at one stroke amongst the serious professionals.'

Mather grinned at her over the lip of his glass. 'Now who's driving a hard bargain? Any sweeteners to the deal? Think carefully now, because I've got news you haven't heard yet.'

'What sort of sweeteners did you have in mind?'

'In Florence you suggested we might work together. Are you still interested?'

'What would you do?'

'Just as you suggested. I set up in Europe. You use me as buyer, seller and fixer. We split commissions. I commute between here and the Continent, so we're in constant contact.'

'Done!'

'Then, so you know how lucky you are, you've just hired the new contributing editor of *Belvedere*.'

'Max, you old fox! I don't believe it.'

'You'd better believe it, *bambina*. I had lunch today with Harmon Seldes. We made a deal for publication of extracts from my Florentine monograph. He also hired me on to the staff. So you see, Miss Loredon, you have a friend on the most prestigious art journal in the world. You've just landed right side up on the trampoline and you're three feet in the air already.'

'How much of this did you have planned before you got to New York?'

'Not a lot, sweetheart. I'm an inspired improviser. Does that bother you?'

'No . . . I'm glad to have you around. I've been feeling very exposed.'

'To what? Or should I say to whom?'

'To everything; but to Bayard in particular. I've been absolutely dependent on his goodwill. I still am.'

'It seems to me he's cut himself a pretty good deal: a lease on his building, his wife's pictures coming to market, an eager and beautiful agent for his own collection. Anything else to add to the list?'

'It's none of your goddamn business, Max!'

'Under the circumstances, it is. I'm not looking for a *ménage à trois.*'

'Why not, Max? From what I know, you're quite comfortable in that sort of arrangement.'

The instant the words were uttered she regretted them. Mather's reaction was strange. He was silent for a long moment, staring down at the backs of his hands. Then he answered quite lightly, 'You're right, of course. I am very good in three-cornered situations, so long as I know the ground rules from day one. I'm flexible, I'm reasonably good-humoured, a live-and-let-live kind of guy. I've managed to stay friends with most of the women I've known.'

She reached out and imprisoned his hands in her own. 'Please, Max! I was bitchy. I apologise. There's nothing between me and Bayard except business. He's made one pass at me, but that was on the first day. Since then he's been very correct, very hard-nosed in our dealings. Still, I know he's attracted to me so I keep my guard up all the time I'm with him. Can you forget what I said? We should both be celebrating, not quarrelling.'

Mather gave her a lopsided grin. 'We should. We shall. But let's talk a little more business first. The Madeleine Bayard exhibition. You're aware that the murder story is going to be revived; how will you handle it?'

'Exploit it for all it's worth.'

'And Bayard will agree to that?'

'Has agreed.'

'He's a nut – and so are you!'

'Ground rule one, Max! Never tell me how to run my business.'

Mather snapped back at her, 'You won't live to run your business if you play psycho games in this town. Haven't you heard of copycat crime? You play it *down*, for God's sake! The elegiac note: "Life is short. Art is long. Madeleine Bayard is immortalised in her work." I'll write the damned copy for you if I have to.'

'All right, Max, all right! I'll think about it.'

'When do you propose to open the gallery?'

'We're at the end of January now. I want to be open by mid-April at the latest. I've budgeted for a premium payment to the contractors if they can make it by the first of April.'

'Which means you should be able to run two exhibitions before the fourth of July. You're opening with the Madeleine Bayard. What's next?'

'Oliver Swann, from New Mexico. He paints landscapes that are so full of raw power you can't believe they exist. He's a colourful character too. He'll make good copy. After that, for the summer, I'm not sure.'

'That could be the time to bring in Niccoló Tolentino to run a month of master classes and lectures. You could charge a stiff admission. Publicise it well enough and you'd have queues outside the gallery. Think about it. If it makes sense I'll get in touch with Nicki right away.'

Apropos of nothing at all, Anne-Marie said:

'You've changed, Max. I'm seeing a different man from the one I knew in Florence.'

'How changed? Better? Worse? More, less?'

'More drive, more calculation. Suddenly you're a man in a hurry. You never used to be like that. You'd drift into town. We'd have fun. You'd drift out again. I liked that. Now I'm not so sure . . . .'

The waiter set down two plates of fettucine in front of them, flourished the pepper and the parmesan, poured the wine, wished them good appetite and withdrew.

They were half-way through the pasta when Mather said casually, 'I was going to ask you a favour.'

'Ask.'

'Would you introduce me to your father? I've got a couple of rather valuable items I'm thinking of selling. I'd like to get some advice – preferably from a friendly expert.'

'What sort of things, Max?'

'Heirloom stuff – a Tompion watch which I am told is quite valuable, an antique ring with a carved emerald . . . a couple of other items. I'm going to need cash to subsidise the sub-lease and renovation of your building.'

'Father won't value the stuff himself, but he'll get you an

expert opinion from within the company. I'll tell him to expect a call from you.'

'Thanks.' He raised his glass in a toast. 'Here's to old times – and to better ones!'

They drank, they ate, they talked. An hour later he walked her the six blocks to her apartment. She didn't ask him in. He did not linger. He kissed her on both cheeks, Italian-style, and turned to go.

Anne-Marie stopped him. 'Max . . . '

'Yes?'

'Are you mad at me?'

'Of course not . . . but I will be if you stand around flatfooted explaining that you've got a headache. I'll call you in the morning – and don't forget to telephone your father.'

'I won't. Good night, Max. . . . '

A blown kiss and he was gone, striding out jauntily and whistling an off-key version of *La ci darem la mano*. He was not too dissatisfied. A little after-dinner sex would have been pleasant, but he could get that by lifting the telephone. The important thing was that his identity, sketchy after a long absence, was now being fleshed out to lifesize. The publication of his material would give him the authority of a scholar. As consulting editor to an important magazine, he could go anywhere and ask what questions he chose. As associate of a new and well-connected gallery, he would be courted by dealers everywhere.

His next need was for local legal guidance – and who better to supply it than Anne-Marie's landlord, attorney for the Art Dealers' Association of America?

Edmund Justin Bayard leaned back in his chair, made a spire of his fingertips and, peering over the top of it, studied his visitor. He liked what he saw: a youngish, handsome fellow, well-groomed, the suit cut by a good tailor, the shirt and tie custom-made, the cufflinks and the watch expensive but not gaudy. He asked, 'Who recommended me to you, Mr Mather?'

'Your name came up in conversation with Anne-Marie Loredon, with whom I dined the evening before last. She told

me among other things that you are the attorney for the Art
Dealers' Association of America. So here I am.'

'And how may I help you?'

'Let me explain first that I'm not an art dealer, I'm a scholar –
a palaeographer and a historian with a special interest in the
history of European art. I'm publishing some material in the
Belvedere, where I've just been appointed consulting editor. Miss
Loredon has asked me to act for her in Europe. I've never done
it before, so I thought I should familiarise myself with the
elements of the law about the acquisition and disposal of major
art works originating in Europe. If I am to recommend a
purchase, I must know the legal requirements on title, provenance, export and import. In this field I'm a complete novice.'

Bayard smiled tolerantly. 'Don't feel too badly about it, Mr
Mather. There are a few simple principles. After that, you're up
to your neck in statutes which change at every national border.'

'I thought perhaps there might be some published guidelines,
a handbook put out by the Dealers' Association?'

Bayard laughed – a dry, barking sound that ended in a splutter.

'My dear Mather, that's a real testimony to your innocence.
Handbook? My God! The main aim of any dealer is to publish
as little as possible, and to promise even less, about the goods
he sells. He's the innocent always, acting in good faith between
a willing buyer and a willing seller. Tell him you picked up a del
Sarto at an auction in Liechtenstein; he'll be prepared to take
your word for it. He'll be deliriously happy if you can produce
some reasonable paperwork. If anyone contests your title to the
work the dealer will step back and leave the two of you to fight
it out. Show him a half-way decent forgery and he'll look at it
with his blind eye and calculate his chances of palming it off. He
doesn't need an abacus to tell you when the statute of limitations
expires on a stolen art work. He makes no guarantees about
provenance even if there is one. What he's selling is what the
owner represents, what the buyer sees. If it fell off the back of
a truck and the owner comes screaming to reclaim it, the dealer
disclaims all responsibility.

'Seriously though, Mr Mather, as dealer or agent your safest
stance is to treat each case on its merits and pass the responsibility on to the buyer. If there's doubt about title or provenance,

just state your reservations; leave the rest to Miss Loredon and her attorneys.'

'Who, presumably, would be you?'

'Not necessarily; though once she qualified as a member of the Association she would have access to my advice. As she probably told you, she'll be buying and selling for my personal collection. So there could be occasions when you and I become directly involved.'

'Would you be willing to take me as a client?'

'If you chose to retain me, yes.'

'I'd like to do that.' Mather offered his card. 'That's my address and telephone number, both temporary. I'm hoping to sub-lease the top two floors of Miss Loredon's building.'

Bayard looked at him with sudden new interest. 'Two floors? That's an awful lot of space.'

'One as my living quarters; one will be a lecture hall and studio. I'm proposing to bring over the senior restorer from the Pitti in Florence to conduct a series of summer seminars on conservation and related subjects. Miss Loredon is keen on the idea. She'd like to participate. If it's a success, I'll bring over other European experts in related disciplines.'

'An interesting project . . . very. You knew Miss Loredon in Florence?'

'Yes. She was there under the auspices of the Belle Arti. I was archivist to one of the old families. We met by chance. I was able to introduce her to local artists and craftsmen; we did a lot of the galleries and churches together.'

'Do I hear romantic overtones, Mr Mather?'

'No. The Florentine lady with whom I was deeply in love died a few months ago. I'm not ready for any new commitment. Miss Loredon has her own ambitions which do not include me.'

'Do you think she'll achieve them here in New York?'

'Probably. She's got good taste and a wide education. She's very determined. People like her. So yes, I'd say she has more than a sporting chance. By the way, she was vastly impressed with your late wife's pictures.'

'I know. That is why I have commissioned her to bring the works to market.'

'Which raises another reason for my visit, but I find it hard to broach the subject without seeming impertinent.'

'Please, say what you want.'

'Miss Loredon and I were discussing the exhibition and the inevitable press stories about your wife's murder. She told me you had discussed it and decided to confront and even exploit the publicity.'

'That's about the size of it, yes.'

'I disagreed,' said Mather flatly. 'I told Anne-Marie so.'

'And?'

'First she told me to mind my own business; then she consented to think about it.'

'What was your objection?'

'Copycat crime – incitement of the unstable by lurid stories luridly told. Besides which, works of art themselves create a potent magic, especially when people congregate to view them.'

Bayard thought about the proposition for a moment, then nodded a guarded agreement. 'I understand your reasoning; I'll talk further with Miss Loredon. Is there anything else?'

'I'd like to ask you a couple more questions.'

'You're paying for my time, Mr Mather.' Bayard was relaxed again.

'What, precisely, constitutes title to a work of art?'

'Possession first. It's still nine points of the law. Then, any evidence of legal transmission: a bill of sale, a deed of gift, a will – even a birthday card.'

'I am told that the title may lapse after a certain period of time?'

'If an article has been lost, stolen or strayed for thirty years, title is deemed to have lapsed.'

'So thirty years after he's robbed you the thief can turn up on your doorstep and offer to sell you the very item he's stolen?'

'Precisely. If you don't meet his price, he can tuck it under his arm and walk away, scot-free. He's protected in two ways, you see. He can't be prosecuted for the crime because the statute of limitations applies, and after thirty years the title to the object is his by right of possession.'

'Next question, then: export and import. Certain countries restrain or altogether prohibit the export of major art works deemed to be national treasures?'

'Correct.'

'Yet most countries will permit the import of illegally exported art works.'

'Not quite, Mr Mather. The proposition is really a negative one. Most countries do not deem it their duty to ask whether or not the export was legal, especially if no other criminality is involved – for example, the objects are not listed by Interpol as stolen. What happens in practice is what I explained to you at the beginning – the dealer, or the auctioneer, doesn't ask. He's satisfied with evidence of title. He's delighted with a good provenance. He's not expected to act as customs officer for the French, the British or the Italians. On the other hand, he's wise not to involve himself directly with any smuggling operations. Also, he withholds all payment until the goods are safely in his own hands, in the land where he proposes to sell them.'

'It seems I have a lot to learn.' Mather gave a wry grin.

'I'm sure you're a fast learner,' said Bayard blandly. 'Now, let me put a question to you.'

'Please.'

'Has Miss Loredon offered you any share in her business?'

'No. Any reason for the question?'

'A simple one. I asked her to consider a partnership with me. She turned me down.'

'I wouldn't take it personally.'

'I'm delighted to hear you say that, Mr Mather. I make no secret of the fact that I have a very great interest in the lady . . .'

'In that case,' said Mather with a grin, 'I'll offer you some advice – free of charge! Don't rush your fences. This is one very independent lady.'

'I'll remember that, Mr Mather, and thank you.'

'Thank you, Mr Bayard.'

As soon as Mather had gone, Bayard lifted the telephone and dialled a number in Murray Hill.

'Lou? Bayard. Another name in the Loredon circle – Maxwell Mather. He knew her in Italy. He's going to be associated with her gallery. I don't think there's anything beyond friendship, but I'd like to know exactly where he fits in her scheme of things. I'll read you the address. What's that? Oh yes, so far I'm very satisfied. She checks out cleaner than I expected . . . '

FOUR

Hugh Loredon, auctioneer extraordinary, was the perfect image of a country gentleman: white hair, ruddy complexion, a taste for tweeds and fancy waistcoats, a roving eye for women, an agreeable wit, an eloquent tongue – and a feral instinct for the taste and temper of an auction crowd. Mather, who was entertaining him to lunch in his apartment, was treated to an hour of dissertation and anecdote.

'Look down on them from the rostrum and they're like a basket of cobras ready to rear up and bite you. So first of all you have to charm 'em, make music, hypnotise 'em into a rhythm of bidding. They've all studied the catalogues; they all know what they want to buy, they're all wondering whether their pockets are deep enough. After a while you learn to read your regulars. If you can get them settled down, they help with the rest of the crowd. I've worked London, Paris, New York, Geneva. Each one is different, but they're all the same: greedy and slippery. Sometimes you get a real sexual current coming up from the floor. There's one woman who bids by touching her left nipple with her right hand, another who keeps opening and closing her legs like a pair of bellows. Very distracting, I assure you, because she's got very good legs. This is a splendid meal, by the way. Where did you learn to cook?'

'I took lessons.'

Loredon nodded approval. 'Wise man. Lots of girls don't like to cook and all of them get hungry.'

Mather laughed. 'The voice of experience?'

'Long, long experience. The only problem with dining in restaurants is that it's a long way back to the bedroom. . . . You said you had some things to show me.'

'Pour yourself a glass of port while I get them.'

Mather cleared a space on the table and laid out his small

68

array of treasures: the Tompion watch, the carved emerald, an enamelled comfit box, a pair of seventeenth-century duelling pistols which he had admired in Brescia and which Pia had insisted on buying for him.

Hugh Loredon took out a pocket loupe and examined each article carefully. His verdict was brief.

'Unless you must, you'd be a fool to sell this stuff. Put it in a bank vault and keep it as insurance for your old age. This watch is a beauty. The inscription indicates that it was made in 1704, the year Tompion became Master of the Clockmakers' Company in London. It's a museum piece. It would have to bring anything from seventy-five to a hundred thousand. I sold one ten years ago for fifty. The jewel . . . it's interesting but not important enough to raise a ripple in a big estate auction. The box is good, Louis XIV. Thirty thousand maybe. The pistols, ten or there-abouts. The value goes up each year you hold on to them. It's up to you. If you like, I'll have our people give them a thorough inspection and then talk to you about a reserve and a suitable date to put 'em up. Alternatively, we could try to negotiate a private sale for you. We've got a pretty extensive international client list.'

'Put them up for auction,' said Mather briskly. 'I'm trying to get some of the clutter out of my life. I'm not pushed for cash yet, though I may be once I sign the sub-lease with Anne-Marie and start creating an apartment.'

'Let me know when you're ready,' Loredon said casually. 'I'd say there's an easy hundred thousand, after commission. On a good day, maybe more.'

'What makes a good day?'

'God knows. For me, it's the way the gavel sits in my hand when I pick it up.'

'There's something else I'd like to show you,' Max told him. 'Even Anne-Marie doesn't know about this. I'm publishing a piece about it in *Belvedere* and I want to keep it quiet until then.'

Hugh Loredon gave him a smile and a shrug.

'You're very trusting. This is the most gossipy business in the world. But I guess I can keep a secret – until I hear the same thing from someone else. Go ahead.'

Mather brought in the Palombini account books and translated the entries for him.

Loredon frowned in puzzlement. 'Don't you find that odd? They were painted in 1505 by a man acknowledged in his lifetime as a great master – and they've never been seen or heard of since.'

'Odd, yes; but not without precedent.'

'And what do you think will happen once your piece is published?'

'The best would be some response that indicates the works are still in existence. The worst, I guess, would be silence.'

'You may get more than you bargain for.'

'I don't understand?'

Hugh Loredon poured himself another glass of port and sliced a small wedge of cheese. He popped the cheese in his mouth and washed it down with a sip of port. Then he patted his lips with the napkin and slowly told his cautionary tale.

'You're talking about treasures here, Max. If you can get forty million at auction for a Van Gogh sunflower, what do you think these items would be worth? Say a hundred million and you're being conservative. If we take them to auction the auctioneers alone get commissions of ten per cent buyer, ten per cent seller – that's twenty million. So we're highly interested parties for a start. Then think of the other cobras in the basket: the dealers, the big collectors, the institutions, the foundations. . . . They're all going to be interested in you. They're going to be waving money under your nose, wanting to retain you, offering finder's fees. More than that, they're going to keep tabs on you wherever you are. Don't you see? It's a cheap exercise. You're the man with the treasure map – a real honest-to-God treasure map, authentic in every particular. Even I would be happy to put a minder on your tail for twelve months, just to make sure my company didn't lose a shot at twenty million commission. So far I'm talking about legitimate interests, but what about the black market boys? There's a millionaire shipowner in Athens who sponsors an art thief all of his own. There's a Colombian collector, a client of ours, who is a well-known receiver of stolen art works. Why shouldn't he be? He's got a mountain fortress and a private army

70

to protect him. There's nothing new in this; in the old days the *condottieri* used to live on booty.'

'Are you saying I shouldn't publish?'

'I have no right to say that. You're a scholar. I'm an auctioneer. We both want to see the things found – each for a different reason. I'm just pointing out that this isn't a parlour game . . . it has nothing to do with aesthetics or absolute values. This is trade – trade in rare and restricted commodities – which is as specialised as the old traffic in spices or the new one in commercial secrets. There's no place for amateurs. The rewards are high. The game is rough, dirty and sometimes downright dangerous. Also, it can cost you a lot of money to buy in . . . I gather you're comfortable, but not rich. From what Anne-Marie has told me, you like the leisure of academic life. I'm just warning you that the next couple of steps you take may land you in hell's kitchen.'

'Let's suppose,' said Max Mather quietly, 'let's suppose I decided not to publish and conducted my own research?'

'You can't.' Hugh Loredon was emphatic. 'It's too late.'

'Why can't I?'

'Because the moment you talked to Harmon Seldes you were already published. He knows what you know. He knows the source of your information. He's already talking it round his money people. I'm the same as he is. I know what you know. All I've engaged to do is keep the secret until it's not a secret any more – which is any moment from now. But because you're a friend of my daughter and you're a good cook and I'd hate to see you get your nose rubbed in the custard, I'm giving you fair warning.'

'I'm an idiot,' said Mather with feeling.

'You're just ignorant,' Hugh Loredon told him cheerfully. 'No harm in that. Stupid is something different. Now I have a favour to ask of you.'

'Name it.'

'I'm worried about Anne-Marie and Ed Bayard.'

'Why, for God's sake?'

'She's tied too closely to him; he's making a play for her.'

'She's a big girl. She knows how to say no.'

'It doesn't bother you?'

'Why should it?'

'I thought you two . . . '

'We're not. Anne-Marie and I had good times in Italy – lots of fun and no regrets on either side. Here in New York the fun times are over and we're just friends doing business together. That suits us both. So if she wants to date the May Queen or the garbage collector, that's her affair.'

'Then let me put it another way.' Loredon was suddenly sombre; his ruddy face seemed grey and shrunken. 'Ed Bayard's wife was a beautiful woman and a fine painter. He was insanely jealous of her. He tried to keep her isolated from her friends, in continual uncertainty about her talent. He would never allow her to exhibit, only to make private sales. He kept her in a state destructive to any artist – continual self-doubt. In the law he's brilliant. In his private life he's a screwed-up sadist. . . . '

'And how do you know all this?'

'Madeleine Bayard and I were lovers.'

Mather gave a long whistle of surprise. 'Did Bayard know that?'

'I believe so. I have no proof.'

'And you let your daughter make a deal with him?'

'I couldn't stop her. She had the whole thing set up before she came to see me: the lease signed, the exhibition contracted. She waved the papers under my nose like a banner, just so I'd be proud of her. What was the point of digging up a shabby little piece of history?'

'You're a bloody fool, Hugh.'

'I know it. I missed the moment.'

'Nonsense. Tell her now. If you don't, I will. Were you never questioned by the police about the murder?'

'Of course I was. But the only thing they could establish was that Madeleine and I were friends who occasionally went to bed together.'

'So it's in the record and it isn't a secret. What else did you tell them?'

'Nothing. You've got to understand that right up to the end I was hedging my bets. I didn't want a scandal; appearances are very important to my company. I had a few other little affairs going, because wealthy women dominate the art scene. I didn't have anything to offer the police except that Bayard made his wife unhappy. It didn't sound very convincing when he was the wronged husband and I was the part-time lover.'

'But Bayard did have a motive for murder.'

'Maybe, but the police ruled him out as a suspect very early in the piece.'

'So why are you telling me now?'

'Because . . . because I'm afraid. I'm as sure as I am of my own name that Ed Bayard is going to use my daughter to revenge himself on me.'

'That's probably an authentic expression of your guilt feelings, but it doesn't fit the facts. Anne-Marie told me herself that she stumbled on the studio through a realtor.'

'But once the deal was mooted, once Bayard knew who she was . . . don't you see?

'I see why you're worried. I don't see what else you can do but tell her the truth.'

'If I do, will you promise to stay close to her? Try to read what's happening between her and Bayard?'

'That's not my style, Hugh.'

'My daughter tells me a different story. That you hung in with your Italian friend until she died in your arms. That you're good in bed. That you're generous to your friends, you don't make scenes and you do clean up in the kitchen. She says there's much more to you than meets the eye.'

'It's a party trick,' said Mather with sour humour. 'Like sprouting mango trees and rabbits popping out of a silk hat.'

'I know that, Max. You know it. But so long as we keep it to ourselves, the illusion works.'

It was the tag-end of the afternoon when Hugh Loredon left, sobered with black coffee, soured a little by memories that curdled in the telling. Mather was left with the impression of an ageing actor who had found a vehicle to keep him working as long as he wanted, but for whom the role had lost all surprise and the performance all conviction. His easy charm and facile cynicism seemed to mask a bleak loneliness.

For Mather himself the luncheon had been a profitable event. The magazine, the auction house, the gallery – all these were patents of respectability. On the other hand, little by little the fictions were being stitched into the facts of other lives from which he had managed so far to isolate himself.

Hugh Loredon's dilemma illustrated something he himself had learned by rough experience: the weakness and the power of the *cavalier' sirvente*, the professional squire. His public existence was a half-life during which his mistress hoisted him like a flag at dawn and then lowered and furled him at sundown. For the rest, he was a possession personal to her: their life together a secret activity in which venery and venality, passion and perversity were compounded in unstable chemistry. The single element that held it in balance was its privacy. Only the squire saw milady's bulges and wrinkles. Only milady knew the cowardice of her attendant. The moment another person stepped into the room, the fragile combination became explosive.

Mather had warmed to Loredon at first because he understood him and could feel for him. He felt for Anne-Marie too, walking so confidently through the minefield of her father's follies. He wanted no part in their affairs, but since he had elected to use them for his own purposes he was like an insect being drawn inexorably into the Venus fly-trap.

He was pottering about his kitchen, stacking dishes, drying cutlery and ruminating on this shift in his perspective, when the telephone rang. Anne-Marie was on the line.

'Max, what are you doing?'

'Right now I'm cleaning up my kitchen. Your father and I have had lunch together. What can I do for you?'

'I'm leaving home now and going down to the studio. The architect is meeting me there. I thought you should meet him too to discuss the plan for your areas.'

'Good idea. Pick me up on the way; I'll be waiting on the sidewalk.'

The ride downtown was a nightmare. The Haitian driver, deaf to all protests and cursing continuously in creole, hurled them through the traffic as though the Ton-ton Macoute were chasing him with machetes. By the time they reached the studio Mather was ready to kill him with his bare hands and Anne-Marie, dizzy with car sickness, was heaving her heart out.

Mather steadied her and made her walk half a block, gulping in fresh air. Then they stood for a while surveying the exterior of the warehouse whose façade was of iron, cast and moulded in the opulent days of the steel barons. It was double-fronted, with a wide door in the centre and barred windows on either side. The door was matched on each level by a hatch through which goods hauled up on a winch could be brought into each storage area.

Inside the whole place had been stripped bare. There was an old-fashioned elevator and a wide stairway. At the rear of each floor was a toilet and a washroom. Apart from these encroachments all four storeys were free space, broken only by the slim cast-iron pillars which carried the weight of the steel floor joists and the roof-load.

They walked upstairs, inspected each level and then rode down together in the elevator. Mather noted with some surprise that the floors had been freshly sanded and the whole interior painted with undercoat. He asked Anne-Marie, 'Did you do this?'

'No. This is how I took it over. The lease says I have to hand it back in the same state. What do you think, Max?'

'It's a steal. The structure is sound. There are no signs of roof leaks, the load is carried on steel girders and iron pillars. The plumbing's old-fashioned but sound. The elevator needs a new motor. You'll want dual cycle air-conditioning. After that it's a partition and paint job, with a good lighting plan. The rest is superficial – a simple office, attractive toilets, a workable kitchen and servery.'

'How does it strike you as a gallery venue?'

'Good. The area is being developed. There's a young, affluent population. You can cover the old-money uptown buyers with advertisements and direct mail. I presume your father can help you build up a good client list?'

'He can. He will. How did you two get along together?'

'Fine. He liked my cooking. I enjoyed his talk. He approves of my working for you; he thinks you can use a minder.'

'I'm beginning to think I need one.'

75

'Any special reason?'

'Not really – except that I'm laying out a lot of money and nothing's coming in, so naturally I'm nervous. Also Ed Bayard's a little more than I need at the moment.'

'More passes?'

'No. It's just that he's so . . . so intense. I spent two hours at his house yesterday, cataloguing the exhibition pictures. At the end of the day I was quite drained. Even here I get an extraordinary sense of . . . of presence.'

'In spite of the clean-up Bayard's done?'

'You mean he's trying to paint out memories.'

'How many New York landlords give you a free scouring and undercoat job on a warehouse lease?'

'You talk as if it's something sinister. I think it's wonderful.'

'You're right. It is. I'll light a candle for him every morning.'

Then the architect was at the door, with an armful of plans and a head full of suggestions for the gallery, the storeroom, the lecture space and a dwelling for Max Mather. Two hours later they were all sitting over dinner in a neighbourhood restaurant run by two Vietnamese girls who called themselves the Trung sisters. The food was good, the service came with a smile. The architect, a new resident in SoHo, was full of gossip.

'I've been spreading the word about the gallery. Everybody's happy you're moving in – takes the curse off the place, so to speak. I'd moved down here just before the murder and for a while realty values took a dive. It was a very bloody business.'

'We know,' said Max Mather curtly. 'We're trying to forget it. You're designing a gallery, not a mausoleum.'

'Sorry.' The architect was all apologies. 'Last words on the subject – ever! Now, to come back to the question of track lighting. . . . '

So by a very narrow margin the meal was salvaged, but Mather was left with the uneasy conviction that silence was more dangerous to Anne-Marie than a blunt statement of her father's follies. Sensitive however to his own secret interest, he decided that he should not make himself the bearer of bad tidings. Such messengers were often killed for their pains and the only reward they got was two copper coins to hold their eyes shut. For him the wiser counsel was to keep his eyes open and his mouth shut and be the good friend of all the world: the Loredons, Bayard, Harmon Seldes, Uncle Tom Cobbley and the girl in the shampoo commercials.

Max sat up late that night, writing a careful letter to Claudio Palombini. It was a simple, straightforward account of the Raphael references, a mention of their forthcoming publication and a plea for help in his future researches:

> . . . Clearly publication of my findings will raise much curiosity about the lost works—if indeed they are lost and not buried in one of the more recondite collections which we know exist, even though the catalogues of their holdings are never published.
>
> It is possible, of course, that you may have knowledge of these works which I do not possess. If so, and you feel free to communicate it to me, I shall be happy to arrange for its publication with appropriate acknowledgment.
>
> I trust you and your family are in good health. The memory of my darling Pia still haunts my dreams. Amid the jangle of New York traffic, I long for the sound of blackbirds outside my window.

It was not all humbug. The nostalgic sentiment was almost genuine. His role as scholar-simpleton was almost authentic. What he could not convey was the excitement of his new enterprise, heady as proof alcohol, the satisfaction of seeing a campaign plan taking shape, watching the field of operations being surveyed for mines and man-traps.

He palmed his tired eyes and settled to the last night-work: the preparation of his notes for the meeting with Harmon Seldes at *Belvedere*.

Seldes gave him a studiously warm welcome: a tour of the office, sherry with the senior editors, lunch with the publisher and in-house counsel who offered him a twelve months' contract as consulting editor at a figure fifty per cent greater than he had expected. After the coffee, Seldes led him to his own office for a private discussion of what he called 'these Raphaels of yours'.

'I've thought this through very carefully, Max. Here's what I propose. We publish you in the April issue. We have a long lead time, so that's the best we can do. Our picture people will be looking out some interesting illustrations. Now, as editor for your piece I'm proposing Leonie Danziger. She's a freelance, one of the best in town. She's read your stuff and has come up with some excellent ideas. She works from her apartment; she's expecting you there at three this afternoon. Is that convenient?'

'Sure.'

'Now as to the Raphael reference, I propose we exclude that from your text. We'll run it as a boxed item properly attributed to you, related to your source material, but introduced by me personally. That way you'll have the full weight of editorial approval and endorsement behind your work. Do you see any problems in that?'

'None at all.'

'I must say, Max' – Seldes was suddenly uneasy – 'you're very laid back about the whole business.'

'I'm a happy hedonist,' Mather dismissed the comment with a shrug. 'I have no patience with academic jealousies.'

'I wondered about that,' said Seldes. 'I looked you up, of course. The academic information is adequate but sparse; the social history is – let's say – interesting!'

Mather's smile was disarming as he spread his hands in a Latin gesture.

'Get it off your chest, Harmon. You're publishing me. You're employing me. You're wondering if I've read the price-tag on the deal.'

'What does the price-tag say, Max?'

'You want to develop the Raphael investigation yourself.'

'How do you feel about that?'

'Content, relaxed, happy – no problem at all.'

'That surprises me.'

'Why should it? I came to you, remember? I came because you are one of the few people qualified to mount and carry through such an extended and expensive piece of research. I'm interested, sure. But I'm not disposed to hard labour. If I can help while I'm doing my own things, I will – but I'm not chasing fame or foundation funds or eating money. I'm happy to share with you whatever information I pick up along the way.'

'That's more than generous of you, Max.'

'Try to believe it's the truth,' said Mather with a grin. 'Then you'll sleep more soundly. There is one thing to remember, however.'

'What's that?'

'Once you publish, the world and his wife will be rummaging in the attic for lost Raphaels.'

'And all of them will be looking to me and to the *Belvedere* to pass judgment on their finds. Anyway, now that we understand each other let me prepare you a little for Danny Danziger. She's quite a formidable young woman. I'm told she has offbeat sexual preferences. That's only hearsay, of course; I never mix business with pleasure.'

Leonie Danziger was, to say the least, a suprise: a tall redhead, thirtyish on the calendar, with green eyes, a classic profile and a figure that would have sent the pre-Raphaelites wild. She wore a brocaded house-gown, horn-rimmed spectacles and Oriental mules. Her greeting was casual, her handshake a cool fleeting touch.

She ushered Mather into a large cluttered loft with a view across the water to the Jersey shore. Having seated him at a Spanish refectory table she perched herself, severe as a mother abbess, in a high-backed chair directly opposite him. Her first words were a flat sentence of damnation.

'You're a bloody dull writer, Mr Mather.'

'I know.' Mather gave her his most engaging grin. 'That makes me God's gift to editors. Anything I can do, they can do better.'

'Have you published much?'

'Very little. In practice I'm an archivist – by preference I'm an idler. Now, where would you like to start?'

'By explaining how I work. First, I get paid for editorial labour, then I get a byline and additional fees for what I write for publication. In other words, I'm not going to ghost your work but I may interpolate it with commentary for which I take credit and for which I get paid. If the commentary distorts or misrepresents your intent, you say so. I'll change it. In this case, I'm the presenter of your wares. Understood?'

'Yes.'

'So now, your material. The substance is obviously accurate. Your comparisons with domestic life today are interesting. Your conclusions are sound if sometimes facile. But you write everything in monotone. I know that *Belvedere* is a stuffy magazine, but it doesn't have to be that stuffy! So what I've set out to do is to choose the best and most interesting parts of your thesis and tie them together with a fairly lighthearted commentary.'

'How come,' Mather leaned back in his chair and studied her like a physician, 'how come I'm a lighthearted guy and write dull stuff – while you're a blue-stocking and you can write lighthearted commentary?'

For the first time a light appeared in the green eyes and a smile twitched at the corners of her mouth.

'Law of compensations. No man deserves to be as good-looking as you are. No woman deserves to be as much a blue-stocking as I am. So you get to be a lousy writer and I get to be a witty editor. . . . Shall we start work?'

He had to admit she was well prepared. She had taken a manuscript of some thirty thousand words, culled from it a score of sequences and put them together into a vivid mosaic of life on a villa farm in Tuscany in the early sixteenth century. She had an eye for lively detail – how wool was dyed and leather was tanned, how the grain that was shipped to Pisa from Sicily was exchanged for Tuscan wine and cheese, how the barrels of tunny fish from Trapani paid for iron from Elba, how woven silks and gentlemen's saddlery were traded for gold-dust from Djerba and black slaves from the Barbary coast.

She had managed to endow his dry prose with the sap of personal experience. Mather, all too conscious of the slipshod work he had delivered on a subject which interested him not at all, was stimulated to critical discussion and lively reminiscence. He had quite lost track of time when she switched off the tape recorder and announced, 'Six o'clock. That's it for today. You talk better than you write. Maybe we should put you on the lecture circuit. I'm dying for a drink. Join me?'

'Love to. Bourbon and water if you've got it.'

'Over there on the sideboard. You can fix me a vodka and tonic. There's a lime in the fruit bowl.'

While he made the drinks she set her papers in order and quizzed him in her offhand fashion.

'You intrigue me, Max Mather.'

'Why?'

'This happy-chappie act. You walk in, I push a pie in your face. You wipe it off and grin at me. You admit you've written a half-assed thesis. There's so little blood in the subject I can't figure why you bothered with it. Then I get you down to work. Lo and behold! Another man: serious scholar in search of excellence. Critical mind applying itself to classic categories. So which is the real you?'

'What you see is what you get.'

'I don't believe that.'

'How do you take your lime – slice or twist?'

'Slice, please. Are you gay?'

He was taken aback by the question, but grinned and answered, 'No. Are you?'

'Yes, most of the time. Didn't Harmon tell you?'

'There was no reason why he should.'

'He doesn't need a reason. He's a natural intriguer.'

He brought the drinks and raised his glass to her. 'However, he did tell me you're a first-rate editor.'

'I can return the compliment and tell him you're a very co-operative writer.'

'Good. He needs the reassurance.'

'You puzzle him. He can't figure out why you're not competing for credit on the Raphael references – they could turn out to be very important.'

'Not to me. I'm not carving out an academic career; I'm a scholar who likes the easy life. Seldes needs the smell of endowment money, the authority of the big institutions, the power of rich foundations. He's welcome to them.'

'No wonder he called you the scholar gypsy.'

'Did he now? Well, it's a clever label but it's a straight pinch from Matthew Arnold.'

'He did add an embellishment of his own.'

'Oh?'

'The scholar gypsy with an iron cock ready to stand at the click of a woman's fingers.'

'How nice of him to say so.'

'Provided, he said, she's widowed or divorced and has a six-figure income.'

'He's a malicious bastard, isn't he?'

'Nature of the beast. He did add that he's heard no complaints about your performance. The ladies all seem very loyal to your memory. On brief acquaintance, I can understand why.'

Mather was nettled by the quite obvious goading. 'Is this all part of the editorial service?'

'It's the part I don't charge for – my private pleasure, the getting-to-know-you game. I like to know my authors – are they married? What's their state of health, their state of mind? All that sort of thing.'

'Well, now,' said Mather evenly. 'Let's see if I pass the test. Married? No. Live-in arrangements? None. Transmissible diseases? None. What about you?'

'The same. Nil return. Please' – she laid a cool hand on his cheek – 'we'll stop the game now. I don't think you're enjoying it.'

'It's a nasty game.' Brusque and angry, Mather moved in for the strike. 'It's cold-blooded and calculated. You play too rough, Miss Danziger. I don't relish pie in the face. I've never liked sadism as a spectator sport – and with Harmon Seldes on the viewing end I like it even less. So I'll thank you for the drink and be on my way. Call me when you're ready for another work session. I enjoyed that part very much. I'll be sure to tell Harmon Seldes how professional you are. Good night.'

He was half-way to the door before she found voice. 'Please wait.'

He hesitated a moment, then swung round to challenge her. 'Wait for what?'

'I got it wrong – I'm sorry.'

'Don't apologise. Explain. About you, Seldes, all of it.'

'Sit down, then. I need another drink. You?'

'Thanks.'

She took her time over the drinks, perched herself on the edge of the table so that she was looking down at him and then began a halting narrative.

'Harmon Seldes and I go back a long way. I was his junior

assistant at *Belvedere*. When he discovered I could write, he used me to draft his speeches and edit his papers for publication. We got along well, because he's not truly interested in women and most of the time I prefer to live in the Sapphic mode anyway. He still employs me because he gets the best job in town. So you come on the scene. He shows me your stuff. I think it's pedestrian, but I agree to take you on. We talk. He tells me how you approached him on the Raphael references. His first thought was that you were setting up an elaborate confidence trick because, as I told you, he felt you were too good to be true. You can't blame him for that. He's been a long time in the business; he's seen every scam in the book. Anyway he checked you out.'

'And how, pray, did he do that?'

'Sent cables to Palombini and to the Library in Florence. Said you were applying for a job at *Belvedere* and had given them as referees.'

'Clever Harmon,' said Mather softly. 'Clever, *clever* Harmon.'

'He didn't show me the replies, but he did say they were A-grade recommendations. He still can't figure how you earned them, but that's another matter. Then he started digging into your social history from Princeton onwards. Apparently you cut a pretty broad swathe as a lover of convenience with ladies in late bloom. Hence the scholar gypsy and the iron cock and all that. . . . Which brings us back to me.'

'It does,' said Mather flatly. 'It certainly does.'

'Oh, God. This isn't easy.'

'It's not meant to be. You walk shit into the house, you have to clean it up. Go on.'

'I'm an editor. I deal with all sorts of writers – men, women, geniuses, idiots, sociopaths . . . you name 'em, I get 'em! So I've had to develop a technique. I put myself in command from the first moment. I try to unsettle them first, then gentle them down. That's what I did with you. Instead you carved me up. I apologise. Now I need another drink.'

'Stay where you are; I'll get it. I haven't finished yet. There's a part of Seldes I don't understand. The Raphael entries in the account books are four hundred and eighty years old. Think how many works of art have been lost, stolen or destroyed in that time. What happened to them is a fascinating speculation, but why should a man like Seldes lose any sleep over it? He writes his pieces . . . there's a spate of correspondence, a few false leads and – *basta!* – we're back to square one.'

'That's where you're mistaken, Mr Mather. Seldes has a lot of secrets locked in his files – and a lot more that he keeps in his head. He consults for wealthy collectors in Europe and South America. He can tell you – but he won't – which well-known items in well-known collections are forgeries. So he can exploit the Raphael information in ways you've never dreamed of. The last thing he wants is an ambitious junior sniffing in his tracks.'

'He'd rather have him rattled by a Gorgon editor?'

'You really are a bastard, Max Mather.'

'I know I am. You know I am but, as Harmon Seldes reports, my women do keep happy memories of me. With a little practice, even you and I might manage to be polite to each other. Thank you for the work. Goodbye.'

It was a flippant and graceless exit and by the time he had reached his own apartment he was ashamed of it. As he showered and dressed he cast about for some words, some gesture of amends.

Then suddenly he remembered a trinket he had picked up one morning after Pia's death. He was in Florence strolling aimlessly across the Ponte Vecchio, totally divorced from the present. In the window of a goldsmith who specialised in reproductions he saw a small cameo pendant of two women embracing. He went into the shop, haggled for half an hour and bought the pendant for fifty dollars. It was only when he walked out with the package in his hand that he remembered Pia was dead and the piece had no further meaning for him. It would sit well on Leonie Danziger, with her red hair and her 'blessed damozel' looks. . . .

Using one of his silk handkerchiefs, he made a gift package in the Japanese style and sent it to her by special messenger. He also sent a note:

An apology for your client's bad manners.
Scholars are presumed also to be gentlemen. I look forward to our next work session.

M.M.

FIVE

That night Anne-Marie was bidden to dinner with Ed Bayard. It was an engagement she could not refuse because she needed to discuss with him the pricing of his wife's pictures and the advertising that would be necessary to bring them successfully to market.

It was the first big test of her skill and judgment as a dealer. If she priced too low, she would lose money and the respect of a client who still possessed an important collection of his own. If she priced too high in a new downtown gallery, she risked an ignominious failure. The problem was compounded because she was dealing with a posthumous exhibition by an artist who had sold only privately through a specialised dealer.

She had already spoken with Lebrun, who had proved at the beginning reticent and faintly hostile. He was a short tubby Frenchman with snow-white hair, small expressive hands and the prancing gait of an old-time ballet master. He was at a loss, he said, to understand why Mr Bayard had not chosen to consult with him directly about the marketing of his wife's pictures. He had nurtured this talent, often under difficult circumstances. He would have thought . . . but there! Perhaps not. He accepted of course that Miss Loredon was blameless in the matter. She was young, at the outset of a career. She was not yet aware of the subtle courtesies of the trade, the need for friendly alliances. He was, however, sufficiently touched by her sincerity and charm to offer a little advice.

The late Madeleine Bayard had been without doubt a fine painter with a special private vision. He had often urged her to exhibit, but she had always declined. Her husband, it seemed, was a repressive character – jealous of his wife's talent, fearful perhaps of losing her. So Lebrun had introduced her work to certain of his clients interested in modern American talent. They might well be interested to increase their holdings in Bayard pieces. He would be happy to introduce them – for the appropriate finder's fee. Prices? Not high while Madeleine was alive – two thousand, five, ten maximum. Of course, with a well-staged vernissage, good advertising and a sympathetic press, then one might move into higher brackets.

Miss Loredon might consider feeding a single picture into the market just before the show was announced, perhaps even having her father or one of his colleagues talking it up to an auction audience. Sometimes this worked, sometimes not. Apropos, what were Mr Bayard's intentions? To disperse the whole collection or hold back certain pieces? Would it be possible to arrange a preview for certain Lebrun clients? One understood the value of a little favoured-nation treatment . . .

Anne-Marie understood very well. She neither understood, nor asked about the precise meaning of Bayard's repressive character or his jealousy of his wife's talent. She called her father and repeated the little Frenchman's suggestion about the introduction of a Bayard piece at auction. She was surprised at his emphatic negative. 'No way, no way in the world! It's a dangerous distraction. Makes you vulnerable to all the gallery gossips. Go for the gold ring, girl! One leap, win or lose. Pricing? Get your client involved. Let him tell you what he'll take. Bayard's got his own access to market information. Good luck.'

Bayard was happy to be involved but he was busy all day at the office, so what better excuse for a quiet dinner *à deux* and a promenade among the pictures afterwards? This time it was impossible to refuse, so punctually at eight she presented herself at his apartment.

They ate in the big dining room surrounded by all Madeleine's pictures. But this time there was no sense of oppression. Bayard was relaxed. The meal was impeccably cooked and served by the Filipino couple. The wines were excellent. Talk was wide-ranging and casual. He had a fund of lighthearted stories about the art world and its more eccentric denizens. Anne-Marie was coaxed into reminiscence of her life in Italy. It was not until the coffee was served that they addressed themselves to the pricing of the pictures. Bayard opened with a bald announcement.

'I've decided on a complete sell-out of Madeleine's works . . . it's the last cathartic act.'

'That's your privilege, of course.' Anne-Marie was carefully neutral. 'However, I should point out that from an investment point of view you could be making a mistake. If I establish a good market for Madeleine's works, you could lose a great deal of money because you hold no reserves.'

Bayard smiled tolerantly. 'How may canvases do we have altogether?'

'Fifty-five. Plus, of course, some seventy-odd sketches and studies of various sizes.'

'So we exhibit twenty major pieces and a couple of dozen minor to catch the lower spenders. The rest we hold back and feed into the market.'

She told him of her visit to Lebrun. He nodded approval.

'By all means let him bring his buyers to a preview. They're a faithful bunch and they trust his advice.'

'I also asked my father whether we might test one piece at auction. He was dead against it.'

'So am I.' Bayard was suddenly tense. 'Your relations with your father are your own affair. But you are my sole representative; I will deal with no other. Understand that?'

'I do, of course.' She was taken aback by his vehemence. 'But I'm very new. I need advice. I seek it where I can and my father is one of the best in the business.'

'I'm not bad myself.' Bayard smiled and patted her hand. 'I've bought a lot of pictures on my own account. So you and I decide together, eh? If we're wrong, so be it. We'll make it up on the next round. Now, grab your notebook and we'll walk round the whole collection. Let's get our individual estimates down first; we'll compare them afterwards. Remember that this first exhibition has to bear an extra loading. You've got to amortise some of your renovations; your advertising bill will be almost double a normal one . . . and what you don't sell becomes dead stock eating up storage space. Now, which do you think is the best picture in the room?'

'There's never been any question in my mind. I want to make "The Bag-Lady" the centrepiece of the exhibition.'

'Very well. How much?'

'Fifty thousand.'

'Is that what it's worth?'

'It ought to bring much more.'

'Then put seventy-five on it. If it doesn't move, we give it a red sticker and in effect buy it back into stock. . . . So we've started at seventy-five. What's our bottom price for a finished canvas?'

'It can't be less than twenty-five.'

'The sketches and studies?'

'Start at fifteen, go down to two thousand.'

'Fine. I'll make my list and you make yours. Then we'll compare the figures.'

The challenge excited her. Her professional judgment was on full test against the knowledge of an attorney who advised the dealers of America, who had himself been buying pictures for more than a quarter of a century. She knew, too, that he was courting her – not in the gauche, uncertain fashion of their first encounter, but quietly, knowingly, drawing her step by step into the charmed circle of his private life.

The decision to sell all Madeleine's pictures was a piece of stagecraft contrived to show her he was exorcising Madeleine from his memory and placing her pictures under the trusteeship of Anne-Marie Loredon – and forty per cent of the proceeds in her pocket.

She could feel his eyes upon her as they moved in opposite directions around the room. She saw the mockery in his smile, but read it as the affectionate teasing mockery of a would-be lover.

There was a small heady triumph when they compared notes and she found that her estimates were only five per cent lower than Bayard's and that their notion of the relative values of the canvases corresponded almost exactly.

'So you're the seller,' she told him with a smile. 'We take your valuation.'

'Now let's do some arithmetic.' Bayard was agreeable but businesslike. 'We have a total of a hundred and thirty pieces of which we're putting one third on exhibition. The face value of that catalogue is one million two hundred and twenty thousand dollars. Let's take a reasonable estimate and say we sell half.

That's six hundred thousand. Your gross is a quarter of a million. How much of that would you estimate for advertising and publicity? Remember, of course, that you have to pay the bills if you don't sell a single damned picture.'

'I've budgeted fifty thousand,' she told him, 'and it puts my teeth on edge every time I think of it. I'm desperately trying to work out how I can pick up freebies. Max Mather has promised to try to get me a notice in *Belvedere*; he's a consulting editor there now. My father's giving me some valuable lists for direct mail. Wally Brent has promised to photograph all the canvases for minimum-scale payment and material costs . . . that's something I've got to arrange with you. Can he work here? There won't be time if we leave it till the studio's ready.'

'Of course. And talking of freebies, I have my own contacts in the press and magazine area. I thought of giving a dinner party here before we move the pictures out. Would you be willing to hostess for me?'

And there it was, the master's move – beautifully prepared, inevitable as death and taxes. She thought for a moment and agreed.

'Subject always to what I said at the beginning of this venture. I have to be seen to be independent. Neither of us can afford gossip, rumours of patronage or romantic interest between you and me.'

'There will be none, I promise you.'

'Then I'll be happy to do as you ask.'

'Good. It will be a very special occasion. We'll work out the guest list together – and remember, our guests will be seeing the pictures as you saw them that very first time. I remember how strongly they impressed you.'

'Even tonight I got the same jolt of emotion. Of course it has something to do with this room, with your personal hand in the display. I hope we can achieve the same thing in the gallery – or at least not lose too much . . . which brings me to a couple of other matters. The catalogue is in hand. Artgravure have given me a good price for the production. What I do need, however, is biographical and personal material on Madeleine herself. If we want to play down the murder story, I must have other material to give to the press. Also Madeleine's personality is so strongly imprinted on her works that buyers and the public will demand to know as much about her as possible.'

Bayard frowned and shifted uneasily in his chair. He poured more wine for himself and drank it at a gulp.

'What the press wants and what I want are two different things.'

Anne-Marie tried to calm him.

'Look, I know this is probably the most painful aspect of the whole project. If you feel you can talk to me, we can work here quietly with a tape-recorder. If that's too difficult, perhaps there are notes, diaries, even published material I can use? But you do see my problem.'

'I see it.' Bayard was recovering his composure. 'I'm ashamed of my fragility, believe me; but I simply could not face a question and answer session – even with you, my dear. What I'd really like is a brief, sparse biography. I'll prepare it for you. My view is that Madeleine's works will say everything that she would wish to be known about herself. Trust me in this, please?'

'As you wish, of course. But I need the answer to one question because the press are going to ask me. Why did Madeleine not exhibit in her lifetime?'

'She never trusted her talent enough.'

'And you, her husband?'

'Could never persuade her otherwise.'

'That's very sad.'

'Sadder than you know.' There was a winter chill in Bayard's voice. 'We hadn't been happy for a long time. We were both robbed of the chance to . . . to reconstruct our relationship. But that's all water over the dam. What I hope for now is a new beginning.'

This was dangerous ground. Anne-Marie dared not linger on it and a melancholy Bayard was more than she could cope with. She stood up.

'Let's leave it at that, then. Thanks for a splendid dinner and for your help on the valuations. I'll print the biography exactly as you send it to me. I'll let you have the catalogue copy for approval – and we still have to fix a time for the photographer. I'll come with him, of course.'

'You're always welcome here, my dear. You know that.'

'Thank you, Edmund. Would you call me a taxi, please?'

'Miguel will drive you.' It was the old imperious Bayard who answered her. 'I hate long goodbyes – I hope the day will come when I won't have to say them.'

He took her in his arms and kissed her on the lips. She did not resist, but her response was cool and passionless. Bayard said nothing. He rang for Miguel, who rode down with her in the elevator and drove her home in silence.

Back in her apartment, she lay for an hour in a hot bath trying to soak the tension out of her muscles; but she could not shake off the notion that clung to her like a burr: either Lebrun or Bayard had lied to her. Lebrun was a fussy little man, piqued that he had not been given the opportunity to continue dealing in Madeleine's work. On the other hand, he was an enthusiast who loved pictures, respected talent and had obviously enjoyed the trust of Madeleine Bayard.

Her husband was a damaged man tortured by guilt, bent rather on expunging his wife's memory than on perpetuating it. And there was the real rub: slowly and carefully he was moving Anne-Marie Loredon into Madeleine's place. The first simple commercial contact was now turning into something else – a trusteeship, a personal responsibility to the living and the dead.

For all the fragility of his emotions, Bayard was a very calculating manager of people and situations and there was an anger smouldering inside him like a smithy fire, damped down but waiting only for the first blast of the bellows to burst into flame. There were faint bruises where he had grasped her arms. Her lips still prickled from the stubble round his mouth. Even so, she could not swear that she disliked him or that she would always reject him.

Max Mather had decided to spend his evening at home assessing what he had so far accomplished, laying out his strategy for the future. First and most important, he was now 'in the business'. He had a clearly defined identity. He had background. He had capital and income. He had friends and peers to vouch for him. He had legal representation on both sides of the Atlantic. He was conducting himself with appropriate humility as the new boy in town. He was free of emotional entanglements – an unfamiliar and occasionally disturbing experience, since he was beginning to understand how quickly greed and ambition could damp down sexual passion. They left so little time for pillow talk, so little inclination to cultivate new company.

As to the future, the priorities were plain. First he must authenticate the Raphaels. He was counting on the publication in *Belvedere* and on Harmon Seldes' researches to flush out whatever copies existed. His whole aim in bringing Tolentino to New York was to have him examine the pieces and deliver his own expert verdict. But before this – long before – he must establish a presence in Europe as he had done in New York. He must make friends, allies, connections in different tribal areas. He was working on a list of Swiss dealers and auctioneers when the telephone rang.

'Mr Mather? Danny Danziger. I have your gift and your note. I'm calling to thank you. Both were unnecessary; it was I who behaved badly. The cameo is beautiful, but I really don't feel I can keep it.'

'Please, you'll embarrass me if you don't. It's an agreeable trifle – a modern reproduction of an antique piece in the Florence museum. It's called "The two courtesans".'

'Do you collect such things?'

'No, I'm a jackdaw buyer with an eye for exotica. I'd like you to keep it. Call it a seal on our truce. We'll be seeing quite a lot of each other. I'm sure we'd both enjoy a quiet professional relationship.'

'Whatever you are, Mr Mather, some woman taught you very graceful manners. Thank you again and good night.'

He went back to his work amused and satisfied. It was another small victory – a potential enemy turned into an ally. On the solitary road he had chosen to walk, even a stranger passing him the time of day was a fortunate encounter. Now he had a tap into Harmon Seldes' network of collaborators and informants.

Shortly afterwards the doorman called up from the foyer. A chauffeur from Carey Cadillac had an urgent delivery for him which must be made hand to hand. It consisted of a note and a locked briefcase consigned from Mr Hugh Loredon, who had left that evening from Kennedy airport on a flight to Europe.

The note was very brief:

Dear Max,

The combination of the lock is 6543. Read what you find inside, then make up your mind how much Anne-Marie should know. You'll have to tell her, I can't. I'll be in touch from Europe. This is an important trip for me.

Best,

Hugh.

His first reaction was rage against Loredon. The man was a shabby trickster waltzing away from the most primitive responsibilities. What more he might be was something Mather did not choose to find out . . . at least not yet. He replaced the note in its envelope and pinned it in his diary. Then he locked the briefcase in his hall cupboard, tidied his papers and began to make ready for bed. He was cleaning his teeth when the telephone rang again. Anne-Marie was on the line; she sounded frightened and distressed.

'Max, there's something strange going on. I got back an hour ago from dinner with Ed Bayard. His chauffeur drove me home. A little later a beat-up green Ford pulled into the street and parked almost opposite my apartment. It's still there, with the driver sitting in the car. The same car has been there on other nights when I've come home late. Tonight especially I'm scared.'

'Why tonight?'

'I'm rattled, I guess. Ed Bayard made a real pass – he's getting serious.'

'For Christ's sake, sweetheart! You're a big girl. You know enough to stay out of the rain. What the hell were you doing at his house?'

'We were pricing the pictures. He works during the day, so it was an evening job. I couldn't refuse. I didn't want to disturb you, but I had to talk to someone. Do you think I should call the police?'

'Not yet. Sit tight. Turn on the late show – I'll be round in a few minutes. I'll give two double rings. Don't let anyone else in.'

'Max, you're an angel.'

'I'm tired and I'm twitchy. Be nice to me when I get there. See you!'

Ten minutes later he was in the street dressed in a tracksuit, jogging down from the Madison Avenue end. He identified the Ford, jogged past it to Park and then doubled back and tapped on the window. The man slumped behind the wheel straightened up and stared at him, startled and hostile. When Mather gestured to him to open the window, he let it down a fraction of an inch and demanded, 'What do you want?'

Mather gave him a wide and friendly smile. 'Are you Mr Bayard's man?'

'I don't know what the hell you're talking about.'

'In that case I'm sorry to disturb you. I have a message for an investigator employed by Mr Edmund Bayard, the attorney. I was told he was on a surveillance job in this street and he was driving a green Ford.'

'You've found him. So what's the message?'

'I was told to ask for your card before delivering it.'

Reluctantly the driver fished in his pocket and brought out a grubby card. Mather studied it a moment and then handed it back.

'Thank you. The message is that you break off surveillance now and call Mr Bayard at his office in the morning for fresh instructions.'

'Fine by me. I could use an early night.'

Mather waited until the car pulled out from the curb and headed towards Madison. Then he crossed the street and gave two double rings on Anne-Marie's doorbell. He wasted no time in preliminaries, but demanded a full account of her evening with Bayard.

She told him of her visit to Lebrun, of his claim that Bayard had prevented Madeleine from exhibiting her work. Then she gave him Bayard's version – that he had never been able to inject enough confidence into his wife.

'And all the time, Max, it's as if he's moving me like a chess piece in his own game plan. He took me in his arms and kissed me good night. I felt like a block of ice, but it didn't matter to him. He was in command. He let me go without a word. That scared me so much I had to call you. And now I find he's had

94

me under observation like . . . like a criminal or a wandering wife. I can't take that.'

'You don't have to take it.'

'What can I do? You don't know him, Max. He's an over-powering character. He takes control of every situation. Obviously that's what he did with his wife. That's what she expresses in her paintings – the sense of entrapment, of yearning for release.'

'What you should do is cut loose from him now.'

'You know I can't do that, Max. We've signed contracts. I've based all my plans on the venture.'

'So here's what you do. You're angry and embarrassed because your private ground has been invaded and violated. So you write and tell him that. You tell him that you need to conduct your future relationship with businesslike formality. In short, you put up the no-go barriers. Write the note now while I'm here. I'll have it delivered to Bayard's office first thing in the morning. Meantime I'm going to call the son-of-a-bitch myself. Give me his home number.'

As she dictated the number, he punched out the digits and waited until he heard Bayard's harsh response.

'Who the hell is this? Don't you know what time it is?'

'This is Max Mather. I'm in Miss Loredon's apartment. You've had a man watching her. His name is Lou Kernsak of the KNK Investigative Agency. He's been parked outside her apartment for several nights. She is frightened and distressed. She called me. I spoke to Kernsak; I told him I had a message from you. He gave me his name and his card; I sent him off. He'll call you in the morning for fresh instructions. You pull him off the job, Mr Bayard, or you're in deep trouble.'

'Mr Mather, I cannot tell you how much I regret this incident but there is a perfectly simple explanation . . . '

'Save it. Just listen. What Miss Loredon decides to do about this is her own business. My advice to her would be to sever all connection with you and sue you on every bloody count she could dig up. And just to close out your record for the evening's surveillance, I arrived here at 11.20 in response to Miss Loredon's summons and I'll be spending the night here to make sure there is no further harassment. Good night, Mr Bayard.'

95

He put down the receiver and turned to Anne-Marie. 'Have you got a drink in the house? I think we're both going to need one.'

Over the drinks he told her of his conversation with Hugh Loredon. She shook her head sadly.

'I'm not surprised. My father's been chasing women all his life; that's what broke up his marriage to my mother. . . . But why he couldn't tell me is something I don't understand. He's never been reticent about his other affairs – one of which was with a girl-friend of mine.'

'This time,' Mather told her firmly, 'there's murder involved – and a jealous husband who is quite powerful in the art world. Also Hugh was questioned by the police in connection with the murder. That's quite a complicated confession to make to your own daughter. Besides, after tonight's episode I'm beginning to believe he could be right about Bayard.'

'I don't know what to think about that. I agree that I should put the barriers up. I can't lose the studio because the lease is already signed. However, if he wants to withdraw the exhibition, it wouldn't be worth my fighting him.'

'You won't lose the exhibition' – Mather was emphatic – 'because Ed Bayard can't lose face. He has to come up with an excuse that will placate both of us – you because he has a big yen for you and me because I'm an eyewitness to the folly he's just committed.'

'But what excuse can he possibly give?'

'Don't try to guess. Let's wait and see. Now settle down and write that note. Make it short, hurt and angry.'

As she began to write, he reminded himself that he too was practising a deception upon her. He had not said anything about the briefcase or Hugh Loredon's sudden flight to Europe. The truth was that he needed time and privacy to see exactly what Hugh Loredon had dumped in his lap – plus the freedom to deny, if need be, that he had ever set eyes on it. The murder of Madeleine Bayard was still an open case on the books and the moment the exhibition was announced the inquiry would be revived. The press would ask questions; the public would respond with a flurry of activity and the old fear of copycat crime would be in everyone's mind – including his own and Anne-Marie's.

That was one side of the argument. The other was that every concealment and half-truth eroded another fragment of their relationship, left her that mite more isolated in a hostile world. So by the time she had finished her letter, he had decided to give her the latest facts.

'Just before you called, a messenger arrived from your father who apparently left for Europe tonight. The messenger brought a note and a briefcase. The note simply gave me permission to tell you what you've just heard. I don't know what's in the briefcase and you mustn't know, in case you're ever questioned by the police. I'm in a different position. I have no direct connection in time or in relationship with the event. Do you understand what I'm telling you?'

'I do . . . and I'm grateful and I've had more than I can take for one day.'

'Let me read what you've written to Bayard.'

He was surprised at the vehemence of her protest:

I am shocked beyond words that you, a respectable lawyer, could commit such a gross invasion of privacy. I am not your wife, I am not your mistress; I am a tenant in a building which you own. I have contracted to exhibit your deceased wife's pictures.

I cannot imagine by what right or what fiction you dare to have a paid spy report on my movements. As soon as possible I shall take legal advice to protect myself from further invasion. Meantime I reserve all my rights to redress for this present intolerable violation.

Anne-Marie Loredon

'That'll do nicely,' Mather told her. 'Now go to bed. I'll hang around for half an hour or so, then stroll home.'

'But I thought you said you were staying?'

'Pure propaganda to deceive the enemy.'

'Please . . . I'd like you to stay. It's lonely in Manhattan when you're scared.'

SIX

Next morning when he left Anne-Marie's apartment, Max Mather called at a pharmacy and bought two pairs of rubber gloves.

Arrived at his apartment he switched on the answer-phone, put on the rubber gloves, took Hugh Loredon's briefcase out of the closet and laid out the contents piece by piece on the dining table.

There were three diaries, each bound in leather and closed with a metal clasp. There were half a dozen octavo-size sketchbooks, two children's exercise books filled with notes, studies and diagrams, and three bundles of letters tied with rose-red ribbon.

The handwriting in the diaries and notebooks was a small, beautifully clear calligrapher's script. Mather, who had spent a large part of his life poring over historic manuscripts, was instantly entranced by the simple beauty of the scripted pages. The sketches – in pen and ink, pencil or brush, some coloured, some not – had the same cursive fluency, the same sureness and economy of line as the script itself. He was so taken with the first rhythmic impact of the pages that for a few moments their subject matter escaped him.

Then it hit him. He was looking at a whole series of erotic narratives, meticulously yet joyously executed in line and wash. Mather was familiar with pornography, ancient and modern; familiar too with all the colourations of the sexual act – triumphant, violent, tender, perverse, destructive . . . but here the overriding tone was joy, orgiac and exultant.

Then he noticed something else. The figures, the faces and the physical attributes were closely observed – images of real characters in a continuing story. One Bacchic figure, regularly repeated, was clearly recognisable as Hugh Loredon. Another was a startling likeness of Danny Danziger. Nowhere was there a personage who remotely resembled Edmund Bayard, but the woman at the centre of every event had to be Madeleine herself.

The notebooks were professional documents in every sense of the word: jottings about the work of other artists, quick reminders of unusual compositions or colour harmonies, a sentence or two on a scene glimpsed in a subway, illustrated by a thumbnail sketch made with an eyebrow pencil. There were erotic themes here too, but they were moments only. This was a craftsman's vademecum in which the object as seen, the vision as extrapolated from the object, the means to attain and record the vision, were the prime matters of record.

Mather himself had been too well trained not to admire the strict grammatical discipline which Madeleine Bayard had imposed on herself. The fluent grace of her sketches was a hard-won triumph. He could not but think how valuable this material would be as an introduction to and an interpretation of the exhibition pieces. He wondered idly what Bayard would do if it suddenly showed up in the catalogue.

Then a new and grimmer thought struck him. If Bayard knew of the existence of this material, he had a clear motive for murder. If he only guessed at it, there was good reason why he had handed over so clean a building – floors sanded, walls under-coated. He had first gutted the place to find where the material was hidden. Mather closed the sketchbooks and turned his attention to the diaries.

They were not chronicles of events but the record of an inward life set down without calculation or restraint. The directness and intensity of their emotion were quite stunning. Poignant phrases leaped from the page:

I am given a talent to show wonders; but I live in a city of the blind.

What Edmund has learned from the law is not justice but tyranny, and the measure of his tyranny is that in spite of all he has done to me, I am still constrained to love him.

None of the other men who say they love me are strong enough to liberate me. Or do they want me captive because the slave girl is better trained and plays more freely than the free?

There is a streak of madness in my husband. The terror is that he recognises it, he nurtures it and calls it up at will like a familiar demon. I suppose one could say that I am mad too – but mine is a happy madness, a meeting of willing bodies, a sleep full of bright dreams.

When I show my canvases to Hugh or Louis or René, they are bored. They see only my body and think only of the pleasure it will give them.

As his eye was carried along by the beautiful calligraphy – without a single blot or erasure – Mather felt himself tossed like a cockleshell boat in a seaway between troughs and surges of conflicting emotions: pity, indignation, sexual yearning, wonder at the mystery of this woman pleading from beyond the grave. And yet she was not pleading. She was simply telling – as though the acts of writing and drawing and painting were in themselves a healing sacrament.

He was too disturbed to address himself to the letters. They could wait until he had identified the writers from either the diaries, the notes or the sketchbooks – or all three. He put the material back in the briefcase and locked it again in the hall closet. This done, he stripped off the rubber gloves, made himself coffee and a cheese sandwich and sat down to think through the situation.

First he gave full marks to Hugh Loredon. The man was a perfect scam artist. In one brief morning he had endowed Mather with the care of his daughter, dumped on him an embarrassing and dangerous piece of murder evidence and then slipped out of the country. Now, quite literally, Max Mather was left holding the bag. Loredon would let him hold it until it suited him to reclaim it. On the other hand, he could deny all knowledge of it. Mather, whose designs needed an immaculate record, would be hard put to prove otherwise.

However there was always a counterplay – a trick to pay back the trickster – and this one appealed mightily to Mather.

Anne-Marie was about to present to the world a new and

hitherto unknown talent. Given a successful exhibition, the price of Madeleine Bayard's works would skyrocket. Biographers and researchers would compete for material on her life. Dealers would pay high prices for autographs, letters and especially for sketches and graphic studies.

And lo, here was Max Mather holding a briefcase full of scandalously precious autograph material and a splendid series of erotica for the underground carriage trade. So obvious ploy: take the stuff to Europe, lodge the originals in a safe-deposit with Artifax and make photostat copies as bait for the big-money buyers. As for Hugh Loredon, he could go dance a jig in Times Square while he figured out how to establish title to evidentiary material which he should not have concealed in the first place and should never have palmed off on Max Mather in the second.

However, there were other characters in the drama and the role of each needed critical definition. First there was himself, Max Mather, home from exile and just beginning to wear respectability with comfort. Max Mather had two Raphael portraits and a set of cartoons that he needed to bring to market without scandal. He could not, dared not, jeopardise this high endeavour for man or woman, or even to indulge his own freakish humour.

Then there was Anne-Marie Loredon, companion and friend of the good days in Florence. She was gutsy and ambitious, but she was learning the hard way that there were no free lunches and very few friends in the market-place.

Which raised the problem of Bayard himself – the attorney whose wandering wife had been murdered by person or persons unknown but whose posthumous testimony, if ever it were brought to the notice of the police, might well put him in the dock. And yet, and yet. . . . How much weight would Madeleine's testimony bear? How would a jury judge between the madness imputed to her husband and the madness confessed by the wife? But there was another question simpler and more immediate: what would Bayard do if he knew that Max Mather was the present holder of his wife's papers? He would be hard put to lay legal claim to them. Would he be secure enough in his innocence to inform the police and force them to take possession? Would he perhaps be ready to kill for them?

As if in answer to this question the telephone rang. Edmund Bayard was on the line; he came straight to the point.

'Mr Mather, I was very upset by our conversation last night. On reflection I recognise that I did a very foolish thing; but it was not without reason. You yourself advised me that the wrong publicity about the exhibition could excite morbid interest and lead to copycat repetition of the crime. I wanted to protect Miss Loredon, not to intrude upon her, but I went the wrong way about it. My only excuse is that I still live in the shadow of my wife's tragic end. I am writing to express my regrets to Miss Loredon and I am telephoning to express my thanks for your stout defence of her interests, also my own personal respect for your prompt action.'

'That's very civil of you, Mr Bayard. I appreciate it; I'm happy to forget the incident.'

'Unfortunately it will not be easy for me to forget. Miss Loredon has written me a very strong note of protest. I understand her feelings. I accept them. However, I do feel it's sad and I am calling to ask your help in restoring our previous friendly relationship. . . . '

'I'd like to offer you some serious counsel.'

'Please.' Bayard was eagerness itself. 'Anything at all.'

'Do exactly as Anne-Marie asks. Leave matters be for a while. Put a little space between you. Let her go about the task of setting up the exhibition. It's a big job, as you know. She'll appreciate some quiet unemotional cooperation. I know this girl, believe me. The reason we've remained good friends is because I've learnt never to push her; I let her walk her own road up to a decision.'

'Then I shall take your advice, Mr Mather, and trust that a change may not be too long in coming. Thank you very much. One other matter. . . . '

'Yes?'

'Anne-Marie has great trust in your judgment.'

'Not really, Mr Bayard. She's sure of only one thing about me.'

'Oh, and what is that?'

'That I'm not about to ask her for anything.'

'But you did ask her for a job.'

'Correction: *she* asked me. Before ever we left Florence, she

102

asked me whether I'd like to play Berenson to her Duveen. I declined. The position is that I represent her in Europe but maintain my own autonomy.'

'I commend your wisdom, Mr Mather. I hope we may one day become friends. Thank you for your patience.'

'You're welcome, Mr Bayard.'

Five minutes later he was on his way downtown to keep his appointment with Leonie Danziger. He found her tousle-haired and distracted with a pile of copy in front of her. She plunged straight into work.

'Here . . . this is my commentary and your text hooked together. Sit down over there and read it carefully. Make your notes in the margin. Then I'll give you a real surprise packet!'

She pushed him into a chair and set him reading and proofing the text. He had to pick his way through a forest of printer's marks and editorial symbols, but it was worth the effort. The document she had produced – selections from his primary text with her own annotations – was fast-moving, clear and authoritative, a world away from his first half-baked version. He pushed the pile of sheets back across the table.

'You've done me proud. Thank you.'

'I'm glad you like it. Now take a look at what our lord and master, the great Harmon Seldes, has done. You've got to hand it to him; when he's good, he's very, very good. Look at the photographic layout. That's what I meant when I said he would exploit this story in ways you've never dreamed of. Read it carefully.'

First there was an editorial, signed by Seldes. It announced eloquently:

In this issue we are proud to publish extracts from a notable research work by Mr Max Mather, a young American scholar who has been working in comparative obscurity as archivist to a noble Florentine family. The work deals with the domestic economy of the Tuscan region at the beginning of the sixteenth century. Compiled from contemporary records – account books of the estate steward, family correspondence and commercial documents – it is authentic, informative and entertaining. Miss Leonie Danziger's brilliant editing and illuminating commentary have reduced the original text to manageable size for readers of our magazine without any loss of continuity.

However, we are indebted to Mr Mather for more than the text. In the account books of the period he found reference to a commission given by the Palombini family to the great Raphael for two portraits and a set of cartoons for an altar-piece. These entries are printed in facsimile in the text; that they are genuine is beyond question.

Mr Mather has the modesty of a sound scholar. He is well versed, though by no means an expert, in Renaissance painting. His real discipline is palaeography. Very wisely, therefore, he decided that the investigation of the fate of the missing Raphaels should be placed in more competent hands. So he came to us at *Belvedere* to seek advice and direction as to how to proceed. Modest man that he is, he waived all claims to credit or reward but promised his full cooperation as a scholar in the work of tracking down and identifying the missing pictures – if indeed they have survived the ravages of four hundred and fifty-odd years.

We are happy now to welcome Mr Mather as a consulting editor to *Belvedere* and to commend this, his first published work, to our readers. . . .

Harmon Seldes.

As he laid down the first sheet, Danny Danziger asked him, 'Well, how does that grab you, Mr Mather?'

Mather shrugged and laughed.

'He's a patronising son-of-a-bitch. But he gives me a useful reference. I'm young – which is nice to know. I'm a sound scholar. I'm modest – which means I know how to suck up to my elders and betters. What more can I want?'

'What he's grabbing for – a lot of kudos and a lot of money if those works ever come to light.'

'Never happen, sweetheart. The trail's been cold for more than four centuries. He's chasing fool's gold.'

'You think so? Read on a bit further.'

He found the place in the text and continued reading.

Presuming that the works are still in existence, where might

one expect to find them? The first and least likely possibility
is that they are gathering dust in an attic or hanging unrecog-
nised in some decaying villa. The second guess would be that
they are in the possession of one of those wealthy but discreet
connoisseurs – Greek, German, Brazilian, Mexican, Swiss –
whose collections are totally unknown to the public. Then
there are those well-known dealers, the elders and lords of the
trade whose holdings in great art are equally unknown, whose
dealings are for the most part secret, who manage by some
miraculous process to maintain a large private stock of masterpieces and yet have a sufficient cash flow to live like Renaissance princes. . . .

'He's covering all bases, isn't he?' Mather was thoughtful. 'He's
sticking to the assumption that the works are still in existence.'

'He's doing a lot more than that. He's tossing bait to the biggest
sharks in the sea – the underground collectors – and to the most
powerful dealers like Berchmans et Cie. Bear in mind that in his
young days Seldes tried to get a job with old Berchmans, but he
was turned down. The snub has rankled ever since. Berchmans,
you also have to remember, is probably sitting on more grade-A
masterpieces than any other dealer in the world. However,
there's a catch. The art appreciates every day, but you can't eat
it and you can't spend it . . . and once you've sold a picture it
passes out of your hands for ever – unless, of course, there's a
chance that you can represent the buyer's estate when he dies
and start the recirculation process. But Seldes knows that there's
always a chance that Berchmans is sitting on the pictures right
at this moment.'

'You make me feel like a hick from Hicksville.'

'Now look at the illustrations Seldes has presented. Raphael
portraits: Elizabeth Gonzaga, Emilia Pia of Montefeltro, Madda-
lena Donni. Raphael cartoons: studies for the Story of the
Madonna, for the Dream of Calvary, for the Terranova Madonna.
All these works were executed in the period 1504–1506. So what
we have here is an identification code which can be immediately
applied to the pictures if they ever turn up. I did warn you never
to underrate him.'

Mather read the piece once more, trying to picture how it

would look if his own photographs were inserted into the sequence. Finally he restacked the pages and passed them across the table to Leonie.

'You're right. He's exploited the information in a way I never could have done. How soon will all this stuff be set in type?'

'It will be ready by Friday. Then it comes back to me for proofing.'

'Will you make sure I get a copy of all the items at the same time?'

'Sure. What do you have in mind?'

'I'll explain later. Would you pass me the phone, please?'

When she handed him the instrument he dialled the number of the magazine and asked for Harmon Seldes.

'Harmon? Max Mather. I'm with Miss Danziger. I've just approved the draft of my stuff and she was kind enough to show me your material. I'd like to compliment you; it's a brilliant approach – no exaggerated claims, a very handy reminder of where any discoveries would have to fit in the *catalogue raisonné*. I found it most illuminating. Complaints? Not a one. My own work often leaves much to be desired – so I admire a man who gets it right the first time. To change the subject for a moment . . . you know of my connection with Anne-Marie Loredon and her new gallery? Well, now that the Raphael piece is done I'd like to work up a piece on her opening show – the posthumous exhibition of Madeleine Bayard. Given all the circumstances, I think it could make an important item. Good, I'm glad you like the idea. Makes me feel I may be able to earn my keep. Do you mind my discussing it with Miss Danziger? I presume you'll want her to keep an eye on my stuff, at least for a while. Thanks. 'Bye.'

He looked up to find Danny Danziger studying him with distaste, as if he were a specimen under a microscope.

'Well, well, well, aren't you the smooth one? Seldes is screwing you blind and you're lathering him with compliments.'

He answered with a grin, '*Biretta in mano non fa mai danno.*'

'You forget,' she reminded him tartly. 'I don't speak Italian.'

'Old Roman proverb: It never does any harm to go cap in hand to the pope.'

'I'm not a papist, so it doesn't signify. But I'm afraid I can't help you with your Madeleine Bayard piece; I've got other commitments.'

'That's my loss, but of course I understand. Did you by any chance know Madeleine Bayard? Are you familiar with her work?'

'I met her briefly; I have a passing acquaintance with her work. It doesn't interest me enough to work *on* it.'

'Fair enough. Then I'll try alone and see how much I've gleaned from you.'

'Won't you ever learn, Max Mather? I'm the last woman in the world to need compliments!'

'Do you know why, Danny D.?'

'Tell me!'

'Because no one ever taught you to accept them gracefully – and that's a bloody shame. Now, do you want to throw me out or do I get a drink before I go?'

Half an hour later he walked out into the raucous twilight of Manhattan. He was the richer – or the poorer! – for a new piece of information: that Leonie Danziger was one of the players in the lethal psychodrama of Madeleine Bayard. He could afford to wait for the answer to all the questions that arose out of that simple proposition. For the present he was glad of the clatter, the mess and the jostle of homing New Yorkers. Their indifference endowed him with anonymity, kept him safe from prying eyes. It also made him feel desperately alone, as if he were the sole mourner at his own funeral.

There were letters in his box and the porter had a package for him. He poured himself a stiff drink and sat down to open them: first a note from the architect, accepting his deposit and agreeing to supervise the construction of his studio apartment; next a brief letter from Claudio Palombini:

. . . to thank you for the courtesy of your communication and to tell you, with great regret, that I can add nothing to the facts you have already on the Raffaello works. It is clear that they were commissioned and delivered to my ancestors, but I cannot enlighten you as to their later history. A great pity, because at this moment I could use the money they would undoubtedly bring in the market.

However, as your own experience will confirm, we Palombini have always been Philistines, trading in material things: wine, oil, hides and manufactured goods. We have sometimes been buyers of paintings, but only spasmodically patrons of the arts. In fact, it helped to refurbish our reputation to have you as our scholar in residence. Be sure we shall welcome you back whenever you choose to come.

Affectionate salutations,

Claudio

The package was a surprise. It contained a small pencil drawing of a building under construction which was signed and dated: Boccioni, Milano, 1910. With the drawing was a card:

An apology and a small token of repentance for my professional indiscretion in respect of Miss Loredon.

I am sure you are familiar with Boccioni's work. I have a portrait and a landscape which I shall be happy to show you when we dine together.

Edmund Bayard

Mather was baffled by the nerve and style of the man. The Boccioni drawing – recognisable as one of the themes developed for 'The Rising City' – was valuable enough to make honourable amends yet not so expensive as to seem a bribe or a solicitation. The choice of artist – a futurist innovator – paid a graceful deference to his Italian connections. The invitation to dine was a deft touch: no date was named, so no immediate decision required. Wondering how Bayard had dealt with Anne-Marie, he called and found her only too eager to tell him.

'There's a long letter of explanation. He was worried about my safety . . . all that jazz. My house is full of flowers; there's a card that says, "But love is blind and lovers cannot see, the pretty follies that themselves commit." It's signed "E.B."'

'He should have signed it "W.S." He picked it up from Shakespeare in the Park.'

'I don't care where he picked it up. It's landed here with at least two hundred dollars' worth of exotic blooms and I'm just trying to figure out how to respond.'

'Easy. Give him the same line of crap he's handing you: "Sir, you do me much honour, but my heart is to the muses dedicate . . . in short, there's no goddamn chance in the world we're going to be lovers." By the way, I've got some news for you—Harmon Seldes has agreed to run a piece on the Madeleine Bayard exhibition.'

'Max, that's wonderful—it's money in the bank already.'

'So ask yourself and then tell me what needs to be said about the woman. I'll be doing my own research, but I'll need all the biographical background I can get—also photographs of the canvases.'

'I can take you to Bayard's house and show them to you.'

'He's already invited me to dinner, but I need the photographs for reference as I work.'

'I'll arrange it. Anything else?'

'Yes. The man's obviously crazy for you, but by me he's crazy, period. So take a cold shower and forget about him. Good night.'

In spite of the jokes and the teasing tone they affected since they had changed from some-time lovers to most-time friends, Mather was worried. Bayard was turning his own discomfiture into a triumph. It was impossible to reject his gestures of amends, and it would be folly for Anne-Marie to turn a powerful penitent into an insulted enemy.

Once again Mather was fatally compromised by his own self-interest. He was engaged in a paradoxical enterprise: to construct a legal trade on a morally dubious act. He, least of all, could afford enemies or ill-sayers. He had to be the little friend of all the world. He could only hope that the web of half-truths which sustained him would not tear apart and dump him neck-deep in a cesspool.

SEVEN

Forty-eight hours later he had a call from Leonie Danziger, with a cool and well-rehearsed little speech.

'Max? I'm calling to tell you that I've changed my mind on the Bayard item. I will edit it for you. I can use the money. You can certainly use my skill. The proofs of your Tuscan piece and Seldes' Raphael article are on their way to you by courier— six copies of each. I've charged the expenses to *Belvedere*.'

'That was very thoughtful of you. Thank you.'

He called Bayard at his office, thanked him for the Boccioni sketch but protested that he could not accept it.

'Its proper place is in your collection. I should, however, be happy to dine with you. We need to talk privately about the exhibition. Seldes has commissioned me to do a piece on it for *Belvedere*, so I need to see the pictures and build up my own portrait of the artist. The sooner I can do that, the better.'

'How does Thursday suit you?' Bayard was brisk but cordial.

'Fine.'

'Then let's say seven for seven-thirty at my place. Just the two of us.'

'Thursday it is.'

'And I insist you keep the Boccioni. No arguments. 'Bye.'

As preparation for the evening, Mather spent a full day in the Public Library reading the press reports of Madeleine Bayard's murder. He also did some discursive reading on Boccioni and the Futurists and copied the *Who's Who* biographical entry on Edmund Justin Bayard. As a final precaution he called Anne-Marie, only to discover that Bayard had already been in touch with her.

'He's very pleased you accepted his invitation. The notion of a *Belvedere* article appeals to him. He feels your friendship and goodwill are important. Will you let me know how the dinner goes?'

'Of course. But more to the point, what are your relations with him now? What did you do about the flowers?'

'Pretty much what you told me: I thanked him for the thought, told him I was happy to continue our association but that I couldn't take any emotional pressures.'

'He understood?'

'Let's say he didn't argue, though I'm not sure how much he understands. But I feel better able to cope with him now.'

'Question: the canvases you're exhibiting are all hung in his house?'

'Yes.'

'What about miscellaneous material – sketches, notes, tentative works, half-finished projects?'

'In addition to the major works, there are about seventy sketches and studies and we'll be exhibiting those too. If there are more, Bayard hasn't shown them to me. I asked about writings; he responded only vaguely. Why do you ask?'

'They're the sort of miscellanea that can dress up an article beautifully. Anyway, I'll ask him at dinner. How is the studio coming along?'

'The place is a shambles but the plumbers and builders are on schedule. The architect has found exactly the lighting we want – oh, and they're already well advanced with your living area. We should go down together and take a look.'

'We shall . . . but leave it until after my dinner with Bayard. It's funny, I feel I really need some training for that meeting.'

'You're right. You can't do this one on a wing and a prayer. One moment Bayard has all the charm in the world; the next, he can be cold and formidable.'

All of which made Mather feel as edgy and uneasy as a student about to take an oral test with a board of examiners. In the event he was totally disarmed. He and Bayard were immediately on first-name terms. The meal was excellent, the wines chosen with care. Bayard was relaxed and open, a thoughtful talker but a good listener who knew how to coax the best performance out of a guest. He was modest about his own collection and quite eloquent about Madeleine's; he was effusive in his thanks for the

Belvedere article which he saw as an enormous asset. By the time they arrived at the coffee and brandy, Mather was hopeful of a good discussion.

He asked, 'Are you ready for question time?'

'I think so.'

Mather took out a small tape recorder and set it on the table between them. He explained, 'Whatever you don't want on the record, we can erase immediately. I need three categories of information from you. The first is for the *Belvedere* article; that's professional and technical background, the artist's mind-set, that sort of thing. The second is publishable material for the popular press; that's biography, gossip, names to drop, what celebrities will be invited. The third is rebuttal, if the rumours circulated in the yellow press at the time of your wife's death are brought up again.'

Bayard was instantly wary. 'Rumours? I was not aware of any rumours.'

'That's understandable. You were in deep distress. You prob-ably did what we all do: half-read the papers and blocked out any unpleasant items. Here's the kind of thing I mean. . . . ' He rifled through his notebook. 'This is from the *New York Post*: "Madeleine Bayard, a beautiful and talented woman, had many friends among the raffish, coffee-house crowd in SoHo. Homicide detectives do not discount the possibility of a crime of passion." The moment the exhibition is announced, that little item will take on a new lease of life. Maybe a couple of names will get dropped into a gossip column: "Once romantically linked . . . " that sort of thing. Someone may turn up with a sketch or a letter. You know that the yellow press pays good money for that kind of item. How do we at the gallery respond?'

'You don't,' Bayard said curtly. 'You let it ride. If I'm libelled and I think I can win, I'll sue. For the rest, you and Anne-Marie and anyone else connected with the gallery buy out of the argument. You weren't involved in Madeleine's life or death. You are concerned only with her genius. Look, Max, I understand the thrust of your questions. I know you need some background just so you don't make fools of yourselves. So let's start with that. Switch off the tape. This must be off the record, way off.'

'Understood; but then you have to be specific about what I can use.'

Bayard waited a moment, then launched into a narration, simple and intimate, more poignant than anything Mather had expected of him.

'Madeleine was born in London, daughter of French parents. Her father was a colonel in the Free French Forces who had set up business in London as a wine-shipper; her mother was on the staff of the French Embassy, attached to the Cultural Section. I was in London devilling for old George Bunbury on a transatlantic commercial case involving US and Canadian clients. The dispute was long and profitable. I stayed in London four months. Madeleine and I met one afternoon at an exhibition at the Royal Academy. She was then a student at the Slade. We fell in love. It was head over heels for both of us. We married before I left England.'

'And then?'

'The honeymoon and the homecoming were wonderful. After that it was a slow decline into misery. I was an ambitious young attorney with an interest in art. She was pure artist – all fire and fantasy, relentless in pursuit of her visions, constantly in need of release and renewal – mostly through sexual encounter. Without elaborating on it, that's the origin of the newspaper reference. My wife was a great painter – and a very promiscuous lady.'

'So that must have determined the thrust of police inquiries into her murder.'

'Of course. I was the natural suspect. Faithless wife. Jealous husband. And I was jealous, make no mistake. I became morbid and tyrannical. I bullied her, put restrictions on her movements, forbade her to exhibit. It didn't help of course. It only made things worse. But it was a simple piece of arithmetic to prove I couldn't have murdered her. I was in conference uptown – I had a secretary call the studio to tell Madeleine I'd be late picking her up. There was no answer. By the time I got to the studio she was dead. I was frantic. I called the police, then I cradled her in my arms trying to revive her. That's how the police found me . . . that's the nightmare I live with.'

'What I can't understand is how you endured the hell you were making for each other. Why didn't you divorce?'

113

Bayard gave him a strange lopsided smile and threw up his hands in a gesture of defeat.

'You're young, Max. You have all the happy talents of a bachelor on the loose. I hope you'll never have to learn as I did that for some people even hell is more tolerable than nothingness. Madeleine and I needed each other, don't you see? We fed on the misery we created in each other. The tension you see in her pictures, the wild impulse to escape, grew out of that misery. Besides, I knew that I had the best of her. It's hung on the walls around you.'

'But what isn't there,' said Mather, 'is the other side of her – the sensual, orgiac side. Did she never paint nudes, human embraces?'

'If she did, I never saw them. Perhaps that was just as well. For me, the hardest thing to endure was the knowledge that other men possessed her body and believed, as I so willingly did, everything she told them in bed. I could have killed for that – oh yes. But I would have killed the lovers, not Madeleine.'

'Did you know who they were?'

'Some, yes.'

'Did she paint any of them? Did she paint *for* any of them? Did she write letters?'

'I'm not sure I see the point of the question.'

'To put it bluntly: is any embarrassing material likely to come on the market during the exhibition?'

'I guess it's possible. Not much we can do if it does.'

'You could buy it in discreetly.'

'I'm not sure I care that much. I'm purging out memories, not acquiring them.'

'Then wouldn't it be best to have them buried or at least kept in a safe place until time takes the sting out of them?'

'You're right, of course. But I'm damned if I'll be the buyer.'

'Then if anything's offered I'll pick it up on my own account. If the exhibition's a success, there will always be a market for it through the gallery.'

'No doubt.' Bayard agreed with cool irony.

After all he had heard from Anne-Marie and Hugh Loredon, Mather found himself trying to match two different portraits of

114

the same man. The problem was to make the disparate images coincide. He asked, 'Are you in love with Anne-Marie?'

'You know I am.'

'Was Hugh Loredon one of your wife's lovers?'

Instantly Bayard was withdrawn and hostile – a domestic animal turned feral.

'How the hell did you know that?'

'Hugh told me.'

'Why would he tell you?'

'He knows Anne-Marie and I are good friends. He's asked me to keep an eye on her. He says he's afraid you'll use her to revenge yourself on him.'

'God Almighty!' The words came out in a cry of anguish. Bayard crumpled as if he had been struck in the belly. Burying his face in his hands he swayed from side to side, moaning unintelligibly. When finally he straightened up his face was a ravaged mask of grief. His voice was unsteady.

'Does Anne-Marie know this?'

'Yes.'

'No wonder she withdraws from me – no wonder she's afraid.'

'That's not the only reason,' Mather told him brusquely. 'You've got a lot of bad habits left from your marriage: you're prickly; you bully people; you're suspicious and, to cap it all, you set a goddamn spy on Anne-Marie. And don't tell me it was to protect her; it was to make sure she wasn't another Madeleine.'

Bayard nodded but did not speak.

Mather pressed the point home. 'So she's angry. She wants you out of her space. You can't blame Hugh Loredon for that.'

'Would you believe,' said Bayard slowly, 'that I don't blame him for anything? I don't blame any of Madeleine's lovers for taking what she offered. After all, I forfeited most of my self-respect to hang on to her.'

'Was Madeleine killed by one of her lovers?'

'Possibly, yes. Probably not.'

'Why do you say that?'

'She never made any pretence of exclusivity. So who needed to kill for what Madeleine handed around like a jar of cookies? At one time I thought that if I refused to talk to every man who'd put the horns on me, I'd have ended up living like a hermit. For a while that's what I did. It's only since I've met Anne-Marie that I've begun to live a half-way normal life.'

'Are the police still active on the case?'

'Active? That's a very relative word. Every few months they come around with a couple of new questions and a rehash of the old ones. That probably won't stop until after the exhibition.'

'Have they explored the possibility that someone hired an assassin?'

For the first time Bayard smiled, a crooked mocking grin of dismissal.

'My dear Max, when they realised I hadn't killed her—couldn't have killed her, in fact—they began to construct all sorts of fantasies. One of them was that I had hired a professional to do the job. The only problem with that scenario is that professional killers don't turn a one-shot job into a slaughterhouse. And I could have arranged a dozen pretexts to keep me out of town on execution day. . . . But hell, what's the point of rehashing the whole bloody affair? Try to understand something, Max, because I'm never going to say it again. Try to explain it to Anne-Marie, if she'll listen. I'm staging this exhibition as a tribute to the best of Madeleine—the part I loved, the woman who kept me captive all these years. After that, she's gone. Out of my life. I don't want vengeance on her killer. I don't want to hate her lovers. I just want to forget her and start living like a whole man again. . . . With Anne-Marie, if she'll have me—without her, if she won't.'

'Then take some advice from a footloose bachelor. Start living without her first. Then she won't feel she's being conned into a one-sided contract.'

'The voice of experience?' There was a new respect in Bayard's tone.

'It works both ways,' said Mather with feeling. 'Women hate a man who's looking for a mother. Men hate the woman who wants a son for a lover. One more question.'

'I hope it's easier than the others.'

'It's money in your pocket; you charge me for legal counsel. How would I go about forming a buying syndicate for works of art?'

'Based where?'

'Based in Europe, but operating anywhere in the world.'

'Point of the exercise?'

'I shall be representing Anne-Marie's gallery. But she's one dealer with her own special policy. Why shouldn't I service five, ten, twenty? Why shouldn't I deal on my own account?'

'No reason – provided your judgment's sound and your credit's good – which on your showing to date they seem to be. If you want, I could set up a syndicate almost overnight.' He broke off to pour two more large slugs of brandy. As he warmed the snifter in his palm, he asked, 'Would you answer a couple of questions for me, Max? Tit for tat, as it were.'

'Sure. Go ahead.'

'What's your precise relationship with Anne-Marie?'

'Ex-lover, good friend – surrogate brother, business associate. We're comfortable and free. Next question?'

'Are you a kept man?'

'No. I've accepted patronage from women – never keep. I've lived on my own resources and helped them to enjoy theirs.'

'It's a fine distinction.'

'As a lawyer, I'm sure you'll understand it.'

'And what's your ambition?'

'To become very rich as soon as possible.'

'And you think you can do that?'

'I'm sure of it.'

'I think,' said Bayard softly, 'I think you just might.'

He raised his glass and made the old toast that suddenly sounded very new and relevant. 'To both of us, Max! Health, money and love – and God give us time to enjoy them.'

Having drunk deeply, they decided it would be a shame not to drink again. Then Bayard pronounced the last unsteady benediction.

'I'm glad you never met my wife. If you had, I'd have lost you as a friend. She stole all my men friends, you see. All the best ones. . . . '

At nine in the morning – three in the afternoon, Paris time – Harmon Seldes received a telephone call from Henri Charles Berchmans the Elder. Their conversation was conducted in

French. Seldes' speech was accurate but fussy and pedantic. Berchmans' still had the rough barking tone of his native Alsace.

'This mess of papers you sent me on the fax yesterday . . . what do you expect me to do about it?'

'Do?' Seldes was bland as honey. 'Do, my dear Henri? Thank me, of course.'

'For what?'

'For the first look at what may turn out to be one of the most provocative discoveries of our time. No one else has seen it – but if you are not interested, of course, we must proceed to . . . '

'Of course I'm interested.' Berchmans the Elder had a notoriously short fuse. 'Don't be stupid. This fellow Martha, Methier . . . '

'Mather.' Seldes spelt it out for him.

'My God, I don't need a spelling lesson! How good is he? Is his work authentic?'

'I've checked all his references with the Palombini family, the library in Florence. He gives the impression of an agreeable idler, but that is deceptive. The work is totally authentic. I have personally inspected the source documents.'

'Which are, however, four hundred and eighty years old. This is cold stew, my friend.'

'Our publication will light the gas under it.'

'So . . . what are you asking of me?'

Harmon Seldes smiled with satisfaction. Old Berchmans was a racing man. He insisted on giving the last riding instructions to his jockeys.

'I ask three questions. First, is there anything in your own collections which might match the description in the Palombini accounts?'

'There is not.'

'Second, can you identify or even guess at matching material in other collections?'

'At this moment, no.'

'Third, do you wish to participate with me in a search for these objects on an exclusive basis?'

'How do you define "participate"?'

'You put up an agreed amount to fund the research. I conduct

118

it. If the articles can be found and brought to market, we do it together . . . and we split fifty-fifty.'

'And if nothing is found – or someone else makes the discovery?'

'Then we are both out of luck.'

'But I am also out of pocket. So we split seventy-thirty in my favour.'

'Sixty-forty and we have a deal.'

'I need time to think about that.'

'You don't have time, Henri. There is only the duration of this call.'

'I must see this Mather fellow.'

'I'll arrange it if we make a deal.'

'Where does he fit in all this?'

'I told you. His scholarship is sound; he himself is a *flâneur*. He has private means, so he doesn't have to work too hard. He is shrewd enough to see that he has neither the resources nor the expertise to do what you and I can do.'

'Would he sign a quit-claim?'

'In my view it would be a mistake, a grave mistake, to ask for it. If we want him to do work for us, I commission him. Already I have him working as a consulting editor. I could probably get him to accept a contract that binds him hand and foot and gives us all the fruits of his labours. But I'd have to approach that very carefully.'

'Why not tie a woman to it?' Berchmans' dry laugh rattled through the receiver. 'Next question: how much do you need to start your researches?'

'First-class travel and accommodation and all outgoings. I'll probably do the bulk of the work during my summer vacation. I presume you can let me use your offices and your scouts?'

'The offices, yes. The scouts we'll talk about as occasion arises. Give me an approximate figure.'

'Fifty thousand to know whether we're on the track or chasing a folly fire.'

'It's too much,' said Henri Berchmans. 'Make it a lump sum of thirty. You pick up all overages.'

'Thirty thousand up front, sixty-forty split of gross proceeds.'

'That's the first time I've heard the word "gross".'

'You didn't expect me to say "net", did you, Henri? Here I am doing you the biggest service of your life and you're still trying to screw me.'

'The gross then.'

'Good. We have a deal.'

'Then why don't you kill the story? Why alert the whole world to what we know?'

'Because there's no way you and I can cover the world, so we stir up the waters and see what bubbles to the surface. You're the doyen of the dealers; it's an odds-on chance the first finds will land on your doorstep – or mine, as publisher of the news.'

'You're probably right,' said Berchmans, never one to pay compliments. 'I'll see you in New York in a week or two. Keep me posted on developments. Anything else?'

'I was wondering,' said Seldes tartly, 'when you were going to say "thank you".'

There was a long moment of silence before Berchmans answered with deliberate contempt.

'We have a deal. I shall do my part. You will do yours. And if we find what we are looking for, we shall both go down on our knees and praise the living God who made us rich and fortunate. À bientôt, Seldes.'

Harmon Seldes put down the phone and looked at himself in the mirror. He saw a jowly fellow in need of a shave and a haircut who had just cut himself a very good deal. At worst his summer vacation was paid for; at best – hell, a man could retire in luxury on half the commission for two Raphael portraits and five cartoons. Henri Charles Berchmans the Elder was a rough-tongued old monster but, like all the great dealers, he did believe in miracles: the shining miracle of genius which could transform a blank canvas into an object of wonder; the Midas miracle of greed, which could turn the object of wonder into gold.

The easiest way to handle the monster was to hand him a victim to rend. He called Max Mather, who at that precise moment was waking to a monumental hangover. His head was pounding, his eyes were full of gravel. His mouth tasted like the bottom of a bird-cage. His response was less than cordial.

'Hell, Harmon, what time is it?'

'Nine-thirty exactly. Did little Maxie have a heavy night?'

'Little Maxie's dying—and you can blame Ed Bayard.'

'He keeps a good table, I'm told.'

'He also pours brandy like a crazy man. What can I do for you?'

'I just want to tell you that old man Berchmans has agreed to finance a search for the Raphaels.'

'I wish you both the best of luck. Now can I go back to sleep?'

'Not yet. Berchmans would like to meet you when he comes to New York in a couple of weeks.'

'I won't be here, I'm leaving for Europe tomorrow. But I can stop off in Paris and talk to him, provided *Belvedere* picks up the Concorde supplement.'

'Why Concorde?'

'Because I'm putting myself out for you and you're picking up the profit.'

'Very well. Put in an expense claim, I'll authorise it. What are your plans?'

'Ten days quiet work on the Madeleine Bayard piece. I saw her canvases last night—they're stunning. And the story can match them. As soon as it's done, I'll send it to Leonie for editing and forwarding on to you. Then I'm going skiing for a week in St Moritz. After that, I go down to Florence. If there's anything you'd like me to do. . . ?'

'I'll call Berchmans now and find out where you can contact him over the weekend.'

'What does he want?'

'To examine your scholar's conscience.'

'Everyone else has. What's another inquest more or less?'

'He's important to us, Max.'

'To you, not to me, but I'll be pleasant to him for your sake. Is there anything else you want done while I'm in Europe?'

'I'll let you know. The important thing is that we co-ordinate our efforts. I can direct you to what I need, but we shouldn't work wastefully or at cross-purposes.'

'I agree, I agree! Now can you get off the line? I'd really like to die in peace.'

*

Five minutes later Max struggled out of bed, rehydrated himself with orange juice and coffee, then called Anne-Marie and arranged to go running with her in Central Park. An hour and a half later they were jogging quietly on the uptown circuit while he explained to her, 'I leave for Europe tomorrow.'

'Why so soon?'

'There's a lot to do. I have to see Berchmans in Paris, set up a company operation in Zurich – that's the one I'll be using for your gallery business. I want to get some skiing at St Moritz too. Then I'll go down to Florence to do some more reading in the archive and make arrangements to bring Tolentino over for the gallery. In between all that, I have to find some quiet time to write the article on Madeleine Bayard and send it back here for editing.'

'Is there any chance of your meeting Father on the way?'

'Only if he's in Zurich while I'm there. I'll call Christies and see if they can tell me where he is . . . but I won't chase him. He should know that. So if he calls, give him that message.'

In the shadow of an ancient maple, she stopped dead in her tracks and kissed him full on the lips. He responded willingly, then held her at arm's length and asked gently, 'What was that for?'

'I'm going to miss you, damn it!'

'I'll miss you too.'

'No, you won't. You'll be too busy.' As they started jogging again, she tossed him a sidelong breathless question: 'Why didn't you and I fall in love, Max?'

'Maybe we did,' said Mather wryly, 'but we were both too busy to notice. Let's run the next half-mile, shall we?'

Edmund Justin Bayard had his own cure for hangovers which, he admitted only to himself, had lately become too frequent. The fact was that while he never touched liquor during working hours, he was tippling solidly over dinner: vodka martinis for cocktail time – one when he got home, one while he soaked in the bath – a bottle of cabernet with the meal, one large brandy with the coffee and another for a nightcap. With a guest for dinner, the quantities increased considerably.

For remedial therapy he would take a brisk walk to a midtown apartment block where a Thai madam and three younger women provided sauna, bath, shave, massage and manual masturbation for lonely or hung-over businessmen. The premises were discreet, the linen clean, the girls amiable and the whole operation comparatively free of risk. Each cubicle was soundproofed and equipped with a phone, so that during the recovery period business could be transacted in reasonable privacy. It was from here that Ed Bayard first broached to half a dozen friends and acquaintances Max Mather's idea of a buying syndicate for art. His argument was simple and it became more persuasive each time he set it out.

' . . . ten participants, no more, each committed for $50,000. That's a working capital of half a million, available for holding deposits on works which become available to us and for which a majority agrees that a ready market exists. Now we're not going to be buying multi-million-dollar master works. No way can we compete in that market. But we all know there are bargains to be picked up in slow seasons around the galleries and low-bidding days at auction. I've got just the man who could run it for us. He's footloose, fancy-free, has modest means of his own and is looking for an opening into the art world. You'll see a couple of major pieces by him in the April and May issues of *Belvedere*: Max Mather . . . that's right, Mather. The beauty of it is that he won't control the funds. We will. He simply advises by fax or telex the item, the price and his recommendation. Then we authorise a holding deposit while we do a quick run around the market. No, we don't have to put the whole $50,000 up immediately; we can underwrite it with a bank. Articles of Association? I've got a couple of sets for your consideration. . . . Splendid. I don't guarantee we'll make a fortune, but we won't lose money and we could have a lot of fun. Thanks! You too.'

By the time he was fully recovered from his hangover and the remedy, he had promise of five contributors and three who would call him back later in the day. He called Mather.

'We're in business, Max. So far five subscribers at $50,000 each. Three more ready to come in. I haven't closed the list because I need to know how you see yourself in the picture.'

'Very clearly. I'm the working member. You get a year's labour out of me for a paid-up share of $50,000. If you want me to continue after that, I retain the paid-up share and we make a new employment contract.'

'That's fair – over-generous, in fact.'

'Then I leave it to you to draw up an arrangement equitable to all concerned. I leave for Europe tomorrow; I'll telex you an accommodation address.'

'You're moving fast.'

'I've got a long action list. By the way, I'd like to use your name as a reference: character only, not financial. My bankers will do the rest.'

'Better still, I'll write a letter of introduction and send it round to your apartment this evening. Oh, one other thing . . . remember that to all intents and purposes the syndicate is in place. There's nothing to stop you talking about it or even using it on your travels. I'll handle the formalities at this end.'

'That's good to know. I'll call you once I'm sure of my movements.'

'Have a good journey, Max.'

His hangover had disappeared. He felt relaxed and ready for a busy day at law. With Mather away, he expected a swifter and smoother courtship of Anne-Marie Loredon. He was enveloped in a warm glow of well-being. He gave the little Thai girl a twenty-dollar tip, patted her affectionately on the rump and walked out into the dusty sunshine of Manhattan.

Leonie Danziger was studiously brisk and businesslike. She was already busy on the background material for the Madeleine Bayard article. She handed Mather two folders sealed with tape.

'This one contains notes of interviews with the senior investigator at the precinct. You can't quote them directly, but they'll give you a pretty clear idea of the police version of the murder. The diagrams are photostats and self-explanatory.'

'How did you manage to get all this?'

'Long practice and a freelance investigative journalist with lots of charm. The New York police department does maintain a public relations section, so she told them of the upcoming exhibition, of the article you were writing for *Belvedere*, the inevitable revival of press speculation over an unsolved murder. They gave her a nice young man who took her up to the precinct. She bought lunch for the officers on the case . . . *voilà*! They wouldn't part with any photographs, but they put her on to the Black Star agency who had a photographer on the spot a few minutes after the police. All of which cost me three hundred and fifty bucks, for which I'll take a cheque or cash.'

'I think you deserve a bonus.'

'I'll accept that too.'

He fished out a small object wrapped in tissue. When she unwrapped it, Leonie found a small figurine of a tarantella dancer in antique capodimonte. Her eyes brightened with pleasure, but her thanks were carefully restrained.

'She's beautiful – and you're very thoughtful, Max. Thank you.'

He wrote out a cheque for three hundred and fifty dollars and handed it to her.

'I'll send you the copy as soon as I can. What I'm proposing at the moment is a portrait of Madeleine Bayard as she reveals herself to me in her paintings, by hearsay, in the record of her life and death.'

'And this time,' said Leonie Danziger gently, 'you'll do it with loving care, won't you? No sloppy work, no writing round a half-thought theme?'

'No, teacher,' he mocked.

'What time do you leave in the morning?'

'Air France Concorde. Ten-thirty. It's an evening arrival. The following morning Seldes has set up a meeting for me with Henri Berchmans in Paris. After that I head down to Zurich.'

'Don't tell me any more. I'm eaten up with envy. Would you believe, I've never crossed the Atlantic – little Miss Manhattan, that's me! I've put everything I've earned into this apartment – and the elements of a blue-stocking education.'

There was a cliché on the tip of his tongue. He bit it back and asked instead, 'Will you act as message centre while I'm away? Commercial rates, of course.'

'All part of the service. By the way, read the police material very carefully, then study the photographs. They open up a wide ground for speculation.'

'Meaning what?'

'Meaning the drug-crazed killer is a sop to the public. The police claim they know the real man, but they can't find proof enough to nail him.'

'Happy thought.'

'Yes, isn't it?'

There was an awkward moment of silence; then, still carefully formal, she held out her hand.

'Travel safely, Max. I don't know what your plans are, but I wish you all the luck in the world.'

'You look after yourself too. I only wish . . . '

She laid a finger on his lips to hush him. 'If wishes were horses, then beggars would ride.'

'Yes, well . . . you look after yourself too. I'll call from Zurich.'

EIGHT

Henri Charles Berchmans the Elder received him with scant ceremony in the galleries of Berchmans et Cie near the Quai des Orfèvres. It was Sunday morning, one of those grey drizzling days when Paris and her people look shabby, unhappy and pinched about the mouth. The only other inhabitants of the galleries were three security guards who looked like middle-aged robots. The interview took place in a cluttered office, devoid of ornament, which on weekdays must have been inhabited by a junior clerk.

Berchmans, a small stocky fellow with iron-grey hair, hard eyes and restless twitching hands, had elevated rudeness to an art form. Mather, whose flight had been delayed two hours in New York, whose hotel booking had been thereby cancelled and who had been forced to spend the night in a room no bigger and hardly cleaner than a broom cupboard, was less than amused. Berchmans' first demand, in French, was all-embracing.

'Well, Mr Mather, what have you to tell me?'

'Nothing, Mr Berchmans. I am visiting you at the request of Harmon Seldes. I have put myself out to do so. I am waiting for you to ask me a question that will justify the inconvenience.'

'Very well.' Berchmans was in no wise perturbed. 'Why Raphael, eh? Why not Caravaggio, Bellini, Boldini? Raphael's fixed and finished. The codex is complete. These references you have found are signposts to nowhere. You're a smart fellow; you must know that.'

'If I were smart,' said Mather, 'I wouldn't be wasting this Sunday morning in Paris. I'm a palaeographer. I stumbled on an entry in a set of Florentine account books. Because I'm a scholar I referred it to a scholarly magazine. Harmon Seldes told me he's made some kind of a bargain with you. I'm not part of that arrangement. I didn't ask to be. I'm paying you and Seldes a

127

courtesy and I find you a very rude man. So if you don't mind, I'll be on my way.'

'Wait!' Berchmans raised a stubby hand to stay him. 'I'm rude. You're angry. Let's start again. These account books – are they genuine?'

'You know they are.'

'I don't know. Seldes tells me so.'

'Don't you believe him?'

'I like to keep an open mind.'

'That's your privilege. Now, if you'll excuse me . . .

'I've made a deal with Seldes. Did he not offer you any part of it?'

'I declined it from day one.'

'You're a fool.'

'I'm wise enough not to play with the big punters.'

'But you wouldn't refuse a stable tip?'

'That would depend on who gave it to me.'

'The owner, maybe. You couldn't do better than that, could you?'

'Unless the jockey were paid off and the trainer was in on the fix.'

'You're insulting, Mr Mather.'

'No. You are, Mr Berchmans. First you try to bully me, now you're trying to buy me. For what? The day we met I told Harmon Seldes that finding the Raphaels is a million to one shot. I don't have the time, energy or money to join the search. I've even promised to pass on any extra information I dig up. But that's it! Finish, done! I've got some interesting projects. I'm scouting for a new gallery. I'll be doing a little dealing at the low end of the market and I'll be continuing my own research programme.'

'I could perhaps put some business your way. Come.'

The old man took Mather's arm and hurried him none too gently out of the office and down into a storage area. He pulled a canvas out of a rack and thrust it at Mather.

'Can you identify that?'

Mather studied the picture for a few moments, then delivered a hesitant verdict.

'It's pretending to be a Frans Hals . . . but it isn't.'

'Why isn't it?'

'The background's too light, the face is weakly drawn, the hair doesn't fit. The costume is elaborate but the lacework is sloppy.'

'Can you put a name to the painter?'

'No. May I ask the point of this exercise?'

'Just to test what sort of an eye you have.'

'Do you want to enlighten me about the painter?'

'No. Except that he's a very good restorer and an excellent copyist who has done a certain amount of work for me.'

'I confess I've seen better.'

'Where?'

'Niccoló Tolentino. I'm bringing him to lecture in New York this summer.'

'Are you an impresario too, Mr Mather?'

'No. I'm a scholar testing his talents in a number of new fields.'

'Then I trust you will send me an invitation to see and hear Signor Tolentino.'

'With pleasure. Is there anything else?'

'Yes. Take my card. Feel free to call me at any time, here or in New York.'

'That's kind of you.'

'I am never kind, Mr Mather. I am rarely even civil. I am a dealer. My sole motive is profit. The fact that I make it by dealing in beautiful things is beside the point. I cannot eat a Poussin. A Cézanne will not feed my horses or pay the jockey and the trainer. It is the profit which does that. I have the feeling that you could be profitable to me – and for that reason only, I am prepared to be helpful to you. On the Raphaels or any other matter.'

'The Raphaels we have already discussed. They are a matter between you and Harmon Seldes.'

'Why are you so obstinate, Mr Mather?'

'Because you are playing games with me – an old man's games, a rich man's games. You're tossing me all sorts of bait and waiting to see which one I'll pick up. I'm as corruptible as the next man, but you're converting me to righteousness very quickly. Now I really must go. I leave at three-thirty for Zurich. I'll stroll back to the hotel.'

'You'll be drenched before you get there. Unbend a little. Let me drop you off.'

'Very well.'

'There now.' Berchmans chuckled and held out his hand. 'Already you feel better. Let's be friends. I like a robust fellow who can fight for himself. That's what makes a good artist, too. He has to be tough to survive the discipline, then the failures and the rejections. Seldes tells me you're doing some work for him. What other interests have you?'

'I've accepted a scouting commission for a new gallery in New York. Hugh Loredon's daughter is running it – you know Hugh, of course?'

'Indeed yes. These many years. His daughter is a friend of yours?'

'We were in Florence together.'

'And what will be your first venture?'

'A posthumous exhibition of Madeleine Bayard. I doubt you've heard of her: wife of a New York lawyer, murdered in her studio.'

'Would you believe I knew her very well, Mr Mather? I bought three of her pictures from my friend Lebrun. I commissioned another, but she died before it was painted. She was a beautiful woman, a great artist.'

'Do you have the pictures here in Paris?'

'No, they're in New York.'

'Would you consider exhibiting them with the rest of the collection? It would do us both good.'

'I might. Who owns the exhibition?'

'Her husband, Ed Bayard.'

'I've done business with him from time to time. He has an interesting collection, but it's like the man himself – fragmented, idiosyncratic.'

'Miss Loredon's gallery will represent that collection as well.'

'Then you, Mr Mather, are in very respectable company.'

'I like to think I'm a useful colleague.'

'I'm sure you are; but you are not of course a specialist in fine art.'

'Absolutely not. My discipline is manuscripts. I did secondary courses in the history of art and appreciation of art. My tradition is the humanist one, which is why I lived very comfortably in Florence. Would you mind if we go now? I have some other matters to deal with before I leave.'

'Of course.'

As they drove back to the hotel, Berchmans made one final strategic play.

'The Palombini family . . . You were their archivist, I understand?'

'Yes.'

'I am not familiar with their art collection.'

'It is not among the great ones. As a matter of fact I had a letter from Claudio Palombini only a few days ago, pointing out that though his family had bought good things from time to time they were, as a matter of historic fact, Philistines. I had written to him with the information I had turned up. His comment was that he had never heard of the pictures but he wished he had them now. He could use the cash value.'

'So you see,' said Berchmans happily, 'I am not such a bad-tempered old fool, am I? You have it from your former master.'

'He was never my master,' Mather told him coldly. 'His aunt was mistress of the household. She and I were lovers until the day she died.'

'*Requiescat.*' The Frenchman crossed himself hurriedly.

'Amen,' said Max Mather.

'Until we meet,' said Henri Charles Berchmans.

On the slopes of the Sonnenberg, overlooking the city and the lake of Zurich, an enterprising developer had built a block of serviced apartments for the use of visiting businessmen. Each apartment had its own garage space. There was a porter at the entrance, a daily maid service, a small but comfortable restaurant with country-style cooking.

It was here that Mather decided to quarter himself for the duration of his stay in Zurich to maintain a residence and an address for future use. He needed a place to be private, to spread his papers without the constant intrusion of hotel staff. Here the developer had provided a small combination safe in each apartment, so that there was a reasonable degree of security. A Mercedes hired from an airport agency made him mobile.

The restaurant would send up meals morning, noon and night and keep his liquor cupboard stocked. Communication was no problem; he was fluent in French and Italian, passable in German. For the rest, his lease was in the name of Artifax and he was at one stroke endowed with anonymity and non-presence. The Swiss were a discreet and disciplined people who minded their own business very well and expected their guests to do the same.

Mather's business was to be conducted with a careful eye to priorities. First he must be introduced around the trade, the old local houses in Zurich and elsewhere who still mopped up huge sums of money in the hard currencies of Europe. Unlike the Americans, they were not gossiped in the local press. Discretion was their stock in trade. They served a tight market: quiet old capital, wary new money. They not only knew every 'von' and 'de' title in Europe, but could tell you to the nearest thousand what the titles were worth in hard cash.

To insinuate himself into this clubbish group would require some careful diplomacy. Alois Liepert and Gisela Mundt would arrange the introductions. His scholar's discipline gave him authority. Palombini, Berchmans, *Belvedere* and Harmon Seldes were potent referees. Access to a half-million dollars in syndicate funds was no small recommendation either, while his association with a new and well-backed gallery in New York had to make an interested buyer in all categories.

By the time he was ready to bring the Raphaels to market he should be, if not an indigenous animal, at least one well adapted to the jungle life. Memory conjured up the image of Berchmans the Elder proclaiming the predator's gospel: 'My sole motive is profit. The fact that I make it by dealing in beautiful things is beside the point.'

Berchmans was now the new element in all his calculations. He had bought and commissioned work from Madeleine Bayard. That was already a seal of market value. If he would consent to hang the canvases he had bought as 'Not for Sale' exhibits at the exhibition, the show would be an immediate sell-out. The man's authority was enormous. Every dealer in town would be following his lead.

The catch was, of course, that Berchmans knew better than anyone the value of his own name. It would be interesting to see what he would charge for the privilege of using it. And that raised another question, whether Henri Charles Berchmans the Elder was recorded in any fashion in Madeleine Bayard's papers.

Mather took out the photographs and the police reports, and began a methodical reconstruction of the murder. Most of the work had been done for him. Leonie Danziger had welded the disjointed police material into a coherent narrative, telegraphic in style but clear in every essential detail, so that there was no possibility of confusing hard evidence with speculation.

You know the location. You have to understand how it was used during Madeleine Bayard's occupancy. The first floor was empty. Madeleine used the two upper floors because the light was better. There were – and still are – two entrances to the building. The rear entrance has a single door which gives on to a loading lane. The front entrance had a buzzer and an amplifier. It could be opened from either of the two upper floors. The approach to these floors was by stairwell or noisy elevator.

Look at the first photograph and you will see how the space was utilised. On the second floor, storage racks for used and unused canvases. Shelves for paper, drawing materials, paints, books. All pretty orderly. A work table with a mitre box for making stretchers. A drafting table for sketches and architectural drawing. Two chairs, a stool for a model.

Print No.2 shows the third floor. A big king-size bed, normally made up with sheets and blankets and a patchwork throwover quilt. According to police – and you can check this yourself – the bed and the cover feature in several paintings. There's a Dutch dresser with cups, ornamental plates, green, blue and red glassware, bowls – the sort of things any artist might use to compose a still life. There's a refrigerator with coke, soda and white wine, also a whisky bottle (half full), a new bottle of bourbon. The easel and the sitter's stool are placed to catch the light from front and back windows. There are no side lights. You will notice that there is a canvas on the easel; it is prepared with a background of blue and umber colour and there is the figure of a man with a naked torso blocked in. The police are still holding this canvas and a number of other sketches and studies. The models for most of

133

these have been identified. Some came from an agency in SoHo, some were pick-ups from Negroni's coffee shop which is a local hangout for models, artists and would-be's.

Now take a look at print No.3. This shows you what Bayard discovered and what the police had to re-set because he had disturbed it by embracing his dead wife and cradling her in his arms. You'll see that the body is rolled like a mummy in the bedclothes. It is lying face upwards on the mattress. It had been stabbed through the bedclothes, so that there was no spouting of arterial blood and no mess other than on the bed itself.

Under all the covering the body was naked. Madeleine's clothes were laid neatly on the back of a chair. There was no sign of sexual assault or sexual congress with a male. There was no semen in the vaginal passage. There was alcohol in the stomach and the bloodstream and traces of a sedative which Madeleine had been taking on prescription. The sequence of events seems to have been that the killer found Madeleine asleep, rolled her in the covers and stabbed her to death.

The weapon was not found. Forensic reports described it as long, narrow, sharp-pointed, with two cutting edges – in short, a dagger of some kind or a dagger-like paper knife. The strokes were delivered from above while the victim was lying on her back. There were three in all and all pierced the heart. Again the medical reports describe the violence as 'precautionary overkill, but not a fury of mutilation'.

The police asked: why a knife, then? Why not some simple, less messy form of execution? The simplest explanation seemed to be that it was a weapon of opportunity and that the killer took it away.

Pass now to prints 4 and 5. These are detail shots: Madeleine's handbag has been rifled, the contents spilled on the dresser. Money was taken and probably her small diary, nothing else. Drawers on both floors have been emptied on to the floor, books have been opened and dropped. All these, according to the police, point to hurried search but not to violence or vandalism. In spite of the hurry there are no fingerprints. The whole situation was premeditated. Yet the police deliberately fostered a story about an addict crazy for drug money. They admit that they took a great deal of care to sell the notion to the press, hoping that the misinformation would make the killer over-confident and reckless.

They also admitted that what really interested them were the things that weren't there: fingerprints, evidence of sexual violence, a murder weapon and, simplest of all – a pocket diary or a personal telephone directory. Madeleine Bayard spent half her life in her studio. Her telephone bills were high. Did she keep all the numbers in her head? Some of the models who worked for her testified that they had seen her using such a book and that she carried it in her handbag.

Along with friends who had visited the studio, they also testified that certain drawings which they had seen pinned up around the walls were gone. The drawings were described as 'sexual in content'. Bayard claimed he might have seen them, but didn't have them in his possession.

Which brings us to Bayard himself. For a long time he was the prime suspect, in spite of his alibi. The first thing against him was that he, a lawyer, should have known better than to disturb the scene of a crime. The instability indicated by the act bothered the police. Worst of all, Bayard made no secret of his wife's wanderings and his own unhappiness, but refused absolutely to name any of his friends or acquaintances as her lovers.

His testimony on this point was clear and repetitive: 'I know she had other sexual partners. I did not seek to know who they were. I saw no one in bed with her. She named no names. Anything I conveyed to you on this matter would be hearsay or suspicion and, in any case, tainted with anger. I cannot do that. I will not do it.' In the end, of course, his alibi remained unshaken. According to the police he is no longer a suspect. However, there is one disturbing phrase which was dropped by one of the investigators: 'We do have a profile of a man capable of violence – even extreme violence.'

Our investigator then asked whether the police had identified any other real suspects. They answered the question in a roundabout fashion. First, they said, Madeleine's life in the environs of the studio was fairly well patterned. She painted in the morning to get the light. About midday she would go to Negroni's for coffee and a snack. She would chat to whoever she found there. Sometimes she would pick up a male and/or female model who interested her, take them back, make a series of studies, then pay them in cash. There were occasional sexual episodes with these models. There were sometimes staged sex scenes which Madeleine sketched. She was as much voyeur as participant. She enjoyed sex with both men and women, but no big affairs developed out of her local village friendships. It is clear that her emotional life was lived on another plane and with other people. All the models, for example, entered by the front door. Yet the lock on the back door was well-oiled and frequently used. Cars could and did park in the rear lane without exciting notice.

Sometimes after midday she hailed a cab and was driven away from the area. Sometimes she stayed at the studio, but always pinned a card to the front door: 'not available until 5.30 p.m.'

This card was still on the door when Bayard arrived on the day of the murder. The front and back doors were still locked. No one had been seen entering or leaving the building through the front door.

All her friends were thoroughly questioned. Some of them apparently admitted to brief affairs with her, but the police were unable to construct a murder case against any of them.

And that's the sum of it, Max: talented lady couldn't get enough sex at home, went prowling to get it, ended in bed with a killer. It's an old cliché dressed up in an artist's smock and set in a garret in Bohemia. Yet, in one way or another, a lot of us are involved in it and we'll be looking to you to make sense of it for us. After all, you're a Bohemian too – a scholar gypsy who may well have insights denied to the rest of us.

Call me if you need more information – and make a great job of this one.

Danny D.

For a long time after he had finished reading Mather sat, chin cupped in hands, staring into blankness. There was something in the whole tone and tenor of the letter that made him uneasy, though for the life of him he could not define what it was. Then,

136

mechanically, he stowed the papers and the photographs in the envelope and locked it in the safe. He looked at his watch: eleven-thirty. New York was six hours behind. She would just be packing up the day's work, pouring herself a drink. He picked up the telephone and tapped out the number.

The phone in her apartment rang and rang. He stood there hypnotised by the sound for nearly three minutes; then he put down the receiver and, numb with fatigue, began to prepare himself for bed.

NINE

At his first meeting with Liepert and Gisela Mundt, Liepert offered a shrewd counsel.

'I note that you have listed as desirable contacts dealers and auctioneers in Zurich. But I think you must be very careful in your first choice of associates. You are, if I may say so, more in tune with Europe than many Americans. I think you should be dealing with those companies where the control has passed from the old ones to the young Turks, the ones who are in contact with new fashion, new money and who take a global view of the market.'

'That makes very sound sense.'

'Let me try to make a little more. You are well recommended, well connected. In a conservative town like Zurich that is valuable. However, I do not want you to dissipate that value by making yourself too available or appearing too eager to trade.'

'Again I agree. How do you suggest we proceed?'

'Let me arrange a small dinner party at my house. I'll invite someone from the bank, two dealers – each a specialist in his own field – and one auctioneer, Swiss of course. That way we create friends and not rivals. I must declare to you at once that I have an interest in this matter. The auctioneer is my client. The others I know in the course of business, but the bank would be interested to have them as clients. For me – a pleasant diplomatic exercise which creates goodwill. For you, it's a springboard from which you jump painlessly into the pool. . . . It's the way business is done in Zurich. You know what they say about the banks here. They have enough colonels to run South America!'

'I've never heard that before.'

'It's true. The bank officers all do Army service together, so they climb up the promotion ladder as friends. Let me call my wife now and see if we can fix an evening.'

After a swift exchange in Schweitzerdeutsch, he turned to Mather: 'Wednesday?'

'Suits me fine.'

'Seven-thirty for eight. If you want to bring a friend, you are welcome to do so.'

'I'm travelling alone.'

'Then permit me to suggest that I invite Dr Mundt as your partner. The others will have their wives. A family affair is easier, you understand.'

'Are you sure this is agreeable to you, Dr Mundt?'

'Perfectly, Mr Mather.'

'Thank you. Now may I ask you both a question. Would you have any means of finding a married couple in Brazil? She is Italian, he's Brazilian of German stock. They were married in Milan in 1947 and then went to Rio de Janeiro.'

Liepert gave him a swift sidelong look. 'May I ask the reason for the inquiry?'

'It has to do with the authentication of the Raphaels. The woman, Camilla Dandolo, was a well-known opera singer and mistress of Luca Palombini. Her husband is thought to have been the local SS commander during the war. A question arises as to whether the Raphaels – or indeed any other Palombini art works – may have been given to the woman as a pay-off or to the man in return for wartime protection.'

'You must forgive the tenor of my next question, Mr Mather.'

'Please go ahead.'

'Are you Jewish?'

'No. I'm not sure I see the point of the question – but no, I'm not Jewish.'

'Sometimes matters like this are raised for other reasons: vengeance for lost relatives, war crimes, recovery of property taken by the Nazis. One has to know before one intervenes.'

'Then let me be specific.' Mather fished in his briefcase and brought out the proofs of the *Belvedere* articles and the letters from Guido Valente and Claudio Palombini. 'Read those and you'll see what I'm driving at.'

Liepert took his time reading the articles. As he finished each page, he handed it to Gisela Mundt. Her expression relaxed into a smile. When the reading was done she folded the papers and handed them back before speaking.

'Well, it seems we have found ourselves a very distinguished client. Alois' dinner guests will be very interested in that material too. Meantime, I can make a start on the Brazilians. They will, of course, be quite elderly people now. We don't want to disturb them unduly and we certainly don't want to be waving large quantities of money under their noses. Why don't we construct an advertisement? "Distinguished scholar is researching work on the divas of La Scala. Would be grateful for any information on career and present whereabouts of Camilla Dandolo, et cetera, et cetera. . . . " There's an agency in Zurich which places this kind of advertisement.'

'Let's do it.' Mather was excited as a schoolboy. 'Who knows what we may prise out of the woodwork?'

'Do you have any of your research material with you?'

'All of it. I'm going on to Italy. I have to return the material I borrowed. I've also brought some pieces to auction here.'

'Why not display them at dinner?' Liepert suggested. 'I know our guests would be interested.'

'If you're sure?'

'Quite sure. They are all young and enthusiastic.'

'I'll do it, then. Now if we may press on . . . the next question is important: confidentiality – between you and me – is guaranteed. I know that. But between me and the friends I meet in your house?'

'There is *Ehrenwort*.' Alois Liepert was very firm. 'The word of honour. This is a small country and in many ways an old-fashioned town. Break faith and you are out of business.'

'That's a refreshing change,' said Mather. The words came out with a smile of regret for vanished righteousness. Inside he felt a pang of wonder that a thunderbolt didn't strike him or the words turn to a bolus of molten lead in his gullet. However, if heaven was silent, Liepert was eloquent.

'Nonetheless, my friend, you are a stranger and we have to protect you. So I advise a rigid protocol. You come and go. You talk business. You explore possibilities. But always you let it be known that the only binding document is a letter from me as your legal representative. You speak excellent German. I imagine

140

you are equally fluent in French and Italian – but you must never presume on the legal subtleties in a foreign tongue. So no handshakes, no "dear old boy" like the British. You say, "I'll have Alois Liepert or Gisela Mundt write to you to clarify and confirm." Keep the words in mind . . . *aufklären und konfirmieren.*'

'I'll brand them on my brain,' Mather laughed. ' "*Aufklären und konfirmieren*", and you're the ones who do it for me. A few more things from my list: you can receive money for me and for the companies?'

'We can receive it and pay it into your bank. We cannot and should not operate your actual accounts. If you choose you can leave me, say, five thousand dollars' impress to cover disbursements – and replenish the balance on validation of my accounts.'

Mather made a swift review of his notes. There remained only one matter to discuss with the attorney, but it was the one on which he needed the clearest instruction.

'Representations made to me or by me as to authenticity, ownership or provenance of objects offered for sale. . . . It sounds a big mouthful, doesn't it?'

'It is a big mouthful,' Liepert agreed, 'and if you don't digest it properly you may have to swallow a jail sentence as well. So let's take things in order. Representations made to you as a buyer: you ask that they be confirmed in writing to me. I'll check them and advise accordingly. It may slow down a deal. It may even lose you one from time to time, but it's the only safe way. You have demonstrated good intent in a legal manner. If a mistake is made or a deception practised, you are in the clear.'

'That's comforting.'

'My father was a judge. He used to say, "There is always comfort for a precise man." It took me a long time to understand what he meant. Now for the second part of the question, representations *by* you: as to title, the right to possess or to sell, this must always be demonstrated. As to provenance . . . there is a wide area of legal tolerance in Switzerland because there is a traditional traffic across our frontiers. That traffic is, of course, immensely profitable. So our own government does not question how the stuff gets here. They will respond reluctantly to official representations about criminal activities, but they refuse absolutely to administer the fiscal or customs regulations of neighbouring countries. So you will find that in the art business a certain reticence is necessary and acceptable. You are not obliged to declare that a wealthy Italian has sold you a picture which he has exported illegally across our borders. Neither are you obliged to tell his name, provided the buyer is content that you are a purveyor of legal goods. But once again our protocol holds. Your clients will quickly appreciate the wisdom of the procedure. Of course the whole thing depends on your disclosures to me; I must be able to rely absolutely upon what you tell me.'

Ten minutes later the conference was over and Mather was striding down the Bahnhofstrasse to see his bank manager, draw cash funds, deposit Hugh Loredon's briefcase and touch, for a few seconds, the coarse waxed canvas that held the Palombini Raphaels.

He needed that touch to stiffen his courage for the game in which they were the golden prize. It had begun in earnest now. He was word-perfect in the rules. He was accepted in the *salon privé*, where there was no limit on bets and no markers were accepted. Now he had to prove that he was fit company for the masters of the game who, if he could not master them, would pluck him clean as a spring chicken and eat him for dinner.

Forty minutes later in Paris, Henri Charles Berchmans was already marshalling his strategic resources and setting out his game plan. The resources were enormous, the game plan was global, because Berchmans was not simply a peddler of expensive art, he was a collector of, and a dealer in, information through a worldwide network of agents and clients.

He made valuations for banks and insurance companies in every major country. He advised on the formation and the break-up of collections. He set trends and fashions in art. He helped to set prices, too, just as the bankers in London and Zurich fixed the daily gold price. He was careful as the diamond dealers of South Africa to control the flow of product, so that the value never fell through the floor. If the auction market were slack, he would intervene quietly with a counsel or negotiate a pre-auction sale that was always published at an inflated figure. If Berchmans bought at that price, the experts said, the picture must be worth it. So the rest of Berchmans' stock increased in value; dealers and auctioneers blessed his name.

With bankers he pursued an expansionist policy. He sold them boardroom pictures at high prices. He put together the exhibitions which they sponsored. He encouraged them to lend money on single art works and whole collections. His argument was very simple.

'I give you a safe valuation for lending – forty per cent below retail. Any work that I have valued I will guarantee to buy in at that price. But if you have to foreclose, I will advise you to go to auction at the right moment and make twenty per cent profit.'

With insurance companies his argument was the opposite.

'I value high, so you can rightly collect high premiums. If the work is destroyed, then of course your pay-out is high. If it is stolen, then I will sooner or later hear where it is being offered in the black market and I will know, better than anyone else, how low to bid for its return. If it is damaged, I can get you the best restorers in the world at the best price.'

In short, Henri Charles Berchmans the Elder was himself a kind of banker, dealing in a restricted market with a tightly controlled currency. Like every banker, he depended upon information delivered daily and guaranteed accurate. He maintained his own data bases in Paris and New York. His offices were united by a computer network. His most valued employees were those who never stepped on to the sales floor or cajoled a client but kept squirrelling away scraps and shards of information on deaths, marriages, divorces, bankruptcies and wills in probate.

So while Max Mather, the novice gamesman, was walking down the Bahnhofstrasse, Henri Charles Berchmans was composing an urgent message to all his correspondents.

The information delivered by Mather and Seldes is accurate as far as it goes. We are looking, therefore, to trace two Raphael portraits of Palombini women and five cartoons – not one of which is even hinted at in the catalogues. There is a plausible reason for this, in that the Palombini were never great collectors and were therefore quite likely to have relegated the works to obscurity. Absent of any description of the portraits, it is my opinion that over the centuries these may have been the subject of wrong attribution . . . as, for example, 'Lady with the Unicorn' was credited to Perugino and 'Portrait of Elizabeth Gonzaga' was exhibited first as a work by Mantegna and later credited to Giacomo Lancia and others. Another possibility hinted at in a letter to Mather from a librarian in Florence is that the works may have been given as ransom or protection payment to an SS official. Please ask our Brazilian contacts for immediate information on Franz Christian Eberhardt, who married one Camilla Dandolo in Milan in 1947 and then went to Rio de Janeiro. Eberhardt's documents showed him to be a Brazilian national, but he could have acquired citizenship after the war. Our insurance and banking contacts may help with this matter. Request information soonest.

At midday he called Seldes, who complained sleepily that it was still only six in the morning in New York. Berchmans ignored the protest.

'This fellow Mather. I met him, I like him. You told me he was an academic idler. He is much more than that. He could be a rogue, but he also could be useful. . . . '

'Then use him, Henri, with my blessing. What else did you wake me for?'

'The Madeleine Bayard exhibition.'

'Mather knows all about that. He represents it.'

'He's not here. He's gone to Switzerland. Do you have an address for him?'

'No. I'm waiting for him to check in.'

'Then you can ask him to call me – and have his people send me immediately a catalogue and price list and a set of transparencies.'

'I'll do that. Anything else?'

'Whom do you recommend as the best textual authorities for Raphael attributions?'

'Hell, I need to take that under advisement.'

'So cable me a list when you get to your office.'

'What are you driving at?'

'I repeat – attributions. We're looking for Raphaels. The folk who hold them may think they're Peruginos. You are not usually so dull, Harmon.'

144

'I'm not usually asked to do business at six in the morning.'

'Don't fall asleep yet. There's more, my friend. Madeleine Bayard . . . what happened to her papers, notebooks, sketches?'

'I haven't the remotest idea. I imagine the police impounded whatever was in her studio. Her husband would probably have the rest. All her stuff will go to him in the end anyway. What's the point of the question?'

'I bought some of the lady's canvases. Lebrun introduced me. We used to spend playtime together whenever I was in New York. I wrote a few letters which I'd like to get back. . . . '

'A thousand regrets, my dear Henri, but with a husband like Ed Bayard – no way! Besides, isn't it a little late in the day?'

'Perhaps. I was reminded only by this new connection between Mather and Bayard.'

'Let me think about this. Mather's writing a piece on Madeleine for the magazine. I know he was looking for papers and miscellanea. I'll raise it with him.'

'Thank you, Harmon. And don't encourage him to expect money. The letters aren't that bad – I've had worse ones splashed across the gutter press!'

'I'll do what I can.'

'Good. You will be happy to know that my people round the world are alerted to the Palombini Raphaels. Now go back to sleep and dream that we are both rich.'

Well satisfied with his morning's work, warmed by the handshake of a banker who was happy with the shape of his enterprise and happier still to offer him overdraft facilities if he needed them, Mather decided to treat himself to lunch in the grill-room at the Baur au Lac.

The food was first-rate. The elderly waiters were good-humoured and efficient. The guests were a cross-section of the financial folk of Zurich – starched, sober-suited, good-mannered but always a little withdrawn from the *Ausländer* like himself. The talk eddied around him in a medley of tongues – French, Italian, Schweitzerdeutsch, High German, Swedish – and all of it dealt with money: interest rates, futures, margins, profit potentials, upside and downside factors. Mather ate a leisurely meal and enjoyed the new sensation of well-being and self-confidence. For the first time in years he felt truly his own man, making his own bargains, risking his own neck. That, he was beginning to understand, was the real attraction of the enterprise. He had been scared all his life, clutching for security at women's apron-strings. Now he was on a tightrope walk without a safety-net. Fear gripped at his guts, but there was a boy's bravado in his silent shout: 'Look! No hands!'

The euphoria persisted until he got back to his apartment on the Sonnenberg. He called Anne-Marie in New York, poured out his news in a spate of enthusiasm, then instructed her: 'Keep in touch with me through Liepert. This place is only living space. I'll be in and out of it all the time, but you've got the number just in case you need it.

'Write immediately to Henri Berchmans. Mention my meeting with him in Paris. Ask him to be kind enough to lend you his Bayard canvases for the show. You'll cover all insurance and transport. You'll give him prominent credit in the exhibition catalogue and all press releases . . . and you'll send him an advance set of transparencies as soon as they're ready so that, in effect, he can have first pick at the show. You won't forget? You won't delay? Good; because I want another set of photographs and catalogues for my Swiss people. Send everything by courier, don't trust the mail. . . . We're really going places, *bambina!*'

'What do I say? I'm thrilled, I'm grateful . . . if I don't sound all that, it's because I'm worried about Father.'

'What's the matter?'

'He's in the London Clinic. He says it's just for a check-up.'

'It probably is.'

'He asked where you were.'

'Call him and give him this address and telephone number.'

'I told him about the briefcase and that you hadn't opened it. He said, "Then he's stupider than he looks. Tell him to study the stuff carefully. It's vital." What does he mean, Max?'

'I don't know. I guess I'll have to open the thing and find out.'

'If you want to call him, he's in room 137.'

'You call him. He'll contact me in his own time. How's Bayard behaving himself?'

'Very well, I must say. He's being solicitous and understanding. I'm rushing around all day and by nightfall I'm dog-
tired. He just calls to say hullo, then lets me be. We had lunch
one day. We went to the Whitney on Sunday and walked in the
park. He dropped me home early. It's very quiet good-friends
sort of stuff, which suits me fine. He's approved the catalogue
notes and is very anxious to see how your story turns out. He'll
be thrilled when I tell him about Berchmans.'

'Better you don't say a word until it's definite.'

'That could be awkward, Max.'

'It will be a damn sight more awkward if Berchmans refuses
to lend the pictures – which he's perfectly entitled to do. You
know what Bayard's like when he thinks he's been slighted.'

'Okay, I'll do as you say. Are you keeping well?'

'Never better . . . but I need the photographs and the catalogues fast.'

'Will yesterday be satisfactory, sir?'

'Barely acceptable. Wish me luck for Wednesday.'

'I do. *Ciao*, Max.'

His next call was to Leonie Danziger. Although it was early
morning in New York she was not at home. He left his contact
numbers on the answering machine and asked her to communicate them to Harmon Seldes. Then he made himself coffee and
settled down to a systematic study of the Madeleine Bayard
materials.

He took the letters first. Madeleine herself had divided them
into three bundles. The first bundle was all erotica – outpourings
in technicolor prose from men and women who had shared a
sexual experience with her. Some were barely literate; some were
unbearably literary. All were signed with a given name or a love-
name: Pete, Lindy, Sugartongue, Ironman. Mather wondered
why she had bothered to keep them . . . then he understood
Leonie Danziger's phrase: 'She was as much a voyeur as
participant.'

The second bundle was made up of letters from artists around
the country with whom she had regular correspondence, but
with whom some kind of sexual relationship had been
established:

147

The thing I love about you Madi, is that you have no professional jealousy. You look at the work. You love it or you hate it and you say so, straight up. Your judgment is tough, but you know what you're talking about because you're at the easel every day. That's why, I guess, I never expected you to be so totally undemanding in love.

Dearest Madi, [this from a woman painter in Arizona] What can I say? I had fire in my fingertips when I came back from New York. You taught me to paint the way you taught me to make love – raw colour mixed on the canvas, all risks accepted, nothing held back.

And from an elderly master, now half-blind but still painting in Vermont:

I've loved you from the first day we met; desired you from the first day we made love in your studio. But I worry about you, Madi. I worry about both of you – the happy one who would like to paint beautiful graffiti all over Manhattan, the sombre one who is trying to paint her way out of hell.

It was in this bundle Mather came upon four letters written in French. They were very short, dashed off in a large emphatic script on hotel stationery and signed only with initials. The form of each one was the same: a single explicit sentence praising her sexual performance, a terse judgment of her work, a dismissive farewell:

Quand tu m'enfourches c'est comme si je m'accouple avec un ouragan et je suis transporté au Paradis. Mais quand je te contemple dans tes peintures, je vois une agonie que je ne sais ni partager ni soulager. Quand même je te convoite nuit et jour. À bientôt, chérie . . . H.C.B.

It took Mather a few minutes to connect the initials with Henri Charles Berchmans. He enjoyed a private chuckle over the irony of the situation, then thought how best to turn it to advantage. There could be no hint of blackmail. Berchmans had had two wives and a string of mistresses. One wife and one girl-friend had taken him to court. A lot of dirty linen had been washed, but the next month when his two-year-old Laurencin won at Chantilly the crowd had given him an ovation.

He must not appear to be toadying for favours. Berchmans would be resentful anyway that some young buck had read his middle-aged love notes. The simplest approach would be the most dignified one: 'I came across this stuff, I'm sending it back to you.' The only problem was that he dared not even touch the originals until he knew why Loredon had passed them to him.

The third bundle of letters had nothing to do with love or sex. They dealt with the economics of the profession, purchases of pictures, invitations to seminars and exhibitions, scholarships, awards and the like. In spite of the fact that she did not exhibit, Madeleine Bayard was well-known and highly respected by her fellow craftsmen.

Now that he had read the correspondence the diaries made much more sense. He could fit real people into the landscape of Madeleine's life. Berchmans' visits, for example, were recorded with a good-humoured affection:

Henri looms over me, a giant shape blotting out the sun. I tell him we have to change places. He laughs and says he is happy to let me do the work. He is potent as a bull and just as brutal, but he never leaves me unsatisfied. There are two of him, just as there are two of me. He will stand silent for minutes on end, looking at one of my canvases, and then turn and stroke my cheek with extraordinary tenderness. He will point to a single corner of a work and say, 'That is well done, almost perfect.' His power can be terribly destructive; but for me he is a healer.

Of Hugh Loredon she wrote with increasing sharpness:

He has become like a partner on the dance-floor who is always looking over your shoulder at someone else. His little box of tricks begins to bore me . . . I know he has paid the same compliments to twenty women. His solicitude is faked: 'You are tired, let me soothe you. Tell Hugh the problem.' He is not bad in bed, but as a man he tries to give me what I get more richly from women.

This Sapphic side of her life was recorded in a different vein altogether:

Paula came today. Her children have left for summer camp. She is so pleased to be alone. I lock my doors and devote myself entirely to her. We make love, we sleep, we wake, we drink wine. I begin to sketch her, stretched naked on the coloured quilt . . . I do a dozen charcoal sketches and one big cartoon in a thin wash. In spite of child-bearing, she is still sleek and white as marble. When I touch her my hands leave paint marks. We both laugh and we begin to paint each other's bodies like children.

There was also a reference to Danny Danziger, of whom she wrote in quite another style:

She tries so hard to make me put into words what I can only express on canvas or by making love. I tell her the words get jumbled in my head, stick in my throat . . . she refuses to understand. So I pin paper on a drawing board, shove a piece of charcoal into her hand and tell her, 'Go on, draw! Draw me, draw the bottle and the glass.' Of course she doesn't know where to begin. So I tell her, 'You can't draw; I can't talk. Now let's go to bed!' Which is what the argument is all about. Except she has to go through the whole dance of the veils before she gets there.

Dotted like raisins in a cake were the references to Bayard:

On days like yesterday, I can almost believe I can be happy with Edmund. We took a couple of my pictures to Lebrun. He bought them on the spot. Then we strolled down Madison, browsing in some of the smaller galleries and finally coming to a craft shop which exhibits the work of American potters, woodworkers, glassmakers and weavers.
    Edmund's attitude to these works is of extraordinary

humility. He says, 'My God, they make me feel so useless, so clumsy. Look at that glaze. . . . Look at that wooden bowl, so simple, yet so respectful of the wood itself.' I ask myself – I would never dare to ask him – why he does not show the same respect towards me and what I do. I know the answer: I am a wayward child who must be punished by withholding approval even from her virtues. He has the understanding eye, but not the understanding heart.

These brief character sketches were interspersed with descriptions of sexual encounters in her studio and in the apartments of friends and acquaintances. But as Max pored over the beautifully scripted pages, he became slowly aware that what he was reading was not in fact a diary but a carefully constructed narrative, part fact, part fiction, of her real and imagined life. The handwriting itself was the clue. It was too regular, too controlled – like a manuscript laboriously copied in the scriptorium of some Rabelaisian abbey. It was a work of art which depicted what her pictures concealed. She manipulated her friends and sexual partners exactly as she posed her models to make the most expressive composition, the most dramatic statement:

Paula and Danny are jealous of each other. I withdraw myself from them and have them make love with Lindy. Then I have Peter join in the play. I explain over and over that love should be fun, not fury. I sketch as they romp. When they look at the sketches they see the beauty of the game and begin to be friends.

Clearly there were deep conflicts in such artificial relationships, but there was nothing to suggest an imminent act of violence until quite late in the record:

Today a horrible fight with Peter. He is suddenly very jealous – obsessively so for a young man. He wants to take me out, show me off to his friends. I refuse. I try to explain that my love-place is private, that I am not a possession to be displayed in public. He calls me terrible names. He hits me, throws me on the bed and tries to rape me. The rape fails because I am only too ready to surrender. I begin to wish Henri would come back. His brutality is always under control.

A few days later came another episode of exasperation:

I ask Hugh to take me to Thursday's auction – important Impressionist items from a Chicago estate. He has told me so many funny stories about sexy women at auctions that I am curious to see them. He says no. Auction days are business days for him. If I want to go, I go alone and stay away from him. I tell him to go to hell. He says, 'Don't push your luck, Madi. This town's full of easy lays.' I hit him in the face. He hits back and walks out. I wonder why the fun is gone out of everything.

Late in the afternoon Danny arrives. She is in a mess too. She has just quarrelled with Harmon Seldes and is thinking of quitting her job as well. I tell her she's a fool. She should stay. The pay is good. Seldes can't afford to lose her. The affair was nothing but a fiction created by two people who couldn't make up their minds about their own bodies.

Mather read the passage three times before its full import hit him. Leonie herself had given him all the clues. He had simply lacked the wit to read them: the connection with Seldes and Hugh Loredon, her identification of Madeleine as voyeur as well as participant, the last words of her report: 'A lot of us are involved and we'll be looking to you to make sense of it.'

He left the rest of the diary unread, turned to the photostats of the sketchbooks and studied them carefully page by page. The manic dancing, copulating figures were real personages now. He could fit names to them from the letters, identify their sexual particularities from passages in the diaries.

On his first cursory examination in New York he had noticed only one image of Leonie Danziger. Now she thrust herself at him from several tableaux: in a Sapphic embrace with another woman, then transformed into a wild-haired maenad pursued through a variety of encounters by rampant fauns who had to be Peter and Ironman.

He left the drawings open on his desk and got up to pour

himself a drink. The telephone rang; Harmon Seldes was on the line, bubbling with goodwill.

'I spoke with Berchmans. You made a very good impression on him.'

'I'm an impressive fellow. You know that, Harmon.'

'How's the Bayard piece coming along?'

'Slowly. She's a hard woman to keep in focus.'

'What sort of material have you been able to find?'

'Not a lot. I'm relying mostly on oral history from Bayard himself and my own reaction to the pictures. This will be mood stuff, not scholarship.'

'No papers, no letters?'

'Not so far. Why?'

'Apparently Berchmans and she were part-time lovers. He wrote her letters.'

'Silly fellow.'

'If any turn up, he'd like to get them back.'

'I'm sure he would. My father had a saying about that.'

'I'm sure it was profound,' Seldes said drily.

'It was,' Mather told him. ' "Do right and fear no man. Don't write and fear no woman." I'd have thought Berchmans was brighter than that.'

'You don't have to be bright,' said Seldes gloomily, 'just rich enough not to care.'

In a private room at the London Clinic, Hugh Loredon sat propped up with pillows and talked with his physician. At first glance they might have been brothers – white-haired, pink-cheeked, blandly eloquent and evasive as only the Boston Irish and the Home Counties English know how to be. The physician made a gesture of helplessness.

'It's rough, Hugh. It's going to get rougher. The secondaries are spreading. You've got very little liver function left. . . . '

'How long?' Loredon asked.

The physician shrugged. 'A month or so of mobility, provided you take things easy. After that you're on the slippery slide. We can ease you along a bit, but at the outside you've got three months.'

'I won't sit still for that.' He was angry. 'If you won't knock me off, I'll do it myself.'

'Yes, well. . . . ' The physician surveyed him with detached pity. 'I understand how you feel; but as things stand in this country, I can't "knock you off". You're a casual patient; I don't have a long history on my books, so I can't build up a consistent overdose of painkillers. As for knocking yourself off, that's easy enough, but let me ask you a question. Do you carry life assurance?'

'Quite a lot,' Loredon answered.

'Who collects the benefit?'

'My daughter.'

'But if you commit suicide, she loses it. Of course it's up to you to decide the issue; I'm just reminding you of the consequences.'

'And that's the best you can tell me?'

The physician spent a long time studying the backs of his soft well-manicured hands. He seemed to be talking to his fingernails instead of to his patient.

'There is another solution. It's not one I dare even hint at with people who have strong religious views, but since you don't appear to have any convictions in that matter . . . '

'I don't,' stated Loredon emphatically. 'I've lived without religion all my life. I can't just put it on like a Burberry to keep off the rain. Tell me.'

'You're still well enough to travel. I suggest you go to Amsterdam. I'll give you a letter to a colleague of mine there who runs an oncology clinic for terminal cases. He'll take you in. . . . And when you feel you're ready, he'll help you to go out. It's swift, painless and more and more doctors in Holland are offering it as a service to their patients. You're a terminal case anyway. So there's no problem with the death certificate. All you need to do is make sure there's enough money to pay the hospital and cremation expenses and have your ashes shipped back home.'

Hugh Loredon chewed on the proposition for a few moments and then asked, 'Amsterdam, you say?'

'That's right.'

'I could fly in, transact some legitimate company business, then put myself into hospital?'

'That's right. The business part is your own affair.'

'It's a charade, but I'd rather my daughter didn't know what I was doing. She's working on a big project. I don't want to upset her more than I can help. No long goodbyes. No mercy flights across the Atlantic. You're sure you can guarantee a pain-less exit?'

'I can't guarantee anything,' said the physician calmly. 'You're a very sick man. You should be following the protocols of treat-ment. You have decided to keep working; you are off to Holland. Like any good doctor, I refer you to a colleague in case you need emergency help. You carry the letter with you. It outlines your medical history. We are all covered. . . . Anyway, sleep on it. We'll talk again in the morning.'

'I've made up my mind,' Hugh Loredon told him. 'Amsterdam it is.'

'Very well. I'll see you again on my early morning round and give you the letter of reference. You can be out of here by ten. I take it you'll be going straight to the Continent?'

'Well, yes. . . . There may be one or two things I have to do before I leave.'

'You're on borrowed time, Hugh. Don't waste it on trifles. If you collapse in London, you'll have to sweat it out right to the end.'

'Point taken.' Hugh Loredon held out his hand. 'Thanks for the service. Now let me make a few calls and see how many friends I've got.'

Max Mather had ordered coffee and sandwiches to be brought to his room. He was anxious to work through to the end of the Madeleine Bayard material and begin some rudimentary drafting on the architecture of the piece.

When he turned back to the diaries, he became aware for the first time of the dates of the entries. It was a matter of visual awareness rather than of any conscious decision to examine a time-frame. He was surprised to find that the final entries ran right up to the date of Madeleine's murder. Clearly Loredon must have gone to the studio on that day and taken away the

155

material . . . which had to make him a prime suspect as the killer, or at least an accessory after the fact.

The last entries in the diary were therefore singularly important. Mather read them slowly, several times:

I saw the doctor again this morning. He gave me a long lecture. He says I cannot sustain the pace of a highly active sex life and the creative drive necessary to produce the amount of work I am doing. He insists I slow down and finish the course of sedatives he has prescribed. He believes I should put myself into therapy, to try to bring some sense of unity into a life which is becoming more and more fragmented. I argue with him, but I know he is right. The only time I feel whole is when I stand alone in front of the canvas, looking at a world which I have created.

Yet people still make huge demands on me. I feel sometimes like Diana of Ephesus, with hundreds of breasts at which the whole world is feeding. The men are bad enough. They are brusque and demanding, but once satisfied they are gone. The women – and I think especially of Danny and Paula – consume much more of me. They demand affirmations and assurances I simply cannot give.

Edmund is daily more concerned. I know that, but when he is concerned he scolds. When he scolds I become bitchy and then he gets angry and bitter and locks himself away from me. There are times when I believe I could goad him into killing me. The sedatives help a little. I could easily become addicted to that soft seductive calm that creeps over me as the dose takes hold. . . . If only I could share it and forget the furies and the jealousies . . .

Mather closed the book and pressed the palms of his hands against his aching eyes. The momentary darkness was a relief from the glare of the paper and the unrelenting march of the script across the pages, but there was no way to blot out the disturbing images conjured up in this sterile Swiss apartment, three thousand miles and twelve months away from Madeleine's studio in New York. Soon he would be living in that same studio. Would he still hear the piping of old music, see the flurry of ghostly draperies? Would the image of Madeleine Bayard still be as vivid as it was at this moment, lying in a drugged sleep, her white body naked on the bright quilt, waiting for the killer to strike?

Not for the first time, Mather asked himself how he had become embroiled in the affairs of all these screwed-up people. One on one was so much easier – squire to indulgent mistress. You walked out hand in hand. When you shut the bedroom door, you shut out the world. Detachment was not so easy now. He was like Gulliver cast up on an alien shore, waking to find himself pegged out and bound by gossamer threads strong as ship's cables.

Sudden and startling, the telephone rang: Hugh Loredon was on the line from London. Mather greeted him without enthusiasm.

'Anne-Marie told me you might call. She's worried about you. What's the problem?'

'It's not a problem, Max. It's a death sentence. Concentrates the mind most wonderfully, they say.'

'Oh, my God! I'm so sorry to hear that. Have you told Anne-Marie?'

'No – and I don't intend to.'

'She has a right to know.'

'It's my life,' Hugh Loredon said curtly. 'The last thing I need is an argument.'

'Is there anything I can do for you?'

'Yes. Meet me at the Amstel Hotel in Amsterdam on Friday of this week. Spend a couple of days with me – we'll look at the Rembrandts, have lunch with a couple of dealers whom you should know anyway. Then on the Monday I'll be going into a clinic . . . I won't be coming out.'

'Oh.' It took a few moments for the message to sink in. 'Does this mean what I think it does?'

'Yes. I've a physician's report and a beautiful set of X-rays. Afterwards there'll be a kosher death certificate and you'll be one of the executors of my will. Ed Bayard's the other.'

'Why us, for Christ's sake?'

'It's a joke: the best and the last I can manage.'

'Talking of documents, I'm already holding a briefcase of yours.'

'Have you read the material?'

'Yes.'

'Keep it.'

'I'd like you to explain it to me.'

'What can I say? For me it's written in sand. The wind and the tide will wash it away. Who cares who gave Gauguin the clap or what knife Van Gogh used to cut off his ear? It's all trivia. Dying dispenses us from it. You haven't said whether you'll come to Amsterdam.'

'I'll be there on Friday.'

'Good. I've already booked the room.'

'You're bloody sure of yourself.'

'I know you can't resist a woman or a hard-luck story.'

'Hugh, listen to me. I understand what you're doing; I think I understand why. But if you want to go out clean, you must let Anne-Marie share this last event with you. If you don't, it's a terrible rejection to lay on your own daughter. How do I tell her that you've called me and not her?'

'Simple, Max. You're just the messenger hired to carry bad news. You stand to get killed for your pains.' He laughed and the laugh ended in a choking splutter. 'See you Friday!'

As he put down the receiver, Mather's hands were unsteady. The notion of optional death was new and suddenly too close for comfort. He wondered how he was going to explain all this to Anne-Marie. The thought of spending the rest of the evening alone was intolerable. He locked up his papers and drove down to the Limmat Quai.

In a dingy night-club called the Venus Room he drank watered whisky and bought gut-rot champagne for a Romanian hooker, then fed her a midnight supper of overcooked steak and under-cooked potatoes. He also paid her a hundred dollars for her stimulating conversation and for having cured him of casual lusts. She was sober enough to tell him that if all gays were as nice as he was, the Limmat would be a much pleasanter place to work.

By the time he got back to his apartment he was convinced that Hugh Loredon had a point. If you were going to end your life with a neat and tidy act, Amsterdam was a much more cheerful place to do it than Zurich.

TEN

Alois Liepert's house was some ten miles out of town – a pleasant country-style chalet set on a wooded hillside overlooking the lake. The interior spoke money – old and new money – and a certain traditional discretion about displaying it. Liepert's wife was slightly younger than he: slim, athletic and very much at ease in social situations.

The dealers were an odd couple: the man who dealt with the moderns looked like a nineteenth-century dominie. The man who handled antiques and old masters looked as though he had just stepped from the pages of a fashion magazine. The auctioneer, who turned out to be a year younger than Mather, had a permanent patina of middle age, like a young Hugh Loredon. Their womenfolk were agreeable but a trifle uneasy and Mather was at pains to draw them into the talk. The banker and his wife were a middle-aged couple of the steady executive breed.

Long practice had made Max Mather an exemplary guest, an attractive listener and a lively raconteur, deft at exciting interest with unfamiliar trivia. All the time, he knew he was under scrutiny and skilled inquisition. He was comforted by the presence of Gisela Mundt, with her easy smile and her fluent transitions from one language to another when the conversation stalled on a point of vocabulary.

However, the disciplines of scholarship held good. He was firmly grounded in the grammar of his own trade and he made no extravagant claims outside it. The *Belvedere* material was impressive. The promise of a flow of dollar funds into the local art market was attractive to everybody. The banker summed it up with a neat little accolade: 'I know you will do well here, Mr Mather. We appreciate *solidität*.'

'I'll get you a good price for the Tompion,' promised the auctioneer. 'All the traditional watchmakers will bid for it.'

'As soon as I get the transparencies, I'll give you a buying order on the Bayards,' said the dealer in moderns. 'And I do want you to have a look at Davanti's work – I think he's ready to break out.'

'Our best man in Renaissance drawings is Gisevius in Basel.' This from the traditionalist. 'When you're ready, I'll make an appointment and we'll go to see him together. He's got a good laboratory. He's very conservative. His word carries much weight in Europe.'

Max's final accolade came from Liepert's wife.

'You've been a most generous guest, Mr Mather. Our friends have enjoyed you very much. Would you be kind enough to drive Gisela home?'

'It would be my pleasure.'

As they drove back to town he felt a warm gratitude for her presence. This was the seal set on his evening, the seal of trust and acceptance in this most conservative of cities. In the classic strategy of old-fashioned warfare, he had driven for the high ground and taken it. In a few days he would have consolidated an alliance with a powerful prince – Henri Charles Berchmans the Elder – again by the classic ploys of placing gifts in his hands, removing a threat. . . . Soon Hugh Loredon's secret would be his. Now he was no longer a client, a dependent, but a man to respect. There would be no more inquisitions. His writ in the trade would run as freely as the next man's. Soon, very soon, he would set down the last elements in the scenario of the Raphaels and begin to put the drama into production.

As they crossed the bridge into the city, Gisela gave him directions to her house – a small, old-fashioned villa near the University. He walked her to the front door. She handed him her key and asked, 'Would you like some coffee?'

'Love some,' Max said. 'Are you sure it's legal?'

'In Switzerland,' she answered him with a smile, 'everything that is not forbidden is legal.'

Which, thought Mather, was one hell of a high note on which to end an evening.

Early the next morning Mather called Berchmans in Paris. He

161

was not available, but a minion promised to deliver a message. One hour later he called back. Mather, accustomed by now to his brusqueness, was surprised to find him good-humoured and agreeable.

'Yes, Mr Mather. What can I do for you?'

'Seldes called me last night. He told me you had an interest in certain Bayard items.'

'True.'

'I have them. Seldes does not know that.'

'Thank you for letting me know so promptly.'

'I am going to Amsterdam on Friday. Hugh Loredon has asked me to meet him there. He's a dying man.'

'I'm sorry to hear that.'

'I'm sure you will treat the information with discretion. His daughter does not know yet.'

'Of course.'

'I propose, therefore – if it is convenient to you – to travel on an early flight from Zurich to Paris tomorrow morning, deliver the items into your hands and take a late afternoon flight to Amsterdam.'

'In that case, permit me to meet you at Orly and offer you lunch at the Veau d'Or. It's only twenty minutes away, so I can have you back at the airport in time for your Amsterdam departure.'

'Good . . . I arrive Swissair 731 at 10.30.'

'A question, Mr Mather. Has anyone else seen these items?'

'So far as I am aware, only the person to whom they were written and the person who gave them to me.'

'Are they originals or copies?'

'Originals.'

'Thank you. I· look forward to our meeting. You continue to intrigue me, Mr Mather.'

Mather landed at Orly half an hour late in a flurry of March wind and misty rain. Berchmans' chauffeur met him and drove him swiftly to a small country restaurant in the direction of Fontaine-bleau. Berchmans was waiting for him in a corner booth, well insulated from the other diners. He was cordial and expansive.

He offered an aperitif. Then he discoursed on the menu: whiting cooked with white wine and breadcrumbs, a breast of lamb with fennel, a rabbit with prunes. He made a ceremony of the wine list. He assured Mather he could enjoy a leisurely meal and be back at the airport with time in his pocket.

Mather was happy enough to be cosseted but he was anxious to despatch the business in hand. So as soon as the orders had been taken he handed Berchmans an envelope containing the letters which he had written to Madeleine Bayard.

Berchmans scanned them swiftly and put them back in the envelope, which he stowed in his breast pocket. He gave a small, shamefaced grin and said, 'Thank you. There's no fool like an old one.'

Mather shrugged and said nothing.

'How did you come by these letters, Mr Mather?'

'Better you don't ask, Mr Berchmans. They are evidentiary material in a murder case which is still open.'

'Wise counsel,' said Berchmans. 'The last thing we want to do is spoil the taste of this excellent food. In this business, moreover, it is best to make friends with the police.'

Then, with hardly a shift in tone or expression, he launched into a series of dazzling anecdotes which lasted from the hors d'oeuvres to the dessert.

He told of the Norwegian cabinet-maker Casperon, who became so good at forging the paintings of Edvard Munch that he painted one under police supervision in three hours. He told how he himself had amassed a collection of excellent forgeries by one Jean-Pierre Schechroun, who came from Madagascar, studied with Leger and could knock off Braques and Picassos, Kupkas and Kandinskys at the flip of a cheque-book. He was clever, Berchmans explained; he never worked in oils, only in watercolours, pastels and sketches – the 'tentatives' of every master in every studio.

His own view of such rogueries was interesting.

'At the top end of the market the effect is minimal. Any challenge to a major work is instantly met by offering a battery of scientific tests. If the work turns out to be a fake, you get a kind of see-saw effect – how clever the criminals are, how much cleverer are the experts. How valuable the original must be, to take so much trouble to forge it.

'In the middle and lower markets, no one sweats too much except the buyer. It's still *caveat emptor* – and *caveat mercator* too, if the dealer wants to stay in business. Hang a David Stein forgery in your dining room and which of your dinner guests is going to tell you it isn't a van Dongen? Mannerisms are easy to imitate. Genius is as hard to catch as a butterfly and it is, after all, the function of genius to make us create our own illusions.'

Then came the sting in the tail of the scorpion:

'Madeleine Bayard had that sort of genius . . . I wonder what you are going to say about her? How are you going to judge her?'

'I'm not sure I understand her yet,' replied Mather. 'There is a schizophrenic quality in her work which still confounds me. I'd like to hear your judgment of her – off the record, of course.'

'I promised you a luncheon, Mr Mather, not a press interview.'

'Let me put it another way then. Did you buy her paintings because you were lovers or because you prized her work?'

'Because I prized the work. No doubt, no question about that. The world is full of junk. I see no reason to pay money for it.'

'Still, she was an exciting lover.'

'That's the second time you've used the word. She was not a lover. She was the classic courtesan, the *poule de luxe*. She gave pleasure with the utmost skill. But that was the end of the endowment. After that she'd devour you if you let her. Not for money, but for reassurance. She was a prisoner, ravenous in an empty room, always looking for escape, not caring who offered it to her or at what risk . . . ' He broke off and looked at his watch. 'Time to go, Mr Mather, if you are to make your plane to Amsterdam. Rushing at airports is a lethal occupation.'

When he had signed the bill, he said quite casually, 'One more matter, Mr Mather.'

'Yes?'

'You have done me a singular service at cost and inconvenience to yourself. What do I owe you?'

'An apology,' Mather said curtly.

Berchmans gaped at him, flushed to the roots of his hair. It seemed an age before he found voice or words.

164

'You're right. That was very uncouth. I apologise. I am grateful for what you have done. Please forgive me.'

He held out his hand. Mather accepted the gesture. He was not sure that he had made a friend, but saw no point in making a powerful enemy.

The evening flight from Paris to Amsterdam was a milk run, crowded and comfortless. Mather gave himself over to dozing and working out variations on the scenario which now was beginning to look more and more feasible, provided he had the patience to wait for the propitious moment.

He had no immediate financial pressure. He could last at least eighteen months living on capital. There was reasonable income in prospect. The master works locked in his bank vault were appreciating every hour – and now there was a new thought to conjure with. As a recognised dealer with a sympathetic banker, he could raise money on the Raphaels without ever having to bring them to market. With the loan money thus raised, he could trade himself into steady profit without ever having to compromise himself. Then, at some later time, he could begin his market forays with the big pieces. Right or wrong, it cost nothing to dream; and before the dream had dissipated they had touched down at Schipol airport.

The road into Amsterdam was greasy, the city blanketed in misty drizzle, but the Amstel Hotel offered warmth and solid burgher comfort. Hugh Loredon had booked him a room adjoining his own suite, so that he had the use of a lounge as well as a bedroom. As always, Loredon was well-groomed and freshly barbered, but his once ruddy face was pinched and drawn and his eyeballs were beginning to yellow. He had ordered dinner to be served in the suite, explaining, 'I tire quickly; I can't cope with crowds. And now, of course, I'm not allowed alcohol. Hell of a note, isn't it?'

'How long have you known about this?'

'I've been fighting it more than a year. I came to England because I didn't want to get caught up in the final protocols of treatments at home. I saw no reason to donate myself as a guinea-pig . . . I'd made up my mind years ago that rather than face a long terminal illness I'd opt out . . . which I'm doing now, courtesy of certain members of the Dutch medical profession.'

'What can I say?' Mather made a small gesture of deprecation. 'It's your life. But I wonder why you can't share at least the last few days of it with your daughter?'

'Because I don't have the right to put her through the misery. I'm an empty man, Max. A one-role actor whose contract's been terminated. The news that you're going to take back is that you left me looking very well. We talked some business together – there's a young Dutch painter whose work you'll see tomorrow who could be a candidate for Anne-Marie's gallery. His name's Cornelis Janzoon. Then before you leave, I'll have a sudden collapse. No time, no warning. I'll be cremated and my ashes will be sent home. Simple, clean, no fuss. Anne-Marie will recover quickly. I've always been a very small part of her life anyway. You've been more important than I have.'

'I'm her old-shoe lover, Hugh, worn out but comfortable, to put on when her feet hurt. So let's you and I stop waltzing around. I've read all the Madeleine Bayard stuff. It's locked in a safe deposit in Switzerland. Now you have to tell me what it means.'

'Before I do that,' Hugh Loredon was harsh and emphatic, 'you'd better be damn sure you want to know.'

'Why?'

'Because knowing's a burden, Max. It's a load on your back and hooks in your heart; and once you've got 'em you'll never get rid of 'em. That's one more reason why I'm taking the high jump. So don't say you haven't been warned.'

'I'm warned. So tell me. Who killed Madeleine Bayard?'

'Wrong question, Max.'

'What's the right one?'

'Why you were privileged to see Madi Bayard's papers and to hear my last confession.'

'Tell me, then.'

'Because you're like me, Max, a maverick, a rogue male – and you're the only one I know who's bright enough, tough enough and crooked enough for me to trust with what's left to be done.'

'Thanks for the compliment.'

'Let's not be sensitive, sonny boy. I'm on the eve of execution;

I don't give a damn for your wounded feelings. Let's start with Madeleine's diary. That explains some of it, but not all.'

'So what's your version, Hugh?'

'It's not a version. It's . . . another facet of a truth that you can't take in all at once. You have to start with Madeleine herself, as she appeared to each of us. I've been auctioning art all my life – great art, good art, valueless junk. One thing I learned: the real thing is a magical object. It raises your own passion, the passion of the crowd in front of you. It's like . . . like a wind rippling across a cornfield. It's the same with the artists themselves. They are magical persons. The air around them is charged with electricity like a storm-cloud. Carl Jung talked about this somewhere. He called it "numen", the aura of power. Madeleine Bayard had it. She was a sorceress, laying a spell on everyone who came in contact with her. Take me, Max. I've been chasing women all my life. Love-'em and leave-'em Loredon! I could read 'em at a glance, from the tip of their pink toes to the twitch of their eyelashes. But Madi Bayard had me so bewitched I'd have walked through fire for her. Even when she got tired of me – which didn't take too long – I was happy to be with her, to be accepted as part of her group . . . the boys and girls and the not-so-young, the talented and the fringe-dwellers. I remember as a boy hearing the story of Circe and how Odysseus came to her castle and heard her singing as she wove wonderful dazzling fabrics. . . . Don't laugh at me, Max. Don't laugh at any of us. Madi Bayard was our Circe. She wove wonderful dreams, but she enslaved us all. She could make us do anything she wanted.'

There was sweat on his forehead and on his upper lip. He mopped it away and reached for a glass of water as Mather waited in silence.

'Problem is, Max, there's good and bad magic. Our Circe, too, turned her guests into swine. Madi's marriage was a mess. Ed Bayard had neither the wit nor the strength to manage her. He turned into a tyrant, a querulous, bitter tyrant . . . She never left him, because he became the excuse for all her aberrations. She hated herself, you see. She knew the talent she had. She respected that. Her pictures were Circe's magic tapestries. But without Ed Bayard she had to explain the ugly creature who lived in her skin when the happy enchantress was absent. That

167

creature played terrible, perverse games. The secrets she heard from one, she would pass on to a rival. She would make love to a woman and then deride her to a man. You've read the diary – which isn't a diary, but facts turned into fictions – you've seen how she herself remained always the centre of her universe . . . the dark goddess who lived by devouring her devotees. Danny Danziger was one of those devotees. You may have met her. She does editorial work for Seldes.'

'I've met her. I've worked with her,' said Mather calmly. 'I can't say I know her very well.'

'She takes some knowing,' said Loredon. 'I probably knew her better than most. She's bisexual, but when I met her all her experience had been with women. I was her first man – which at the time I was very proud of – a special kind of victory! Jesus, how naïve I was! The encounter was a mess for both of us. It also created a big problem with Madi. She was jealous of any interest that wasn't centred entirely on her. Me she could threaten by gossip and denigration, but she was very canny about that because I knew too much and was always ready to snap back – slap her about, if necessary, because she needed violence sometimes as other women need caresses.

'But in Danny Danziger she had an easy prey. You remember that piece in the diary where she described introducing Peter into a lesbian encounter between Paula and Danny? It wasn't at all the way she described it. Peter was a model hired from Negroni's – a professional stud, a nasty piece of work. The whole episode was painful and humiliating for Danny, but Madi managed it so that it made Danny more and more dependent on her – more self-conscious, more stricken with self-contempt.'

'I'm getting the picture,' said Mather. 'It isn't a pretty one.'

'It's exactly what she expresses in her paintings,' Loredon said wearily. 'Her unsuccessful flight from an untenable habitation, an unhappy and destructive self.' He gave a small humourless chuckle. 'That's a good phrase; you're welcome to use it in your piece. No charge, just pour a libation to my ghost.'

'I'll use the best scotch,' Mather assured him. 'Go on, for God's sake.'

'It began with Danny. Early one afternoon, about one-thirty, she got a call from Madeleine asking her to come down to the studio. According to Danny she sounded strange – a little drunk maybe, cajoling, making sex talk. She wanted Danny to model for her, to have a drink, to make love. Danny made excuses. She couldn't face a long, draining session. Then she began to be worried. She knew Madi was on sedatives; she wondered if she'd taken an overdose. So she went to the studio.

'She found Madi on the bed naked and snoring. She'd obviously had a woman visitor because there were two glasses smeared with lipstick and the dregs of a bottle of champagne. There was an unfinished canvas of a male figure on the easel, but a whole series of nude sketches of the woman visitor – someone she'd never seen before . . . probably a pick-up from Negroni's. It was clear that Madi had called Danny to stage an encounter with this woman, but she had passed out and the woman had left. She had obviously gone through Madeleine's wallet and taken whatever cash was in it.'

He broke off and took another swallow of water, holding the glass in both hands. Mather waited in silence until Loredon forced himself forward into the narrative.

'Danny was obviously shocked by the whole scene. She said Madi looked like an obscene doll tumbled on the bed. She was shivering and twitching and muttering in her sleep. Danny rolled her in the bedclothes and propped up her head so she wouldn't choke. She told me that it was at that precise moment she decided to kill her, because she took the pillow away and laid Madi flat on her back. Then she went into the washroom and found a pair of rubber gloves which Madi used to protect her hands from turpentine and etching acids. On Madi's desk was a present I had given her. It was an antique poignard, a dagger with a basket hilt that she used for a paper-knife. With that weapon she killed Madeleine.

'Then she called me. It was then about a quarter to three. I told her to wipe everything she'd touched, put the weapon in her handbag, get the hell out of there and walk six blocks before taking a taxi back to her apartment.

'I hotfooted it to the studio, parked in the lane and cleared out every incriminating document I could find – diary, sketchbooks, notes, porno pieces and, of course, Madi's telephone directory. I wore the same gloves Danny had used. Then I went up to

169

Danny's and talked her down out of shock. I took the dagger from her, washed it carefully and took it home. Later in the year I put it up in an auction of antique arms. The damn thing fetched two thousand dollars!'

'How the hell did the two of you survive twelve months of police investigation?' asked Mather.

'Because Ed Bayard was the principal suspect and because I'd got rid of a whole slew of embarrassing documents . . . but most of all because Danny Danziger kept her nerve. That's one very special woman.'

'So now you've told me all this,' said Mather, 'what do you expect me to do with it?'

'You're going to create a myth,' Loredon stated with sudden fire. 'The myth of Madeleine Bayard: beautiful woman, soul of fire, great artist cut off in her prime. That legend will establish Anne-Marie's gallery and make Madeleine Bayard canvases worth more than Rothkos or Pollocks. You're going to make money out of them, too – and while you're doing it you're going to make damn sure Anne-Marie never marries Ed Bayard.'

Mather stared at him in amazement, then burst out laughing. 'Hugh, you're a genius! In a well-ordered society they'd string you up for gallows meat. But, no doubt of it, you're a genius.'

'You brighten my last dark days,' Loredon told him with a grin.

'You are also a bloody liar!'

'What the hell do you mean?'

'This is all private talk in a hotel room. In a few days you'll be dead. So none of it can ever be proved. You're doing the old disinformation trick – I'm to be your red herring, stinking up the scene of a crime. Danny Danziger did not kill Madi Bayard.'

'Can you prove that?'

Mather laughed again and got up to pour himself another drink. He said gently, 'In my business, Hugh, there's a thing we call internal evidence. You work through a manuscript claimed to be authentic – third, fourth century maybe. You become aware of little things that don't fit . . . stylistic usages, notions that were not current at the period in question, glosses and interpolations of other texts. The moment you stumble on one of these interpolations you know you're dealing with a cooked-up job.

170

Your story's a cook-up . . . I've seen police photographs of what was found in Madeleine's studio. The pictures show a whisky bottle half full, a bottle of bourbon full and in the refrigerator coke, soda and white wine. There's no mention of champagne or glasses with lipstick. Why the fiction, Hugh?'

Hugh Loredon shrugged and gave a grin that turned into a grimace of pain.

'Because you're being thick-headed, Max. You're not thinking straight. You mustn't know anything – anything at all – about Madeleine's murder. You were in Italy, for Christ's sake, as was Anne-Marie. What's in the briefcase is evidence from the police point of view. From yours it's treasure-trove – sketches, notes, studies, diaries, letters which will be worth a fortune very soon.'

Hugh Loredon heaved himself out of his chair and limped over to the door to admit the waiter with the dinner service.

They ate lightly. Mather could not face a heavy evening meal. Hugh Loredon had no appetite at all; he was content to nibble at cheese and crackers and turn the talk back to his own imminent departure.

'It's crazy when you come to think of it. Forty-eight hours from now, I'm paying a perfectly respectable Dutch doctor a very respectable professional fee to kill me. I met him today. He's very charming, very compassionate. Took a lot of time to make sure I understood what would happen and that I'd put all my affairs in order.'

'And how does he explain what happens, Hugh?'

'Very simply. I'm in bed. He comes in, chats for a moment, wishes me a pleasant journey, gives the injection. It's quite pain-less, he says . . . he compares it with stepping on to an aircraft, strapping yourself in and falling instantly asleep.'

'And then what dreams may come?'

'No dreams, Max. No anything. That's the beauty of it.'

'But don't you think Anne-Marie will grieve for you? Don't you believe your friends will feel your loss?'

'I doubt it, Max. I doubt it very much. On auction days I was king of the castle. I stepped up on the rostrum with my little gavel and the whole room focused on me. But when the last bid was taken and I stepped down, it was as if I'd never been there. The buyers would be inspecting their purchases; the disappointed bidders, the gawkers and the kibitzers would all be on their way home. What I needed most at that time was a woman, just to remind me I was real.'

'Hugh, would you like me to be with you at the end?'

'No.' He was very emphatic about it. 'Definitely not. I'd like you to wait in Amsterdam until it's over. That keeps everything tidy. The doctor's very punctual. He names a time and that's when it happens. Go to a bar, have a drink for me. Then call Anne-Marie. Say gentle things. You'll find the words. She'll get a letter from me forwarded through the US Consulate. There'll be one for you too. Now tell me about yourself.'

'You know all there is to know, Hugh. I'm finding a niche for myself in the business. I think I'll be able to operate quite profitably from Europe.'

'What about the Raphaels?'

'The article will be published at the beginning of April. I imagine there'll be a flurry of correspondence and whatever activity that provokes. Meantime Seldes and Henri Berchmans have joined forces.'

'That's a formidable team. And where do you fit, Max?'

'I don't, I'm the floating particle. I like it that way.'

'Don't float too long, sonny boy. You get out of the habit of stable living. I always thought I had a good line with women – always a quip or a jest or a compliment that got me a bed for the night. It took me a long time to realise that all I needed was four words: "Do you? Don't you?" So that made things a lot easier. But the hard thing – and it got harder every year – was what to say to them afterwards. I was going to take you out on the town tonight, Max, but I'm beat. I'd better call it a day.'

Next morning they were out early, strolling in the spring sunshine along the Prinsengracht and the Keizersgracht, with their red-brick houses and their high step-gables and the linden trees making dark blotches on the oily water. In a garret studio near the old St Nicholas Church they found the young Cornelis Janzoon, who was working with Hogarthian exuberance to document the new sub-culture that had sprung up in the old city – the addicts, the pimps, the whores, the polyglot peddlers of coke and heroin and every other drug in the underground pharmacopeia.

He was a scrawny, scraggly youth in his mid-twenties, but his drawing and his composition were as assured as any of his elders and his palette was lively with extraordinary confections of modern colour chemistry that leapt from the classic backgrounds of sea-mist, weathered brick and dun Lowland skies. His first exhibition had been enormously successful, but the critics had made a meal of his second, so he was brusque and defensive.

'They say what I am doing is old-fashioned expressionism. What do they mean? I live here, I express what I experience. What do those bastards know except words? What label do they invent to describe "The Nightwatch"? Take a look at it when you go to the Rijksmuseum this morning. You don't put labels on a thing like that. You just look . . . and you listen, too, because you can hear that damned drum beating.'

He brightened immediately when Mather bought two small canvases and asked for transparencies of some other works to be sent to him in Zurich. Ten minutes away they called on a young woman, born in the tulip lands of Aarlsmeer, who was turning her memories of tulips in bloom into extraordinary optical assaults that made one think of the primal wonders of an emerging creation.

As they left her and strolled towards the Rijksmuseum, Hugh Loredon said, 'I've been asking myself how much longer I could endure survival – which means, I guess, how much pain I'd be prepared to pay – to use a talent like that. Part of my problem has always been that I never stretched for anything. . . . Money, yes; a woman, sometimes. But the attainment was always a disappointment. Seems to me the artist is always stretching for something else, something better.'

'"Their works drop groundward",' Mather quoted softly. ' "But themselves, I know, reach many a time a heaven that's shut to me. . . . " '

'Browning,' said Hugh Loredon. 'Andrea del Sarto, the Perfect Painter. I sold a del Sarto once, in London. Somebody put me on to that poem and I used it in my spiel . . . I used to say it probably put thirty per cent on the price. I'm getting tired. Do you mind if we take a taxi to the Rijksmuseum?'

'We can go back to the hotel if you want.'

'No, I really want to see the Rembrandts. That's my going-away present to myself.'

The which, it seemed to Max Mather, were the saddest words he had heard in his life.

ELEVEN

Forty-eight hours later in a clinic on the outskirts of Amsterdam, the life and times of Hugh Loredon were terminated by a lethal injection. The death was certified, quite truthfully, as 'cardiac arrest'. The news was passed to Max Mather in his room at the Amstel Hotel. Immediately he called Anne-Marie. Their talk was brief and bleak.

'Max – how nice to hear from you. Where are you?'

'In Amsterdam. Listen, I'm afraid I've got some bad news for you.'

He heard her sudden intake of breath and then her voice, very small and childlike.

'How bad?'

'The worst. Your father collapsed last night. He'd been suffering from terminal cancer. I got him into a local clinic. He died a few minutes ago. I'm sorry, love, I'm dreadfully sorry.'

'Why wasn't I told before? Why didn't he call – or you, Max?'

'He wanted it this way – no farewells, no mourning. He loved you too much to inflict them on you.'

'No, Max.' There was anger in her voice now. 'That wasn't it. He just couldn't face anything unpleasant . . . What happens now? The funeral, the . . . the arrangements?'

'All in hand. Hugh left everything very tidy.'

'Except me, Max. I'm his daughter. I'm not tidy. How the hell did he think I would take this?'

'He loved you, sweetheart. You have to believe that.'

'In his fashion, sure. But not enough to think I might need to kiss him goodbye. Just that, Max – kiss him goodbye. It was you he called, not me.'

'Would you like me to come back to New York? I could be with you in ten hours.'

'No. Stay there. Keep things tidy – above all, keep things tidy.

175

I'm going to hang up now, Max. I need to cry, but I seem to have mislaid my tears.'

An instant later she was gone and Mather was left to pour a last lonely libation to the pale ghost of Hugh Loredon. Then out of some dark well of folk memory came the conviction that there were other ghosts to be laid and that the most baleful was the ghost of Madeleine Bayard. She was too potent a spirit to be dismissed with spilt wine. She had to be summoned up, confronted, challenged to declare herself good or evil, exorcised with bell, book and candle.

Mather sat down at the big buhl desk, pulled out a pile of hotel stationery and began to write.

I never met Madeleine Bayard. I have encountered her only in her canvases, in conversations with her friends and lovers, in police documents, in the austere landscape of memory which her husband now inhabits. Yet I am haunted by her. She is like a beautiful kestrel, graceful yet sinister, hovering between me and the sun.

I must summon her down, coax her to perch on my wrist, be still long enough for me to put the jess on her and then have her converse about the high blue kingdom she inhabits. For this is no ordinary wind-hoverer, this is a magical bird, a rider of the storm, a challenger of the Sun-God . . .

A surge of energy infused him and the images began forming and re-forming in his mind like flames in a fire. The words poured from his pen and the manuscript piled up beside him, clear as Madeleine Bayard's own text.

Three hours later it was done. He did not reread it, but pushed it straight into a manila envelope with a covering note to Leonie Danziger:

Dear Leonie,

Hugh Loredon died here in Amsterdam today. It was a peaceful but lonely end for so gregarious a man, but that's the way he wanted it to be. We had long and intimate talk before he died and you will find echoes of it in the following pages.

176

He spoke of you too; I will tell you about that when we meet again.

Here written in blood and tears – not all of them mine – is the memorial on Madeleine Bayard. It is, I promise you, as honest and as good as I can make it. I leave it to your absolute discretion to decide whether it should be published or suppressed. If you opt for publication, then you have similar absolute discretion over the editing. When you are satisfied pass copies to Bayard, to Anne-Marie Loredon and to Harmon Seldes.

I would like you to take up with Seldes the question of whether the piece might not find a better home in the *New York Times Review*, which has a much shorter lead time than *Belvedere*. I would like it to have the best impact for Anne-Marie's show. It would be a kindness to call her. Hugh refused to bring her to Europe for what he called a death watch. Naturally she is very upset. We all need the purging of shared grief . . . which brings me by a round turn back to Madeleine.

You knew her. You received at her hands both joy and pain. In my memorial I have tried to respect your privacy and everyone else's. I hope I have limned a portrait that you and others can accept as authentic. Please call, or write me in Zurich. I leave tomorrow for St Moritz for a few days' skiing, then I'm off to Italy for a week.

Affectionate greetings,

Max

He walked downstairs and consigned the package to the concierge for transmission by overnight courier to New York. Somehow it was a terminal act. Enough of other people's games and the stale taste of other people's parties. It was time to set himself on the road again, about his own exclusive business. He had still to find an ending to the tale, but he was confident he could devise one. First he needed to clear his head, tone up his body and order his future to sane and simple ends. The best place to do that was on the last snow on the last high pistes before spring came to the Engadine.

*

There were good falls that weekend. Badrutts Palace was almost full. This was the time the regulars loved, the last flourish of winter, the first chancy promise of spring when the thaw threatened and great plates of snow were loosened. In the old days Max had come here with Pia. He still held his membership in the Corviglia Club. The hotel staff recognised him and gave him the welcome of an honoured guest. Not that he was alone this time. Still depressed by his experience in Amsterdam, still troubled about Danny Danziger, he had invited Gisela Mundt to join him for the weekend. Skiing, she agreed, was a wholly legal pursuit in St Moritz. The preludes and the postscripts to this act might be marginally objectionable, but certainly not illegal. Therefore, yes, she would be delighted to be with him.

On the drive up, she began very tentatively to propose a new plan for the disposal of the Raphaels.

'Look at it, if you like, Max, as a worst case solution. Although we are colleagues, I'm not as sure as Alois that you can bring the Raphaels to market without litigation . . . I've told him this. There's no secret between us. Whatever the price we're talking about – one hundred million, two hundred – it's a glittering prize. The best legal brains in the world would be scrambling to work on the case and I swear to you it could go on for years and would certainly bankrupt you if you lost it – which, with appeal after appeal, you might well do.'

'So what are you suggesting?'

'That you take at least a passing look at the ten per cent solution.'

'Which is?'

'The formula every insurance company works on – that it's cheaper to pay ten per cent to recover lost or stolen goods than pay the full value of the insurance. It's a simple choice really. Which would you rather have: ten million or twenty million guaranteed, or a hundred million at risk on a crippling lawsuit?'

'I'd like to take that one under advisement,' Mather told her.

'You're the client,' said Gisela Mundt amiably. 'I offer advice, but in the end I accept your instructions.'

Late next morning Mather and Gisela shouldered skis and rode up to the Corviglia Club, to have lunch and then ski home. There was the customary round of introductions to members from Italy, France, Great Britain and West Germany. For Max it was one of time's sweeter revenges. He had come here first as the dependent lover of a wealthy widow. Now, by some strange mutation, he was accepted as another creature – newborn but full grown – whose past, like the past of so many in the Corviglia Club, was seen as a natural stepping-stone to the present. Old money and old lineage still counted for something – but what club in the world could survive without new money and the headline glamour of the arrivistes? Mather and his escort fell somewhere in between – a clerkly pair who understood the manners of the club and court and knew how to eat soup without making a noise or a mess.

Gisela Mundt was an instant attraction. A group of eager young members formed about her, while Mather himself was pinned in a corner by an elderly Italian whose name was synonymous with wines and who was lecturing him tediously on the follies of the Palombini clan and how none of the present generation could hold a candle to Luca the Swindler.

'You knew him then?' Mather was always a good listener.

'Very well. He was fifteen years older than I, which would put him well into his eighties by now. But when I came home wounded from Libya – *Dio*! That's a long time ago – and started work on our estate, he was very kind to me. He bought a lot of our products, helped me push our exports in Europe. A hard man, but loyal. He said every fool deserved one good lesson; if the fool didn't learn from it, there was no hope for him. You and he would have got along very well. By the way, I must say this: there is much praise for the way you treated Pia . . . '

'What else could I do? I loved her.'

'That, of course,' said the old man drily, 'is what took some time to understand.'

'Apropos Luca . . . '

'Yes?'

'He had a famous girl-friend, didn't he?'

'He had a lot . . . sometimes two or three at one time. Were you thinking of anyone in particular?'

'Camilla Dandolo.'

179

'The opera singer? Oh yes, I remember that one. In fact some of us have very special memories of her . . . no great singer but with so many other talents! What do you want to know about her?'

'Didn't she marry a Brazilian?'

'No – a German, naturalised in Brazil. A lot of us had a hand in that *combinazione*. He was SS, very high up, very troublesome. We made a deal with him that if he'd get off our backs, we'd get him out of the country to South America before the Allies got to him. Camilla was part of that deal . . . Camilla and various other items. He was head over heels and gone for her, so that end of the bargain was easy. The extraordinary part was that he came back in '47 or thereabouts and married her. What's your interest in the lady?'

'I'm doing some preliminary reading for a book on the divas of La Scala. Her name came up.'

'Fascinating subject – I wonder why nobody's thought of it before. Come and see me when next you're in Italy; I'm sure I could dig up some of our own family material for you. All our menfolk were opera buffs, although most of their interest was not in the divas but in the promising young sopranos. Let me give you my card.'

'Thank you. About Camilla Dandolo – is she still alive?'

'Alive and living in Milan. She's an old lady now. Her husband died a few years ago. She cashed in his Brazilian estates – which were fairly substantial by all accounts – and came home. The local *anagrafe* would have her address. I'm sure she'd be more than happy to receive you. Old troupers always love an audience.'

Later as they sat over lunch Gisela remarked, 'You look like a cat with cream on his whiskers. What's happened?'

'I've decided to take your advice.'

'About the Raphaels? Why not? It's a ticket in a lottery. You can't win unless you buy one. Now you can answer some questions for me?'

'About what?'

'Pia Palombini. You were lovers, it seems. Very famous lovers.'

'Famous, I wouldn't know. Lovers, yes.'

'And she got very sick and you nursed her until she died.'

'Yes.'

'Were you in love with her?'

'I loved her. It's not quite the same.'

'How old was she?'

'Forty-six . . . eleven years older than I.'

'I approve that.'

'You do?'

'Equal opportunity. If older men can chase young women, I'm all in favour of older women taking young men – most of whom need a lot of education anyway. Didn't your Mr Benjamin Franklin have something to say about that?'

'I believe he did, yes.'

'Am I embarrassing you, Max?'

'Yes.'

'Good.'

'Why good?'

'Because it confirms something I've felt about you ever since we met. You're a man who for a long time has had very little confidence in himself, who always felt not quite good enough to compete in the challenge races. That's why you always went for older – and richer – women.'

'I think this has gone far enough.' Mather was terse. 'It started as fun. Now it's mischief. Finish your lunch and let's do the run.'

'It's not mischief.' She laid a cool hand on his clenched fingers. 'I'm really working up to a compliment. I see a man with a rock of confidence building inside himself. At the Corviglia Club you were one who had earned his place . . . I admire that, and I'm glad I came to the Engadine with you.'

'You'd have no trouble finding someone to take you home.' Mather gave her a rueful grin and relaxed. 'I didn't mean to snap. Forgive me.'

'You're entitled. If I made mischief with my brothers, my father would bite my head off.'

'What did your father do?'

'He was a hill farmer – which meant, of course, that he had to be a master of all trades: mason, blacksmith, carpenter, animal midwife. He was also a *maler*, a rustic artist who painted pictures on the walls of houses. I used to think he was better than Dürer.

181

That's why I was fascinated by all that dinner-table talk at Alois Liepert's.' She hesitated a moment, then blurted out, 'I'm glad to be part – even a small part – of what you're doing in Switzerland. I don't mean the Raphaels but the rest of your plan.'

'Why do you exclude the Raphaels?'

'Because I find myself involved in a very difficult conflict of interest.'

'Which is?'

'You have a perfect legal right to do what you are doing. I've undertaken to defend that right. But as an old-fashioned country girl, I find your conduct reprehensible. There, now it's said. You can sack me as your lawyer and put me on the next train to Zurich.'

Mather shook his head. 'You don't escape that easily. You told me the first time we met that I had to decide the moral issue for myself. So what's new?'

'Nothing. Except that for my own conscience I had to tell you.'

'You've ruined my lunch,' he said with a shrug. 'Let's move. It's a long schuss home.'

It was not a schuss. It was a series of traverses each with its own special risk, but when they hit the town, apple-cheeked and breathless, Mather felt a slow surge of hope. Of all the women in his life, this was the least complicated, the least . . . he groped for the appropriate word . . . the least tainted by social displacement and the alien speech of the acquisitive societies. As he trudged down to the hotel, carrying her skis as well as his own, he found himself responding with less and less reserve to her questions.

'What did your father do, Max?'

'He was a schoolmaster – a very good one.'

'What did he teach?'

'European languages. Comparative languages. English literature. He was a versatile man.'

'And your mother?'

'My mother was a lady – she came from a well-to-do family – who always felt she'd married beneath her.'

'Oh dear!'

'She always wanted more than we had. She bullied my father unmercifully. He retreated further and further into his scholar's world. In the end it was hard even for me to reach him – and I loved him very much.'

'And your mother?'

'I loved her too. I knew I could never match her ambitions for me, but I depended on her for my own security. It was she who somehow scraped together the money for Princeton – but it was my father who prepared my mind for it. I loved them both. I never understood why they couldn't make each other happy.'

'You've had a lot of women in your life, Max.'

'I guess. I've never really counted.'

'And now you've got me.'

'On a weekend pass only.'

'Granted, on a weekend pass; which doesn't count. Which of your women were you really happy with, Max?'

'It's the wrong question.' Mather was suddenly withdrawn. 'I'm not sure I've ever learned what happiness really is.' Instantly he shrugged away the sombre thought. 'I'm going to have a sauna and a swim – join me?'

'Sure. Then I'm going to bed for a couple of hours. Join me?'

Which of course made for a pleasant Saturday afternoon, but solved not one of the problems of Max Mather.

That evening they dined in the Stübli, where it was not necessary to dress formally. The place was crowded and noisy with a gaggle of languages. Half-way through the meal there was a sudden lull in the talk and then, from a nearby table, came a clatter of Italian. The voice was familiar . . . Mather slewed round in his chair to find himself staring at Claudio Palombini, who was seated with two other men in a banquette near the window. He excused himself to Gisela, got up and went to greet him.

'Claudio, how goes it?'

'Max!' Palombini was instantly on his feet, embracing him. 'What a surprise! What are you doing here? This is Gianni Ruspoli, our financial controller; Marcantonio, my cousin, who runs things for us here. Bring the lady over and join us. Now, from the beginning. What brings you to Switzerland?'

It was easy to share with them the clubbish euphoria of the moment. They were interested to hear of the gallery project, the job on *Belvedere*, the buying syndicate. Gisela was a ready sharer in the talk.

It was, however, much less easy to stifle the pangs of guilt as Max sat face to face with the man he was depriving of his patrimony. Only long practice in dissembling enabled him to do it. The talk went round the table, fluent and facile, until Mather asked his own question of Claudio.

'And how's business? You sounded unhappy when you wrote to me.'

'Boh!' The word came out in a sharp explosion of sound. The gesture that accompanied it expressed futility and despair. 'We are here to talk to the gnomes. My darling aunt – God rest her! – your beloved Pia, left me a tin of worms for a legacy. We had hoped for some salvation from the art collection, but that, as you know, is worth very little. Three months from now we shall be in real trouble. Without an extension of our loans or a new injection of capital, we may be forced to sell off some of our holdings and regroup. In today's market that's not going to be easy.'

'I'm sorry to hear that.' Mather was genuinely concerned. 'I had no idea.'

'How could you?' Claudio was instantly on his dignity. 'It was – it is – a family matter.'

'Of course. Forgive me.'

'We need a miracle.' Gianni Ruspoli tried to relieve the momentary tension. 'Like the loaves and fishes.'

'Or those Raphaels about which you wrote me.' Claudio laughed as he said it, but the laughter had a hollow sound. 'I've been dreaming about the damned things. They dance in front of me, just out of reach. Do you think there's any chance of their turning up?'

'After all these centuries?' Marcantonio was sceptical. 'That would be a bigger miracle than the loaves and fishes! Besides, how do you establish ownership after nearly five centuries?'

'Perhaps it wasn't five centuries,' said Gisela. Everyone turned to her. She smiled at them over the rim of her glass. 'The very first time I heard this story I felt that it had ended too soon.'

Claudio was immediately alert. 'Perhaps you could explain that more clearly, Signorina?'

'Certainly. Check me, please, on the details. Max is working as archivist in the Palombini household. He is engaged on a private research project as well. His employer – your aunt Pia – dies. His employment is terminated. He returns to the United States but continues his researches, in the course of which he discovers an entry in old account books concerning the commissioning of works by the master, Raffaello Sanzio. An article or series of articles on that discovery is in course of publication. Right?'

'In every detail,' he agreed. 'Now what?'

'That's my question,' rejoined Gisela. 'Has any further investigative work been done to trace the history of the pieces? If they were sold, are there any receipts? Were they given away as a gift? The occasion must have been important enough to note somewhere. When was the last time, if ever, the collection was listed? It seems to me that you let your most important asset escape you. Who else in the world knows as much about the Palombini archive as Max Mather?'

'*Madonna Mia!*' Marcantonio breathed a long sigh of surprise. 'We come to ski in the Engadine, we meet the Cumaean Sibyl. She's right, Claudio. There's been a lot of history since 1500.'

'A lot of recent history too,' Ruspoli put in. 'The Fascists, the Germans! Luca *l'ingannatore!*'

'The point is made,' said Claudio curtly. 'Let's not labour it.' He turned to Mather. 'Max, this is a matter which you and I might discuss in Florence. I realise that you have commitments and ambitions in other directions, but perhaps . . . ?'

'Let's discuss it by all means,' agreed Mather.

'But since you pay me to advise you,' said Gisela cheerfully, 'I'll draw up the contract.'

'Are you a lawyer, Signorina?' Marcantonio asked the question.

'A very expensive one. I also teach jurisprudence. I'm especially good on mediaeval concepts and their development into modern law. Try me on chattels – what paintings are and women used to be. I know all about trover and retinue and finder's rights and replevin. But it would pay you much better to retain Max. Now if you'll excuse me, gentlemen. I know you have business to talk and I've had a very long day. So I'll say good night.'

When she had gone, Palombini ordered another round of drinks and talked trivia until they arrived. Whatever the vices of the Italians – and they had many – the big virtue they had was style: style in adversity, style in friendship, style in love. They might not have two coins to rub together but their shoes would be polished, the threadbare suit pressed, the shirt-front immaculate, the pinched cheeks barbered. When they took you to their hearts they created a whole family about you. When they hated they did so in the grand manner.

Claudio Palombini, scion of the banner-bearers of Florence, was going down the drain with the bath-water; yet he was doing it with a flourish and half a hope for a miracle, while Max Mather, scholar, man of intelligence and respect, drank his liquor, smiled like a very Iago and wondered whether to bless or curse Gisela Mundt.

Marcantonio passed him his drink and began quizzing him. 'That's a smart girl you've found, Max. What do you think of her idea?'

'Great in theory. In fact, it's a million to one shot. Claudio here knows what that archive looks like . . . It's thousands and thousands of books, folios, bundles of decaying paper. Your odds against finding any relevant items in it are millions to one. You couldn't pay me half enough to look at a job like that. But let me explain what is going to happen and what neither you nor I has any part in.'

He explained in careful sequence how Seldes and Henri Berchmans had teamed up and how, with their worldwide contacts, they would be combing the market for any trace of the missing master works. He read a brief lesson on statutes of limitations and provenance and the difficulties of proving title. Then he said, 'But once Seldes and Berchmans find access to the pieces, you can forget any idea of repossessing them. Those two will keep you dangling and dancing for twenty years, and the Raphaels will have gone underground before you can say Sanzio. Have you any idea what that whole suite of pieces is worth in today's market?'

'Millions,' said Ruspoli.

'But how many millions?' inquired Palombini, and added the

gloomy postscript, 'Just for the record, we need twenty in ninety days!'

'The portraits are worth not less than fifty million dollars each. You might conceivably get a hundred. The cartoons not less than a million and a half each. So what you have to ask yourself is what reward or what commission you would be prepared to offer to get them back – verified authentic and undamaged. Remember it can't be less than ten per cent, because that's what an insurer would offer on an article which he had covered.'

'Ten, fifteen, twenty – what does it matter?' asked Marcantonio. 'You're only paying on results – and I'd happily pay twenty to have eighty million in our pockets right now. Think about it, Claudio.'

'I am thinking about it,' Claudio told him. 'I'd like to hear if Max here is also willing to think about it.'

'I might . . . on certain conditions.'

'Which would be?'

'Only if there were a clear contract that we could both wear.'

'I'm sure we could come to that quickly.'

'And only if I have a free hand with no questions asked.'

'I don't understand that,' Gianni Ruspoli objected. 'If we're paying the money, we must have the right to . . . '

'You won't be paying a cent unless and until the articles are available,' Mather interjected. 'If someone has legal title to them, there's no way you're going to get them for less than the market price. But if someone has bad or dubious title, then maybe – only maybe – you can work out the ten per cent solution. But the condition will inevitably be: no questions, no answers. Impossible to work any other way.'

'Let's say fifteen per cent and close with the offer,' suggested Ruspoli.

'Let's not say anything until Max and I have talked in Florence.' Claudio was in command again. 'I think I understand Max's position. He declines to solicit us. He has profitable projects of his own. If we want him, we must offer the contract. Right, Max?'

'Right, Claudio . . . now, I'd like to buy us all a nightcap.'

'And maybe you'll tell us where you really found that little Gisela?'

'Why does nobody believe me?' asked Mather plaintively. 'I told you. She's my lawyer in Zurich.'

'And I always thought the Swiss were such dull dogs – Swiss lawyers especially.'

'It pays to keep an open mind,' said Mather. He raised his glass. 'To our continued good health!'

As he drank the toast he understood with stark clarity the nature of damnation: that it was self-inflicted and irreversible. You ate the meal you had cooked though it turned to fire in your gullet. You drank the traitor's cup to the dregs, but before you set it down it was filled again with gall and wormwood. The lies you told were graven on stone and you carried them at arm's length above your head as a sign of infamy.

When they arrived on Monday morning at Zurich station, Gisela thrust a thick envelope into his hands and told him, 'This is my thanks for a wonderful weekend.'

'What is it?'

'Three hours' work while you were asleep. It's my version of the only contract you should sign with Claudio Palombini. I think it's a good document – I'm proud of it.'

'And how do I tell you my thanks?'

'Just kiss me – and call me!'

He did the one and promised the other. Then they scrambled into a taxi and held hands until they arrived at her house, where she changed instantly into the *Fräulein Doktor* Mundt, attorney-at-law, lecturer in jurisprudence and authority on European law relating to chattels.

Back at his own apartment Mather found messages, letters and packages awaiting him. A Miss Loredon had called from New York, also a Mr Bayard. They would be soundly asleep now, he would call them later. There was also a note from Henri Berchmans in Paris:

You paid me a singular courtesy. The least I can do is return it. Please inform Miss Loredon that I shall be happy to exhibit my Madeleine Bayard canvases as 'Not For Sale' items at the opening of the gallery. I look forward with pleasure to that occasion.

There was a package of transparencies from Anne-Marie, together with proof copies of the catalogue and the biographical notes. He called the young dealer to whom he had promised them. The dealer arranged for a courier to pick them up. He was impressed with the speed and efficiency of Mather's response and would endeavour to be equally brisk. He presumed there would be the normal dealer's discount if they did business together? Naturally, Mather agreed; and that matter was laid to rest. Finally, there was the letter, sent by transatlantic courier, from Leonie Danziger:

My dear Max,

Your piece on Madeleine Bayard arrived on Friday. I read it immediately; then I read it three times more during the day. I was stunned by it. I could not understand – indeed I still cannot – how you, who had never met her, were able to grasp so swiftly and surely the essential nature of the woman and the extraordinary influence she exerted on so many people, myself included.

I am certain I never spoke to you of my relationship with Madi, but it is clear that you must know of it, clearer still that you have come very close to understanding its complex nature. You expressed a fear that I might feel invaded by your text. On the contrary I am enriched by your understanding. I cannot speak for others, only for myself.

I gave a copy to Bayard, as you asked. I delivered it by hand and explained the discretion you had given me as your editor. He asked me to wait in his office while he read the piece. It had the most extraordinary effect on him. His expression changed from moment to moment. He smiled, he frowned, at one instant I thought he was going to burst into tears. When he had finished he took off his spectacles, wiped his eyes, then cleaned the lenses . . . a whole series of little moves designed to delay his comment. The only thing he said was, 'How the devil could he know so much?' When I told him he should be thankful for so graceful an epitaph, he simply nodded. He was still too moved to say much, but he did approve publication.

Which brings me to Anne-Marie Loredon. I called on her as you asked. She was very quiet, very reserved, still trying to come to terms with the fact that her own father had excluded her from his last rite of passage. I could have explained it, I think, had she been willing to listen, but the hurt is too deep. She needs you to reason through the pain with her.

Last of all on my list, Harmon Seldes. I put it to him that the piece could sit better in the *New York Times Review* and would be much more helpful to the Bayard exhibition. He did his little dog-in-the-manager act. You're his contributing editor, you'd cleared the piece with him . . . all of which is true. It's also true that he knows it's beautiful, touching, sensational – and he doesn't want to let it go. We argued for an hour, then he agreed to print it as a special loose-leaf insert for the April edition provided – and this is the sting in the tail – Anne-Marie Loredon would pay for a back-page advertisement on the lift-out. She'd already recognised the importance of the article and readily agreed to the outlay. So it's all arranged. You can have reprints at cost if you want them – very useful for provincial and overseas selling.

So comes the question, my dear Max. Now what? For me it's easier to answer than I expected. With Hugh Loredon dead there is no one left to mock my follies and make me feel less than myself. What you have written lifts me up, as you have lifted Madeleine Bayard, to a higher place from which I can see the pattern of things. I have found a new friend. Her name is Carol. She is an artist, like Madi. She has moved in. We are learning to be happy together. I hope you will like her.

More, much more when I see you. I can say now what I never could before. I love you, Max, in my own special way. I wish you better things than you allow yourself to hope for.

Danny

It was the first time she had used the pet name to him. The look of it on the page moved him strangely. It told him that this one time – if never before and never again – he had broken through the dry crust of scholarship and told a truth about the tears of things.

He lifted the telephone and dialled the number of Niccoló Tolentino's studio at the Pitti Palace in Florence.

The voice that answered was ten times as big as the gnomish little man who owned it – a rich, velvety baritone that welled up from the soles of his shoes.

'This is Tolentino. Who's speaking?'

'Max Mather.'

'Max, dear friend. What a pleasure! Where are you?'

'In Zurich. I'm coming down to see you the day after tomorrow. Everything is arranged. You are coming to New York.'

'I don't believe it.'

'I promised.'

'I know you promised, but most promises are like Madam Butterfly – "one fine day".'

'This time the dates will be firm, the tickets will be bought. You'll be staying in my apartment. Now, here's my programme: I fly into Milan Wednesday morning early. I pick up an afternoon flight to Pisa, then drive into Florence. Can we have dinner?'

'Certainly. Nine o'clock. The Gallodoro. Would you like me to call Guido?'

'No. This time it's just you and me. We have lots to discuss, big decisions to make.'

'Incredible!' said Niccoló Tolentino. 'Just when I have become a contented infidel, a miracle happens.'

Max Mather himself had need of a miracle. His next call was to the international operator in Milan to identify in the telephone directory the number of a widow whose name was Eberhardt but who could now have reverted to her maiden name of Dandolo or to a combination of the two.

This was not in itself a monumental task, but Italian operators were notoriously short-fused and at the slightest hint of difficulty or confusion they left you dangling on the end of a line, deafened by a 'busy' signal. This time the miracle happened. The operator was cheerful and attentive. She found the number in twenty seconds flat: the Signora Camilla Dandolo-Eberhardt, Via del

191

Orso 81. Mather copied down the address and the number and flirted with her for fifteen seconds more until she giggled and threw the switch on him. Then, with a silent prayer for one more miraculous intervention, he dialled the Dandolo-Eberhardt number. After what seemed an age, a maid-servant answered. She demanded to know who was speaking and the nature of their business. In his best Tuscan accent, Mather explained himself.

'An old friend of the Palombini family . . . from America . . . writing a book about the great divas of La Scala . . .' Thus and thus until the maid, overwhelmed by his eloquence, consented to pass him to her mistress. Camilla Dandolo sounded spry enough, but touchy and suspicious. Mather had to go through the whole pavane again and answer another twenty questions before she consented to receive him at eleven on the Wednesday morning. He promised to call her from the airport if there were any flight delays.

Then Mather drove down to Alois Liepert's office. Did he know a reliable travel agent? He did. Could he have his girl make a series of bookings and find him a hotel in Florence? All possible. All immediately in hand. Finally, asked Mather tentatively, could Alois Liepert cast an eye over a draft contract? Now, if possible? Liepert read the document with great care and then cocked a quizzical eye at Mather.

'From your point of view, it's a wonderful contract. It gives you exclusive rights to deal for the family over the Raphaels. You can't sell them or mortgage them if you find them, but you don't have to hand them over until you're paid. You're not obliged to declare how they came into your possession. You can make what representations you like, short of a criminal act . . . And nobody can go past you to the family. The only thing I ask myself is why anyone would be fool enough to make that contract with you.'

'But you'd agree it's worth a try?'

'If Palombini signs it, I'll buy you the best dinner in Zurich.'

'You're on. Could you have it engrossed and copied for me, please?'

'One minor question: who drew it up for you?'

Mather grinned. He also had the grace to blush.

'Gisela Mundt. We've just had a weekend skiing in St Moritz.'

Alois Liepert threw himself back in his chair and laughed immoderately.

'My God, my wife was right after all. She told me there was electricity between you two. I didn't believe her. She's an inveterate matchmaker. Well, what can I say? I'm delighted – I hope it lasts.'

'And you don't mind about the contract?'

'Hell, no. All I can say is I wouldn't have the gall to draw it; but if you get away with it you owe the lady diamonds.'

'Only if the Raphaels are genuine.'

'That, of course, is the big if.' Liepert laughed again. 'I'll raise the bet. I'll buy you both a dinner.'

The travel documents and the contract in his pocket, Mather went to the bank, drew money for the journey and then withdrew from the safe-deposit the photographs he had taken months before of the Raphael portraits and the five cartoons. He knew it was a risk to have them in his possession, but if Palombini signed the contract the risk would vanish immediately. If he did not, then another strategy would have to be devised and for that he might well need the photographs.

Back in his apartment he made three calls to New York. The first was to Bayard in his office and his first question was about Anne-Marie.

'How's she holding up?'

'Holding back is the word,' said Bayard unhappily. 'She's very controlled, very withdrawn and working around the clock. How long are you going to be away?'

'A couple more weeks. We're pretty well organised here. I sent you stuff from Amsterdam and Zurich.'

'The Janzoons were great. The prices are right too. We'll talk about him as soon as you get back. And, Max?'

'Yes.'

'Your memorial to Madeleine – I read it. I was deeply moved. I still can't understand how you came by such insights. I want to ask . . .'

'Don't ask, Ed. Let the document stand on its own merits.'

'You're right, of course.'

'I have good news for you. Berchmans will allow his pictures to be shown and acknowledged at the exhibition.'

'That's fabulous. Money in the bank. How did you manage it?'
'Gentle persuasion.'
'I'm sure. There's something you should know, Max.'
'What?'
'I had a visit from the police yesterday.'
'Any special reason?'
'Yes, they were asking whether there was any connection between Max Mather and my late wife.'
'And you assured them there was not.'
'Of course. The reason for the inquiry was a letter written by Hugh Loredon two days before his death and lodged for transmission with other documents by the US Embassy in The Hague. The letter apparently stated that on your return to the United States you would be in a position to make certain disclosures which would effectively close the case. Have you any idea what that means?'
'A very good idea. And I don't like any part of it.'
'Can I help?'
'Maybe, later.'
'What do you suppose Hugh Loredon was trying to do?'
'I'm still reserving judgment on that one – and observing discretion on the telephone. Until we meet, then.'
'Until we meet.'
His next call was to Anne-Marie. He was unprepared for the sudden rush of urgent affection when she answered.
'Max, thank God you called! I've been going crazy. After the way I behaved the other day, I thought you'd never want to talk to me again. I knew I was acting badly but I couldn't help it. You were the last one in the world I wanted to hurt – you know that, don't you?'
'Sure. I know it. How are you feeling now?'
'All the better for hearing your voice.'
'I've got some good news for you.'
'Tell.'
'Berchmans will lend his pictures for the opening.'
'Wonderful!'
'I've just sent the transparencies to our Swiss friend. We'll have to provide a gallery discount – I'm sure he's a buyer. There's a wonderful young expressionist in Amsterdam called Cornelis

Janzoon. I'm sure we could get him to exhibit with us . . . and I'm leaving on Wednesday for Florence to finalise arrangements for Tolentino's visit.'

'That's great news, Max . . . Thank you.'

'How's the building coming along?'

'Faster than I expected. The elevators are installed, all the plumbing's in and most of the electrics, alarms and so on. Your apartment is almost finished. Most of what's left to be done is superficial. We'll be ready for opening, which is now the second week in April.'

'We'll make it a smash hit.'

'I read your article.'

'I hope you liked it.'

'That's the wrong word. It moved me. It made me, in a way, very jealous. It was almost as though you'd been in love with her yourself. But it's a wonderful piece and it will do wonderful things for the show. You got some of it from Hugh, yes?'

'A lot of it.'

'How much did he tell you?'

'More than I wanted to hear.'

'And the stuff he wanted you to read?'

'What stuff?'

'You know, in the . . . oh!' She gave a small gasp of surprise and recognition. 'Forget it, I must have been thinking of something else. I've got so much on my mind these days.'

'We all have, sweetheart. And how are things with you and Bayard?'

'Quiet. He's been very protective, very considerate. I know he's relieved that Hugh isn't around any more, but I don't blame him for that.'

'And you? How do you feel?'

'Until you rang I wasn't feeling at all. You must have been my wake-up call. How's your love-life, by the way?'

'Don't pry, sister Anne – remember what happened in Bluebeard's castle.'

'Can I ever forget it?'

She said it lightly enough, but the way she spoke made him wonder whether Hugh Loredon's secret was a secret any more. That bloody ham actor couldn't make a clean exit to save his

195

soul. He was born to be the rear end of a pantomime horse – going out with a fart and a lurch and a last twitch of his goddamned tail . . .

TWELVE

The flight to Milan was delayed fifteen minutes at Zurich and another fifteen by a stack-up over Linate airport. Another twenty minutes were lost in immigration because a visitor from Lebanon had an out-of-date visa. Mather had just time enough to buy a basketful of wilting violets, scramble into a taxi two steps ahead of a murderous mob and make a flustered arrival a quarter of an hour later.

Camilla Dandolo's apartment was on the second floor of a nineteenth-century palazzo with high vaulted ceilings and stairwells cold as charity. A gorgon of a maid admitted him and left him to cool his heels in a *salone* full of heavy mahogany, photographs in silver frames and romantic landscapes in gold ones.

'It does look terrible, doesn't it?' Camilla Dandolo spoke from the doorway. 'But I rent it furnished and the price is right.'

She was a very old lady, but still a very grand one. She was dressed in a brocaded house-gown. Her feet were shod in gold mules, her white hair tied back with a gold ribbon. The hand she held out imperiously to be kissed was covered with rings. Mather almost expected to hear an angelic voice intoning 'Celeste Aïda'.

No mean actor himself, he played back to her without shame: the low bow, the lips barely brushing the old parchment of her skin, the speech full of honorifics. Even so there was a moment when he was up to his hocks in trouble. The lady was not easily flattered. She was shrewd and short-tempered. She cocked her head on one side like an elderly parrot and demanded to know: 'How would someone as young as you know about Camilla Dandolo? Do you remember any of my roles, any of my leading men? I'm sure you don't.'

Mather gave her a disarming smile and a lame explanation.

'I came to know you in a very romantic fashion, when I was archivist at Tor Merla for the Palombini family. I was fascinated by the stories the old servants used to tell of your great love affair with Luca. So last weekend your name was mentioned – with great affection, I must say – by a member of the Corviglia Club in St Moritz. It was he who told me your husband had passed away and you were now living in Milan.'

'Ah, now it becomes clear.' She was amused and flattered. 'So this book is not about the divas but about the scandals of La Scala?'

'Not at all. It will be an accurate work. I know, for example, that you sang Olga in *Fedora* with Gigli in 1939; that Guarnieri conducted you in *L'Amico Fritz* and you sang Mimi with Malpiero . . .' He broke off with a laugh. 'You see, I really have done my homework! However, my interest in you is different. You were a friend of famous and powerful men like Luca Palombini. You were not only a beautiful woman, you were powerful in your own right. All this I have in fragments and hearsay; I would like to hear it from your own lips, record it in a series of taped interviews.'

'It sounds much too formidable for me. I'm an old woman. My memory is not so reliable any more.'

'For that,' said Mather with a smile, 'we interviewers have all sorts of tricks, little association games that open doors in the memory . . . May I show you what I mean?'

'Please do.'

'Close your eyes, please.'

He reached out to take a silver-framed photograph from a tabouret and held it directly in front of her.

'When I ask you to open your eyes, focus on the object in front of you and tell me everything about it. Open now.'

She took a moment to focus and then recited like a well-drilled schoolgirl: 'That is a photograph of my husband, Franz, and myself on our farm near Brasilia. The other people are the German Consul-General and his wife. The Indians in the background are labourers, the buildings are barns and machinery sheds.'

'Thank you. Now let's try again. Close your eyes.'

This time he held in front of her one of the Raphael photographs – that of the Maiden Beata Palombini. She opened her eyes, focused again, stared at the image for a longish moment, then said vaguely, 'It looks like a picture we had in our house.'

'Let's try again. Close.'

He held up the other portrait, that of Donna Delfina.

'Open!'

This time there was no hesitation: 'That's definitely one of ours.'

'Tell me about them.'

She shrugged irritably. 'What can I tell? I was never very interested in art. My husband was the collector.'

'Tell me what you do know then.'

'Franz acquired two pictures during the war from Luca Palombini. I don't know the details. He was always shopping around for things during his campaigns. He took them with him to Brazil and when we married and went there to live those pictures were still there. They were in our house until he died. Then – because I didn't want to cart stuff back to Italy – I sold them with the rest of the estate. They turned out to be very valuable – Joaquin Camoens, who is one of our most important dealers in Rio, gave me a very good price for them.'

'You see?' Mather gave her a smile of happy approval. 'You see what I mean about association? Already there is the background of a whole story: your husband, what he did in Italy during the war and afterwards, his relationship with Luca as well as yours. Suddenly a whole history begins to shape itself.'

'I'm not sure that's such a good idea,' said Camilla Dandolo. 'I really would have to think about it very carefully.'

'Which is precisely the purpose of this visit,' said Mather soothingly. 'To introduce the idea and see how you react to it. If it's a burden, simply forget it. No harm will be done – and I have had the pleasure and honour of meeting you. I'm going on from here to Florence. Would you like me to convey your greetings to the Palombini family?'

'I think not.' The old lady was very definite. 'Luca's family believe I robbed them. The fact is I saved their skins more than once. But you still haven't told me; where did you get those photographs?'

'They were sent to me by a dealer in Paris.' Mather told the lie without a flicker of remorse. 'He didn't tell me where he got them, but he did ask me to establish a provenance for the pictures. Your Mr Joaquin Camoens must be offering them to the international market.'

'But how did you connect them with me?' This was one doughty old campaigner. She would let nothing pass her without a challenge.

Mather rose to it gallantly. 'That's the simplest answer of all, dear lady. I knew a lot about Luca's business deals . . . also, like you, I loved a Palombini.'

'Which one?'

'Pia. She died last year.'

'Then we should let her sleep in peace,' said Camilla Dandolo. 'The world will not perish because you do not write your book. A pleasure to meet you, Mr Mather. A pity I'm too old to pursue the acquaintance. My maid will show you out.'

Mather had now established beyond doubt what he had always recognised as a possibility: that a copy or copies had been made of the Raphael portraits. He had no present means of knowing whether the pieces in his possession were the originals or the copies. One thing he knew for certain – the moment he brought them to market, the others would appear as if by magic and the inevitable fight over authenticity would break out. He could not win it single-handed, so he decided to take out some insurance.

There was time to kill before his flight left for Pisa. He went to the post office at Linate airport and made a call to Henri Berchmans in Paris. Berchmans was on the floor with a client and it took some persuasion to have the secretary call him to the phone. He was his usual brusque self.

'I hope this is worth your money and my time.'

'You are being rude again, Mr Berchmans. I promised to pass you information on the Raphaels. I am doing just that. Do you have time to receive it?'

'Of course, of course.'

'I am in Milan. At the airport. I have just been to visit Camilla Dandolo, who returned to Italy after the death of her husband in Brazil.'

'How did you find that out?'

'I went skiing in St Moritz where I met one of her old flames. May I go on?'

'Please do.'

'After a long runaround I have established that her husband acquired two Raphael portraits on undisclosed terms from Luca Palombini. These pictures were sold with the rest of their art collection to a dealer in Rio called Joaquin Camoens.'

'I know him,' said Berchmans with feeling. 'A crook. He'd sell his grandmother's corpse for the gold in her teeth. Anything else?'

'No. That's the lot.'

'What are you doing now?'

'Going on to Florence to visit old friends. By the way, thank you for the loan of your Bayards.'

'My pleasure.'

'Now you can thank me for this expensive phone call and this valuable information.'

Berchmans gave his harsh cackling laugh. 'You expect too much, Mather. Send me a bill for services rendered. It's far less trouble.'

As he sat in the bar with a beer and a stale sandwich, sweating out yet another delay, Mather tried to work out Berchmans' next move. First he would have to locate the pictures in Brazil, then do a full authentication, then acquire them by option or outright purchase and finally, bring them to market. All the time he would be wondering—as Mather himself was wondering—whether Luca Palombini had dumped a fake on Franz Eberhardt. He would be wondering how many fakes there were and how quickly they would start to pop up in the market.

And this was the real purpose of the alliance with Niccolò Tolentino. He was the only person in the world who could make an absolute determination between the original and the copy.

The problem was, of course, that the more people who became involved in the affair of the Raphaels, the more vulnerable Max Mather became. Which brought him one step nearer to that most ancient and paradoxical of remedies: open confession. How simple it would be to say: 'Look, I've been a greedy fool. Take the stakes and wash me out of the game. Just let me keep the small reputation I own by right, give me a modest profit on the deal and I'll be content.'

But it wasn't as easy as that. He was subject to the same divine irony as the rabbi who played golf on the Sabbath and made a hole in one. The recording angel demanded punishment. 'Wait!' said God. 'Whom is he going to tell?' So it seemed Max Mather's penalty was to go on building his fine tall house worth millions of dollars, knowing all the time that it was founded upon sand and that a single flash flood might tumble it down.

Then, because he was back in Italy and the orchard trees were in bloom across the Lombardy Plain, and Palombini might just be fool enough to sign the contract that would keep him out of trouble, and tonight he would be eating pasta and pollo al diavolo and drinking Tuscan wine with Niccoló Tolentino, he said to hell with it all and ordered another drink.

Take-off was an hour and a half late. On arrival the autostrada to Florence was jammed with commuter traffic. The approaches to the city were noisy with horns and shouting drivers. By the time he reached the comparative quiet of the hotel, he felt like a man from Mars set down on a mad planet. He shaved, bathed, changed into casual clothes, unpacked, sent a suit out for pressing, called Palombini to make a luncheon date for the morrow, then very slowly, like a decompressing diver, came back to normal. He armed himself for the evening with the gallery catalogue, the proofs of the *Belvedere* material and the Raphael photographs, then set out to walk to the Gallodoro.

His first gambit was to reaffirm the visit to America with Tolentino.

'We open the gallery in mid-April. If we could have you there for the opening it would be wonderful. We would aim to begin the lecture series no later than a week after that. You can live in my apartment or lodge elsewhere, as you choose. Fares paid both ways, a guarantee of a thousand a week for four weeks, plus fifty per cent of profits – and any private commissions you get are yours to keep. How does that sound to you?'

'Like heavenly music,' said Tolentino. 'Fiddlers and flutes and a chorus of cherubim. You will never know what you are doing for me, Max . . . But you also have to explain what you want me to do for you. I will need to prepare. My English is okay, but that is not enough; I must do honour to you and the people who pay to hear me . . . also to this city and the great ones who have worked here. So tell me what you expect.'

'I want you to teach and to demonstrate. There will, of course, be students in the audiences – many, I trust – but I'm hoping to have a big enrolment of senior professionals: teachers, curators, restorers. They will want to share your experience, see your techniques, enter into dialogue with you. They will want to discuss forgers and their methods, the dealer as patron and middle-man. What I'd like you to do is draw up a four-week programme of three sessions a week. I intend to charge a lot of money, so I don't want to over-expose you. If the thing's a success, we can always extend. You'll have the whole of the second floor above the gallery. It will hold easily fifty or sixty people. If we get a rush of bookings, we'll have to double up on sessions. How do you feel about that? Could you bear it?'

'I still feel wonderful,' said Tolentino.

'Can you get leave from the Pitti?'

'Any time.'

'Great! Now, can I ask you a very delicate question?'

'Certainly. Go ahead.'

'You have to apply for a US visa. Is there anything that could cause a problem?'

'Like what?'

'Like a police record in your youth perhaps?'

'Never!'

'There was gossip – we spoke of it – about forgery. The gossip said you were very good at it.'

'The gossip said one thing. The facts say another. Let me explain . . . No, don't worry. I know why you need this, so I am not angry. I have told you before. I am not a forger, I am a copyist – probably the best in the world. I can copy any painting you put in front of me and, given the right materials, I can copy it so well that the master who did the original would almost believe it was his own work – right down to the signature. But that is not forgery. A forgery is when I pass off my copy as an original. I have never done that. Others may have done it with my works, but never with my knowledge or consent. Now, wait . . . I say never. There were moments in wartime when Goering's agents and Himmler's people as well were rushing about pillaging works of art, bludgeoning people into parting with them for a song. Then, yes . . . I was very young and not nearly as good as I am now, but I did some very good forging. Does that answer your question?'

'Yes, thank you. I can now sign the formal invitation for you to enter the United States in association with the gallery. You'll present that when you apply for your visa.'

'We should have another drink on that.'

'Let's wait for the wine. I've got something else to show you. Close your eyes – open them when I tell you.'

'They're closed.'

Mather laid the two Raphael photographs on the table in front of Tolentino and told him to open his eyes. The instant he saw them his face lit up with pleasure and recognition. His deep voice dropped to a conspirator's whisper. 'My God. All this time and now it is you who bring them to me! How? Why? Where are they?'

'Not so fast, old friend.' Mather snapped up the photographs and put them in his pocket. 'It's very important that we do this systematically. What do these photographs represent?'

'Two portraits, mother and daughter, Palombini women painted by Raffaello in 1505.'

'Where are they now?'

'I don't know.'

'But you've seen them?'

'Seen them? Max, my friend, I lived with them for weeks on end. I copied each of them stroke for stroke.'

'For whom?'

'Luca Palombini.'

'You must have been only a boy at the time.'

'I was twenty-six. The war was on, but I was unfit for military service. I had just arrived here and was working under old Cesarini. He was great in his day, but by then his hand wasn't too steady and his eye for colour was getting uncertain. So he passed the job to me . . . he still took half the fee though, by God!'

'So you made only one copy?'

'That's right.'

'What did Palombini do with the copies?'

'I don't know; I didn't ask. It was never politic in those days to ask too many questions. I presumed he palmed them off on someone.'

'If you had the originals and the copies lying before you on this table, would you be able to tell the difference?'

'I could – but you couldn't. In fact I'd defy most of the so-called experts to tell the difference except after long and exhausting experiment . . . . Unless they knew my little trick, of course.'

'And what's that?' Max pressed the point roughly. 'I have to know now, Nicki.'

Tolentino pulled his sketch-pad towards him and drew a basic monogram

Then he explained it. 'Tolentino, Niccoló: my initials. On every picture I have ever painted, those initials appear somewhere. That, you see, was my defence if anyone ever accused me to my face of forgery. I was copying a master – that after all is my trade – but even when I copied his signature on to the copy, because after all it was part of the whole, I signed my own work. I do it even with a restoration, except I sign that on the back, thus:

Restauravit: Tolentino, Niccoló.

He fished in his waistcoat pocket and brought out a loupe. 'Now let's take another look at those photographs. Come round next to me; you'll see better.'

Mather got out of his chair and stood behind the old man, peering over his shoulder as he used the tip of his pencil as an indicator.

'Take the mother first . . . Donna Delfina. I put my monogram in the landscape background, in one of the tiny windows. Now the daughter. My mark should be just on the edge of the lowest fold of the gown.'

He examined both photographs carefully, then invited Mather to examine under the glass the spots he had indicated. Max shook his head. 'I see nothing.'

'I can't see anything either,' said Tolentino. 'The reduction in size is too great.'

'But if your mark is not on them?'

'Then they are the originals.'

'Not necessarily,' Mather objected. 'There could be other copies than yours.'

'Not possible,' Tolentino was emphatic. 'I know the Raffaello brushstrokes by heart. I'll tell you one other thing, too. The panels on which I made my copies are different from the orig-inals. Mine are on seasoned oak. The originals are on cedar . . . now perhaps you'll tell me what all this means?'

'I will,' Mather promised. 'But not yet. I need you absolutely unprejudiced – and able to swear that you are.'

'You mean . . . '

'I mean you're coming to New York, where you're going to be famous overnight and you're going to forget you've ever seen these photographs until I stand you in front of the pictures themselves and ask you to tell the world which are the master works.'

'And that's all you're going to tell me?'

'For the moment it's all I *can* tell you. But as soon as there's more you'll be the first to know. One last question: could you come to Zurich at short notice?'

'I could leave now,' said Tolentino with a grin, 'except that I owe you dinner – the happiest dinner of my life.'

'I'll buy tomorrow night,' Mather suggested. 'We have to talk once more before we leave. I'll get Guido along. We'll celebrate together.'

Even as he said it, he breathed a silent prayer that there might be something to celebrate. If what he held in Zurich were copies, then he had wasted a lot of time and money. If they were orig-inals and Claudio Palombini failed to retain him on contract, then he would be sailing very, very close to the wind.

Mather's lunchtime reception at Tor Merla was much less exuberant than at the Gallodoro. The womenfolk of the house-hold were away, there were fewer servants in evidence. The villa environs had a rundown look and the interior of the house had changed: there were fewer pictures on the walls, the furniture seemed more sparse. He was received by Claudio Palombini, his cousin Marcantonio and a young man he had never seen before, introduced as Avvocato Stefano Stefanelli.

Claudio was apologetic. 'You see what is happening? We are cutting back wherever we can. Still, we are eating from the land and the cook's wages are paid.'

Mather asked permission to salute the staff. He found them warm but diffident. They, too, were smelling the wind from the battlefield. Only two embraced him. Matteo the major-domo and Pia's personal servant, Chiara, wrinkled as a prune but still combative and resentful.

'It was different when the Signora was alive and you were here. Even when she was dying there was something to laugh about. Now it is like a graveyard after midnight.'

Mather kissed her, patted her cheek and went on to join the others at the lunch table. The food was still good. The estate wine was maturing nicely. Claudio insisted they talk no business until the fruit and the cheese. Then he opened the dealing.

'Clearly we need someone to represent our interests and make active searches for the Raphael pieces. Equally clearly, you have certain important qualifications to do that. You would, as you have said, be willing to consider a contract.'

'This contract,' said Mather, and laid it on the table. 'Only this one. Take your time, read it. I'll have some more coffee, if I may.'

The document was only half a dozen pages but it was ten minutes before anyone lifted his head to make a comment. It was the advocate who spoke first.

'If you'll forgive me, Mr Mather, this seems – may I say it – a very arbitrary document.'

'It is.' Mather was mildness itself. 'It is also non-negotiable.'

'May one ask why?'

'Of course. Item one: the discovery of the Raphaels and their return to the Palombini is at best a highly speculative enterprise. Item two: in the present financial circumstances the Palombini cannot afford to underwrite one penny of the cost. Item three: once my article is published at the beginning of next month – an article of which you were given ample notice – there will be a veritable gold rush in the art market. Item four: I shall be dealing in a jungle, with very evolved animals; I need all the protection I can get.'

'All of which we accept without question,' said Claudio Palombini. 'But our lawyer feels that certain premises should be established as a preliminary to the contract.'

'He has a right to ask that; I have an equal right to refuse. May I call your attention to the opening terms of the contract: "The said Maxwell Mather makes no affirmation as to competence, special knowledge or qualification, or special circumstances relating to the task he undertakes. He makes no solicitation that this contract be entered into by other parties. He offers no guarantees other than a best effort performance whose expenses shall be borne entirely by himself." That seems to be clear enough, gentlemen.'

'It is, of course, very clear,' said Marcantonio, 'but would you be prepared to answer a few questions on it?'

'No,' Mather was very definite. 'Because any answers I gave could then be regarded as a representation and subject to any interpretation you care to put on it at a later time.'

Claudio was affronted. 'Do you think we are as brutal as that?'

'History tells me you are, Claudio,' Mather told him with a grin. 'I don't blame you. We shouldn't quarrel about it. But you've been merchants hunting bargains for centuries. You don't change. There is no reason why you should. But I'd be a fool to offer you a hand and let you bite it off.'

'You exaggerate, Max.'

'Do I? Let me remind you I had to fight you to get in a day and a night nurse for Pia. I had to battle to arrange for her a daily visit from the physician. You drive hard bargains. Fine, I know that. So this is the only bargain I'll make with you. Take it or leave it. I'll stroll over to the tower. Let me know your decision when I get back.'

The walk to the tower was a mistake. It brought on a dizzying rush of memories: of Pia offering him the first freedom of the domain, of Pia the prisoner of her own illness, of his own flight with the Raphaels stuffed in his luggage, sweating out every minute to Switzerland. When he got back to the house, Claudio offered him a snifter of brandy and a pair of amendments to the contract.

'We think fifteen per cent is too high, considering the millions involved.'

208

'No deal. If someone is in illegal possession of the pictures, that person has to be frightened and paid off. Ten per cent is a normal insurance offer. Then I have to be paid for my trouble. If you think you can deal more cheaply, I'll step back and let you go it alone.'

'Very well. Fifteen it is. But there has to be a time limit to your representation.'

'How long do you suggest?'

'If you can't do anything before the end of June we are dead – three months?'

'On the other hand, if I am showing results even though a return of the works has still to be effected, you can certainly get an extension from your bankers. I want nine months – to the end of the year.'

Claudio looked to the lawyer, who nodded.

'Nine months it is,' said Palombini. And for the first time he smiled and asked, 'Now you can tell us, Max, what are our chances?'

'Let's sign first' – Mather was adamant – 'then I'll tell you!'

With the contract in his pocket he felt better and worse, like a fever patient swinging between shivers and sweats. The contract would keep him out of gaol. He could not be accused of wrongful possession, of fraudulent conversion, of larceny as a servant. Until his fee was paid, he remained in undisturbed and unchallenged possession of the Raphaels. On the other hand, he was now obliged to act. He could not withdraw from a situation that was tainted at source.

As he drove back to town in a rented car that threatened to collapse at any moment, Mather wondered why the situation bothered him so much – why a social conscience, dormant so long as to be almost atrophied, had wakened into so lively and prickling a bedfellow.

Then out of a clear blue sky came the memory of his father, yellow and shrunken with the cancer that finally killed him, sitting at the window of his bedroom and looking out at the russet fall of the autumn landscape. He was explaining himself, begging for a tardy understanding.

'I knew what your mother needed, I knew what she wanted for us; but for me the price was too high. It involved a betrayal of the only integral possession I had – myself. I couldn't face that. I couldn't bear to look in my mirror every day and see a stranger . . . or perhaps a double image, never knowing which was which.'

It was the simile of the double image that plagued him now. The Max Mather reflected in the eyes of his women was not the whole of him but the image they chose to select. The images that Berchmans had, and Liepert, were different again and just as illusory. Now he would have to go back to Zurich and face Gisela and see her eyes light up when he told her the contract had been signed . . . and then what? The question was still unanswered when he arrived back at the hotel. He stopped at the desk to ask the concierge to make bookings back to Zurich for himself and Niccoló Tolentino. He called Guido Valente to invite him to dinner. Then he stripped off, soaked in a hot bath and dozed fitfully until it was time to go out.

Guido Valente, Custodian of Autographs at the National Library, was in a happy mood. He rejoiced in the good fortune of his friend Niccoló who was going to America. He himself would be going, though not at the same time, on an exchange fellowship arranged by the American Libraries Association. He would be based in Washington, but would travel extensively, studying American library methods, their latest storage and retrieval techniques and inter-library exchange programmes. He hoped he was not too old to profit from the experience, but the arrival of a new secretary in his office had convinced him that lust was still a happy possibility.

He then enquired solicitously about Anne-Marie. He might, just might, arrive in time for the opening of her gallery. Now he had some good news for his old friend Max. Thanks to the generosity of a certain Marchesa – an American lady long married to an Italian – a *borsa*, a fellowship, had been established at the Library for American post-graduate scholars. The amount was substantial, the terms fell well within Max's discipline. He would be happy to recommend his old friend for the first award. The fact that this same old friend had procured the Palombini archive for the Library could not fail to count strongly. So . . . ?

So Max Mather was touched. He promised to think deeply about it and respond as soon as possible. Guido would understand that he had a number of options open and that this was a critical time for him. It was so critical that he thought they needed more wine. Niccoló agreed. But before he drank, he too had an announcement to make. He had been much exercised on what kind of gift he should make to his good friend Max. Finally he had settled upon this. He brought out a small flat box in which, nestled upon a bed of tissue, was a small copper rectangle incised with the head of a boy.

'This, my dear Max, is the first etching I ever made. The head is of my brother who died in the war. I give it to you because you are like my brother, open and generous . . . and under here,' he lifted the plate, 'are prints numbered one to five which I did especially for you.

'Eh, bravo!' Guido Valente blew his nose violently. 'I keep saying to you, Max, you are a man much loved.'

Far gone in wine, Mather was very near to tears himself; while the imp on his shoulder kept nagging him sardonically: 'If only they knew, little brother; if only they knew!'

In Zurich it was Friday, high noon on a bleak March day, with a cold wind whipping across the lake and the citizens still muffled to the ears. There were large patches of snow on the lower peaks. Winter was at an end but it was not yet truly spring. Niccoló Tolentino was perched on a bollard on the quay, sketching. Max was in the kitchen of his apartment laying out a lunch of cold cuts and salads for Gisela Mundt. She had warned him she would be late. Her Friday lectures did not finish until noon, so it would be twelve-thirty before she arrived. This he had decided must be the day of truth – Black Friday or Good Friday, according to the outcome. He could no longer tolerate this see-saw existence, rocked between the bright promises of the future and the accusing voices from a past which refused to be buried. Safe now from arraignment because of the Palombini contract, he could begin to negotiate, if not a peace, at least a truce, with his residual conscience.

Gisela arrived, flushed and breathless, demanded to be kissed and then offered a drink. They toasted each other, then the contract. She was in no hurry to eat, so Mather plunged head first into deep water:

'I'm going to tell you something.'

'Oh. Confession time, eh?'

'If you like, yes.'

'You show me yours; I'll show you mine.'

'It isn't funny.'

'I know it isn't – I can see by your face it's deadly serious.'

'It's about the Raphaels . . . '

'So?'

'I've decided. We take the ten per cent solution.'

'I think you're wise.'

'I'd hoped,' said Mather with a grin, 'I'd hoped you'd tell me I was good and noble and no longer reprehensible.'

'How would I know, Max?' She gave him that happy beguiling smile. 'I've enjoyed your body, I delight in your company. But I've still seen very little of your soul.'

To which he made the tart reply, 'As to that, my dear *Doktor*, it's for sale like everyone else's – provided the price is right!'

That same afternoon, just before close of business, Max Mather went to the safe-deposit vaults of the Union Bank on Bahnhof-strasse with Gisela, Liepert and Tolentino. There, with unsteady hands, he pulled the wax from the canvas satchel, unpicked the lacing of cobbler's thread and laid the contents on the glass-topped table in the alcove between the tiers of boxes. He kept the cartoons covered to protect them from the light but displayed the twin portraits of the Palombini women – Donna Delfina and the Maiden Beata.

In the hush that followed, Niccoló Tolentino held them at arm's length and gazed at each for a long time. Then he took the loupe from his pocket and examined every square centimetre of the surface. He put the loupe away and, with a small pocket-knife, scraped a tiny area of wood on the back of each picture, carefully spreading the dust on the palm of his hand before blowing it away.

This examination completed, he laid the portraits down and re-covered them. He carried the drawings to the dark corner of the alcove, made Mather stand in front of the light source to cast a deeper shadow; then reverently, as if he were handling a

Communion wafer, he held each of the sheets up for inspection. Finally he laid them down and covered them again. It seemed an age before he spoke, and even then his deep voice was husky and unsteady.

'These are the real ones, from which I made the copies.'

He broke off. Mather was shocked to see that he was weeping. He laid a protective arm round the humped shoulders. The old man recovered slowly and gave a shaky laugh.

'*Son' pazzo*, I'm crazy. Every time I look at something so wonderful, I know there has to be a God – else how could an ugly animal like man make such beautiful things? I was worried about the cartoons, but they are standing up well. The air-conditioning in these vaults is about right for them. No more light though! Imperative there should be no more light. Put them back in the canvas, but don't reseal it. There is no need.'

'The next thing we must do,' said Alois Liepert, 'is go back to my office and take a deposition from you, Niccoló, that you have seen and identified these things and that they are authentic and in good order and condition.'

'While we're there, I must ring Berchmans,' said Mather.

'Is that wise?' Liepert was dubious.

'I think it's necessary. If I don't let him know that the pieces in Brazil are copies, then he'll think I conned him. He's one I don't want as an enemy.'

'Just be cautious,' Liepert warned him. 'Don't tell him too much over the phone. And if he wants to get deeper into discussion, refer him to me.'

'*Für aufklären und konfirmieren*, right?'

'Right!' agreed Liepert. 'Gisela has given me strict instructions about you.'

'I have a question for you both,' said Gisela tartly. 'Who's carrying the insurance on these little items?'

Tolentino did not seem to hear. He was busy replacing the pictures in their covers, handling them like tender infants.

Mather and Liepert looked at each other. Liepert said, 'Let's discuss it back at the office.'

The deposition which Liepert drafted in Italian for Tolentino's signature covered a lot of ground.

On this day I, Niccoló Tolentino, citizen of the Republic of Italy, presently and for the past thirty-seven years employed as resident copyist and restorer of paintings at the galleries of the Pitti Palace, Florence, went to the safe-deposit vaults of the Union Bank situated in the Bahnhofstrasse, Zurich. I was accompanied by Advocates Alois Liepert and Gisela Mundt and Mr Maxwell Mather, official agent for the family Palombini in Florence. I inspected two portraits on cedar-wood panels which I believe to be autograph works of Raffaello Sanzio and five cartoons by the same master. I was familiar with the portraits because I had been commissioned in early 1941 to make copies of them for their then owner, Sig. Luca Palombini in Florence. The cartoons I had never seen before but I identified them, like the portraits, as most probably the work of the same master. The said works were in excellent condition and were being cared for in adequate conditions of dry air, stable temperature and minimal light exposure. I was not offered, nor did I ask for, any information as to their recent provenance. I was not offered, nor did I seek, any fee for my services which were given as a mark of respect for the Palombini family and their representative, Mr Max Mather.

Next came Mather's phone call to Berchmans in Paris. This time it was made on conference phone and announced accordingly to Berchmans.

'Max Mather here again. I'm calling you on a conference line from my lawyer's office in Zurich. Mr Berchmans, Mr Liepert.'

'Good-day to you, Mr Liepert. Now may we get on please. Why the formality?'

'About the Brazilian items.'

'What about them?'

'They're copies. Good ones, but copies.'

'I'd need proof of that.'

'Then I simply suggest caution until I have the opportunity to lay the facts before you.'

'Dealing at this distance with Camoens, I'm at a disadvantage. He may try to set up an auction with me providing the floor price. So I have to ask, Mr Mather. How good is your information?'

Liepert interposed quickly. 'I offer a laywer's opinion, Mr

Berchmans. The information is Grade A. The informant is impeccable.'

'In that case, I thank you both. Has Harmon Seldes been informed?'

'No,' Mather took this one very quietly. 'My position with Seldes is equivocal. He employs me to provide certain services. Our communication is coloured by that fact. On this matter I have dealt only with you, but you are free to communicate my information to whomever you wish.'

'There is, however, a change in Mr Mather's personal situation of which he wishes you to be aware.' This from Liepert.

'And what is that?'

'Mr Mather has been approached by the Palombini family to place his academic knowledge at their disposal once more and to act for them in the matter of the Raphael portraits. I have just negotiated his contract which provides, among other things, that Mr Mather shall be the sole intermediary between the family and the market on this matter. He wishes me to tell you that you are the first to have this information, which will be made public in due course.'

'Which means,' said Berchmans in his brutal fashion, 'he's cutting me out.'

'On the contrary,' said Mather. 'You are in exactly the same position as before, except that you have a friend at court – if you choose to regard me so. That's up to you. Nothing changes except that I become the point of reference for the family and am remunerated by them, not by anyone else.'

'In that case,' Berchmans beat a reluctant retreat, 'thank you for telling me. We should stay in touch.'

'That would be wise. À bientôt, Mr Berchmans.

As he put down the receiver, Niccoló Tolentino puffed out his cheeks and gave vent to an explosive sound.

'Boh! So much talk. So much greed! These are beautiful things, the work of a great master. They are not bones for dogs to fight over. Forgive me, I get angry too quickly these days. I think I should go for a walk and talk to the ducks.'

'You can't,' said Max Mather firmly. 'We have to work out your travel arrangements to New York, draw cheques for you, write a letter to accompany your visa application. . . . Alois, can we have your secretary take some notes, please?'

'A tyrant.' Tolentino raised hands and eyes to heaven. 'A tyrant, mad with the lust for money.'

THIRTEEN

Advance copies of the April edition of *Belvedere* were delivered to Harmon Seldes' desk ten days ahead of publication. He called the staff in to look at it. Everyone agreed it was a slap-up job—first-rate material, handsome layout, accurate colour definition. His editorial sat well, the photographs were as provocative as he had intended them to be. Mather's stuff on domestic economics in Tuscany smelt of the lamp, but the Danziger commentary helped it along.

The surprise of the edition was the lift-out on Madeleine Bayard. Instead of running a conventional advertisement on the final page, Anne-Marie Loredon had elected to fill the space with a full colour reproduction of 'The Bag-Lady', centrepiece of the forthcoming exhibition. It made a splendid display piece and exactly fitted the highly emotional tone of Max Mather's memorial.

Now there was a surprise! In one leap, with the same issue, the plodding scholar was turned into a poet. Several of the senior editorial staff remarked on it—though careful to give full credit to the wisdom of Harmon Seldes, the maker and breaker of talent. The mutual admiration society was still in session when a call came through from one of the senior vice-presidents at the mother house, passing blessings and compliments from on high.

Enough then of compliments! There was work to be done. Seldes pushed everyone out of his office except his secretary, with whom he settled down to that most tantalising of pastimes: 'making a market'. This began with those favoured souls—directors and curators, major dealers, reviewers—who were privileged to receive advance copies of the magazine, prefaced always by a ritual telephone call from the master himself:

'Charles, my friend!' or 'Anna, my love! Harmon Seldes. I have some real surprises for you this month. Yes, it's on its way

217

to you by courier this minute. Take particular note of the stuff on the Palombini Raphaels. Of course you haven't heard of them; they're a *Belvedere* exclusive. A Harmon Seldes exclusive, really; but there. Modesty forbids. Believe me, you should not discount this. Henri Berchmans and I have teamed up to do further research. Also, take a look at the lift-out . . . Madeleine Bayard. This might be a first and last chance to pick up a bargain.'

In the middle of this agreeable exercise, Henri Berchmans called from Paris to tell him that Max Mather had been contracted to represent the Palombini. Seldes was outraged.

'Well, after all his protestations of disinterest! And what are his qualifications anyway? The man's a palaeographer. He knows nothing about art. He's a pretentious puppy!'

Berchmans gave his harsh braying laugh. 'It seems your puppy may have grown into a mastiff. How much progress have you made in your researches?'

'There's hardly been much time, has there? The advance copies of our April edition arrived on my desk only half an hour ago.'

'You miss the point, my friend. Already Mather has traced copies of the two portraits in Brazil. I have a hold on them, but I do not expect too much. What impresses me is the man's ingenuity and industry.'

'I wish I could say the same about his honesty.'

'I begin to be impressed with that too,' said Berchmans. 'He has dealt very openly with me.'

'Not so at all with me.' Seldes was beginning to be petulant. 'After all, I am his senior editor – I do keep him eating.'

'Try getting him to eat out of your hand. He likes polite people.'

'In my present mood I'd rather fire him.'

'That could be an expensive mistake. I'd much rather keep him on our side.'

'I wonder what other little surprises he has in store for us?'

'I'm waiting to know what his evidence is and where his sources are.'

'You asked me about Raphael attributions. Passavanti is still the best and most up-to-date authority. It might pay you to get him to look at the Brazilian material.'

218

'I have to get my hands on it first. Camoens drives a rough bargain. He won't budge an inch without money in his fist.'

'You could, of course, send me down to Rio to talk to him.'

'I'll think about it. And cool down, Harmon. Our young friend is doing all the work for us. But he'll never get within a shout of the market. In the end the Palombini will drop like peaches into our basket.'

Seldes was still chewing over that interesting proposition when Leonie Danziger walked into his office and announced briskly, 'I need some help, Harmon.'

'For you, Danny – anything. The issue looks great, doesn't it?'

'One of the best. Congratulations!'

'You're not happy about something?'

'I'm not happy. Period. Do you keep your office diaries?'

'Of course. Best lesson I ever learned: don't dump the records. You never know when you'll need 'em. What date do you want to check on?'

'February 18th last year.'

'What's the significance of the date?'

'It's the day Madeleine Bayard was killed.'

'Oh!'

'The police want to know – I need to know – what I was doing from dawn to dark. I've been over this with them a dozen times before. They seemed to accept that I had no alibi, but now they're back again. I can remember less now than I could at the beginning. I throw out my diaries as soon as they're used. And don't read me a lecture, Harmon; I can't bear it. Just . . . just look up your entry. See if you have me down for any meeting, any assignment.'

'Sure. Relax now. You know where the liquor is, pour yourself a drink.'

'No, thank you.'

Seldes opened a cupboard and immediately located the diary. He turned back the pages and read the entry for February 18th.

'Aspen . . . Aspen . . . Aspen . . . all the week. That was the Moulton skiing party, I remember. I brought back the story about the sale of their Vanvitello collection – the only one outside Italy. Now that's a thought for Max Mather . . . minor eighteenth-century Italian landscapists . . .'

'Please, Harmon. This is serious. What assignments was I working on that week?'

'It doesn't show here, Danny. And if it doesn't show you could have been working anywhere, couldn't you? I was away from the office. But in any case you're a freelance. We meet. We set an assignment. You go. You don't come back until it's finished.'

'Thanks for nothing, Harmon.'

'Please! Don't be like that. I want to help. What are the police fishing for this late in the day?'

'I don't know, but they certainly have quite a lot of background on this.' She waved the Madeleine Bayard lift-out under his nose. 'That's what they were quizzing me about—Madeleine's love-life, her sex habits, her friends.'

'Of whom you were one, as I remember?'

'As who wasn't, Harmon, when Madi was really swinging?'

'I don't believe our article brought this on.'

'I don't either. The police mentioned a communication of some kind from Hugh Loredon. It was written before he died; sent on from the US Embassy in Holland. They seem to be using it as a text for this new round of interrogations. They mentioned Max Mather too. But there's no way in the world he could be involved.'

'Our golden boy is really getting around,' said Seldes with marked distaste. 'He's due back in a week or so; you'll be able to ask him yourself. Meantime I'll have a check run on all our records for February 18th last year, just to see if we can pin down your location. Try not to worry.'

'Thank you, Harmon. And congratulations on the April edition. It really is very handsome.'

'Thank you, Danny my love.'

But 'Danny my love' was already out of the door and striding towards the elevators. There had been a moment when the paper scissors on Seldes' desk had looked exactly like a dagger and the temptation to use them had been almost irresistible.

In the studio building in SoHo, the painters were putting the last coat on the interiors, the electricians were testing the track circuits and pushing screens about the floor to test the spots. In Mather's apartment on the top floor, carpet was being laid and curtains hung. Anne-Marie was in her office with a pile of invoices and a stack of letters on the desk, the two homicide detectives drinking coffee and making polite but persistent conversation. She had names firmly fixed to them now: the young and good-looking one was Sam Hartog; the older, more rugged and less polished was Manny Bechstein. They were a well-practised team. Hartog led the dance with deferential attitudes and carefully placed queries. Manny put in the tricky moves, reversing over old ground, twisting and twirling an answer until it sounded like something quite different.

Sam Hartog sipped his coffee and worked patiently through his questions.

'So your father told you he was going into the London Clinic for tests? After that he went on to Amsterdam?'

'Right.'

'Why did he go there?'

'I presumed for business. High category auction goods and auction clients come from all over the world. My father travelled all the time between auctions.'

'I understand. Then your father asked Mr Mather to meet him in Amsterdam?'

'Yes.'

'Why Mather and not you?'

'As Max explained it to me, although my father was feeling very threatened and lonely, he didn't want to upset my life. He knew that Max and I looked after each other . . . so he called Max.'

'But your father did write to you – a letter which was transmitted with other correspondence from him through our Embassy after his death.'

'That's right.'

'Would you be willing to show me that letter?'

'Sure. I have it here.'

She fished in her handbag and brought out the envelope with the Embassy stamp on it. Sam Hartog opened the letter, glanced at it and handed it to Bechstein, who nodded and passed it back. Hartog summed up the message briefly.

'Your father knows he is dying. He apologises for being an

indifferent parent. He tells you he loves you – and begs you at all costs not to marry Edmund Bayard . . . '

'Which I have no intention of doing.'

'In spite of the fact that you are good friends and will be doing considerable business together?'

'It might be more accurate to say because of that fact.'

'Why did your father dislike Bayard?'

'He had a long affair with Madeleine. He thought Ed Bayard treated her very badly – a fact which Ed admits freely and regrets very much. My father always saw him as a man of uncertain temper and an unsuitable husband for a much younger woman.'

'But he saw no problem in your doing business with him, leasing the studio, arranging an exhibition of his wife's pictures?'

'My father had nothing to do with those arrangements. I made them without consulting him.'

'But he did try to talk you out of them?'

'Without success. Now, Mr Hartog, I think you owe me some explanation. I've been very open with you.'

'You have. We appreciate it.'

'I think, therefore, that you should be equally open with me.'

For the first time Manny Bechstein stirred out of his silence.

'It's not always possible for police officers to be open, ma'am. But let's go as far as we can. At the same time as he wrote to you, your father wrote a letter to us at NYPD. He had the letter notarised at the Embassy, so it has weight as a document in evidence. It is an account of the murder of Madeleine Bayard and his connection with it.'

'And what was that connection?'

'Accessory after the fact.'

'Which means?'

'Someone else killed her. Your father assisted that person to evade detection.'

'Who killed her?'

'We can't disclose that – and we haven't proved his accusation yet.'

'You mean he could have been lying?'

'It's possible.'

'But why? Dammit, he was a dying man!'

'Which doesn't mean he was telling the truth,' Manny

Bechstein pointed out. 'Only that he could say what he liked and get away with it.'

'That's why,' said Sam Hartog mildly, 'we have to be careful about mentioning names or giving out information. When is Mr Mather coming back to New York?'

'Within a week.'

'We'll catch up with him then.'

'But what possible connection . . .'

'That's the problem with murder,' put in Manny Bechstein. 'It connects the most unlikely people. Thank you for your help, ma'am. We'll be on our way.'

'My card,' said Sam Hartog, 'in case you want to get in touch. And, before I forget, Manny and I would like to be invited to your opening.'

'I'll send you cards. It will be a black-tie affair.'

'I approve.' This surprisingly came from Manny Bechstein. 'My mother used to say, "It makes for respect." She was an artist too. She used to engrave crystal for Corning. Some of her work was museum quality. See you, Miss Loredon.'

When they had gone, she shrugged resignedly and turned back to the pile of work on her desk: bills, advertising layouts, the draft of a circular on Tolentino's seminar, guest lists, phone calls to be answered, correspondence with artists and their agents. Somewhere far in the back of her skull a warning bell was ringing. This addiction to work, this refusal to address any personal questions, this compulsive flight from quiet were abnormal symptoms. Her grief and her rage had never been properly purged. The puzzles of her relationship with Bayard had never been worked out. Her dead had never been laid to rest in proper fashion. So, the vague bells rang; but she shut out the sound and wished that Max Mather would come soon to share the burden of Hugh Loredon's last cryptic communication:

. . . I know I haven't been much of a father. I've never been much of anything except an auctioneer and an entertaining bed-mate. But even there I always functioned best with women who didn't take me or what we were doing too seriously. Now it's all too damn serious and too damn short to do anything except to tell you that in my very odd fashion I've always loved you and always admired the good job you are making of your life.

Also I must tell you – and take my word for it – Bayard is the wrong man for you. He's all screwed-up. He's intelligent. He wants to be open and pleasant. He can't be. There's no joy in him. Madeleine didn't help, of course; she was screwed-up too. They both had highs and lows, but never in sync. If they'd been able to hit the crest of the same wave just a few times they might have made it.

Madi and I managed to have some good times, but I was never a horse for the long ride. I liked the short gallops and a quick change of scenery. With Madi, I know, I hung around too long and all sorts of things got balled up. I've written a letter to the police that I hope will straighten things out. Let them close the record and let you get on with your life.

Max Mather will know what I'm talking about. He'll answer your questions. I like Mather very much, but I'm not sure that he's a stayer either. That's all for now. I was never much of a writer. So just let me say it once again: I love you. I've made a will. Whatever's left is all yours. Don't grieve. Drink a toast and then break the glass.

Hugh

The first time she read it she had wept bitterly. Now it made her angry. It was too flip, too facile – a tawdry performance by a bad actor to an audience for whom he lacked respect. The problem was that she, his daughter, could not yet find the grace to forgive him. Max Mather's note, written a few days later, had chided her gently but firmly:

Hugh escaped me at the end because that was the way he had come to terms with termination. He wanted to be alone with his executioner. I don't think any of us would deny another that last indulgence. Besides, much as we may want it some-times, we have no right to possess our parents. They have as much need to escape us as we them. And after all, Hugh was a great escape artist, a latter-day Houdini. Be angry if you must, smile if you can, but in the end, for your own peace, you must forgive him. I hope you will forgive me too, your unwilling surrogate in the last passion of Hugh Loredon.

Love, Max

That was the hardest and most bitter mouthful to chew on. Max, too, was escaping her. Dear faithless, unreliable Max – companion of carefree hours in Tuscany – was changing into someone quite different. He had purposes of his own now and would not long be content to be a junior lieutenant to Anne-Marie Loredon or, indeed, to any other woman. If she wanted to hold him, and she was still not sure that she did, then she would have to reach out and grab him before he waltzed away with another woman – like that Leonie Danziger who had called to offer sympathy and had seemed to know a great deal more than she told about Hugh Loredon and the Bayards.

On the other hand, Anne-Marie wasn't really sure she wanted anyone just at this moment. There was too much to do. She wasn't eager for sex, though she could use some soothing. Ambition seemed to chew up an awful lot of adrenalin – and besides, she had always enjoyed sex most when there was a laugh in it . . . just like the late Hugh Loredon.

For Edmund Bayard, the renewal of police inquiries was no surprise. It had been clear from the first that the exhibition of Madeleine's canvases, on the murder site itself, would raise gossip and rumour all over again. It was equally clear that the police had to move in order to protect themselves against criticism.

The fact that Hugh Loredon had made some kind of death-bed confession did not surprise him either. All his life the man had been a mountebank, a woman-chaser, an irresponsible meddler in other people's lives. Whatever he had written – an act of tardy repentance or a final testament of malice – would still have a nuisance value; but it would have no strength in law unless it could be confirmed by other evidence which Bayard could not see forthcoming. His own alibi had been tested and re-tested. It still stood rock-solid.

What bothered him in the new line of police questions was the

225

mention of papers belonging to Madeleine and the fact that he could not identify them. The suggestion was, clearly, that Mather had seen them and had been thus enabled to write so poignantly about Madeleine's life and work. Given the existence of such personal records, given that they could fall into the hands of the press, his own privacy – that small place of quiet still left in his existence – was immediately threatened. His fragile self-respect could be shattered at one blow; and all the king's horses and all the king's men would never put it together again.

This was the real threat hanging like a hurricane cloud over his life. Madeleine had made him a cuckold hundreds of times over. Worse still she had made him a fool, an object of scorn to her lovers and cronies. He had survived it once and come within a shout of salvation with Anne-Marie. But if that failed and she made no answering call to him, then would come the true horror and his world would take on a doomsday look.

He had suffered this dread before. It was a symptom of the depressive illness that had affected him in recurrent cycles throughout his life but which had only been clinically identified in later years. He had learned to master the wild swings from mania to depression, riding them as a sailor rode the swells, taking them on the shoulder, never on the snout of the ship, sliding down and clawing up but never letting the sea batter him to pieces . . . But now the sea was rising mountains high and sanity seemed a frailer craft than it had ever been.

If only Anne-Marie would bend to him. If only he could break through the hedges of measured affection to the well of passion that lay beyond them. She must have sexual needs. She could not always live like a nun. She had not always done so; Max Mather was witness to that. What then? Who, then, was his rival? He would give Anne-Marie until the exhibition, then he would, he must, force her to declare herself.

Which brought him back, face to face, with Mather. The man had all the talents of an attractive rogue: an adequate education, good taste cultivated at the expense of others, a charm of deference, with a handsome face and an athletic body thrown in for a bonus. It was too much for one man. It was more than too much that he should have written so intimate and accurate a portrait of Madeleine and depicted so tragic a picture of her

226

doomed and destructive marriage. Worse still was the fact that there was no malice in Mather's work; yet its very compassion was an affront. Client Mather might be, friend of Anne-Marie, valuable associate in the business of the gallery, but at this dark moment he became the focus for all the dreads and distrusts that had once been centred on Hugh Loredon. Cool reason told Bayard this was a folly, urgent and dangerous; but inside the hurricane cloud there was no reason – only turbulence, darkness and the seeds of destruction . . . The buzzer on his telephone startled him into reality. He snatched up the receiver to find a member of the buying syndicate on the line.

'Ed, the boys have all had a look at the transparencies from Holland – what's the guy's name, Cornelis Janzoon? They like the stuff very much. They want to know what's the possibility, and when, of staging an exhibition in New York. If that could be arranged, then clearly we ought to buy some stuff now and hold it.'

'I know that Max did discuss an exhibition with Janzoon. He probably hasn't raised it yet with Anne-Marie. Her father died very recently, as you know. But leave it to me. I'll get on to it. If we do buy, how much would you authorise for the syndicate?'

'With an exhibition – fifty thousand. Sixty tops.'

'I'll talk to Anne-Marie and get back to you. We're expecting Mather here in a week or so.'

'Are you all right, Ed? You sound rattled.'

'I've had a bad morning with a troublesome client.'

'Don't let 'em get to you, Ed. You're the guru, so keep 'em ignorant and humble. Have a nice day!'

Bayard put down the receiver and then called Anne-Marie at the studio. He asked, 'Have you had a chance to look at the Janzoon material that Max sent from Amsterdam?'

'I have, yes. It looks very interesting.'

'Interesting enough to offer an exhibition?'

'It's too early to make that decision, Ed. We have to see how we go with Madeleine's work. Then we're signed for Oliver Swann – that's two figurative artists in a row. I think we have to consider a fairly wide excursion for our third show. We've got several options. I'd like to keep them all open. So I don't want to be pressed on this matter until we're launched.'

'I know. It was just that members of our syndicate are very interested in Janzoon.'

'And they'd like to do a little punting and let me hike the market for them! I won't play that game, Ed. I'm sure Max won't, either.'

'He's a member of the syndicate.'

'But he also represents me; so if there's any conflict of interest it had better be declared right now!'

This was getting out of hand. Bayard tried to mollify her.

'I'm sure there's none. Max has acted quite properly. He's sent back recommendations. Now it's up to the syndicate to decide what it wants to buy – it's up to you to decide what you want to exhibit.'

'Just so everybody knows the rules!'

'Be sure they do. Can I offer you lunch? Dinner?'

'I'd love it – if you give me a rain-check until the end of the week. I'm up to my eyes in work right now.'

'Why don't you hire some help?'

'Because I'm trying to keep overheads down and I can do it cheaper and faster myself. By the way, I had a visit from the police today.'

'And what the devil did they want?'

'Comments on a letter my father wrote them before he died.'

'Did they offer to show you the letter?'

'No.'

'Then I hope you declined to make comment.'

'More or less. They also asked when Max would be back.'

'Let me repeat my advice. Don't allow them to draw you into comment or speculation about material they're not prepared to display to you.'

'I'll do just as you say. Call you Friday, early morning.'

'I'll look forward to it. Have you heard from Max?'

'Just a long fax message about Niccoló Tolentino, with a list of his twelve lecture subjects. That's another thing I have to start promoting. Max expects to arrive Sunday afternoon on Air France from Paris. It'll be nice to see him again.'

'Very nice,' Bayard agreed. 'Very nice indeed.'

*

In Zurich it was the end of the day. Niccoló Tolentino had been embraced, encouraged, documented, supplied with travel funds, sworn to silence and shipped back to Florence on an afternoon flight. Max Mather and Alois Liepert were conferring on the next steps in the Raphael strategies. Liepert's recommendation was clear and emphatic.

'Now we need a waiting period – a cooling-off time. You know you have the originals. You can produce them at any time. Palombini doesn't have to meet his notes until the end of June. The articles are published now. Curiosity – and, therefore, market value – will rise. So sit tight, Max. Possess your soul in patience. You need to go back to America. Go! Leave me a power of attorney and I can do anything that needs to be done. The companies function by procuration, so they can perform legal acts without you. If you are going to be a good dealer, Max, you must learn one lesson: patience. You are not – as history proves – a very patient man.'

'I agree, Alois. So be it, then. I push off to America. You're in charge here. But what am I going to do about Gisela?'

'Forgive me, my friend, but you are rushing that one too. This is a very bright, very modern but also very traditional Swiss girl. This is still Reformation country here. Calvin and Zwingli walk the mountains. Gisela loves you. She approves of an active sex life between lovers. But any hint of sharp trading in business and she bridles. Now that we have our contract, I can wear the Palombini situation. I've worn much worse with many other clients. As a lawyer, Gisela wears it too – indeed, she constructed it; but she dropped a phrase to me the other day which gave me pause. She said, "In a marriage you need 'compatibility of conscience' ".'

'I get the message.' Mather shrugged ruefully. 'I guess that's what I'm trying to do now: work out a way of paying debts – financial and emotional – without bankrupting myself or ruining the reputation I'm just beginning to build.'

Liepert nodded a sober assent. 'I approve that. There are few absolutes in human affairs – and the law is often a braying ass.'

'I totally agree.' Gisela swept in, apple-cheeked and wind-blown after her walk from the university. She kissed them both, then collapsed into a chair. 'What do you have to drink, Alois?'

229

'Whatever's in the cabinet. Help yourselves. I'll be back as soon as I've signed the mail and . . .'

The telephone rang. Liepert picked it up, listened for a few moments, then handed it to Mather. 'America on the line for you.'

Without thinking, Mather pressed the conference button and Leonie Danziger's distorted voice crackled about the room.

'Max, this is Danny. The police are here. They've arrested me for the murder of Madi Bayard. This is the one phone call I'm allowed. Help me, please!'

'I will. Now be very calm and answer me clearly. Have they read you your rights?'

'Yes.'

'Then stand on them. Be silent. Don't say a word until I can get an attorney to you. Understand?'

'Yes.'

'Is Carol with you?'

'No. She has classes.'

'Ask the arresting officer if he'll let you leave a note just to tell her what's happened. Tell her to expect a call from me. I'll leave here as soon as I can get a flight. Then we'll see if we can get you out on bail. What's the exact charge?'

'Murder in the first degree.'

'Oh, God, it's not possible! Ask the arresting officer if he'll speak to me, please.'

There was a short pause, a murmur of unintelligible talk and then a neutral voice answered.

'Sam Hartog speaking. Who is this?'

'Max Mather. Is the charge as Miss Danziger states it?'

'I'm afraid so. Murder one.'

'I'll be calling an attorney for her.'

'That's wise.'

'Naturally he'll be applying for bail.'

'Naturally . . . When do you expect to get back, Mr Mather?'

'Tomorrow—the next day, as soon as I can get a flight.'

'We'd like to talk to you as soon as you get in.'

'The wish is mutual; give me a number. Thank you. Where are you taking Miss Danziger now?'

'To the precinct. The sooner you can contact her attorney the better. Would you like another word with her?'

'Please . . . Danny, it's all in hand. I'll have an attorney for you within the hour. And very soon I'll be with you. Courage, now!'

'Oh Max, how can I thank you?'

'Hang in there. I'll be with you as soon as I can. 'Bye now.'

'I'm impressed,' said Gisela. 'Sir Galahad, instant to the service of a damsel in distress. You will be explaining all this to us?'

'I will. Now pipe down and let me get on.'

He was already dialling the number of Ed Bayard's office. Bayard—the secretary informed him—was in closed conference with a client.

'Then please get him out of it! Tell him Max Mather is on the line from Zurich and this is a grade A emergency!'

Bayard came on the line. He was curt and irritable. 'What the hell is this emergency!'

When Mather told him, he was shocked into silence.

'So I need a good attorney, *now!*'

'I can't help you, Max. We're a commercial law partnership, not a criminal practice.'

Mather exploded into fury. 'What the hell kind of answer is that?'

'A prudent one.' Bayard was cold. 'The victim was my wife. It would seem wise and necessary to maintain an arm's length position from the accused, wouldn't you say?'

'So maintain it. Give me a number, Ed; I'll sort the rest out when I get back to New York.'

'Wait a moment.'

He waited three long minutes before a secretary came on the line with the information.

'The name you require, sir, is George Munsel. The code is 212, the number is 735 4141. Do you have that?'

'I have it,' said Mather and slammed down the phone.

'Can I help?' Gisela asked.

'Not yet. Just pour us both a drink.'

He dialled the Manhattan number and was connected to a cool university club voice that identified itself as George Munsel. Mather plunged straight into a brisk recital of the circumstances

231

and the needs of Danny Danziger, at the end of which Munsel asked, 'And how did you find me?'

'I asked Ed Bayard, who represents me. He suddenly invoked prudence and conflict of interest. I chewed him out. His secretary came back with your number. I have to underline the fact that he didn't recommend you.'

Munsel laughed—a relaxed sound. 'Who's footing the bill?' he asked.

'I am. You'll get a cheque as soon as I arrive.'

'Bail?'

'She's got steady and lucrative employment, owns her own apartment. I just can't see her as a fugitive.'

'How much do you know about this business?'

'I wasn't involved in it, if that's what you mean—I was out of the country all of last year and the year before. But because of my connection with Anne-Marie Loredon and her late father I've been sucked into the undertow. Also, I'm sitting on Madeleine Bayard's private papers.'

'Where are they?'

'Here in Zurich.'

'Leave them there. Bring a set of notarised copies: I repeat, *notarised*.'

'Got it. I hope this means you'll take the case?'

'First I have to talk to Miss Danziger. I should be on my way now. Call me when you hit Manhattan.'

'Will do. And thanks.'

Gisela handed him a large whisky. His next call was to Anne-Marie Loredon at the gallery. She had just heard the news on radio and was almost incoherent with shock.

'This is terrible for us, Max. Three weeks from opening and now this bloody mess! I need you here, I just can't face this by myself.'

'I'll be there tomorrow. Sit tight. We don't cower under the threat, we exploit it. As soon as I get in we'll call a meeting of our advertising agents and PR people. Have you heard from Bayard?'

'No. Have you?'

'Yes, I spoke with him—asked him to find me an attorney for

232

Danny Danziger. He ran for the hills. You can tell him from me, he's a shit.'

'That's not fair, Max. This woman's accused of murdering his wife. How can you expect him to set up her defence?'

'Let's not argue, lover! There's worse to come. We need to stand together. I'll call you as soon as I arrive. We'll have drinks and a council of war at my place.'

'What do I say to the press?'

'You're surprised; you're shocked; you can't believe it. You hope justice will be done . . . and there's a strange echo of Greek drama which they, too, will catch when they see the exhibition – which will most definitely start on time. Write that down before you forget it. See you!'

'And another stricken woman takes heart from the presence of this young knight.' Thus Gisela Mundt with operatic gestures. 'That's two so far. How many more?'

Mather laughed in spite of himself.

'Well, I might have to go to one of my wealthy widows to raise bail. If she won't do it, then I'll just have to work through my black book. Seriously, though, this is quite macabre. It's the story Hugh Loredon told me in Amsterdam. I called him a liar. But clearly the letter he wrote must say Danny Danziger was the killer. Why? Why would a man lie when he's facing certain death?'

'Because there's no more perfect time,' Gisela suggested. 'You can get away with anything. Now let's ring Swissair and see what flights they're offering to New York.'

There was one seat left on an 11 a.m. flight to Kennedy, which left him just enough of the afternoon to go to the bank and arm himself with money, photostats and documents. He ordered a car for 8.15 a.m. and had Swissair book him a limousine at Kennedy. Which left only one more call to make before they walked out of Liepert's office.

Mather insisted on calling Berchmans in Paris. The old man's reaction was subdued. 'Do you think she did it?'

'I know she didn't.'

'Can you prove it?'

'I hope so. One thing I do have to tell you. I am taking copies of Madeleine's papers and sketchbooks. They may be subpoenaed in evidence. You appear in both, though not too conspicuously or scandalously.'

'No way you can pull me out?'

'I'm afraid not. Frankly, the most the media could do is poke ribald fun.'

'Can I trust your judgment on this, Mr Mather?'

'You must, I'm afraid.'

'Good. I'm coming to New York shortly. Call my office there, they'll let you know the exact date. We should meet again. I've made arrangements for the two Brazilian Raphaels to be shipped under bond for inspection. I'd like you to see them with me.'

'Thank you. By then I hope to have further news of the originals.'

'Which, of course, have to be verified?'

'Of course.'

'We should talk about how they may be coming to market.'

'That too.'

'Now I owe you a piece of advice. Watch Seldes – he doesn't like you. He's jealous. He can be dangerous.'

'Thank you for telling me.'

'One hand washes the other,' said Berchmans and hung up.

FOURTEEN

George Munsel, attorney for the defence of Leonie Danziger, was something of a surprise. He was six feet three inches tall, thin as a beanpole, with big hands, big feet, a square-cut Scandinavian face, a shock of blond hair and a smile of childlike innocence. The biggest problem in his life seemed to be to accommodate himself to the scale of ordinary mortals. He stooped going through a door; he sidled past furniture; he sprawled in a chair; he bent to listen to people. Mather had the impression of some ancient Nordic sage bowed in compassion over the commonfolk. In Mather's small apartment he stretched his long legs under the dining table, laid out his notes and his brief-pad and delivered his report in a deep baritone recitative.

'A quick rundown. The client accepts me, I accept her. I need an opening retainer of ten thousand. We haven't come to disclosures yet, but the DA's office must be pretty confident to lead off with murder one. The girl denies the charge, but admits damaging involvements and circumstances: a lesbian association with the victim, quarrels, a visit to the studio on the day of the murder, a call to Hugh Loredon. My guess is we'll be offered a plea. My instinct is to refuse it, ask for reasonable bail and fight the case.'

'Bail,' queried Mather. 'How much?'

'Too early to say – and it's not your responsibility to raise it.'

'I want to help if I can.'

'Because she's your editor?'

'Because she's a damned good editor – and I owe her for that.'

'That's an interesting point of view. The lady is, on her own confession, lesbian.'

'It's irrelevant,' said Mather. 'What's next?'

'What's next in your story, Mr Mather?'

Max Mather told it quietly and without embellishment, marvel-
ling as he did so how deeply he had become embroiled – and in
so short a time – in the lives of all these people. Munsel listened
for the most part in silence, interrupting only to clarify an element
in the story or to give himself time to record a point. Then he
made Mather retell, twice over, every detail of his meetings
and talks with Hugh Loredon from their first luncheon in the
apartment to their parting handshake in Amsterdam.

Next he turned his attention to the letter which Danny
Danziger had written him and the photographs she had sent
covering the police inquiries. His comment defined the uneasi-
ness which Mather had felt but could not put a name to when
he himself had first read them.

'This bothers me,' said Munsel. 'She writes with total detachment, as though she is simply summarising information from
others. The only concession is in the phrases "a lot of us are
involved in it" and so on. In short, the letter is in essence a
falsehood.'

'It bothered me too when I read it,' Mather agreed. 'But I didn't
know then what I know now. If you read Madeleine Bayard's
diaries, you'll see a possible reason for the lie . . . Take your
time; I'll fix us a drink. What will you have?'

'Vodka tonic, please.' He was already deep in his reading.

Mather served the drinks and then went into the bedroom to
call Anne-Marie. Their conversation was brief. She was delighted
he was back. She would join him for dinner at eight. Oh, and
would he please call Ed Bayard at home? Why? Ed was feeling
very badly about his conduct. He'd like to apologise and make
friends. On the principle that even friends like Bayard were a
shade better than enemies, Max agreed to make the call next
morning. Then he telephoned Harmon Seldes, and was surprised
to find himself welcomed effusively.

'My dear Max. Delighted to have you back! My God, the timing
couldn't have been better – we publish your Bayard piece; they
arrest Danny Danziger. Terrible mistake, of course. It has to be.
We're all rooting for her.'

'In that case, I'm sure it would help if you supported her bail
application.'

'How would I do that?'

'Attend the court. Be prepared to testify that she's in permanent employment, is of great value to the magazine . . . that sort of thing. It would be good for staff morale too, Harmon!'

'I'll see what I can do. Now tell me about the Raphaels. Berchmans says you're making lots of progress – and, you old fox, you've hooked yourself up with the Palombini again.'

'They asked me to represent them. It would have been churlish to refuse.'

'Of course. When am I going to see you?'

'The arraignment won't take long. Let's talk after that. I have a suggestion for a follow-up on the Raphael story.'

'Let's talk about it by all means. Meanwhile I'll do what I can to support the bail application. I can't wait to hear where you're at with the Raphaels. I know you've been talking to Berchmans, but he doles out information as if it were money . . . You and I must make time to talk. It's very important. Once again – welcome back!'

George Munsel was still absorbed in Madeleine Bayard's manuscripts and sketch books. He looked up as Mather entered and asked abruptly, 'Why did Hugh Loredon give you this material?'

'I've never quite figured that out. I believe he viewed it as a weapon against Bayard. Once I saw it I was inclined to agree.'

'Why did you hang on to the stuff? Why didn't you give it back?'

'He told me to keep it.'

'Did he give a reason?'

'Yes. He said: "For the police it's evidence; for you, it's treasure-trove." Which, given the circumstances, it is.'

Munsel gave his big, innocent smile. 'But why did he give it to you and not to his daughter?'

'Because he knew we had been lovers. He saw me always as a kind of protector.'

'The police are going to ask you another question.'

'Which is?'

'Mr Mather, do you understand the meaning of misprision of a felony?'

'I do. It means concealing knowledge of a crime.'

'So what do you reply to the police?'

'Madeleine Bayard's papers make no reference to a crime – only to the follies of her friends and intimates.'

'Which of course could be relevant to the crime that took place.'

'But I am not, and was not, competent to judge of that relevance.'

'Hugh Loredon obviously thought you were.'

'Did he? How would that be established?'

'Good answer, Mr Mather. How did you read Hugh Loredon's intention?'

'I couldn't with any certainty. My guess is that he wanted to protect his daughter from distress and scandal after his death. He may well have wished to enrich her with valuable document-ation on Madeleine Bayard – but he couldn't do so directly without involving her in the concealment of evidence. So he turned to me, confident I would protect her interests.'

'I could use another vodka,' Munsel said. 'This time, hold the tonic.'

'Coming up.'

'So now let me make a small suggestion. Suppose – just suppose – Hugh Loredon was playing one last devious game.'

'To do what?'

'To bring down the man he feared and hated most: Edmund Bayard.'

'And to do that he incriminates an innocent woman with a cooked-up story? That's crazy.'

'Not so crazy. You watch what happens after the arraignment. The prosecution has a notarised confession which is also an accusation. The accuser is dead and can't be questioned. Absent any other evidence – and my hunch is that they have some, but not enough – they're in a very awkward spot. Especially when I produce a rebuttal document as strong as this stuff I've got under my hands.'

'But that's all before the fact.'

'Except for the man who will interpret it.'

'And that is?'

'You, Mr Mather!'

'I don't see where you're leading me.'

'You're a scholar, Mr Mather. I've looked you up. I've read your two pieces for *Belvedere* to which Danny Danziger pointed me. Your discipline isn't fine art but palaeography, the study of manuscripts ancient and modern. According to my encyclopaedia that study is to read correctly the handwritings of the past, to examine manuscripts in the light of internal evidence (to wit, the contents) and external evidence provided by other available documents. You've already been through Madeleine Bayard's papers several times. You have produced a moving and illuminating article. I want you to go through the same material again, as a palaeographer, looking for internal and external evidence about the life and death of Madeleine Bayard. If my guess is right, I could make you the star witness for the defence.'

Mather gaped at him in amazement.

'Do you realise what you're asking? This isn't a game. It's a gamble on a woman's liberty – not only on my skill, but on the vagaries of a dead woman's mind and the fantasies she constructed to amuse or shock or mystify. I couldn't even attempt this!'

'Not even if I direct you a little?'

'I don't see how you can.'

'Try this, then.' Munsel flipped forward through the diary to the last two pages. 'This is the beginning of the entry for the last day of Madeleine's life: "It is bitterly cold. The studio is like a tomb. I turn on every heater. Even so, my fingers are not as completely under control as they should be for this scribe's work. Yet old habit determines that it must be done, at this hour and in this fashion, else the rest of my day will never flow smoothly." Interpret that for me, Mr Mather. Give it to me off the top of your head. First skim off the cream, so to speak.'

'Well . . . ' Mather scanned the lines three times before he answered. ' "This scribe's work" . . . that's exactly what it is. For the diaries she uses a very formal and reglar hand based on an old French Gothic style called *écriture financière*. The form is called *ronde* or rounded and, because it is rounded, upright and accented in the downstrokes, it is slower to write and needs much more care than cursive or running hands. "At this hour and in this fashion, else the rest of my day . . . " That says to me that she used the diary as a kind of warm-up exercise for drawing and painting. Also, knowing something of her domestic background, I would say it probably constituted an act of release

239

and outpouring after a night of marital tensions. There is a hint of superstition—the ritual must be performed, otherwise the day goes wrong. "The studio is like a tomb" . . . What was the heating anyway? It certainly wasn't central.'

'Bravo!' George Munsel cut him off with a burst of solitary applause. 'That's great. That's exactly what I'm talking about. Will you have a go at it? We can meet every day or two and discuss what you're finding.'

'It's worth a try . . . but what do I say to the police when they put me on the griddle?'

'One more question before I answer that one. Where are the originals of these writings and drawings?'

'In a safe-deposit in Switzerland.'

'Who owns them?'

'The company to which I disposed of them—Artifax SPA.'

'What if the police ask to see them?'

'I'll be happy to put them in touch with the lawyer who deals for the company.'

'Good. And since I'll be sitting with you at that interview, you'll take your cues from me. I'll also call the police and arrange the time and venue with them. You are going to be available but very hard to isolate.'

'When can I see Danny?'

'With luck she'll be bailed at the arraignment tomorrow. If not, I'll arrange for you to see her immediately afterwards. However, after reading this stuff and hearing what you have to say, I believe bail will be set at a reasonable figure; the girl does have enough assets to make arrangements with a bail bondsman. I'd rather not have you encumbered or tied too closely to her. I need you as an expert witness, which is how I'm going to present you at the trial.'

'You realise that my testimony will touch a lot of other people: Ed Bayard most of all, Anne-Marie because of her father, not to mention all the other men and women who pop up in the diaries and in her drawings?'

'Let's take them in order. Ed Bayard? He takes his soup as it's served. We're not pursuing him, we're defending a client. Anne-Marie Loredon? That's rough. Her father will certainly be discredited. She may lose insurance benefits if the company decides to deem Loredon's death a suicide. Again it's rough; but she's free and our client is in jail and will still have to face trial. The rest . . . It's their problem, isn't it? One of the problems of the swingers' circuit—leaving out AIDS, herpes, chlámydia and syphilis—is that you get caught up in a whole gaggle of other lives and you never know who or what is likely to come knocking on your door. In this case it's going to be a little man with a subpoena offering a fun day in court. Any more questions?'

'What gave you the idea of using me as an expert witness?'

'The stuff you wrote for *Belvedere*—and Leonie Danziger's own estimate of your talents.'

'And what's your estimate of her?'

'I'm not sure I've arrived at one yet. She's intelligent, well-educated, passionate—affectionate, which is somewhat different. She's fiercely independent, yet desperately needs someone to depend on. She's also capable of deep attachments—she's already developed one for you in spite of her lesbian tastes—and in my view she would be capable of murder. But then we all would, given the provocation. In short, she's a highly complex character, not yet fully formed in my mind, and I have no intention of putting her on the witness stand. So now tell me how you feel about her, Mr Mather?'

Wearily Mather explained, 'Harmon Seldes gave me Danny as my editor. He also told me she was a blue-stocking who had unusual sexual preferences.'

'And did she?'

'Yes.'

'How did you confirm that?'

'She told me so.'

'And. . . ?'

'And nothing. We continued working together. She's a first-rate editor. She's helped me greatly. I can't walk away from her now.'

'What if she's found guilty? She could be, you know.'

'What do you expect me to say? There but for the grace of God goes Max Mather?'

'You'll do,' said Munsel. 'I'll see you at ten o'clock in Part No. 3. Thanks for the drink.'

He gathered up his papers, uncoiled his lanky body and sidled

241

out of the room. It was six-thirty – Mather had an hour and a half to lay in provisions and prepare a meal before Anne-Marie arrived.

This meeting promised to be a difficult one. He had no intention of conducting it in a public place. So far as Anne-Marie was concerned everything she had was on the line: her family name, her inheritance, her career, her business and her personal relations with Ed Bayard. For himself, the issues were equally important. His career was being rebuilt on the twin foundations of the Raphaels and his representation of a reputable gallery in New York. The arrest and trial of Danny Danziger was like the first rumbling of an earthquake which could wreck all their carefully-built projects.

Like an earthquake, crime produced extraordinary random effects. The murder of Madeleine Bayard was changing the lives of people in Florence, in Zurich, in Paris, Rio and New York. The affair of the Raphaels assumed a new dimension in the context of a New York courtroom. His casual relations with Anne-Marie now coloured his growing attachment to Gisela Mundt. Ed Bayard, whom he had chosen as his own legal counsellor, had turned suddenly hostile and, with equal suddenness, was now suing for a truce. George Munsel was a new catalyst, setting off all kinds of chemical reactions to construct a defence for his client. And Max Mather himself had become a mutable man, a very chameleon – changing his colour, altering the configuration of his presence to merge himself more perfectly with the background and protect himself from the predators who hovered always over the scene of a catastrophe.

His shopping completed, he walked back, set the table and began laying out ingredients in the kitchen. This was a deliberate ploy to keep himself busy during the opening gambits with Anne-Marie. The last scene he wanted to play was a confrontation of interests or opinions. Besides, he intended to convey comforting echoes of Florence, when he would serve cocktails on her terrace and afterwards take over her kitchen to prepare the evening meal. A little nostalgia now might take the rough edge off the evening. The harsh truths of the situation might sound a shade more comfortable in Florentine slang . . .

All of which careful stage-management fell apart when Anne-

Marie arrived with Ed Bayard in tow. Mather was furious, but managed to damp his anger down to a frigid politeness.

'It's one drink, I'm afraid, Ed; then I throw you out. Anne-Marie and I have a lot of business to discuss and I have to face the arraignment and police interviews tomorrow.'

Bayard was clearly embarrassed.

'I didn't want to intrude, Max, but Anne-Marie insisted. I really do want to apologise for my conduct when you called from Zurich. I was caught by surprise—a difficult conference, shocking news, your assumption that I could pull defence counsel out of the hat. Anyway, I'm sorry it happened. If there's anything I can do . . .'

'Thank you, no; but George Munsel seems a bright man.'

'I'm afraid I didn't choose him. My secretary did.'

'Then I'll call and thank her.'

'She'd appreciate that.'

There was an awkward pause, then Anne-Marie made a stammering request. 'Max . . . Ed was wondering whether he could look at the material my father gave you.'

'I'm afraid that's impossible; I don't have it.'

'Where is it then?'

'In Switzerland.'

'Max, I hate to insist on this,' Bayard was trying hard to be polite, 'but my wife's papers are part of her estate, of which I am the executor. I must ask that they be returned to me.'

'Two answers to that, Ed. First, Hugh Loredon claimed they were given to him by Madeleine. If that is true, he had a perfect right to give them to whomever he chose—in this case, me. Any other claim would have to be proved in court. Second answer: in your own house I suggested there might be material like this floating about and that you should contemplate buying it in. You said, if I remember rightly: "I'm damned if I'll be the buyer!" I then told you that I would pick it up on my own account—my exact words . . . Do you remember that conversation?'

'I do now, though I had forgotten it. So in effect, you are claiming that Madeleine's papers are now your property?'

'No longer. They have passed out of my hands. If you wish, I can put you in touch with the attorneys who represent the present owners.'

'That won't be necessary. You've obviously studied the papers, otherwise you could never have written that portrait of Madeleine for *Belvedere*.'

'I've studied them, yes.'

'What . . . what sort of picture do they give of me and of our marriage?'

'It's very intimate' Mather said quietly. 'Intimate and, I have to say, damaging.'

'Do you or the present owners have any intention of publishing them?'

'I do not. The present owners may have, but I don't think they will. However I think it's entirely likely they will be subpoenaed as evidence for the defence. George Munsel has already discussed that with me.'

'Have you seen or do you know what Hugh Loredon wrote to the police?'

'I haven't seen it. I only know what he told me in Amsterdam, and that I am prepared to disclose only to Anne-Marie.'

'I want him to hear it, Max!' Anne-Marie cut swiftly into the talk. 'He has a right. Everything that happens now touches him. I'm selling his wife's pictures. I represent his collection. My father's testimony affects his life . . . Madeleine's papers were given to you.'

'To me. Exactly.' Mather was suddenly hostile. 'So whom I tell is my choice. I don't recognise Ed Bayard in this transaction—only you. What you tell him afterwards is your affair.'

'That's silly and obstinate.'

'No, my dear.' Bayard was himself again, measured and urbane. 'Max is being perfectly reasonable. It was a mistake for me to come. I'll call you in the morning at the gallery.' He set down his glass and moved towards the door. 'I must say, Max, you've changed since we first met.'

'It's been a painful process.' Mather's smile had little humour in it. 'I'm obviously a late developer.'

The door had hardly closed on the unwelcome guest when his control snapped and he rounded on Anne-Marie.

'What the hell do you mean, bringing him here without warning, without permission? This is my house, for Christ's sake!

You're a guest. You're a friend I'm trying to help. Bayard's bad news. You're stuck with him. I want him at arm's length.'

'He just wanted to apologise . . .'

'The hell he did! He wanted to know what I found out in Amsterdam, what's in Madeleine's papers, what sort of mess he's in. No way! He set the ground rules when he wouldn't lift a finger to find me an attorney for Leonie Danziger. He wanted to maintain an arm's-length position. He's got it. Now, why don't you fix us both a drink while I get dinner.'

'I don't want dinner. I want to talk to you.'

'Then I'll eat alone. You can talk while I'm cooking.'

'Max, this is too serious to fight about.'

'You're right. It's death and disaster. So why did you bring Ed Bayard into my living room? To make it worse?'

'I'm sorry. It just seemed natural and useful at the time. Max, please don't scold me any more. You don't know what it's been like, with Hugh dead and you away and the whole weight of everything pressing down on me. Today, for instance. Every-thing seemed to be going well. I'd got through a lot of work . . . your Tolentino stuff went out, the invitations to the opening. I'd coped pretty well with the press, I thought. Then I decided to walk through the place from top to bottom. It looks good, Max, it really does. The workmen have done a fine, clean job. Your apartment looks lovely. And it was while I was there that the horror hit me. That it was there it had all happened. The place seemed to change before my eyes. It was as if Madeleine were there clutching at me, trying to tell me something. I panicked, I ran downstairs and called Ed. He promised to come down right away. I went over to Negroni's and waited until he arrived. Then we walked around the place together and everything was normal again. So when he suggested I bring him to see you, it seemed the most natural thing in the world. I'm tired, Max. I'm scared of everything. You could sell me the Brooklyn Bridge if you just talked gently to me.'

'All right. Get the drinks, then sit up here on the stool and keep me company . . . I'll talk sweet and tender.'

Which wasn't an easy promise to keep when her first question was so basic and brutal. 'How did my father die?'

'He was terminal. He couldn't face a painful end so he opted for mercy-killing in a Dutch clinic. I offered to be with him. He wanted to be alone with the doctor who did it.'

'How was it done?'

'By injection.'

'I can understand why he didn't want me there. What did he write to the police?'

'I don't know; I'm guessing that it's very much the story he told me.'

'I have to know, Max.'

'You have to be patient while I explain the background, the kind of life Madi lived, the private world she constructed in that place.' He worked as he talked. The mechanical processes of preparation – the washing, chopping, mixing – gave distraction from the sombre line of the narrative, but try as he might he could not avoid his own grim conclusion: Hugh Loredon had denounced Leonie Danziger for a murder he had committed himself. He dared not put it into words, but he had the odd feeling that Anne-Marie had already understood.

It was a strange little tableau: Mather in a butcher's apron behind the servery counter, holding a chopping blade, Anne-Marie perched on a stool opposite him, pale and still as a stone sculpture.

Finally, she said in a small distant voice, 'I hear what you tell me, Max but I can't . . . I can't take it all in. I want to, but I can't. May I have another drink?'

'Sure. And you can pour one for me.'

She paused with the bottle in her hand and the glass still empty, to ask:

'Is this all . . . I mean, are you going to say all this in court?'

'I must.'

'So you're the real executioner, aren't you? You're the one holding the chopper, because nobody else knows as much as you do.'

'You expect me to let an innocent woman go to prison?'

'That's the problem, Max. Nobody's innocent. Everybody had a hand in Madeleine's death – Bayard, Hugh, Madi herself and all those nameless lovers. Everybody, Max, except you and me. But now, because I'm selling Madi's pictures, I've stirred up all

246

the mud again. And because my father told you truths and lies in the same breath, you're the man with the power of life and death.'

'But not over your father. He's out of it now.'

'What do you think is going to happen to Ed Bayard?'

'I don't know. I can't understand why Hugh didn't point the finger at him too. He was so much against your marrying Bayard that he would have done anything to break it off.'

Anne-Marie poured the two drinks and handed Mather his. She still seemed sunk in puzzled reverie, almost talking to herself.

'Ed Bayard's a sad man. He has no lightness, no laughter in him. Being close to him is like standing outside a prison and watching a face – a gentle, kind face – that peeps through the bars and then disappears. But my father's the one who escapes me utterly. I knew him and I loved him as the dashing, feckless, romantic fellow who stood up on the rostrum and sold things worth millions at the tap of a hammer. He bought me extravagant presents and made me understand what it meant to be flattered and courted as a woman. If you're a girl that's what fathers are meant for, Max. But this other side of him – the frightened one, the dark, vengeful, intriguing one – I don't know at all . . . I don't know how to place it in my life.'

'You don't try,' said Mather firmly. He began working on the food again, trimming the veal, flattening it with a mallet, making deliberately florid gestures. 'You have your future to think of and that's bound up in the gallery. You and I are going to take on this town – the press, the critics, the buyers. We're going to turn these goddamn disasters into a triumph. I'm going to the arraignment tomorrow. After that, I'm available full-time to work with your PR and advertising people and take media interviews. We both have dead to bury. Let's put 'em underground, say a prayer and leave 'em to God.'

'And what about the living, Max? What about Ed Bayard?'

'You're the one he's in love with. How do you feel about him?'

'Protective, grateful . . . impatient!'

'I don't hear eager, passionate, sexy . . . '

'Of course not!'

'Then you're playing games, aren't you? You're using him as

a life-raft. He's not going to be happy with that for ever. He's been there before with Madeleine. And remember that your father's last message to me was to make sure you never married him. What more can I say? You're a big girl now.'

'You could say you loved me and it would be nice to be back in Florence right now, drinking cocktails on the terrace and watching the sun go down behind the bell towers.'

'I could,' said Max Mather quietly. 'But it wouldn't be true. I'm hoping to get married.'

'My God!' Anne-Marie choked on her drink. 'That's one for the book – Max Mather getting married. Who is she, Max? She has to be rich. How old is she . . . do I know her?'

Then all of a sudden she was weeping uncontrollably, and when he tried to hold her she beat on his breast with her fists and thrust him away and rushed into the bedroom, locking the door behind her.

Mather was shocked by her outburst of emotion. His notion of his own worth had been so diminished and eroded by the traffic of casual affairs, even by the affectionate ease of this one, that he accepted and expected to be taken for granted as a piece of furniture in Anne-Marie's life. She could move it, sell it, give it away and no complaint would lie against her. He was reminded of the old Browning piece 'On a Toccata of Galuppi's': 'what was left of soul, I wonder, when the kissing had to stop.'

For the first time, Mather began truly to understand what was happening between himself and Gisela. This was no lightning-strike. Rather it was a slow and steady flowering of a kind of love which was new to him. Gisela was demanding more of him than any other woman had done. The kissing and the passionate coupling were fine, but not enough. She was reaching far beyond and inward to touch and hold his heart and his will.

For his own part, Mather was aware of new dimensions in himself. He was combative about the woman. He was jealous of the attention other men paid her. Her tough-minded scholarship challenged him to higher levels of personal accomplishment – and, he had to admit, to shame for his too facile conscience about life and loving.

He was fond of Anne-Marie. He hated to see her hurt or

threatened. But with Gisela he was a lover and in love, a suitor eager to prove himself.

When he called Anne-Marie for dinner an hour later she was calm again, her hair tidy, the tear-stains wiped away. She was ready to shrug away the outburst.

'I needed that, Max. You understand, don't you?'

'Sure.'

'You haven't told me about your wife-to-be.'

'For a good reason: I haven't asked her yet!'

'Who is she?'

'She's my lawyer in Zurich, Gisela Mundt. She's young, she's bright, she's pretty. She also lectures in law at the university. She's wakened both my heart and my sleeping conscience. What's more to tell?'

'That says it all, I guess. Does she know about your lurid past?'

'I haven't offered her a recital of the full score. But yes, she knows.'

'Where would you think of settling?'

'On the Continent – Zurich or Florence.'

'Which means we could keep on working together?'

'Of course.'

'Tell me about this syndicate of yours.'

He told her. Then she told him about Bayard's request for an exhibition of Cornelis Janzoon. Mather was furious.

'God, how I hate to be managed like a riding-school hack! Trot, canter, gallop. I'll have no part of that nonsense. On the other hand, I'd advise you to put in a bid for Janzoon. He's in the great genre tradition of the Dutch masters.'

'I can't afford any more outlay yet, Max. Right now we're absolutely dependent on the Bayard exhibition.'

'So let's talk about the campaign. What happened yesterday with the press?'

'Mostly it was phone calls – people trying to get a hook on a twelve-months-old story. I told them to call Ed Bayard, who has a very good defence system at his office. As far as we were concerned, I told them we'd hold a press conference as soon as you were back and have a special press preview at which further questions would be answered. You'll have to handle those functions, Max.'

'It's not going to be as easy as that. You may be quizzed about your father and his association with Madeleine Bayard. How will you answer?'

'My father lived his own life. I'm living mine.'

'Good. Now tell us, Miss Loredon, where does Ed Bayard fit into your life?'

'He's my landlord. I am selling his late wife's pictures and I represent his personal collection.'

'No special relationship?'

'None.'

'He says he'd marry you at the drop of a hat.'

'It takes two to do a hat-dance. Ed Bayard is a good friend and, as I hope he will tell you, I'm a very good art dealer . . . How am I doing, coach?'

'Great. Just hold that line.'

'Now what's your contribution to the interview, Max?'

'I feed in the market information: strong overseas interest, offer of new artists and, of course, Niccoló Tolentino. I'd like you to consider letting him open the show.'

'With all those Manhattan piranhas? They'd eat him alive.'

'Don't count on it. This is a very rare man who's spent all his life in the company of the great masters and can still weep at the wonder of them. I don't think the piranhas will even snap at him.'

'Let me think about it. People expect a fairly standard routine at an opening.'

'I know. Grab the grog and a canapé and a catalogue, wander around looking wise, making smart-ass comments and hoping somebody's looking at you instead of the pictures. Let's give 'em something a little different. Whether you like it or not, it will be different anyway.'

'I'm scared we're going to bomb, Max.'

'We won't let that happen. We may get people there for the wrong reasons, but we'll get people. How are you placed financially?'

She gave him a swift searching glance. 'That's not a question I'd expect from you, Max. Why do you ask?'

'Bear with me a minute. Did your father carry life insurance?'

'Yes. About half a million worth.'

'Which I presume comes to you?'

'I'm told so. Why?'

'Because if the manner of your father's death ever became public, the insurance company might—just might—institute an action claiming it was suicide, and then your claim could be in dispute.'

'Is there any reason why it should become public?'

'I'm the reason. I'm a witness for the defence in the trial of Danny Danziger. I have to answer whatever questions are put to me. This one may not come up; but if it does you may be damaged by the answer.'

'Well, it's still not quite the end of the world. Surprisingly, there is a trust fund worth about a quarter of a million. I didn't know of its existence until a couple of days ago when I got a letter from Lutz & Hengst, the attorneys who are trustees for the fund. Apparently I'm entitled to the income from it. The capital can only be touched with their consent. However, it's the cushion if I need one.'

'I think you may have to budget some larger funds for advertising and public relations.'

'I've thought of that. I'm prepared to spend if we have to.'

'Who set up the trust?'

'My father. About twelve months ago—which must have been about the time he first knew he was threatened. You and I were in Europe then. Your Pia must have fallen ill about the same time.'

'Thereabouts, yes.'

'Do you ever think of her now, Max?'

'Sometimes.'

'How?'

'Very tenderly.'

'That's good to hear.'

'It's odd . . . One day during the last bad times, she said: "You know, Max, I couldn't have been more trouble to you if I'd been your wife!" We laughed about it but she was right. Those were the times when we were closest—nearest, I guess, to a marriage.'

'You're a strange man, Max.'

'I can get stranger.'

'For instance?'

'Tomorrow, with luck, Danny Danziger will be out on bail. I'm going to bring her to the opening of the gallery.'

She gaped at him in utter disbelief. 'You can't!'

'I can. I will.'

'Max, for God's sake! It's my gallery. It's Bayard's building. We're exhibiting his dead wife's pictures—and you propose to waltz in with the woman who's accused of killing her? What are you trying to do to me?'

'Make your show a sell-out instead of a freeze-out. I intend to blow it up into the most scandalous success of the decade. There'll be lines around the block and wall-to-wall coverage in the media. Question is, whether you've got the nerve to carry it off?'

'You know me—little Orphan Annie. I always come through. But what about Ed Bayard?'

'Same question. Can he handle himself, or can you handle him?'

It was a long time before she spoke; then it was not to answer but to ask her own sombre question.

'Why is it, Max, that we're such good friends and yet you're suddenly so threatening to me?'

The arraignment of Leonie Danziger was strictly a non-event. The press left it to the regular court reporters who, on the principle that the arrest had been covered and the fireworks would come later, gave it minimal notice. The only members of the public in court were Harmon Seldes, Max Mather, a plain plumpish girl in a track-suit who introduced herself as Carol and half a dozen early morning gawkers who came inside for the warmth.

The prosecutor read the charge. George Munsel pleaded his client not guilty, promised a most vigorous defence, then asked that the accused be released on bail into his custody. He pointed out that she had an unblemished record, was gainfully employed by a distinguished magazine, owned her own residence in Manhattan and had never applied for a passport. The prosecution raised no objection. Bail was set at five thousand dollars. The case was set down for hearing in three months' time.

Leonie Danziger seemed dazed. She embraced Max Mather, thanked Munsel and Seldes, then surrendered herself to the girl in the track-suit like a convalescent to her nurse. As they filed out of the building, George Munsel issued a series of curt directions.

'Carol, you answer the phone. Danny is not, repeat *not*, available to any of the media. I want Max and Danny in my office at ten sharp tomorrow morning. Allow two hours at least for discussions. Max, I want you to bring the documents we were discussing yesterday and I need a complete minute of all your conversations in Amsterdam. That's all.'

He strode off—a tall, flailing figure towering above the local pygmies. Carol announced in firm, no-nonsense fashion. 'I'm taking Danny home now.'

She whistled a passing taxi, hustled Danny Danziger into it and was gone without a backward wave.

'Mother hen with her new chick,' commented Harmon Seldes. 'Our Danny was rather subdued, I thought?'

'She's in shock, for God's sake . . . and two nights behind bars is no fun.'

'Danny's tougher than she looks.' Seldes laughed. 'So are you for that matter, Max. I underrated you.'

'You wanted to talk about the Raphaels?'

'Indeed, yes.'

'How much has Berchmans told you?'

'That you have traced two Raphael copies to Brazil and that you are now the accredited agent of the Palombini for negotiating the recovery of the originals. I don't, of course, know any details.'

'Well, the appointment was the result of a coincidence. Palombini was in St Moritz at the same time I was. He made the suggestion then. I wasn't too keen; I'm busy on my own affairs. But he pressed the point and made a good offer. I accepted . . . simple as that.'

'But the copies in Brazil: copies of what?'

'The two portraits. The cartoons are not yet in question.'

As he retold the now familiar tale, Mather spun it out with endless details and anecdotes intended to divert Seldes from the fundamental question: how could the copies be classified as such without comparing them with the originals? But Harmon Seldes was too bright for such childish ruses. Inevitable as death, the question came again. Mather answered with deliberate care.

'Niccoló Tolentino was the key. He was a young man then, of course. He was commissioned by Luca to copy the two portraits. He handed the originals and the copies to Luca. He believes that the copies were taken to Brazil. It seems natural that Luca would want to hang on to the originals. But Tolentino has an infallible method of identifying his own work – a personal cipher built into the picture itself.'

'And do you know what that cipher is, Max?'

'Yes, I do.'

'How could you, if you've never seen copy or original?'

'Oh, ye of little faith!' Mather mocked him. 'This is the man who copied the damned things. Weeks and months of work. He sketched them for me from memory, showed me exactly how to identify the cipher and where to find it.'

'Could you show me?'

'I'll show both you and Berchmans when the pictures arrive from Brazil . . . But aren't you missing the point, Harmon? We're both scholars. We both committed ourselves to print on this subject; so far our theories are proving out beautifully.'

'What I'd hate to see,' Seldes was less than happy, 'is we two scholars proving our hypotheses and Henri Berchmans strolling off with the rewards.'

'I can't speak for Berchmans, but I fail to see that I'm any sort of a threat to you. I'm paid directly by the family only if and when the pieces are recovered by the family. I don't know the details of your arrangements with Berchmans, but it seems to me they have to be on a dealer or auction level. In which case, I don't see that there's any conflict of interest between you and me.'

'Only this, Max: fine art, Renaissance art, is my discipline. It's been my whole life. I'm better at it than you can ever be. It was my name which lent authority to your piece in *Belvedere*. I was the one who opened the pages to you anyway. I introduced you to Berchmans. I accepted your piece on Madeleine Bayard – and I have no part in that action at all.'

'No quarrel with any of that.' Mather was mildness itself. 'But make your point, please. Are you asking me for a percentage of what the Palombini pay me – if they ever do? Are you asking for some reward or bonus or whatever on the Madeleine Bayard situation? That's out of my hands, as you know. But you're clearly unhappy. What can I do to make you feel better?'

'In a word, Max, for a man of modest accomplishments you're riding too high. You're an upstart!'

'I'm sorry if it appears that way.'

'It does, believe me. I've dealt with Berchmans all my life. I've spent millions with him from the galleries. Now it's you he calls and not me. You make a big fuss of a copyist at the Pitti. God, I've known and bought and sold the biggest names of our time . . . I'd have thought it would have been the smallest of courtesies to bring my name forward to the Palombini.'

'Now cool down, Harmon. Shut up and relax before you say the unsayable. You're a great Renaissance scholar. Admitted. No question. I'm a much humbler animal, a not-bad palaeographer. But one of the things I'm very good at is method . . . you can't follow my trade without it. There would have been no point at all in my mentioning your name or Berchmans' or those of your Swiss colleagues with whom I've become very friendly. What do any of you represent to Palombini at this stage? Nothing except very expensive names – future commission takers! He's a merchant, for Christ's sake! He lives and breathes profit and loss. Me, he understands – I'm an old family retainer, old family legend. He knows where I fit, what I do, how I deal. In short he trusts me. He will also trust me when, or if – knowing where the Raphaels are, how they can be procured and sold into the market – I tell him it's time to bring in the experts like you and Berchmans and perhaps Hürliman in Zurich. But it isn't that time yet, Harmon. I haven't even told him about Eberhardt and Dandolo or the pictures in Brazil. And there's good reason for that, too, but I don't feel free to disclose it at this moment. That's all, Harmon, except to repeat that I know Palombini and he knows me and I believe this is the best way to deal with him. If that makes me an upstart, I'm sorry.'

'Please, the expressions were intemperate. But I'm sure you understand my anxieties?'

'Of course. Now let's forget the squabbles and talk about a follow-up piece on the Raphaels.'

'This time,' said Seldes, 'I'll do the piece. That will leave me free to speculate in a way that you, representing the family, may not care to do.'

'You're the editor, you hand out the assignments. Do you want to see my notes on the other subject: "Art and Criminality"?'

'Of course. Let me know when you have them ready and we'll talk. I must be getting back to the office. Split a cab with me?'

'No thanks, I'll stroll a while longer. You've given me a lot to think about.'

And what loomed largest and darkest in his mind was the thought that Harmon Seldes, with his affronted scholarship, his bruised vanity and his transparent greed, could make life very complicated for Max Mather. It took very little imagination to see that once Seldes began to meddle with the delicate mechanisms of information and negotiation which he had set in motion, the whole machine would disintegrate.

Max worried over the thought for half an hour; then he drank two cups of coffee, ate one soggy doughnut and headed uptown to his apartment to call Gisela Mundt and Alois Liepert.

FIFTEEN

'Have you got it all, Alois?'

'Every single word.' Liepert was beginning to sound frayed. The call had been going on for twenty minutes.

'Read it back to me once more, please.'

'Item one: in order to guard against any possible move to seize or distrain the art works, the portraits and the cartoons are to be placed in three separate deposits.

'Item two: the cartoons go to Gisevius in Basle to authenticate and then accept temporary museum custody and care at our expense. We will be responsible for insurance. Which at this moment we can't afford.

'Item three: if Gesevius accepts custody, then you keep one of the portraits in your own safe-deposit. We accept custody of the other.

'Item four: I will call Claudio Palombini and tell him we think we're on the track of the works. We ask him to hold himself ready to respond to your call for a conference either in the United States, London or Europe.

'Item five: I inform Palombini that you will provide authentication for the works and conduct negotiations with the present possessors. You will also be conducting exploratory discussions with Berchmans in New York, with Hürliman in Zurich, with Christie's in London and such other persons as you think may be suitable, to bring them into market once they are returned. You will at the appropriate moment introduce Palombini into these discussions, but only when a satisfactory negotiating position has been defined.

'Item six: I report to you urgently on progress or problems. I draw down funds for expenses and fees.'

'That last one is an interpolation, Alois.'

'But I know you'd want me to eat, my dear Max.'

'I do, but never to excess.'

'Now perhaps you will tell me why you are complicating your own life and ours.'

'Because if we come under any sort of threat – by default, by delinquency under the contract – we're holding insurance. We deal with one object at a time.'

'Why are you suddenly so anxious?'

'Probably because I'm back in New York. This is a very litigious town. The atmosphere gets to you very quickly.'

It was half the reason, but when he put down the phone the other half presented itself and it was not pretty to contemplate. The greed was getting to him now. He was as prickly and sensitive as a hungry hound, fearful that someone might snatch away his food-bowl. He needed the few minutes of love talk with Gisela to make him human again: her rush of emotion, her half-laughing, half-crying confession.

'I couldn't believe it, Max. The minute you left there was this big, black hole in my life.'

'There's not a hole in mine. There's just this room with me in it and a mirror I don't like looking at and a lot of people I hope won't come, but who keep crowding in. I wish you were here with me.'

'I can't be. So you have to come to me. Tell me what's happening.'

He told her, but the narrative lacked reality because he was suddenly aware of the insecurity of the telephone lines, the danger of casual intrusion upon his valuable secrets.

Gisela seemed to understand that and cautioned him, 'Max, I'm afraid for you. We've talked about this before. You're very impatient. You think every action by someone else requires a new answer from you. That makes you terribly vulnerable. Sit quietly, contain yourself, wait. . . . '

'I'll try.'

'I think you're doing the right thing to split the works and hold them with separate custodians. If necessary I can deal with one lot myself – and if you need a courier?'

'You'll be first on my list. I love you, *Gisela mia*.'

'I love you, Max. Call me soon again.'

'I promise.'

The rest of the day stretched before him, barren of comfort but full of busy, greedy demands. Calling George Munsel, he caught him just as he was going out to lunch. He told him of his evening's session with Anne-Marie Loredon. Then he made a suggestion.

'First, can you check whether any American insurance company or reinsurer has refused or deferred payment on euthanasia deaths in Holland? Second, Anne-Marie says there's a trust set up by her father about twelve months ago and administered by Lutz & Hengst. It occurred to me you might make a lawyer-to-lawyer inquiry about the consequences of any evidence I might give on the euthanasia issue, then find out who settled that trust and where the funds came from. Knowing Hugh Loredon's high-stepping style, I doubt he ever had two hundred and fifty thousand dollars at any one time in all his life.'

'You have some offbeat ideas, Mr Mather.' Munsel seemed amused. 'But I'll check it out. I'm glad you called. After our discussion tomorrow morning, we have a meeting with the two investigating officers on the case. I have their names here – Hartog and Bechstein. We should be through by one. After that, I thought you'd like to buy me lunch.'

'I'd be delighted.'

'Good. I also have a summary of the evidence in the Danziger case from the DA's office. In the light of what I've got, your record of the talks in Amsterdam and your interpretation of the diaries become vitally important.'

'I'll be ready with the notes on the talks. The diaries will entail a lot of slow, careful work.'

'You'll have time for it. The trial is three months away. See you at ten, Mr Mather.'

After that it was time to stroll round to Gino's for a gossip at the bar and a one-dish lunch and afterwards to plunge into Bloomingdales to buy himself some casual clothes, for the summer heat was still three months away. For the first time since he could remember, he was without a woman and ashamed to go chasing one. He remembered one long twilight evening, sitting on the porch with his father, and the young-old shrunken man telling him:

'You're alone coming in, son. You're alone going out. All your

259

life you're trying to escape the loneliness. You never do until you accept it. One day you sit down by yourself in a quiet place and start whistling a little tune or humming to yourself, or maybe just reciting nursery rhymes to cheer yourself up. Then, lo and behold, you're not by yourself any more. There are people just as alone as you listening to the small music, joining in, picking up the beat. You walk away . . . they follow you. It doesn't help too much because their heads are still buzzing, like yours, with their own business. But you're not alone any more. You may be lonely, but you're not alone. Am I making sense?'

Well, maybe he wasn't making sense at the time . . . but now? It would have been pleasant to buy him a drink and a plate of pasta at Gino's.

Back in his apartment, he telephoned the galleries of Berchmans et Cie. It took him ten minutes to establish that yes, Mr Berchmans had arrived; that yes, Mr Berchmans was expecting his call and yes, yes, yes, Mr Berchmans would certainly get his message as soon as he returned from lunch. Pending which Max Mather took out his note-pad and began, line by line, to reconstruct his dialogues in Amsterdam with the late Hugh Loredon.

At four in the afternoon Henri Berchmans called. He would be at his gallery until six. If Mr Mather would care to pass by he would be happy to receive him and show him beautiful things . . . which had to mean that the pictures had arrived from Camoens in Rio and Berchmans was feeling very good about them. Mather set down the last page of his Amsterdam dialogues, spruced himself up in grey slacks, blue blazer and club tie, then strolled uptown along Madison, window-shopping as he went to calm himself and damp down his jangling nerves.

This meeting would be the crucial one: his first encounter with the great white shark, when all his strength would be tested to the limit and all his weaknesses exploited without mercy. He passed a small store selling expensive optical ware. On an impulse he went in and bought himself a loupe. A block further on, he turned into a novelty store and bought a miniature pocket-knife which he hung on his key-chain. Then, as a salute to simple sentiment, he went into a flower shop and ordered an expensive arrangement to be sent to Gisela in Zurich and a small indoor plant as a welcome home to Leonie Danziger. As a final gesture of defiance, he bought a red rose for his own buttonhole; then, with a jauntiness he did not feel, he walked up the steps to Berchmans' gallery, a greystone mansion on Seventy-third between Madison and Fifth.

A uniformed doorman received him with gravity. A pretty girl welcomed him with a smile and rode up with him in a small ornate elevator to the second floor, where Berchmans received him in a long gallery from which every canvas had been removed and in which stood two easels, each covered with a velvet drape.

'So, my young friend. As usual your timing is excellent. This morning our ladies arrive from Brazil; this afternoon you present yourself. Let us look at these beauties together. Afterwards, we talk.'

He unveiled the pictures with a flourish and steered Mather to the spot on the floor where they could be viewed to the best advantage. Mather looked at them for a long time while Berchmans looked at Mather.

'Can you put names to them?'

'This one on the left is Donna Delfina; the one on the right is the daughter, the Maiden Beata. Excuse me just a moment.'

Using the loupe, he examined the Donna Delfina portrait. In the right-hand upper corner was a cluster of buildings dominated by a square crenellated tower whose walls were pierced with romanesque arched windows. In the topmost window, miniscule but clear, was the Tolentino monogram,

$$\text{ᚿ}$$

Mather turned to the portrait of the girl and, in the shadow of the lowest fold of the gown, found the same symbol.

'What are you looking for?' Berchmans was intrigued.

'I haven't finished yet. Hold this one for me, please.'

Then, as he had seen Tolentino do in Zurich, he scraped away a tiny area on the back of each panel, just large enough to distinguish the grain and texture of the wood. This was pure theatrics. He himself knew not enough to distinguish ash from birch from oak from a hole in the ground, but the monograms had told him what he wanted to know.

261

As he replaced the pictures on the easels, Berchmans said grudgingly, 'That was an interesting performance, Mr Mather. Now tell me what it means.'

Mather handed him the loupe and indicated the places he should inspect on the pictures.

'What am I looking for?'

'First tell me what you see.'

Berchmans took a long time to focus the lens and examine each painting. He repeated the process. Then he asked, 'And you scraped the back to see what kind of wood was used?'

'That's right.'

'I could have told you that at a glance. It's oak.'

'Now tell me what you saw in the paintings.'

'It looks like some sort of cipher.'

'It's a monogram.' Mather took out a card and sketched it. 'Like that?'

'Just like that. What does it signify?'

'It's the personal cipher of the man who copied these from the originals – which, by the way, were painted on cedar, not oak. His name is Niccoló Tolentino.'

'And you can verify that?'

'You can verify it for yourself, Mr Berchmans. I'll be bringing Tolentino to New York in mid-April.'

'Meantime, Mr Mather, I think you and I should begin to talk serious business.'

'My thought exactly.'

'Let's go into my office.'

He was just about to flip the velvet covers over the paintings when he paused and remarked, 'This Tolentino is a fine painter in his own right. You should do well with him in New York.'

'He commands respect,' Mather said quietly. 'He makes me examine my conscience.'

'An uncomfortable exercise,' Berchmans commented drily. 'Let's talk business.'

For the first time in their patchy acquaintance, Berchmans unbent sufficiently to call him by his first name and invite him into the private office where he dispensed hospitality and advice to wealthy clients. It was a small chamber panelled in white ash upon whose walls were displayed a Gauguin, a Manet and two

Cézannes: a still-life of plums and peaches and a version of the rocks at Estaque which Mather had never seen before. Offered whisky, Mather settled for mineral water.

Berchmans asked, 'So Max, where are we with our scandal?'

'Danny Danziger is out on bail. Munsel looks good as defence attorney. There's no way we can stop Madi's diaries being cited in evidence. However, what I can do is get you a photostat of the passages which refer to you. Then at least you'll be forewarned.'

'I'm very grateful.'

'Then you can do something for me.'

'If I can, of course. What's the problem?'

'Harmon Seldes. You told me he was jealous. He thinks – and has said – that I'm an upstart poaching on his preserves and taking over his relationship with you, which I gather has some financial basis.'

'It does.'

'He thinks I'm a threat to that. I am not. He also proposes to write a follow-up article on the Raphaels. He's perfectly entitled to do that. However, he may well make a fool of himself – and of you.'

'And what do you expect me to do about that?'

'Tell him what I am about to tell you . . . or as much as you think prudent.'

'I take it you have a proposition for me, Max?'

'No, Henri, I'm going to give you some information and you're going to give me some advice. It may well be that out of that exchange a profitable situation will develop.'

'Profitable to you or to me?'

'To you. My contract is directly with the Palombini. They pay me. I cannot accept kick-backs, over-riders, considerations of any kind from anyone else.'

'In short,' Berchmans' tone held a hint of mockery, 'a situation of purest morality.'

'Not exactly,' Mather laughed. 'A situation with certain flaws in it which, for that reason, requires very legal handling.'

'I'm intrigued,' said Berchmans. 'Please go on.'

'First, I'm the agent of the family, accredited by written contract to find the Raphaels and negotiate their sale. I cannot, however, make the final contract. They must do that. They will be introduced when a groundwork of discussions has been laid. Am I clear so far?'

'Admirably,' replied Berchmans. 'What is not so clear is why an ancient merchant family would appoint you as agent instead of handling matters themselves?'

'A number of reasons. This generation of Palombini was unaware of the existence of the Raphaels until I discovered the reference in the archive. They were also unaware – and chose to remain so for political reasons – of many transactions made by their wartime patriarch, Luca *l'ingannatore*. Luca survived by all sorts of stratagems, not all of which smell too good today. The deal with the German Eberhardt is a case in point. So nobody wants to dig up family skeletons. They prefer to leave them undisturbed in the vaults. However, I'm one of the family skeletons; I was the lover of the last matriarch, Pia. With me the family had no fear of blackmail. I organised a gesture that sat well with the Italian government: the donation of the Palombini archive to the National Library in Florence. Also – and this is important to them – they do not wish to raise any question for the Belle Arti about illegal export of national treasures. Therefore I am a useful emissary – I clear the streets before the procession passes!'

'I understand.' Berchmans nodded a ponderous agreement. 'It makes a devious kind of sense. But why, even before they know where the damned things are, why are they talking sales?'

'That's the simplest answer of all,' said Mather with a rueful grin. 'They were hit by the market crash in October; now they're twenty million dollars in the red and their notes fall due in June. When I wrote telling them what I'd discovered in the archive, they were hardly interested. Later, when we met by accident in Switzerland, they changed their minds. Now they're hoping the Raphaels will be their life-raft.'

'Provided they're found in time. But if the family is broke, how do they find money to buy them back? And then resell them at a profit? Whoever's got them must know their value and must have built up some title to possession.'

'I'm guessing.' Mather made no attempt to rebut the argument. 'I'm guessing that title is non-existent, weak or at best disputable. You know yourself there have been a number of recent cases where US courts have ordered the return of art works alienated during the Nazi occupation. Anyway, it's the best hypothesis I've got.'

'So far that's *all* you've got, isn't it Max?'

'Not quite,' said Mather with a smile. 'I know where one picture is – that's Donna Delfina. More than that, I'm sure I can make a deal to acquire it or – more correctly – ensure its return to the family.'

'Who will immediately offer it for sale.'

'That's right.'

'How will they prove it's authentic?'

'I've already had it checked by Tolentino. It is the one from which he made the copy you have downstairs.'

'So what are you asking of me?'

'The same advice as I'm asking from a small list of auctioneers and dealers: the best proposal to bring the Raphaels to market. When I make my recommendations on those proposals, Claudio Palombini decides who gets the selling contract.'

'And who are my competitors in this rather curious lottery?'

'One other dealer: Landsberg in Zurich.'

'I know him – a good man for this period.'

'Two auctioneers: Christies in London, Hürliman in Zurich. In New York, yourself.'

'Why did you pick the two Swiss candidates, Max?'

'Because, according to my information, they have a good clientele and are extremely discreet in their dealings. The one shadow that still hangs over this transaction is the Sovrintendenza delle Belle Arti in Italy. I don't want them to claim that the pictures must be imported back as a national treasure. After all, the Palombini live there. The last thing they want is a long lawsuit with the government. So I'm prepared, as indeed are the Palombini, to have a slightly muddy provenance.'

'Which doesn't help if you want a good price at auction.'

'But which need not be an impediment in a private sale – the kind of transaction in which you and Landsberg are experts. So my questions, Henri. Would you be interested to deal privately for us?'

'Yes.'

'At what percentage?'

'I need to take that under advisement.'

'Remembering, of course, that if we go to auction we pay twenty per cent.'

'But remembering also that the auctioneer is selling to me and people like me who trade for big institutions such as Getty and the Metropolitan – and sometimes with unique items there's an agreement to keep the price within reason.'

'A ring, in other words.'

'My dear Max, that's libellous!'

'Of course. My point is that the seller's commission must be competitive and there has to be a floor price to protect the interests of my client.'

'For objects of this value and rarity a syndicate of dealers might be advisable. Each big dealer has his own exclusive list of clients. A syndicate means that you can tap into a wider market without the publicity of an auction. But all this is predicated on three requirements. One: that you can offer clear title to the picture. Two: that it can be authenticated. Three: that whoever gets the first picture and makes a satisfactory market for it, gets first shot at the other items as and when they become available.'

'I would advise Palombini to accept those conditions – provided the first commission figure made sense.'

'I wonder,' said Berchmans, 'whether you understand what that commission pays for?'

'I think so.' Max Mather was singularly respectful. 'To quote Whistler: "the experience of a lifetime, the credit of a lifetime". Believe me, I don't underrate that. I would hope one day to have a fraction of that experience and credit; but to do so I must act as I am acting now to protect the interests of my client. I'm very small beer, Henri. I've wasted a lot of years playing around. But I'm not playing now . . . I'm doing my damnedest to learn from a master.'

'I'd say you're a fast learner.' It was hard to tell whether he was offering a gibe or a compliment. Mather waited for the rest of it. 'However I don't take pupils or apprentices. I have two sons who will inherit the business, so I use outsiders only to serve my own purposes. However, those whom I do use must merit my trust.'

'Then we understand each other. You have twenty-four hours

266

to respond on the commission figure. Otherwise I shall assume you are not interested. There is one other condition: satisfactory escrow arrangements for the passage of funds and the delivery of the pieces.'

'The Berchmans name is usually good enough.'

'The signature on the Raphael pictures in your studio is perfect . . . it is still not genuine.'

'And how would you know if it's perfect, Max?'

'I've seen the original. I've held it in my hands. During the escrow period it will lie in my safe-deposit. So you see why I make the point.'

'I also see,' said Henri Berchmans slowly, 'that you are much further along the road than I believed. In that case my commission will be twenty per cent.'

'Would you be open to a syndicate operation?'

'Reluctantly – and it could well be unnecessary. The two copies downstairs are splendid sales aids. It may well be that I shall come back to you with an offer very soon.'

'In that case I'll have a suggestion to make to you – something to add a little style to the deal, a little old-fashioned panache.'

'And what kind of nonsense do you have in mind, Max?'

It took some time to tell it, but Henri Berchmans listened to every word and at the end Mather thought he saw a twinkle in the dark shrewd eyes. On the other hand, it could just as easily have been a trick of the light reflecting off the granite.

When he left Berchmans, fatigue hit him like a hammer blow. Manhattan was his battlefield now. Every hour meant a new foray, a new skirmish. There was no longer any woman to whom he could turn to borrow strength or solace. He ate a quick taste-less meal in a coffee-shop, then went home, soaked in a hot tub, climbed into pyjamas and dressing-gown and settled down to yet another analysis of Madeleine Bayard's diaries. This time he decided to analyse her accounts of all the people in her life and compare her versions with his own experience. Ed Bayard was the first on the list, not only because he was her husband but because every day's entry took its key from their last encounter.

Not all were hostile or even abrasive. There were moments of serenity, more rarely of tenderness. The odd thing was that the abrasive encounters were followed by lively, even joyous entries, while the gentle ones segued into flashes of anger and frustration:

Last evening was so simple, so pleasantly bourgeois that it was almost comical. Ed was working over a brief, I was sketching and listening to Claudio Abbado playing a Mozart piano concerto. I kept saying to myself, I hope nothing happens to spoil this. And nothing did. We went to bed, we made love, we fell asleep. But this morning I couldn't wait to get out of the house! I am oppressed with ennui; it weighs on me like a leaden cape, stifling me. I look at the sketches I made last night. Dull, banal and academic. It is only when I am in this empty space that I take fire. Last night I was looking at Ed with love and tenderness. This morning over the breakfast table I could hardly be civil to him. I wish he would do something to outrage me, but no, he chips away like a sculptor trying to hew an angel out of this impossible piece of rock. All he succeeds in doing is call up the devil. I have called Peter to model for me this morning – now there's another kind of devil: mindless, stupid, vain, cruel – but his body is perfect and while I pay him he is all mine. I have learned to tame him with contempt, because I can buy twenty like him and he knows it.

A few days later the emotional tone reversed itself completely:

Whenever Ed is harassed in business he demands from me an instant concern. I must understand immediately the complexities of the problem, the clashing personalities. I must shower him with sympathy and solicitude. I tell him I can't do this. My mind, my emotions, don't work like that. I wouldn't expect him to nurse me like a child every time I was having problems with a canvas. If he needs that sort of comfort, he can buy it in a bath-house or with a call-girl. I wouldn't mind. I do mind and I do resent very much his tugging me this way and that as if I were a rag doll. But the moment I am back here I am calm again. I call Danny. She says she will come and sit for 'The Woman at the Window'. While she poses we talk. She tells me all her problems, with women and with men. I soothe her by gentle words. It gives me so much pleasure to see the taut muscles relax and her white body begin to transmit its fluid image on to the canvas. When it is over, we kiss a little and drink a little and make comforting love.

In another place there was mention of the manic aspect of Bayard's character:

He does not indulge in crude violence. He does not strike out or smash things. Sometimes I think it would be healthier if he did. Rather his rage turns inwards and is translated into something else – a studied menace like that of a villain in high tragedy. Except that this is not drama, but reality, and I confess that it frightens me terribly. It is like looking into the face of Siva the destroyer. I tried to catch the image in a sketch, hoping to exorcise it by putting it on canvas, but my hand balked and my memory went blank. I simply cannot face the studio alone today. I should go out, but that would mean I am defeated by Edmund. Instead I decide to call Hugh Loredon. He comes as always at the click of my fingers – but I know that he would respond in the same way to any good-looking woman. Hugh represents no triumph to me; I can summon him up like a court jester, certain that he will make me laugh – at myself and at him. But when I tell him about Ed and his black rages, he shakes his head despairingly and tells me, 'If you don't get away from each other, one of you is going to get killed – you mark my words, Madi. I don't know how you put up with this life. It's like a witches' brew, simmering and bubbling over the fire.' I tell him he exaggerates, but deep down I know he is telling the truth. I would like him to make love to me, but he's in a hurry to be off – to a viewing, he says, but I know he is saving himself for one of his women clients. Holding him is like trying to hold quicksilver.

The one area of their life that seemed to be safe from desecration was their mutual passion for collecting art. Madeleine's comments on a buying expedition were illuminating:

269

It is like changing partners in the middle of a dance. The moment he sees something that he likes – in this case a Georgia O'Keeffe, bleached rocks and a cactus flower, gigantic on a desert floor – he is suddenly transformed. It is like an exorcism: the devils cast out, the man left empty and innocent and trembling. He turns to me and says, 'I love this. Can you live with it? Tell me.' I always agree. I would be a monster to do otherwise, because his instinct is so right. I too admire the work, but between me and it are all the barriers of knowledge and – let me say it – all the jealousies of one artist envying the gifts of another. I tried to explain this to Henri Berchmans when he came to spend a few hours with me. He only laughed and told me: 'You artists are the spoilt children of God. He lets you peep into heaven. You still want to make mud pies in hell!' Then he made love to me like a farm boy in a hay-loft, fast and brutally. Yet he, too, makes me laugh and in a strange way helps me to forgive myself. That's the problem with Edmund. When the exorcism is over and the house is calm and empty, the devils come back – more numerous than before and terribly, terribly unforgiving.

And there, it seemed to Mather, was the whole key to the tragedy: two people who could never forgive each other for being what they were. Madeleine was just as implacable as her husband. Even the act of love became an act of vengeance. The pictures she painted were all of captives trying vainly to escape. It was strange that the only truly happy pieces were the erotic fantasies in which the participants were like playmates in some primal Eden. But even this illusion proved too fragile for comfort:

I know that Edmund buys the sex I refuse him; just as I buy or command or seduce the lovers I need instead of him. Henri Berchmans is right. We are both God's spoilt children, loaded with gifts that we do not know how to share. Hugh Loredon came to see me today. He told me that he had cancer and that the prognosis was not good. I knew he needed comfort. Suddenly I had nothing to offer. The presence of illness repelled me, I shuddered at his touch. He was terribly hurt. I have never seen anyone so frozen in anger, so filled with loathing. Yet I could not help myself. For the first time since I had known him, Hugh had nothing to say. There was a half-finished canvas on the easel. The model was a young girl from Negroni's, a dancer. Hugh looked at it in silence, then snatched up a brush and blotted out the image with great daubing strokes. Then he said, 'Somebody will kill you one day, Madi. Maybe I'll give myself the pleasure before I die.' From a man like Hugh it sounded like a Biblical curse. When he had gone, I cut the painting off the stretcher and began a new work altogether.

Mather marked the passage, knowing as he did so that it was too easy and too tempting an explanation for Madeleine's death. Hugh Loredon would have read it anyway, and might well have used it as a cue-card for the creation of his own fiction. It was midnight. Mather's eyes were burning. He was just about to close the book when another passage caught his eye:

The boys and girls from Negroni's are always experimenting with drugs of one kind or another. I have made it a rule that inside my doors nothing will be used. Peter, the stupid one, has tried to defy me: he smokes pot, he sniffs coke. This morning he made a big display while Danny and Paula were here, so I ordered him out. He refused to go. When I walked to the phone and dialled the police number, he tried to snatch the phone from my hand. I picked up the dagger which I use as a paper-knife and held the point against his crotch . . . he let go and walked out. I told him, never, *never* to come back. This and the rape incident were too much.

Paula left soon after, but Danny stayed. She was very angry. She reproached me in bitter words: 'I loved you, Madi. I would have done anything in the world for you. I trusted you. I played your little games because I believed they had meaning for us both. I thought you were the most beautiful, talented woman in the world. Look at you now! You're tearing yourself and everybody else to ribbons. You're looking like a slut; you haven't done a decent piece of work in weeks.' Furious because I knew she was right, I flew at her and slapped her. She snatched up the weapon and came at me with it. I dropped my arms and stood there. She froze in her tracks, then she tossed the dagger on the table. I begged her to stay and have a drink with me. Then we would start everything afresh: new pictures, new friends. She shook her head and walked away. I took a clean white canvas from the rack and began to prepare the background for a storm picture. About half an hour later Edmund walked in. It was the first time he had ever come unannounced. He said, 'I had the strangest feeling you might be in trouble. I thought I'd pick you up and take you home with me.' I thanked him and told him I was pleased he had come and that I was quite ready to leave.

Mather closed the book and put it in his briefcase with the rest of the documents ready for the morning conference with Munsel and the later meeting with the police. He was bone-weary, but after the reading his mind was racing like a buzz-saw. He poured himself a whisky, switched the television to a late-night Western and settled back to unwind. Then the janitor phoned. He was English, a recent migrant doing his best to lend a little tone to Manhattan. It seemed there was a Mr Bayard in the foyer. Was Mr Mather at home?

'Send him up,' said Mather wearily.

Bayard was a little drunk, but he looked fresh enough and he smelt of cheap bath soap and massage oil. He said:

'I know I'm intruding, but it's a bib . . . biblical counsel: "Never let the sun go down on your anger." The sun's down, but the moon's up. We were both angry last night.'

'Now we're just tired. Let's not prolong the agony, Ed. What can I do for you?'

'Anne-Marie called. She said you wanted to bring the Danziger woman to the opening.'

'That's right.'

'I just wanted you to know I concur . . . that's the word. I heartily concur.'

'I'm glad you see it that way.'

'Only possible way, Max. Innocent until proven guilty . . . justice seen to be done . . . all that. Very proper. I could use some coffee. This place I use, the women are expensive but the drinks are free. I drank quite a lot, so my performance was a little inhibited. You know what I mean?'

'I'll get the coffee.'

Bayard followed him into the kitchen, still talking.

'I agree with your policy on the exhibition, Max. The fat's in the fire now. Let it sizzle . . . make a blaze. What have we got to lose? Nothing. What have we got to win? Nothing but money. So I said to Anne-Marie: go for broke! No sugar, no milk, just black and strong! Another thing I wanted to say, Max . . .'

'Let's take our coffee inside, shall we?'

'Sure. Another thing I wanted to say, Max—I'm glad we're not rivals any more.'

'As far as I know, we never were.'

'I thought we were—which comes to the same thing. Now I hear you're marrying a Swiss miss?'

'So?'

'So congratulations.'

'Thank you.'

'And I'm going to ask Anne-Marie to marry me right after the exhibition.'

'It's probably wise to leave it until then; she's under a lot of stress right now.'

'But your being back is a great help, Max, a great help. Now about the other poor girl. Danziger . . .'

'What about her, Ed?'

'She didn't do it.'

'I know she didn't, Ed; but that has to be proven in court to a New York jury. If you know anything that can help her defence . . .'

'I know she didn't do it.'

'You said that. How do you know?'

'The blow, Max. The weapon. All wrong for a woman, especially this woman.'

'Then why did you bawl me out when I called from Zurich?'

'Because I hadn't had time to think about it. It was like getting a smack in the mouth.'

'Are you prepared to give evidence at the trial?'

'Max, Max, you're very thick in the head tonight. What I have is an opinion, not evidence. That's more than useless in court. But if anything else crops up I'll certainly be in touch.'

'Ed, it's very late, long past my bedtime. What did you really come for?'

'Oh, that? Yes, well, a number of things.' He began counting them off on his fingers. 'First, black coffee which is doing me a lot of good. Second, to tell you about Anne-Marie and myself. Third, to congratulate you on your engagement. Fourth, to tell you I'd rather not have your Florentine friend introduce Madi's pictures; Lebrun will do it very prettily. And fifth—what the hell was fifth? Oh yes—to invite you to dinner at my place next Wednesday. It's a sort of private preview for the exhibition, cream of the cream of Manhattan's connoisseurs. Twenty people, black tie. Anne-Marie will be my hostess. I'll be pairing you off with Mrs Lois Heilbronner. She tells me you once knew each other quite well.'

'Oh God,' Mather prayed in silence. 'Why now? Why me?'

But he knew the answer already. God was a practical joker who took care of drunks and madmen like Bayard but had no mercy at all on talented Casanovas like Max Mather.

SIXTEEN

'Y ou will sit at the head of the table, Miss Danziger.'
George Munsel was setting the scene for the morning's
conference. 'Max will sit to one side of you, slightly
removed; I will sit opposite him. Effectively you will be isolated
as you will be in court, as each witness is on the stand. That in
itself is a test of nerve and concentration. This morning, for the
purpose of this exercise, neither Max nor I is your friend. We are
old-fashioned inquisitors, interrogators intent only upon arriving
at the truth. Each of us has information which you do not
possess, so what you tell us will be tested against what we know
already. Is that clear?'

'Yes.'

'There will be no concessions in the questioning – no politeness. Are you prepared for that?'

'Yes.'

'If I choose to put you on the stand in court – and I haven't
decided that yet – you will be under oath. A false answer will
be perjury. You will answer now as if you were under oath.
Agreed?'

'Agreed.'

'How long had you known Madeleine Bayard?'

'About two years.'

'How did you meet?'

'I was working on a *Belvedere* piece called "Artists and Models".
Seldes had dug up some old photographs and prints of Montpar-
nasse and the Via Margutta in Rome and the Café de Paris in
London. He wanted to show the continuity with SoHo and the
Village today. One of the places I came to was Negroni's. One
of the people I met and talked to was Madeleine Bayard.'

'You became friends?'

'Yes.'

275

'You modelled for her occasionally?'

'Yes.'

'How long before you became lovers?'

'I suppose a couple of months.'

'Are your sexual preferences exclusively for women?'

'They were not then. They are now.'

'Why the change?'

'I think because I am no longer trying to be what I am not.'

'Was your relationship with Madeleine Bayard exclusive?'

'No. She had other lovers.'

'And you?'

'I followed her example.'

'You enjoyed the variety?'

'No. I found I . . . I wasn't built for it.'

'Can you explain that?'

'I felt that I was cutting myself up in little pieces like a wedding cake and handing myself out to be eaten. I was afraid the pieces would never come back together again. I needed . . . I need the security of a one-to-one relationship.'

'In other words, you are very possessive?'

'Yes.'

'Jealous?'

'Yes.'

'How jealous? Very, madly, insanely?'

'Very.'

'Enough to kill someone?'

'Enough to wonder if I could kill someone.'

'Yet you willingly took part in a variety of sexual entertainments with people of both sexes. These entertainments were organised and directed in the studio by Madeleine Bayard.'

'I took part. Not always willingly.'

'You protested?'

'Mostly I resented, silently.'

'When did you protest?'

'When I was forced by a man I did not like to do things I didn't want to do.'

'While Madeleine watched?'

'Yes.'

'And encouraged the performance?'

'Yes.'

'But when you protested?'

'She called a halt.'

'And how did you feel?'

'I hated her.'

'Ever afterwards?'

'No, I don't have that talent either. I can't love or hate too long or too deeply.'

'With your permission, George,' Mather cut into the interrogation, 'I'd like Danny to comment on certain notes I have. They're verbatim quotes from Madeleine's diaries. Did you know she kept a diary, Danny?'

'Yes. But she would never let me or anyone else read it.'

'Let me try some passages on you: "Paula and Danny are jealous of each other. I withdraw myself from them and have them make love with Lindy. Then I have Peter join in the play. I explain over and over that love should be fun, not fury. . . . " Does that refer to the occasion you have just mentioned?'

'Yes.'

'Would you say it's an accurate record of what happened?'

'Definitely not. It makes it sound as though it were a carefree romp, with Madi as . . . as mistress of ceremonies. But it wasn't at all. It was crude and cruel and . . . and dangerous.'

'Try this, then.' He read her the long recital of the drug episode and her own attack on Madeleine with the dagger. 'Is that a true recital?'

'No, it isn't. First of all Paula wasn't there – only Peter and Madi and myself. Madi is lying when she says she didn't allow drugs in the studio. She'd never have been able to stage her parties without them. But she never used them herself. She was too afraid of what they might do to her work – which was the only thing she respected. But yes, the kids from Negroni's brought them in . . . on this occasion Peter offered me coke. I refused it. It's too great a risk for me too; I depend on one talent. Then Peter began to get difficult. He had a kind of routine. He would coax first, then get playfully cruel, then quite violent. Madi just stood by and watched. I grabbed the dagger in one hand, a jar of raw turpentine in the other. I threw the turpentine in his face. It blinded him. Then I ran out, leaving Madi to clean

277

him up. I don't know what the date of that entry is, but I never went back to the studio until Madi called me on the day she died.'

'So what you are saying,' George Munsel picked up the interrogation, 'is that Madeleine's diary is an unreliable document?'

'I'm saying it's not a document. It's a story she made up each day to make it possible to live with herself. Look, she knew my weakness for her; she knew my indecision about my own sexual identity. But she was pandering me to this . . . this muscle-bound thug, Peter. Then of course it got out of hand. I could have killed him—or he could have hurt me very badly.'

'Could you have killed Madeleine?'

'A few times, yes.'

'Did you?'

'No.'

Munsel consulted his notes and then, in the same dry detached fashion, continued his inquisition.

'The day of the murder was February 18th. Tell me exactly what you did on that day.'

'I can't tell you exactly. The morning is clear enough, but the afternoon is a blur.'

'Tell me then what you remember.'

'I got up at seven and jogged until eight. Up Fifth to Seventieth Street, across to Madison, down Madison to Grand Central, across town and home.'

'What was the weather like?'

'Clear, but bitterly cold.'

'Then?'

'I showered, made breakfast, went down to the Public Library to look up a reference.'

'On what?'

'Michelangelo's forgery.'

'I'm not familiar with that.'

'Michelangelo spuriously aged a statue of a sleeping cupid for a Milanese dealer, who sold it as a genuine antique to Cardinal San Giorgio.'

'So you found the reference. Then?'

'I stopped at a stationery store to buy some manila envelopes and some gummed labels. Then I had some coffee.'

'Where?'

'Somewhere around Forty-seventh Street. After that I caught a cab and went home. There was a message on my machine from Madi, asking me to call her.'

'And you did?'

'Not immediately. I had been free of her for a while. I really didn't want to get involved again.'

'So why did you call back?'

'There was something about her voice that bothered me: it was slurred and stumbling, as if she were drunk. Then I wondered if she was having a stroke . . . I had seen that happen to an aunt of mine. I remembered it very vividly.'

'So finally you did call back?'

'Yes.'

'And Madeleine answered?'

'Yes.'

'How did she sound then?'

'Better, but still not herself. When I asked what she wanted, she said she wasn't feeling well and would I come down and have lunch with her. I asked if she were alone. She said she was. I agreed to go down and see her.'

'What time was this?'

'About noon.'

'Before or after?'

'Just after.'

'How do you know?'

'I switched on the radio as I came in; the twelve o'clock news had just begun.'

'How did you get to the studio?'

'By taxi.'

'What time did you arrive?'

'About ten to one.'

'How did you get in?'

'By the front door. I rang the bell and Madi let me in.'

'How was she dressed?'

'As always on a working day: a smock over a jumper and slacks.'

279

'What was she doing when you came? Painting, drawing, writing . . . what?'

'Painting. There was an unfinished canvas on the easel.'

'But you said she was unwell.'

'No. I said she sounded unwell and she told me she was unwell. She looked pasty and puffed around the face and her speech was definitely not normal.'

'So then what?'

'I asked her what was the matter. She told me the doctor had put her on sedatives, but she complained they were too strong and were slowing her down. I saw the whisky bottle and the glass. I warned her she shouldn't drink with sedatives, but she said she'd only had one small drink. Then I made her take off her smock and shoes and lie down. I covered her up and sat on the edge of the bed talking to her until she fell asleep. I didn't know quite what to do. I didn't want to stay there. I didn't want to leave her. So I went downstairs and hung the "Not back till 5.30" notice on the door. Then I called Mr Bayard at his office. They said he was out for lunch, would I leave a message? I thought better not. Then I tried Hugh Loredon. I knew they'd had a big fight over something, but Hugh was always very protective of her – and of me, for that matter. We'd made love a few times together and while it wasn't great it wasn't too bad either. Hugh was in his office. He told me not to hang around, just make sure Madi was covered and the heaters were left on. He'd be down in fifteen to twenty minutes, he said. I was glad to leave. Ever since the Peter episode I'd been wary of the bunch at Negroni's. So I let myself out of the back door, walked half a dozen blocks and took a taxi uptown.'

'With your permission, George,' Mather cut across the narrative, 'I'd like to ask about the heaters. That place is a great, cold barn. We've had to install air-conditioning to make it habitable. What was Madeleine Bayard using?'

'Gas heaters,' said Leonie. 'Those with a gas bottle on a trolley. You can move them from place to place, adjust the height and focus the heat. There were three on the second floor and six on the top floor, because there was no insulation under the rafters and the place cooled down very quickly.'

'So,' said Munsel, 'you've given us your story. Now let me

280

give you the one the prosecutor is going to put to the jury, with certain supporting evidence. Then Max here has another set of variations on the same theme. But just before we come to that, he has another question for you.'

'You sent to me in Zurich a summary of the police and press reports on the case. You sent me photographs. But you mentioned not one of the facts you've just revealed now. Why?'

'Because I had no idea I was under suspicion. I saw no reason to complicate my life with unnecessary revelations. And our relationship – yours and mine, Max – was on a strictly limited basis.'

'That's clear. Thank you. Over to you, George.'

'The case for the prosecution, as you will hear it outlined in court, is as follows. First, the time. A witness who was drinking coffee in Negroni's will testify that you entered the front door of the studio at ten minutes after two. The late Hugh Loredon testifies in a notarised statement made just before his death that you called him about a quarter to three and told him Madeleine was dead. That he told you to take the weapon, leave the studio by the back door and walk some distance before you took a taxi home . . . he would take care of the rest. Later in the day – that part of the day you're not very clear on – Loredon came to your apartment, where you told him how it all happened and he advised you to sit tight and say nothing and everything would turn out fine. So, the prosecutor will ask, how do you like them apples, Miss Danziger?'

'It's not true. It's simply not true.'

'But how do you prove that? You were seen going in to the studio more than an hour after the time you say you arrived. You admit you called Loredon. He says you were still there when he arrived and that you admitted killing Madeleine. The weapon was one you were familiar with. According to the diaries you had already threatened Madeleine with it. Even in your version, you threatened Peter. You say you called Ed Bayard first, but you didn't leave a message so there is no record of the call. Loredon's statement says he came to your apartment later. You say you remember very little of what happened that afternoon. Why is that?'

'I went to Roxanne's.'

'And who is Roxanne?'

'It's a club, a women's club. They call it the Sapphic Spa. I met some friends and we had drinks – too many drinks. Some of us decided to walk ourselves sober; the walk turned into a giggling bar-crawl. The only thing I remember clearly is coming home quite late and having to borrow my cab fare from the doorman.'

'And you have no recollection of Hugh Loredon's visit?'

'No.'

'Come back to Madeleine. You say you put her to bed with her clothes on?'

'Yes.'

'The police say she was naked and her clothes were folded neatly on a chair. The suggestion is, of course, that she had been entertaining a lover – a female lover, since there was no evidence of congress with a male. Now you two did have such encounters in the past, didn't you?'

'Yes.'

'And sometimes, as you have told us, they ended in quarrels?'

'Yes.'

'As this one did?'

'We did not make love. It happened exactly as I told you.'

'If you didn't kill Madi, who did?'

'The watcher in Negroni's. Hugh Loredon himself. How can I possibly know?'

'Who was the watcher in Negroni's?'

'It had to be Peter. He hated me enough to set me up for this.'

'But how could he know you would be there?'

'He could have persuaded Madi to invite me. He'd done it before. Madi was working on a male figure. It's possible he was the model.'

'Look at the other possible – Hugh Loredon. Can you see him as the killer?'

'I could never read Hugh very well. At first I liked him; everybody did. He . . . he was good for me emotionally at a very bad time. He was great at first aid, but never at after-care. But yes, there was a dark side to him and sometimes I think Madeleine awakened it.'

Once again Mather interpolated himself into the dialogue.

Holding up the sketchbooks to George Munsel, who nodded a silent assent, he explained them to Danny Danziger.

'These sketchbooks go with the diaries. Have you seen them?'

'I don't think so.'

'Then be prepared for a jolt. When you're over that, I want you to put a name to every person you can identify on every page.'

He passed the books to her. Both men watched her intently as she absorbed the first shock, then with deliberate care began to turn the pages. Finally she closed the books and looked up. She said coolly:

'They're like the diaries – wishful thinking, passion remembered long after passion was spent. They're like Beardsley drawings – exquisitely polished, no redundancies, no false steps. But if you'd ever watched her first thrusts at a subject, the bravura, the careless mastery. . . . Where are those sketches now? I know they existed because I was there when some of them were done.'

'Perhaps,' suggested Munsel mildly, 'she destroyed them herself after translating them into the form you have before you.'

'It's possible.' Nevertheless she sounded very dubious about it.

'Now,' Munsel directed her, 'let's go through the sketches again. You put a name to every face you know.'

When that was done, Mather made another incursion into the talk.

'Something bothers me. We can postulate a motive for Hugh Loredon to murder Madi. But why would he set you up to take the rap? No, don't say anything for a moment . . . I want to read you what he said to me in Amsterdam. This is not quite verbatim, but it's near enough: "I was her first man – which I was very proud of – a special kind of victory. Jesus, how naïve I was! The encounter was a mess for both of us." True or false, Danny?'

'True.' She was coldly angry. 'It was a mess – a scrambling humiliating little episode. He laughed it off. That was his way. I was sore inside and out. I hated him for that. Why would he set me up? He'd have set up his own mother if it suited him. But where does all this get me? Madi and Hugh are dead. Who speaks for Danny Danziger?'

'I do,' George Munsel smiled for the first time. 'And Max here is doing a splendid support job. You've stood up well to a rough session, so I think you're grown-up enough to listen to some straight talk—and at the same time not to start building false hopes. The fact is I don't want this case to go to trial at all. Nobody will come out clean; a lot of people will be smeared for life; the press will have a field day and justice will not be served. As of this moment the State's case isn't strong, but neither is ours. Between now and the trial date we've got to put together a brief that I can slap on the prosecutor's desk and convince him that he'd be a fool to proceed. . . . Not easy, mind you, not to bet on; but we'll be trying.'

'And what do I do in the meantime?'

'You work. You live a normal life. You keep a low profile, stay away from places like Roxanne's and don't discuss the case with anyone but me.'

'Not even Max?'

'Not even. He's a witness. I'm your attorney . . . which means . . .'

'Moses coming down from the mountain with horns of fire!' said Mather with a grin.

'It also means,' said Munsel, 'that Miss Danziger now pays you a cheque for ten thousand dollars, in repayment of the fees you advanced to me.'

'Can you afford it, Danny?'

'I can afford it,' she told him. 'But I'm still in your debt, Max. I can never thank you enough.'

Mather shook his head. He reached out to touch her hand.

'No debts. We're square now. We can afford to be friends. Also, we have work to do together.'

'Now go home,' said George Munsel briskly. 'Max and I still have our work to do.'

She was hardly gone when Munsel plunged into a new topic.

'Mercy killing at the request of the patient in another jurisdiction . . . to date there has been no litigation by United States companies to classify this as suicide. If the death certificate issued by the jurisdiction in which death occurred is in order, the demise will be accepted as normal and the insurance will be paid. So we should have no qualms about disclosure to the police on the manner of Hugh Loredon's death. Next question: the quarter-million trust fund established by Hugh, admin-

284

million trust fund established by Hugh, administered by Lutz & Hengst to the benefit of Anne-Marie Loredon. The original settlement was two hundred thousand dollars; the rest is accrued interest. The settlor was in fact Hugh Loredon.'

'Which doesn't help us much, does it?'

'Wait, my eager friend. Wait! The fund was opened with a banker's draft on Citibank. And that draft was paid for by a debit against the personal account of Edmund Justin Bayard. The date of the transaction was February 25th.'

'One week after Madeleine Bayard's death?'

'Precisely.'

'And that tells us . . .'

'It tells us nothing.' Munsel raised a cautionary hand. 'But it makes us ask a question: what consideration could Loredon, a notorious spendthrift, offer to Edmund Bayard in return for two hundred thousand dollars?'

'This was more than twelve months ago,' Mather reminded him, 'when Anne-Marie was still living abroad but Hugh had received the first intimations of a death sentence.'

'Let's meditate on it,' Munsel said. 'Very shortly you're going to have to front up to our two homicide investigators, Hartog and Bechstein. Your stance is full co-operation under advisement from me. Since you are being presented as an expert witness, they have to tread warily and you can be as friendly as your sunny nature dictates.'

'My sunny nature needs a cup of coffee.'

'While I'm getting it,' said Munsel, 'try this for size. . . . Hugh Loredon has got the big C. He's under sentence of death. Ed Bayard is serving a life sentence with a brilliant but bad-news wife. Loredon has also had his problems with the same lady, therefore he proposes a no-loss deal: "I'll knock her off if you set me up with a nest-egg for my darling daughter". . . . Cream and sugar?'

'Black, please.'

When Munsel returned with the coffee, Mather read him the passage from the diaries describing Loredon's announcement of his illness: 'I shuddered at his touch . . . I have never seen anyone so frozen in anger, so filled with loathing . . . He said,

"Someone will kill you one day, Madi. Maybe I'll give myself the pleasure. . . . "'

Munsel pursed his lips in doubt, then put the doubt into words. 'You can't have it both ways, Max. If you say the diaries are part invention, you can't suddenly turn them into factual evidence.'

'Then try this, George.' He turned back to his notes. 'I've had conversations with Bayard, once over dinner in his house. We were talking about Hugh Loredon. Bayard said, "I don't blame him for anything. I can't blame any of her men for taking what she offered." Question: why was Bayard so tolerant of a man who had made him a cuckold?'

'Not enough to hang a case on, Max.'

'We try, brother! We try!'

'Indeed you do. Now let's walk along the corridor and see how you handle a brace of New York's finest.'

Hartog and Bechstein were a very practised pair. Mather presented himself as a co-operative subject. George Munsel laid down the ground rules like a sensible umpire.

'Mr Mather is here of his own free will to assist you in any way possible. Since he will be an important witness for the defence, I must, however, instruct him from time to time on his responses. Clear, gentlemen?'

It was clear. Sam Hartog opened the dialogue.

'What is your relationship to the accused, Miss Danziger?'

'She is the editor appointed to me by *Belvedere*, the magazine for which I work. She's very good at her job. Our relations are amicable and productive.'

'Your relationship with the late Hugh Loredon?'

'Arose from a prior relationship with his daughter whom I met in Italy and with whom I now work. It was she who introduced me to him.'

'Did you have a close relationship with him?'

'No, but he knew I was a good friend to his daughter. He saw me in a . . . a protective role.'

'Protecting her from what?' It was Bechstein who asked the question.

'Business mistakes. She was just starting out on a risky enterprise.'

'Did you know he was ill?'

'Not until I spoke with him in London, before I joined him in Amsterdam.'

'Before he left New York, he handed you a briefcase.'

'That's right.'

'Containing what?'

'What I later discovered to be diaries, letters, notebooks and sketchbooks which had once belonged to Madeleine Bayard.'

'Were you not aware that this was evidentiary material in a murder case?'

'It was not represented to me as such. The murder took place more than a year ago when I was working in Italy. I saw the material as invaluable background on the life of a fine artist whose work was about to be exhibited posthumously.'

'In fact,' said George Munsel, 'the investigation having issued in an arrest and an indictment, this material will be used in defence evidence and will be exhibited to the prosecution at the proper time.'

'Your visit to Hugh Loredon in Holland.' This was Bechstein again. 'How did that come about?'

'When I spoke to him in London, he told me he was in the terminal stages of cancer. He was going to Holland to die. He didn't want his daughter to know or to be there. So he asked me.'

'To do what?'

'Hold his hand, hear his last confession.'

'Like a priest, you mean?'

'Something like that.'

'So what did he tell you?'

'A cock-and-bull story,' said Mather flatly, 'about how Danny Danziger murdered Madeleine Bayard, then called him and he told her to leave while he dressed the scene for the police. That's the broad outline. I have detailed notes.'

'Not just at this moment,' said George Munsel.

'And what was your reaction to this information?' Sam Hartog asked the question; Bechstein was watchful as a cat.

'I told him he was a bloody liar,' Mather replied. 'That his story was as full of holes as a Swiss cheese.'

'And his answer to that?'

287

'He admitted it.'

'Why didn't you report this to us? You knew we had an ongoing investigation.'

'Because I knew Hugh Loredon would be dead the next day. He'd arranged a mercy killing in the Dutch style. What evidence did I have of a one-to-one conversation? What I didn't know, of course, was that he had written to you denouncing Danny Danziger as the killer.'

Bechstein looked up sharply. 'That's an odd word, Mr Mather – denouncing.'

'I lived a long time in Italy. That's the phrase: you make a *denuncia*, you report someone. In the old days in Venice you slipped an anonymous note into a lion's mouth. After that the Council of Ten took over.'

'It's an interesting metaphor,' said Munsel. 'What you have, gentlemen, is an accusation written in *articulo mortis* by a man who's paying to get himself killed . . . and a perjured declaration from a witness at Negroni's.'

'How the hell do you know who our witness is?' Sam Hartog was visibly shaken.

'I'll show you a picture.' Munsel was mildness itself. 'Not yet of course, but when we're a little further down the track. I'm going to advise Mr Mather now that he's answered your key questions and should reserve the rest of his information for the court. That is, of course, if we get to court.'

'Meaning?' Bechstein, a good hunting hound, was instantly at the point.

'The courts are overcrowded, the judiciary is overworked. You've got mobsters and murderers walking free. If you really want to see justice done, you'll talk to the Man, tell him he hasn't got a case and that we'd be happy to prove it to him privately before he makes a fool of himself in public.'

'If you want to take a plea?'

'No plea.' George Munsel was suddenly grim. 'No deal. Your sources are tainted. Your case is bad. You're sitting on dynamite.'

'We'll talk to the Man,' Bechstein said.

'He won't like it,' said Hartog.

'He doesn't like it now,' said Bechstein. 'But that doesn't say

288

he'll change his mind. His middle name is Billy. Show him a stone wall and he'll try to butt it down.'

'Feed it to him,' suggested Munsel cheerfully, 'one spoonful at a time.'

Afterwards when they were strolling out to lunch, he handed Mather a slightly different proposition.

'We said true words and brave words. They're not enough because the law doesn't work that way. The boys know they've got a flawed case, so does the prosecutor. But he also knows that we don't want orgies and lesbian lovers and messed-up marriages spread all over the tabloids. So what he's going to calculate is whether it's worth taking a beating in court to stage an old-fashioned witch-hunt – sex in SoHo and all that. It will take time to work out the mathematics: elementary justice or a well-staged human sacrifice.'

Two days later Max Mather went through his own form of ritual death – moving himself and his possessions into his studio apartment in SoHo. The movers he hired were the 'nice Jewish boys' who advertised in *New York* magazine, who guaranteed to preserve him and his belongings from all harm and leave him relaxing in luxury at the day's end.

It was not their fault that it rained, that there were grid-locks on the crosstown arteries, that the trucks were late, that two movers and shakers had bad backs and another had wife problems. Neither was it their fault that it was after midnight when Mather dumped the last bag of trash at the collection point, vacuumed the last nap from the new carpet and found himself alone, like a lost animal in unfamiliar territory.

Below him were two empty floors smelling of new paint. The elevator grilles gleamed with polished brass and black ironwork; the ground-level doors were bolted and deadlocked, the windows grated with steel bars. Outside was an alien skyline and alien tribes moving in hostile streets. His only companion for the night was the fragile, faint piping ghost of Madeleine Bayard.

He was trying to read himself to sleep when the telephone rang. Anne-Marie was on the line.

'Max? Where are you? I'm sorry it was such a foul-up with the movers. I'm sorry I couldn't help, but I was racing about all day . . . I bled for you. I can't bear the thought of your spending your first night alone in that great barn. I've just picked up a champagne supper at the Chantilly. We'll have our own private housewarming. Don't worry, I've got a limousine. . . . The driver will wait at the door until you let me in. Don't fall asleep before I get there.'

The which, he told himself without too much conviction, was not forbidden fruit but an unsolicited gift which it would be churlish to refuse. In a dog's world, you had to give thanks for small mercies and always to keep a warm spot on the mat for the unexpected guest.

It was a kind of love feast. They did get sentimental about shared memories – the clamour of Sunday bells in Florence, drinks in Harry's Bar on the Lung'arno, summer sailing at Porto Santo Stefano; all the shared hopes that now, in strange and tortuous fashion, were becoming realities. They ate caviar, drank champagne and walked the empty building together, planning where to hang this or that picture, how to make the auditorium look like an assembly place for scholars and disciples. They rode upstairs in the elevator, tidied the supper mess and, because there was no other way to finish the evening and sign off from nostalgia, nestled together in the wide bed, turned out the lights and watched the big yellow moon setting over the roof-tops. They made love, laughing in the dark as they remembered old encounters and bed-habits. But afterwards came the slow insidious sadness and the silence of untold secrets.

Anne-Marie drew close and told him: 'I'm glad we had this, Max. It was a good way to sign off, wasn't it?'

'The best, *cara*. The best. It gives us both a clean start.'

'Not yet, Max. I know you've been trying to nurse me through the exhibition. I know that when it's over you'll be gone and we'll just be friends and colleagues. But it won't be as easy as that, Max. You can't leave me walking in the middle of a mine-field, not knowing when something's going to blow up in my face. You have to come clean with me now, otherwise this place will be enemy territory for the rest of my life.'

'You're asking me to hurt you – hurt you badly.'

'Better now, Max, better here, than later with another man who doesn't understand.'

He gathered her body close to his own and then, without gloss or excuse, he told her about her father, about Madeleine and Edmund Bayard and Leonie Danziger – and even about the final dark suspicion that hung over the trust fund. During the whole recital she said not a word. Her only response was the wetness of tears on his breast and the tremor as she absorbed each separate shock like a boxer under a rain of killing blows.

When the long sorry tale was ended, she lay huddled against him as if the slightest move would expose her to new pain. The first words she spoke had a strange Sibylline ring.

'Remember old Guido Valente in Florence? He used to read my palm at dinner. He said what was written there was the graffito of God and we were too stupid to read it.'

'I remember. Guido's coming to your opening.'

'I'm not sure I can face it, Max.'

'You can. You will. The worst is over now.'

'Not for Ed. He's lost everything, hasn't he? Including me. He's going to ask me to marry him . . . you know that.'

'So you wait till he asks and tell him gently: no thanks! That will be the end of it. Now curl up and go to sleep; it will be morning soon.'

SEVENTEEN

Morning brought a call from Alois Liepert in Zurich. Everything was going according to plan. Gisevius in Basel had been especially helpful over the cartoons. He was so pleased to have them, even in temporary care, that he had included them on his own insurance list free of charge – to encourage, as he put it, the idea of a later exhibition. Palombini was on notice about an early meeting. He was also becoming increasingly restless and curious. Liepert had had to remind him of the stringent provisions of the contract to settle him down. Then it appeared that his anxieties had been exacerbated by a cable from one Harmon Seldes asking for a special exclusive interview for *Belvedere* magazine.

Mather exploded. 'The bastard – that's the last thing we need.'

'Precisely what I told Palombini, who has sent a curt refusal and directed him to deal only through you.'

'He'll get more than a curt refusal from me.'

'Take it easy, Max. Everything is in good shape here. Where do you want to see Palombini?'

'In Zurich. I need you there – I'll call you tomorrow with a date. How's Gisela?'

'Well . . . and anxious to hear from you.'

'Tell her I'll call her first thing in the morning, Zurich time.'

'That means you're keeping late hours in New York, Max?'

'I've just moved into my new apartment. I'm still trying to find my way around it. By the way, call your friend at the gallery and tell him we expect active trading at the exhibition. If he wants to reserve any pictures from the transparencies we sent, he should let me know by telex and I'll reserve them for him. Also, pass a message to Hürliman that I may want to confer with them when I get back. But don't mention Palombini yet.'

'You sound like a busy boy, Max.'

292

'More than busy. The opening's just around the corner. We've got Danny Danziger out on bail, but the case still has to be fought.'

'No offence, Max; but that should double your sales.'

'You have the morals of a grave-robber, Alois.'

'It's the art business, Max. It seems to attract rogues and vagabonds. What else do you need done?'

'Get in touch with Tolentino. Make sure he's got his visa and his ticket; let me know his arrival time and I'll pick him up at the airport. Also call the National Library in Florence and see if they can give you a contact point in Washington for Guido Valente. If he's in the United States, I'd like him to be at the opening too.'

'Are you bringing Gisela over?'

'Yes. But she doesn't know it yet.'

'You'd better clear out all the other ladies before she gets there, Max. She's devoted to you, but if she catches you looking at another woman you'll find she's got emerald eyes and snakes in her hair!'

'I'll remember.' Mather laughed. 'Thanks for the help – I'll be in touch.'

When he called Henri Berchmans and told him of Seldes' indiscretion, Berchmans swore volubly. Mather added some terse comments.

'Palombini has cabled him to deal only through me. If I call him, I'll blow my stack and that will give him an excuse to fire me. I don't need the money, but my position at *Belvedere* is useful to us all at this moment. Useful to him too, only he's too dumb to see it.'

'Let me see if I can explain it to him.' Berchmans was measured and mild. 'That occasion – that piece of business we discussed. Would you have any objection to giving him a part in it . . . something to soothe his injured vanity?'

'Not at all. So long as he does as he's told.'

'Let me put it to him,' Berchmans suggested quietly, 'so that he consents to do as he's asked.'

'I am reproved.' Mather gave a small sour laugh. 'But thanks, Henri.'

'You're new in the business.' Berchmans was tolerant as a schoolmaster. 'You're suffering from first-night nerves.'

Mather's nerves were even more jangled when he rode down to the second floor to take the press conference which Anne-Marie and her public relations people had set up for him. Anne-Marie looked tired. There were dark hollows under her eyes, but she was very composed and there was a new, distant dignity in her bearing and in her speech. He took her hand and drew her to a quiet corner of the big room, out of earshot of the journalists who were filing into the rows of chairs.

'How are you holding, *cara*?'

'I'm fine, Max, I promise you. I'm in control now; the ghosts don't frighten me any more.'

'Some of them will pop their heads up in a few minutes.'

'I'm not scared – just bruised.'

'What's the name of the PR lady?'

'Chloe Childers.'

'My God, I don't believe it.'

Chloe – big, brusque and brash – collared him for final instructions. 'There are the usual warhorses from the arts pages, but most of this lot are news. All the TV stations are here and radio as well. I'll be chairperson and control the meeting. You field the questions. Ready?'

'Christians to the lions,' said Max Mather. 'Let's go.'

It was only when he stood at the lectern without a single note in his hand that he understood what a bad joke it was. These were the predators: young, fast on their feet and hungry for red meat. The first question set the tone.

'Mr Mather, what is your connection with the Liberation Gallery?'

'I represent it both as buyer and seller, especially in the European market where there is already lively interest in this exhibition.'

'How lively, sir?'

'I'm just off the phone. I'm awaiting confirmation of several orders from a Swiss dealer.'

'Madeleine Bayard was murdered in this building.'

'That's right – on the floor above.'

'May we see the place?'

'I'm afraid not. It's now my private apartment.'

'Is it haunted?'

That one got a laugh but he decided to take it quite seriously.

'Yes, it is. This whole building is haunted by the memory of a tragic woman of enormous talent. In a few days the first floor will be hung with her creations, some of which are illustrated in the photographs which you have been given. It's a vulgarism to think of haunting only in terms of terror. We are haunted also by beauty – and by what Wordsworth called "intimations of immortality".'

'What can you tell us about her death, Mr Mather?'

'Nothing.' Mather was curt. 'If you need that information, you'll find it in your own files.'

'And what about the woman who is accused of killing her – Leonie Danziger?'

'She has pleaded not guilty and has been released on bail. Her case is *sub judice* and I have no comment to make, except that she will be here on opening night as a guest of the gallery with the full knowledge and consent of Mr Edmund Bayard.'

They liked that. It was a piece of the raw meat they needed. They began to show some respect to the fellow who tossed it to them with ill-concealed contempt. This time the questioner was a woman.

'Mr Mather, Madeleine Bayard is said to have lived a very colourful and . . . well, promiscuous sex life. What have you to say about that?'

'First, madam, in spite of my obvious youth I'm an old-fashioned man. I was brought up never to kiss and tell and never to speak ill of the dead, who can't defend themselves. Also, there's the question of the living who, as you well know, can still sue for libel.'

'But, Mr Mather, don't you think. . . . '

'Please, madam. You asked the question. Let me answer it. In a very real sense, Madeleine Bayard's morals are irrelevant. When you look at the splendour of the Sistine Chapel, does it bother you that Michelangelo was an agonised homosexual? Who remembers or cares that Caravaggio was a riotous and quarrelsome fellow who killed a man in an affray and died as a result of violence? That is the kind of stuff you use to play Trivial

Pursuit . . . and this is an art gallery, not a coffee-shop. What we're privileged to sell is the stuff of dreams, which in the end are all we have to leave.'

'Talking of dreams . . . ' – this, Chloe whispered, was the *New York Times* – 'you appear to have a few of your own, Mr Mather. I understand you're going to stage a series of seminars at the gallery?'

'In this room,' he replied. 'Our first guest will be Niccoló Tolentino, who is recognised as one of the great restorers of Italy. He'll be doing a series of twelve lectures in the form of master-classes, on all the aspects of his craft.'

'And you think there will be an audience for that sort of thing?'

'It seems so. I know that since our first notices went out we've received more than a hundred applications for enrolment – about half from senior students, the rest from working staff at various collecting institutions.'

'Mr Mather, in this month's *Belvedere* you published a paper in which reference was made to works by Raphael, now lost. Has that brought any response?'

'Surprisingly, yes. Copies of the two paintings – that is to say, one copy of each – have been traced and identified.'

'You mean forgeries?'

'No, I mean exactly what I say: copies. I can't tell you any more at this moment because confidentiality is involved, but further announcements may be expected shortly.'

'About the originals?'

'We hope so.'

There was a momentary lull in the questioning, but it was only the calm before the storm. A girl in the back now held up a sheet of drawing-paper.

'This, I am told, is a sketch made in her studio by Madeleine Bayard. It's very erotic; some might even call it pornograhic. Any comment, Mr Mather?'

'I'd give you a piece of advice. Hang on to it – it's going to be very valuable, very soon.'

'Was Madeleine Bayard a pornographer, Mr Mather?'

'If you're asking me did she paint or draw erotic studies, I'm sure she did. Unfortunately we don't have any in our exhibition and so far none has been offered to the gallery. Again, I fail to see your point. J.M. Turner was a voyeur who used to visit the London brothels to draw the scenes he witnessed. John Ruskin, who wasn't very good in the sex department, took it on himself to destroy them. Loss or gain? Important? Or just another footnote to a great painter's legacy? Up to you to decide.'

'Mr Mather?' A plaintive voice from the middle of the hall belonged to a tall angular woman of indeterminate age but with a very determined jawline. 'It seems to me you're lecturing us. Why are you doing that?'

Suddenly all the tension in him dissolved. He grinned, shrugged and made amends with an eloquent gesture.

'Why? Because I'm the new boy and when someone pushes me, I push back. But the real reason is in front of you.' He stepped back, whipped off the white sheet that covered the easel and displayed the centrepiece of the exhibition: 'The Bag-Lady'. 'Take a good look at it, ladies and gentlemen, then decide what's relevant and what isn't.'

As he stepped down from the rostrum there was some scattered applause and then a concerted move to examine the picture while the cameramen jostled to get their shots. Chloe Childers gave him a discreet thumbs-up sign. Anne-Marie pressed his hand and whispered her thanks.

So, for good or ill, it was done. He lingered awhile for photographs with Anne-Marie, for TV dialogue shots and some puff-pastry questions from the gossip girls; then he retreated upstairs to call George Munsel and make his confession.

'You should know I had a long session with Anne-Marie Loredon last night. Ed Bayard's going to ask her to marry him – I felt she had to know the full story.'

Munsel's reaction was milder than he had expected. 'I doubt it was prudent. I agree it was probably necessary. How did she take it?'

'Pretty well, I think.'

'What's she going to do about Bayard?'

'Decline with thanks.'

'Question arises later; what are *we* going to do about him?'

'In what sense?'

'Warn him or whack him with it? We're back, you see, to misprision of a felony. Always awkward, mostly borderline. You

297

don't have to worry too much – I just want you to know that I'll be the one with the nightmares.'

'Why else does the client pay you, George? I'm only a witness serving the cause of justice. I've also just come from an exhausting press conference.'

'I hope you were discreet?'

'I was.'

'I'll be interested to see what they do to you.'

'Chop me up for hamburgers, I expect.'

'Before they do, I need you to finish your analysis of the diaries. If you need computer assistance I can offer some.'

'Thanks, but I'll do it the old-fashioned way: coloured pens and ruled columns. I'm not very educated, George.'

'I know. You get by on native cunning. It's an awful risk. Have a nice weekend.'

That brought him up short. This was Friday. He had no desire to spend a solitary weekend in SoHo. He looked at his watch. It was coming up to midday – six in the evening in Zurich. He called Gisela.

'If I stay here over the weekend I shall go out of my mind. I'm going to try to get a night flight to land me in Zurich early tomorrow morning. We could have the weekend together. Meantime, I'll give you Claudio Palombini's number. Track him down, wherever he is. Tell him it's life and death that I see him in Zurich on Monday – at my apartment and alone. Start on it now, will you, sweetheart? I'll call you back in two hours. Yes . . . of course I'm coming in anyway. You were right. This city's too full of temptations for a country boy. Oh yes, the latest news is that you're coming to New York for the opening of the gallery . . . Alois will give you leave. You can skip one university lecture, go sick, whatever. I'm picking up the tab. I know I'm spending money like a drunken sailor, but after Monday I'll either be rich or in jail.'

When he told Anne-Marie, she gave a small start of surprise and then nodded.

'I understand. But you will be back for Ed's dinner party on Wednesday? I couldn't face that one without you.'

'I couldn't face it without you either.' He told her about the ghost from his gaudy past, Mrs Lois Heilbrunner, and he was delighted to hear her laugh.

'That's the Max I used to know. I was afraid I'd lost him altogether. You were so formidable with the press this morning. Boy, they weren't prepared for what you dished out to them. Chloe's saying that while some of them may roast you, the gallery will get a good run and the TV segments will look great.'

'Name of the game.' Mather shrugged. 'They think they can make or break you. They can, but only if you let 'em. In the end, it's what's hanging on the walls that counts. Dream stuff is very durable.'

He had grace enough to realise that the phrase sat strangely on the lips of a man who was playing dice games for a hundred million dollars' worth of Raphaels. As he packed for the journey – clothes, documents, the Madeleine Bayard diaries, every relevant scrap of paper – a small cold finger of fear probed at his heart. It was one thing to play the publicity stakes in Manhattan, but to step into the spotlight and play truth and consequences with the moguls was another game altogether.

The overnight flight from New York landed him in Zurich at nine in the morning. Gisela, typically, was there to greet him and whisk him off to his apartment for bath, love-making and lunch in very extended order. It was a tardy but true admission that one of the things he had missed most in his life was a sense of homecoming, of being, after however long an absence, among the gods of one's own household. The household might be a moveable place, but the deities and the matron figure who kept the lamps trimmed before them defined the hearth and heartland of the dwelling.

Gisela had organised the weekend with a certain Swiss precision.

'Saturday is free for us, just us. Sunday we drive out into the country and spend the day in the place where I was born and which is now my dowry. You didn't know I was a land-owning lady, did you? The couple who run the place for me will serve us lunch. Alois Liepert and his family will join us, because I think you should talk to Alois before you meet Palombini on Monday. He gets in at ten and will come straight here. Alois suggests that he take you both to lunch at the Jägersverein.

299

Monday night's for you and me. Tuesday I've booked you back to New York. Now, tell me everything that you've been doing. . . . '

It was a long and often disjointed recital, but it led in the end to a question from Gisela.

'What do you really want to do with your life, Max?'

'That's not easy to answer. Let me try to reason something out with you, because I'm just beginning to come to terms with myself. I've told you about my father and my mother and the lifelong conflict between them. I couldn't face that kind of battle in my own married life. So the simple solution was never to get married and always maintain the liberty to walk away from an unsatisfactory relationship. Fine. But what was really satisfactory to me? In spite of everything, I'm not a bad scholar, I'm well grounded. My doctoral thesis wasn't bad. I got all that from my father – a fundamental respect for learning. From my mother I got a lot of unfulfilled desires and the notion that the world owed me a better living than I had . . . and frankly, I set out to collect it. You ask me what I want to do with my life. Two things. I want to repair the holes in my scholarship — and at the same time pay my way, and yours, with my own skills. I'm enjoying what I'm doing now – the hustle, the bustle, the horse-trading. And I'm best when I believe in what I've got – like the Bayard collection. I understand Niccoló Tolentino and Guido Valente. I think I understand you; but I do know I love you. You're the kind of people who keep people like me honest. So, in an ideal world, what would I like to do? Make enough money from what I'm doing to marry you and raise a family. Have enough leisure to take the fellowship that Guido Valente's waving under my nose and begin to tidy my academic mind . . .' He broke off, laughing a little uneasily at himself. 'That's the game plan. God knows if I can make it work.'

'I'm sure you can, my love.' Gisela laid a cool hand on his cheek. But none of it will happen until . . . '

'Until the bride price is paid and I've been washed clean in the blood of the lamb!' Max interrupted. 'That's what you're trying to say, isn't it?'

'Don't, Max! That's cruel. To yourself and to me.'

Her eyes were full of tears. He took her in his arms and held

300

her close for a long time, staring over her shoulder into a very uncertain future.

When Claudio Palombini arrived at the Sonnenberg apartment at a quarter to eleven on the Monday morning, Mather was waiting for him with fresh coffee and a small tabulated pile of notes and documents. He served the coffee and then, without preamble, made the opening move.

'Claudio, we're very near to success. I've asked you here because the next moves are crucial and there has to be complete understanding on both sides before they are made. Whatever is said in this room is private and can never be proved in a court of law. Am I making myself clear?'

'What you are saying is clear, Max. The reason for it is still a mystery. We have a contract, signed and notarised – I trust there is no requirement to vary it?'

'None,' said Mather. 'That's our starting point. Now take a look at these.' He laid out on the table the photographs of the two portraits and the five cartoons.

Palombini stared at them in wonderment. 'You mean . . . ?'

'This is your ancestor, Donna Delfina. This is her daughter, the Maiden Beata. These are five cartoons for an altar-piece for the votive chapel of St Gabriele which used to exist in the grounds of the Palombini villa.'

'I never heard of such a place.'

'It did exist. It was the scene of the rape and murder of a peasant girl. In the seventeenth century it was deconsecrated and destroyed.'

'And you know where these things are?'

'I do. I've seen them . . . I've authenticated them. I've even seen copies of the two portraits. But refresh your family memory with this.'

He handed Palombini the letter he had received weeks before from Guido Valente. Palombini read it slowly, then handed it back. Quietly, he said, 'I said a long time ago, Max, that I underrated you. Please go on.'

'Eberhardt died in Brazil. While we were both in St Moritz, I heard that Camilla Dandolo had returned to Italy and was living in Milan. I went to see her. I showed her the photographs. She recognised the two portraits as those which her husband had acquired from Luca Palombini during the war. After his death she sold them to a Brazilian dealer. They are now in New York on offer to Henri Berchams of Berchams et Cie, of whom you have no doubt heard.'

Palombini's face fell. 'So we've lost them.'

'No. I have personally verified in Berchams' presence that they are copies. The copyist's cipher is painted into both pictures and the wood is oak, not cedar. Now read this.'

He handed him a copy of Niccoló Tolentino's deposition made after viewing the portraits. Palombini read it and began hitting his forehead with the heel of his hand.

'Stupid, stupid! All this in our own city under my own silly snout and I see nothing. For the first time I begin to see what I am paying for. Now the big question: where are these things now?'

'All in safe custody in separate locations. The cartoons are in special care under museum conditions.'

'Who owns them?'

'A company which deals in art works – and other things.'

'Will they sell? Will they deal at the figure you specify in your contract – ten per cent recovery fee?'

'I have reason to believe they will.'

'Then what are we waiting for?'

'The solution to a problem – two problems in fact, though one is subordinate to the other. The first problem is title and provenance. Suppose you acquire these pictures now and you want to make a deal in the market – a legitimate deal, mind you, not a black market discount – you have to show clear title. You can prove that from the original document of 1505. You can prove it acceptably up to Luca during the war. After that there's a huge gap of more than forty years. Now even on a private sale, without the publicity of an auction, that's going to worry a big-money buyer. He's never going to be sure that his ownership is beyond challenge. The second problem, which is minor, because the pieces are *de facto* outside Italy, is the question of the export of national treasures; but with a forty-year gap in history, that difficulty can probably be sidestepped.'

'Which says to me,' Claudio Palombini gave him a long approving nod, 'that you have already worked out a solution.'

'It's the best you'll ever get.'

'Already you frighten me,' said Palombini. 'Remember that at the end of June I am bankrupt anyway.'

'Bear with me, Claudio . . . *pazienza!*'

He began laying out documents on the table.

'Item one: Valente's letter, Tolentino's deposition, clearly point to a wartime export traffic of various kinds by Luca Palombini. The family itself has had a continuous business presence in Switzerland for a long time. That more or less takes care of the export situation.

'Item two: Pia and I were lovers. From time to time she made me expensive gifts. These are the cards in her own handwriting; Here are two of her gifts – an antique watch valued at at least 100,000 US dollars; a comfit box, Louis XIV, valued at thirty.

'Item three: the photostat of Pia's holograph will which you gave to me on the day it was read at the villa. You will note that among her legacies to me is an object in the archives, provided it is not a manuscript and does not damage the sequence of the family history.

'Item four: this is the object I chose – a canvas bag covered with wax, sewn with cobbler's thread, which I carried, sealed, out of the country. No one – not even you, Claudio – bothered to ask me what I had chosen. You were perfectly prepared to alienate your whole family's archive to the National Library and this bag could have gone with it.

'Item five: the legal procurators of the company which now owns the art works will do exactly what its shareholders instruct.

'So there, if you care to use them, are your title and your provenance. If you care to dispute them, you will of course be disputing against your own interest, any immediate deal on the pictures will be impossible and the taint of the dispute will carry over for decades.'

For a long while Claudio Palombini sat staring at the papers and photographs spread in front of him. Mather refilled his coffee cup and passed it back to him. Palombini sipped the lukewarm liquid, then dabbed at his lips with a silk handkerchief.

Finally in a dead, cold voice he asked, 'Does all this come

under the original contract? If not, how much more does it cost
me?'

'The contract says fifteen per cent of what you receive – that
is to say, after auctioneer's or dealer's commissions.'

'That's right.'

'You know they will take twenty.'

'Yes.'

'For doing far less work than I have done. Without me,
Claudio, these things would have passed out of your hands
altogether and I'm advised that these documents give, inside or
outside Italy, a defensible claim to the art works. A holograph
will is a very potent instrument, as you know. The scale of Pia's
gifts was always high . . . I was not simply her lover, I was her
faithful body servant.'

'You're a *mascalzone*, Max, a crook.'

Mather smiled and shrugged.

'I can say that, Claudio. You can't, because the documents say
the opposite. I'm a trader like you – a sharp trader, but always
one step inside the law or half a pace outside it like Luca *l'ingannatore*, eh?'

'Oh, for Christ's sake – let's finish this comedy. Name the
price.'

'Five per cent.'

'That makes twenty all up – just to you.'

'I'll admit it's steep; but without me you wouldn't have
anything, would you?'

'Let's not argue any longer. How do we arrange this?'

'First . . . ' Mather was mildness itself, 'first we go to the
Jägersverein for lunch with Alois Liepert. Then we go to his
office where some documents await your signature. The first
document acknowledges that the Raphaels passed to me, in part
by gift and in part by legacy from Pia. The second document is
a bill of sale, whereby for the sum of five million dollars I sell
you the Raphaels. The third is a quit claim signed by us both,
acknowledging that no further claims will be made by either
party. The total cost to you is five per cent of market price, only
a third of what you're committed to pay me under the existing
contract.'

Claudio Palombini stared at him in utter disbelief.

'I don't believe this. You're passing up the best part of ten million dollars. Where's the catch?'

'The catch is in what happens if we don't do it. On the basis of the documents, I have better claim than you. You wrote me a letter disclaiming all knowledge of the Raphaels, remember? Also, I'm not amenable to the Italian government . . . you are. Even so, my claim could be disputed, so the whole transaction could end in limbo. From my point of view, I figure I've earned what I'm claiming because you simply couldn't have done what I did and built the Raphaels up to a high profile market item. *D'accordo?*'

'*D'accordo!*' Palombini agreed. 'But there's only one catch: I don't have five hundred *thousand* dollars to spend, let alone five million.'

'That's easy,' said Mather with a laugh. 'We hold the pictures until they're sold into the market. Alois Liepert holds the documents and demonstrates them as needed. One thing, though . . . you'll have to decide who's going to market the pieces and where. I've got some suggestions about that . . . and one of them is that you come to America.'

'Save them for lunch,' said Palombini. 'What I need at this moment is a stiff drink.'

'That makes two of us.'

As he was pouring the drinks, Claudio demanded, 'Why, Max? You're away free. You come back and make a lousy deal like this. Why?'

'I read my Dante.' Mather grinned at him over the glass. "*O dignitosa coscienza e netta.*" I've just discovered mine.'

For the first time Claudio returned the smile and raised his glass in a salute. 'The Palombini belong to another age. We cut our teeth on Machiavelli.'

The lunch at the Jägersverein was followed by a visit to the vaults to inspect the portrait of Donna Delfina, which was now the only one of the Raphaels left there. Palombini's reaction was almost the same as Tolentino's. He held the picture at arm's length, staring at it with tears in his eyes. Then he turned to them with a tremulous smile.

'You have to forgive me, but at the moment she looks like a miraculous ikon, the Madonna of Perpetual Help. I cannot tell

305

you how I felt these last months, watching the enterprises that my ancestors built go down the drain. . . . I have to apologise, Max. I called you a nasty name . . . Yet this is the second time you have brought succour to my family.'

'I'm an easy touch, Claudio.'

'We should all be so easy,' said Alois Liepert. 'Let's get back to the office and sign those papers.'

'You take Claudio with you. I'll join you later – I'm going out to buy an engagement ring.'

'Go to Barzini's,' Claudio advised. 'It's just a few doors down from here on the left. Hand them this card and they'll give you a decent discount. We own the place – or we will, after Master Raffaello of Urbino pays off our mortgage!'

That night at dinner, Mather slipped the ring on Gisela's finger and said quietly, 'I'd like you know, my love, that you're the most expensive woman I've ever bought. Today you cost me ten million dollars!'

To which, in her staunch country fashion, she answered, 'I'm sure you'll find me worth every cent of it – and I'm damn sure I'll last longer than the others did.'

EIGHTEEN

The moment he arrived at Kennedy, Mather telephoned
Henri Berchmans and arranged to call at his gallery on the
way downtown. Their talk was brisk and businesslike.

'Palombini now has clear title to the Raphael items, subject to
a payment to me,' Max began. 'So I still have control of the
situation. The provenance is clean and documented, though we'd
rather not have it published.'

'And all the documents are kosher?'

'Absolutely: a holograph will, gift notes, deed of sale. . . . '

'And my position?'

'Palombini is flying in for the Bayard exhibition, but principally
to see you. I have already put him in touch with your Swiss
colleagues, because I hope to do business with them later as well
as with you. My suggestions have been either a co-operative
effort over the three works or a division of the works between
you. Your conference with Palombini may produce other
solutions. I have done as I promised. It's over to you.'

'I appreciate what you have done. You've been very precise.'

'There's more. Palombini is bringing with him the original
Donna Delfina. He'll have his own guards on the plane but he'll
need your security people at this end, safe storage in your vaults
and extra protection at the showing. You may care to use the
occasion to interest a buyer – especially with Tolentino there.
We're agreed on the procedures at the exhibition?'

'Of course.'

'Mention will be made of your generous loan of early Bayard
works.'

'Thank you. I'll blush prettily,' Berchmans responded.

'Harmon Seldes will do the honours when I introduce Tolentino upstairs?'

'He was highly reluctant at first – he's still very upset with you

307

– but now that he smells money he'll become a pussycat again. By the way, for a pair of novices you and Miss Loredon didn't score too badly with the press; and the television shots of "The Bag-Lady" were splendid. I've already reserved that for myself.'

'Then I think that's about as tidy as we can get for now.'

'How tidy is the rest of it, Max? The police, the Danziger girl, Bayard himself?'

'There are still a lot of land-mines lying around. I hope none of them goes off before the exhibition. Oh, I almost forgot. These are photostats of the sections in Madeleine's diaries that refer to you – and these are a couple of sketches that might be useful for advertising!'

Berchmans scanned them quickly, then gave his harsh braying laugh. 'At least she gives me full credit for potency. My God, what testimonials!'

'I'm glad they make you happier.'

'Put it this way, Max: I won't have to spend any hush money on them.'

'There's Palombini's flight number and ETA. If you'll send the limo and the bodyguards we'll stop off here first, then you can deliver him to the Pierre. Now I must be going. À bientôt!'

'À bientôt . . . and again my compliments. Very precise, a very tidy mind.'

'A reminder, Henri.'

'Yes?'

'Palombini is now out of the woods. So don't try to squeeze him too hard.'

'You are wise beyond your years.' Berchmans waved him on his way. 'Go teach your grandmother to suck eggs!'

Anne-Marie was busy, tousled and happier than he had seen her for some time. She now had an assistant in the office, a fresh-faced junior with a pleasant smile and outgoing manner. She showed him the first press clippings, which spread over eight pages of a scrapbook. Most were good-humoured, a few were quite flattering and all made mention of the sudden theatrical effect of unveiling 'The Bag-Lady'.

'We couldn't really have expected better, Max . . . and already we've sold five pieces. Your Swiss people came in for three. Berchmans wants "The Bag-Lady" and one of the people at the press conference was an art editor who is also a collector. He bought one of the smaller canvases, "The Boy at the Pigeon-loft". It seems our luck is starting to run.'

'I'm sure it is. What do you hear from Ed Bayard?'

'Not too much. He's sent me a list of his dinner guests. They're all from the big collecting institutions—MOMA, the Metropolitan, the Whitney, the Guggenheim—and a few of the big dealers. I notice he hasn't asked Berchmans. I wonder why?'

'Don't ask. Has there been any more talk of marriage?'

'Not directly. He keeps talking about having discussions, seeing where we stand—after the exhibition, of course. He desperately wants your approval, Max. Now that he knows you're engaged to someone else, he seems to be making you into a kind of elder brother or father figure for me. Also, he tells me the police have been around to talk to him again; I feel dreadful, knowing what I do . . .'

'Don't think. Don't feel.' Mather was imperative. 'You promised to keep your mouth shut. Now do it and get on with the job.'

'Why are you so brutal about him, Max?'

'It's not about him. It's about you. Pity can be as deadly as hemlock for Anne-Marie Loredon. Now come upstairs while I unpack and I tell you some good news. We are going to have the best opening night New York has seen for years: a double feature. . . .'

'No, Max, please.'

'Please me no pleases, woman. Wait till you hear what I have to tell you.'

She listened, she protested; he argued; she finally agreed. There would be a double-headed evening. When the invited guests had made their ritual circuits of the exhibition and it seemed there were no more red stickers being requested, everyone would proceed to the conference space on the second floor to meet Niccoló Tolentino and hear him introduce his seminar programme.

This was a risk. Not only would the audience be drowsy with champagne, canapés and critical diarrhoea, but Manhattan art buffs were never noted for their tolerance or their good manners. Still, as Anne-Marie said after a couple of drinks, 'What the hell, we're riding our luck. Let's ride it till we take a fall!'

And then, as a wry little afterthought, she raised her glass in a toast. 'So my Max is finally hooked. I hate your Gisela in advance. But I wish you both the very best, Max. Truly I do.'

Edmund Justin Bayard's dinner party was a metaphor for the man himself: formal, punctilious, rich with professional talent, redolent of money, old and new. The talk was clubbish and cliquey; the focus of interest always somewhere over the shoulder of one's partner. In the case of Mrs Lois Heilbronner this was a mercy, because she was concentrating on a new young dealer from 57th Street rather than upon Max Mather, whom she relegated to the honour roll of 'dear friends and clever people'.

And yet the gathering was shrewdly put together. There were four major dealers. The rest were the heads of collecting institutions and their womenfolk, the ones who headed fund-raising committees and groups of volunteer guides and drives to canvass new members. These were the arbiters of taste, if not always of fashion. What they bought today would be blue chips in the art market tomorrow, though what were durables and what time would consume only time itself would tell.

The ritual of the evening was a fair copy of diplomatic procedure. Bayard and Anne-Marie received the guests, the waiters presented them with champagne and canapés and ushered them discreetly into the salon where Bayard's own collection was hung. This was sufficiently large and varied to break up the crowd and provide them with conversation pieces and pegs on which to hang a malicious comment or two. Nothing so vulgar as a name-tag was in evidence. This was the true family of elders to whom Max Mather addressed himself with assiduous courtesy. 'We haven't met. My name is Max Mather; I work with Anne-Marie.' If he was lucky it produced a trickle of talk; if he was unlucky, all he got was a polite murmur which left him free to retreat into obscurity with a fresh glass of champagne.

Dinner was served in the big dining hall where Madeleine Bayard's pictures were being displayed for the last time – a stroke of theatre which brought gasps of approval from even the most case-hardened cognoscenti. Attention was constantly divided between the plates and the pictures and there was a genuine warmth in the compliments that were passed to Bayard at one end of the table and Anne-Marie at the other. Clearly a speech – if not an oration – was called for; and between the dessert and the cheese, Ed Bayard delivered it.

'My dear friends, thank you for sharing this evening with me, the last evening which I shall spend in this room with Madeleine's canvases. Tomorrow they will be moved to Miss Loredon's gallery, to be placed on public exhibition and offered for sale. For me this marks the end of one life, but I trust it may be the beginning of a better one. We are all friends here. It is no secret that Madeleine and I never succeeded in making a happy marriage; but, strange as it may seem, it was a stable one and out of it grew, like poppies on a battlefield, the wonderful, truly wonderful works which surround you now. This toast which I now give you combines my salute to the woman who painted them and my thanks to the courageous young woman who has risked all that she has to exhibit them in her new gallery. I join them both in this toast because the artist cannot live without a patron to present her and, without the artist, the patron is left – as I shall be – with an empty room. To Madeleine, hail and farewell! To Anne-Marie, welcome!'

Even to Max Mather, who knew so many secrets, it was a moving performance. Several of the women wept openly, while the men blew their noses and echoed the toast a shade too loudly. Mather stole a glance at Anne-Marie. She was ashen-faced, hands clasped on the table, staring down at her bleached knuckles. There was a long pause when he was tempted to rise and make a short speech of thanks for her, but he thought better of it. This was Bayard's personal convention; let him handle it in his own fashion. Finally the man from the Whitney got to his feet, made a short but adequate and tactful response and sat down to a round of well-bred applause.

The rest, it seemed, was epilogue. Coffee was served, liqueurs were offered. Nobody wanted to smoke. The party declined to a decorous close. To Mather's surprise, Anne-Marie was one of the first to leave, driven home by Bayard's manservant. She did not offer him a lift but said in a quick whisper, 'Call me when you get home' before hurrying out.

When Mather came to take his leave, Bayard held him back. 'Don't go yet, please. I need to talk to you. Go through to my study – there's coffee and brandy.'

There was no good reason to refuse. He did as he was asked. When Bayard came in a few minutes later, he seemed sober enough but he was frayed and tense.

'Anne-Marie was upset by my speech: angry and embarrassed, was how she put it. She told me she needed to be alone for a while. Did I say anything offensive?'

'Offensive, no; I thought it was a very appropriate and dignified speech. But it was a little tactless to join the two women in one toast.'

'Oh, God, I hadn't thought of it that way – I meant what I said.'

'That was evident.'

'Especially about the new beginning . . . is that possible, do you think?'

'In general, it's always possible.'

'But for me in particular?'

'Ed, that's an unfair question. What do I know? How can I tell what your needs are, what would make a new start for you?'

'You know one thing – marriage to Anne-Marie.'

'I know you want to marry her – but that's not quite the point, is it? Come on, Ed. It's late. . . . ' He tried to make a joke of it. 'I'm not in the marriage market. After all, I'm bespoken now and I've just bought a very expensive ring for my Gisela, whom you'll meet at the opening.'

'I hope she's not an artist.'

'No, she's a lawyer, like you. She teaches jurisprudence in Zurich.'

'Then you have a chance.' Bayard's self-control began to break down. There was a manic intensity in his look and in his speech. 'Madi and I didn't . . . not a snowflake's chance in hell. You see, Max, artists are different from us. They belong to another plane of being. They're sacred, magical – like temple prostitutes or the vestal virgins. That doesn't mean they're good or bad – they're different. They don't need us. When they're sad or glad or frightened, they don't turn to us; they climb up to their tower of silence and look out on landscapes we'll never know, and when they come down they're purged and refreshed and they bring their works like a talisman of comfort. But not for us, Max. We're still grieving for them and for our own loss. With Madi it wasn't the infidelities, the perversities. I could wear those . . . I did. But I could never endure the separateness, the difference, the never, never sharing. Do you know anything about mythology, Max?'

'A little. Why?'

'Nemesis, Max. Nemesis was woman. She was the Daughter of Night, the avenger of those who were insolent to the gods, who failed to understand and respect the order of things. Madi was my nemesis. I thought I could change what was graven into the granite on the first day of creation. I tried to turn the sacred into the ordinary, the magical into the banal. Tonight I was trying to reverse the act, put back the magic, lift up the sacred signs again. But it didn't work. So the Daughter of the Night stalks me to exact retribution.'

'Ed, my friend, it's late. We're full of food and wine and this is very heady stuff. Let's call it a night, eh?'

'I'm sorry. We will. We must. But I need one answer from you, Max, just one.'

'Let's hear the question.'

'If I ask Anne-Marie to marry me, will she say yes or no?'

'I can't answer that, Ed. Ask the lady.'

'I tried to, tonight. She broke up and demanded to be taken home.'

'You can hardly blame her. That was a very emotional speech you made and it broke up a lot of people. Imagine what it did to her.'

'Can't you imagine what this is doing to me? I'm on my knees, Max, I'm begging. Is it too much to ask to be spared any more humiliation? You know her mind, Max. She's told me that: "Max understands. With Max, I don't have to make long explanations. Max accepts . . . " So tell me, Max, do I have a chance? Is it worth waiting?'

There was a sudden chill silence in the room. The only thing Mather could see clearly was Anne-Marie, white-faced and

313

distraught, sitting in Madeleine's place at the dinner table. His mouth was dry, it was an effort to shape the words.

'No, Ed, you don't have a chance. She'll never marry you.'

'Has she said why?'

'You and I know why, Ed.'

'Yes.' Suddenly Bayard was calm. The transformation was eerie. 'Yes, I suppose we do.' He stood up and held out his hand. 'Thank you for coming, Max. Thank you for being honest with me. You can tell Anne-Marie she won't be bothered any more. I'll see you at the exhibition – you can introduce me to your Swiss lady.'

'You're not going to supervise the hanging of the pictures?'

'No, that would be inappropriate. They're out of my hands now . . . everything's out of my hands. Would you like my man to drive you home?'

'No thanks. I'll walk a while and pick up a cab. Thanks again for the evening.'

'You're welcome. Good night, Max.'

Mather did not go straight home, but walked round to Anne-Marie's apartment. She was in dressing-gown and slippers, sitting in front of the television with a drink beside her. She offered him a brandy. He refused and asked: 'What happened tonight? Why did you run off like that?'

'It was the speech, Max. It was weird. It was as if, with all those people, he was walking me into a web and I knew that once I was trapped I would never get out. Then, while everyone was milling around after coffee, he called me into his study and offered me what he called a good-luck gift for the opening. It was Madi's engagement ring . . . that was the last straw. I had to leave or have screaming hysterics. I'm dreading the next few days.'

'You needn't. I spoke for you . . . I told him you'd never marry him.'

'How did he take it? Was he angry? Hurt?'

'He'd been fairly manic when we started, but by then he was very calm. It's done, girl. Don't go back trying to trim the hedge and make it all look neat and tidy. It isn't, it's a ragged mess; but you're out of it. Now stay out. Are you hearing me?'

'I'm hearing you. Do you want to stay the night? It's a long hike downtown.'

'I'd better push along; but thanks, anyway.'

'Does this mean you're a reformed character, Max?'

'It means I'm trying to be. I've been lucky and scraped home by the skin of my teeth. If I foul this up, I may not get another chance. *Sogni d'oro, bambina*; golden dreams!'

Niccoló Tolentino arrived the next day and was lodged in the guest bedroom of Mather's apartment. They spent a couple of hours going over the protocols of opening night and discussing the content of the seminar lectures, then Mather handed him over to Anne-Marie to lend a critical eye at the hanging of the Bayard pictures. The old man nodded approval of what he saw, then launched into eloquent praise of a talent cut off so early.

Mather went uptown to sit in on the first meeting with Palombini and Henri Berchmans who, freebooters both, fenced carefully and respectfully until the Donna Delfina was unpacked and displayed under the lights. Then they both fell silent. Palombini crossed himself. Berchmans breathed what sounded very like a prayer: *'Mon Dieu! Quelle merveille!'* When they began to talk again, it was no longer a fencing match but an almost reverent assessment of how this miraculous survival should be exposed to buyers. His task completed, Mather left them to it and walked over to the *Belvedere* offices to make his peace with Harmon Seldes.

The gesture had an immediate effect – not unaided by the fact that Seldes was now a sharer in a very profitable Berchmans deal. He was flattered also by the invitation to present Tolentino – and even more interested in Mather's suggestion that *Belvedere* should sponsor the seminars as an ongoing project. The conjunction of this proposal and the discovery of the Raphaels gave him instant access to top management and he promised an early answer which, if it were favourable, would be announced on opening night. As for Max himself, obviously in view of all that had happened some upward review of his arrangements could be contemplated if he were willing to continue on the magazine.

Max was willing. His luck was running. He had no alternative but to run with it. The only negative – large enough, in all conscience – was George Munsel's report on his first conference with the prosecution.

'So far, they're holding firm; they swear they've got a good case and are prepared to fight it to a finish. They're willing to let us plead to a lesser charge, but that's as far as they'll go at this moment. However, it's early days yet. Have you done any more work on the analysis of the diaries?'

'Not yet. I've had a lot on my plate.'

'I've got a woman's life and liberty on mine.'

'I'm sorry, George. As soon as the exhibition's launched you'll have my total attention. Which reminds me . . . I'm bringing Gisela across for the opening. Could you pick up Danny Danziger and escort her? It's probably an appropriate pairing – counsel and client.'

'Very appropriate,' Munsel agreed. 'Now tell me about your dinner party with Bayard.'

He listened intently as Mather talked him through the evening's events and then asked for a replay on both the speech and their final dialogue in the study. His comment was anxious.

'Problem with Bayard is that he's a sentimentalist.'

'Come again, George?'

'It's a phrase that's stuck in my mind for twenty years. George Meredith . . . does anyone read him nowadays, I wonder?'

'What the hell's he got to do with Bayard?'

'Somewhere, I think it was in *Sandra Belloni*, he wrote: "Despair is a wilful business . . . native to the sentimentalist of the better order."'

'That's a very snobbish piece of phrase-making!'

'I wonder if it is.' Munsel was thoughtful. However you define it, despair is a terminal event. The old divines used to call it the sin against the Holy Spirit. Anyway, we'll see. I'd better telephone Danny Danziger and arrange to do my Prince Charming act.'

'You'd have more hope as a princess, George.'

'I know, but I don't have the build for it.'

So far it was all rehearsal time, lighting and walk-through, with nerves frayed and people snapping at each other for no reason at all. Niccoló Tolentino absented himself with sketchbook

316

and paint-box to set down his first impressions of Little Italy. Guido Valente called from Washington to say he would be arriving late, but would most certainly be present. A temporary foul-up in the track lighting was soon fixed and the pictures looked great against the neutral panels. Mather drove out to Kennedy to pick up Gisela, who was as excited as a schoolgirl at her first sight of Manhattan. Anne-Marie gave her a more generous welcome than he had expected and whispered in passing, 'Nice work, Max. Congratulations!'

Three hours later the overture began when a Brinks van pulled up outside the gallery. After a small army of security men had positioned themselves around the approaches and on each floor of the building, two of Berchmans' minions carried two carefully wrapped packages inside, unwrapped them on the second floor, laid them on twin easels and covered them with linen sheets. In Mather's apartment Anne-Marie and Gisela dressed in one bedroom, while in the other Mather knotted Tolentino's bow-tie and fumbled with the pearl studs in his old-fashioned starched shirt-front. By six-thirty the guards were in position, armed and watchful; the caterers were standing by with drink trays and canapés. The visitors' book was laid open with a gold pen on a little gold safety-chain. A clerk sat ready to record purchases. Anne-Marie, Ed Bayard and Max Mather took their places in the receiving line, while Niccoló Tolentino took Gisela on his arm and led her to a safe distance from the entrance, proud as an Italian uncle. As if they had appeared out of the woodwork Hartog and Bechstein arrived – Hartog dapper as a fashion plate, Bechstein crumpled and uncomfortable in a stiff wing collar. Then suddenly it was curtain time and the tragi-comedy of a new Manhattan opening began.

Anne-Marie had been afraid of a freeze. Instead they had a near riot. Every name on the guest list showed up. The street was jammed with gawkers and would-be gate-crashers, drawn by the unusual spectacle of a black-tie affair south of Houston, with enough hired muscle to police a prize-fight. The ceremonial opening was set down for seven o'clock, but it was seven-fifteen before the doors were closed and Mather made his way to the microphone to begin proceedings.

'Miss Loredon has asked me to speak for her tonight and to

welcome you all to this first show at the Liberation Gallery. There are reasons for her choice: I work here, so I have to sing for my supper; I'm taller than she is and my voice is bigger – though I'm not nearly as good looking; finally, she doesn't want to talk about this exhibition, she believes it speaks for itself. However, both Miss Loredon and Mr Bayard felt that it would be appropriate to have the exhibition formally opened by the man who was the first, the very first in New York to buy a Madeleine Bayard canvas – Mr André Lebrun!'

However, before he brought Mr Lebrun to the microphone he wanted to call everyone's attention to a singular event on the programme. At eight o'clock, after everyone had had time to enjoy the Bayard canvases, a bell would sound and they would be asked to proceed upstairs in an orderly fashion, to witness a unique and historic event in the art world. This event had been arranged by courtesy of the Palombini family and of Mr Henri Berchmans, who had kindly lent his own Madeleine Bayards to grace the exhibition. It would be introduced by Mr Harmon Seldes, editor of *Belvedere* magazine, the sponsors of the forthcoming Tolentino seminars. Now, without more ado, he would call upon Mr André Lebrun to open the exhibition. . . .

Lebrun was a mistake but a long way short of a disaster. He was excited. He was prolix. His accent was distorted by the microphone. But there was no doubting the sincerity of his praise and the underlying pathos of the story he could not tell. The audience gave him a solid round of applause before dispersing to continue their rounds of the exhibits.

Henri Berchmans tapped Mather on the shoulder and growled his approval.

'That was good – brief and to the point. You look at pictures. You don't audition them. See you upstairs.'

Anne-Marie gave him news on the wing. 'Fifteen red stickers already and they're busy at the desk. Keep your fingers crossed.'

'How's Ed Bayard?'

'Fine, I think. We've exchanged a couple of words, that's all.'

'Berchmans approves.'

'I know. He's signed firm for "The Bag-Lady".'

'Great.'

'I'm having good comments all round.'

'I too. You're launched, my love.'

'God bless this ship . . . '

' . . . And all who sail in her.'

They touched glasses and drank just as Edmund Bayard approached, smiling and relaxed.

'Can we have that toast again? I'd like to drink it with you.'

They drank again. Bayard said, 'My compliments, my thanks to you both. This is a splendid night. I never expected anything half so good.'

'It's Madi's material, Ed.'

'Plus a lot of loving care. The sales appear to be going well.'

'Very.'

'You won't mind if I slip away before the ceremony upstairs? I could use a little quiet time after this – I'm sure you understand.'

'Of course. Do you need transport?'

'No. My man's waiting.'

He detached himself from them and slipped away through the crowd. Then George Munsel came over with Danny Danziger and Carol. He was smiling and in good spirits but Danny was tense and restless.

'Carol is taking me home now. I'm finding it all too much – Madi's pictures first and then the stares and whispers as I pass.'

'You wouldn't stay for the Raphaels? After all, you had a big hand in that.'

'I'd like to, Max, but truly . . . '

'She's had enough,' put in Carol brusquely. 'I'll get her home. Congratulations on the show, it's great. Maybe I can talk to you some time about my own stuff?'

'Any time,' said Anne-Marie. 'Drive safely.'

Mather looked at his watch. 'Time to get 'em upstairs. I'll go and give the signal.'

It took nearly ten minutes to get them all to the second floor, free of glasses and eatables, and assemble them in the rows of seats facing the pair of easels under the watchful eyes of the security men. Berchmans and Palombini stood at the back, chatting amiably. Mather collected Gisela and went to join them. Palombini was delighted to see her again and Berchmans' dark eyes brightened with approval. At a nod from Mather, Harmon Seldes mounted the rostrum and in his slightly pompous style

319

related the history of his first meeting with Mather and the decision to publish his material in *Belvedere*. He did a brief song and dance about the power of the press and the surprising outreach of even an eclectic publication like *Belvedere* – which, he was happy to announce, would be sponsoring the seminars.

Then, before he unveiled the pictures, he said, 'Now, ladies and gentlemen, all of us here are educated in the fine arts – some more, some less; but all of us are capable of making up our minds about the authenticity and basic value of a work. I am going to show you two portraits – portraits of the same subject: a sixteenth-century Florentine matron. One is an authenticated original by Raffaello Sanzio of Urbino . . . it is one of the lost Palombini pieces to which I have just referred. The other is a copy by one of the acknowledged modern masters of this craft, Maestro Niccoló Tolentino who is here tonight. I shall invite your opinion by a show of hands as to which is the original and which the copy. You may come up and inspect them both, but you will please refrain from touching the surfaces. Are you ready? *Voilà*!'

He lifted the sheets and there was a gasp of surprise as the two panels were revealed. It was a mass reaction, a theatrical response to an essentially theatrical moment. Then, marshalled by the guards, the audience filed slowly past the portraits studying them in silence. When they were all seated again, Seldes called for a show of hands to indicate the original. The votes were six to four in favour of the copy.

Then Niccoló Tolentino took the stage and with a very Florentine flourish acknowledged the vote as a tribute to his own skill – but regretfully passed the honour to the Maestro Raffaello from Urbino. They liked his style. They applauded. They listened in dead silence as he explained the history of the commission, the technical demands upon his skill as a painter, the search for traditional pigments and media, the preparation of the panels, the differences between one timber and another . . . the difference between a copy and a forgery.

As a *confèrencier* he was an instant success. His small crooked figure radiated strength and authority while his heavy accent lent charm to a lively and exotic discourse, but his final peroration held them spellbound.

'What is the difference between me and the long-dead Master

320

who painted this panel? Brush-stroke for brush-stroke, line for line – nothing. I know as much as he did – in fact, I know more. I have a wider range of supports, of pigments, of media, of solvents than he ever had. I have at my fingertips a far wider range of instruments and techniques. But still, when I stand beside the Master, I am a pygmy beside a giant. I am primal clay before God breathed into it the breath of life. I watched you all tonight in the gallery below, reading your catalogues, talking prices and auctions and who sold what for how much. Who cares? What does it matter? What matters is that you were moved as I was by the living spirit of a woman dead too soon to reach the full flowering of her genius. Or perhaps not. Perhaps she had said all she needed to say – and who will be bold enough to claim that the full-blown rose is more perfect than the opening bud? I presume, I know. I come to this great city in your new world and I presume to make sermons to you. But there is a reason. I stand every day before the works of great masters: a small crooked man who cannot remember when he did not have a brush in his hand and yet, infidel though I am, I make a cry to God. "Why, oh Lord . . . why to them and not to me? Just once, just once before I die, give me light!"'

After which, as George Munsel remarked in his dry fashion, all else was postscript – and dispensable. The guests filed out slowly, pausing to make another circuit of the Bayards before leaving. The security men marched back to the van with the Raphaels, true and false, carried like precious relics in the centre of the phalanx. The caterers packed away their plates and glassware. The two night-watchmen came on duty. Anne-Marie Loredon's staff and the small temporary family which had grown up around her – with Hartog and Bechstein roped in as a goodwill gesture – gathered for one last drink.

After all the excitement it was hard to believe it was still only nine-thirty, harder yet to believe that in three short hours they had sold twenty canvases and put four more on reserve for public galleries. What was even more notable – but not even mentioned – was that Berchmans and Palombini had settled on a guarantee of forty million for the Donna Delfina, which a little Japanese in the audience, moved by Tolentino's eloquence, had already bought for fifty because his company had an embarrassing number of devalued dollars to be spent in a hurry.

Palombini, flush and footloose in New York and happy to find that Anne-Marie spoke fluent Italian, proposed a celebration supper in Little Italy where a distant relative owned a restaurant called La Cenerentola. So, leaving the address with the night-watchmen against the unlikely event that anyone should call to reserve a canvas, they trooped out into the street where the last of the limousines were waiting to transport the new plutocracy to their watering-place.

Edmund Justin Bayard stood in the dining room of his apartment and looked about him. Stripped of the pictures, the wallpaper was a patchwork of light and dark rectangles created by uneven exposure to light and to the dust motes from the air-conditioning system. The whole place looked intolerably shabby. It would have to be redecorated, he decided. And then what? A new collection? Commission a suite of frescoes like some Renaissance prince? Not impossible. An agreeable fantasy for a wealthy bachelor. Only one problem: who would share the fantasy, who would even take the time or the trouble to understand it?

One good thing: there was nothing left of Madeleine now. It was as if her ashes had at last been scattered to the cleansing winds. Not without honour, mind you. Not without piety and respect. Tonight had been a worthy occasion, like the old translations of sacred relics from secret places to great basilicas, for public veneration. And, by God, there had been veneration and respect. That crowd tonight was a real college of surgeons, eager to declare the body clinically dead so that they could begin to dismember it. But there, in that place where she had died, Madeleine was alive – dominating the spectators as once she had dominated him.

That was the problem, of course. To dominate, you had to be indifferent . . . to the infliction of pain, to the deprivation of pleasure, the diminution of rights. He had thought himself tolerant. In her rages Madeleine had screamed that he was a tyrant. In fact he was neither; he was an intelligent man, but made of a clay too fragile to be fired in the kilns of passion. So he had emerged, cracked and flawed, while Madeleine, with all the dross burned away, was like a perfect Sung vase, *pai Ting* with teardrops in the glaze.

He had no tears left to shed. He was conscious only of calm . . . the calm of a great desert, cold and windless under a white moon. All sense of guilt was gone. Nemesis, the Daughter of Night, had accepted his amends knowing that the mulct would be paid in full.

As for Anne-Marie, she was a might-have-been for whom, even in the windless calm, he could still feel a small chill of regret. May and September? Well, it might just have worked. Beauty and the Beast? Sometimes, more rarely, that worked too.

Max Mather? Now there was a strange one. A tightrope walker, teetering on the high-wire without a net, making it in one last skittering run to safety. A man to envy, perhaps, but not emulate.

So, as he undressed and put on his best silk dressing-gown, the accounts seemed to tally at last. The Daughter of Night beckoned. It was time for the final tribute. He went to the bathroom and took from the medicine cabinet a plastic bottle full of sleeping pills. Then he went to his study, poured himself a whisky and put on the tape of Mahler's Ninth. From the bookshelves he took down a volume which had belonged to his father – *La très joyeuse, plaisante et récréative histoire du bon Chevalier de Bayard* – and as he began to read, picking his way through the archaic phrases, he sipped the whisky and swallowed the tablets.

The last words that registered on his fading consciousness were those of an old proverb: 'Whenever a man dies, somewhere another is grateful. . . . ' It was a proposition he found perfectly acceptable.

'Your client's still on the hook.' Bechstein was contesting every inch of ground. 'She had motive . . . sexual humiliation by Madeleine and her playmates, jealousy, all that tangle of emotions. She had opportunity. She was alone with Madeleine at the relevant time – about which she is lying, because we have a witness who puts her arrival an hour later. Then we have the written testimony of the late Hugh Loredon who says the following: Danny called him. He told her to leave immediately.

Later he came and found Madeleine dead, took the weapon and cleaned out her papers. You've got a copy of the letter in your hands.'

'Question.' This from George Munsel. 'Why would he bother to write that letter at all? He knew he was going to die. It wasn't a confession; it was an accusation against Danny Danziger.'

'Our view is that he did it for exactly the reason he expressed to Mr Mather here. He didn't want his own daughter to think her father was a killer.'

'That's not enough.' Mather was beginning to be angry. 'It doesn't explain why he would frame Danny Danziger. As the act of a man who's just about to make his exit from life, it doesn't make sense. It's too . . . too cold-blooded!'

'By me,' said Bechstein, 'it's a common enough syndrome: rejected lover, rejected rapist, male unsatisfied for whatever reason demands revenge by the humiliation or destruction of the female.'

'Loredon was a born liar; I called him so to his face.'

'His answer, Mr Mather?'

'All he said was, "Prove it".'

'And that's exactly what we're saying.' Sam Hartog was back in the talk. 'For Pete's sake, we're not trying to crucify the girl, but you must give us more than we've got. Bayard's suicide leaves us in a worse mess than before. He didn't leave a single scrap of paper -- no goodbyes, no whys or wherefores. . . . '

'We're about to show you why,' George Munsel told him, 'and this evidence is documented.'

'Then please let's have it,' said Bechstein wearily.

'You lead, Max.'

Mather spread out before him the diaries, the sketchbooks, the notebook and the bundles of letters, identifying each as he did so. Beside them he laid his own notes on the Amsterdam talks and his analysis of the manuscripts. Then with academic care he began.

'We distinguish first between internal evidence – that which is recorded or implied in the documents – and external evidence, which is available elsewhere. When the two coincide, we are on very solid ground. You'll agree that proposition?'

Hartog and Bechstein nodded.

'Let's begin with the period just before Madeleine's death. Internal and external evidence coincide on the following points: the Bayard marriage is a mess; Madeleine is living a highly promiscuous life with lovers of both sexes; Hugh Loredon is one of the males, Danny Danziger is one of the females. Why don't the Bayards divorce? All the evidence points to a strange perverse dependence on each other . . . the vices of one excuse the failures of the other.'

He read them a series of brief passages from his conversations with Bayard and from Madeleine's diaries, then he asked, 'Are we agreed, then, that what we have is an apparently stable but highly explosive situation both in the marriage and in Madeleine's private world?'

'I'd agree that,' said Bechstein. Hartog nodded.

'Now,' said Mather, 'let's take a very careful look at the internal evidence. Bayard's conversations first. He's a lawyer. He's trained to be very careful about the *form* of what he says. He tells me, for instance, that he holds no rancour against Loredon or any other of his wife's lovers for taking what she offers. He says he has unreserved admiration for Madi's talent. But his actions belie what he is saying. He won't let Madi exhibit. In domestic life he is querulous, bitter and destructive. Now turn to Madi. The diaries, the notebook and the sketchbooks each tell us the same story from a different angle. They tell us the truth. They don't necessarily give us a truthful rendering of fact.'

'A nice point.' Munsel approved.

'You've lost me,' Sam Hartog said.

'My uncle is a rabbi,' remarked Bechstein cryptically.

Mather picked up the thread of his argument once more.

'Madeleine was an artist. Like every artist, she rearranged things – in her own mind, on the canvas. She changed the light, the emphasis, the composition, the order of events and their emotional tone.'

Turning back to his notes, he read both the diary version and Danny's version of the invasive episode with Peter. Then he turned the pages of the sketchbook and showed them her pictorial version of the same incident. All the ugliness was gone out of it. All that was left was a beautifully drawn slightly comic version of Priapic frenzy.

'Do you see my point, gentlemen?' Mather asked.

'We do,' said Bechstein. 'It's well taken. But think about it a little longer. Madeleine has staged her pornodrama. She's got her picture. Peter has got his model's fee and his fun. But Danny Danziger has effectively been raped – and acquired a very good motive for murder.'

'Which she didn't commit,' Munsel put in.

'Prove it to me,' challenged Hartog.

Mather pointed to the male figure in the drawing. 'That's your witness, isn't it? That's the guy who's prepared to swear he saw Danny arriving an hour later than she actually did.'

Bechstein and Hartog looked at each other. Bechstein said, 'That's the one.'

'Now,' said Mather, 'let me read you what Madi writes about him.' He gave them Madeleine's version of Peter's attack on her line for line, then turned back to his Amsterdam notes. 'With all that in mind, I want you to listen very carefully to Loredon's version of Madeleine's death in which he casts Danny as the killer.' As he read them the notes they listened intently, sometimes exchanging covert glances. Then he began to comment on the story.

'Hugh Loredon is very clever, because Madi is still the one setting up the encounter but this time the partner is a woman. Listen to the description of the scene. It's very carefully worked up – two glasses smeared with lipstick, the dregs of a bottle of champagne. Did you find those when you first went in? I'm damned sure you didn't. The police photographs prove they weren't there. Then there are the nice details about the rubber gloves and the dagger and Danny's disposal of it. I note all that's in the letter he sent you. According to his version, all this took place between two-thirty and three in the afternoon. Right?'

'Right,' agreed Bechstein.

'When Bayard called to report the murder of his wife, what time was it?'

'About six-thirty.'

'And you got there when?'

'Fifteen minutes later, more or less.'

'Bayard was nursing his wife's body and was covered with fresh blood?'

'That's right.'

'If it had been lying in one place for nearly four hours, wouldn't the blood have congealed enough to be sticky and viscous?'

'What are you saying?'

'That the murder took place much later than three – and Hugh Loredon staged it. He stripped Madi, who was still in a drugged sleep, then laid her clothes neatly on the chair and wrapped her in the quilt to prevent any spurting of blood. He rifled her purse, scanned the studio to find the diaries and sketchbooks, killed her just before Bayard arrived and left by the back door, taking the weapon with him.'

'You can prove that?' It was Hartog's question.

'Yes. When I accused him of lying and he admitted it, he told me that he himself took the weapon and later got rid of it by putting it in an auction of antique arms at Christies. He said it brought two thousand dollars.'

'That should be easy enough to check,' said Bechstein.

'I've already checked it,' Mather told him. 'The piece was bought by a collector of antique arms in Connecticut. He will make it available for police examination.'

'It won't show anything. The important thing is whether Loredon put it up for sale.'

'He did. That's in the record.'

'So there's a good break for your client. What else can you give us?'

'A motive for Loredon to kill her.'

'Which was?'

'Money. He was broke, or nearly broke as he always was; but now there was a difference. He had received a death sentence and wanted to leave something for Anne-Marie. It shamed him to think he couldn't.'

'But he was Madi's lover.'

'By this time a very bitter one. I have some notes on that too.'

'Don't bother, just tell me about the money – how much and who paid and when?'

'Two hundred thousand dollars,' said George Munsel, 'paid by Ed Bayard seven days after Madeleine's death into a trust fund administered by Lutz & Hengst to the benefit of Anne-Marie Loredon.'

'You can prove that?'

'Chapter and verse,' Munsel said. 'And Bayard knew I could.'

'How would he know?' Bechstein was as persistent as a ferret.

'Because,' said Munsel patiently, 'when Lutz & Hengst gave me the information they told me they would, as a matter of protocol, report my inquiry to Bayard.'

Hartog weighed in with a comment: 'And Bayard, being an old-fashioned gentleman, decided enough was enough and took himself out of the game.'

'He wasn't a gentleman.' Bechstein, it seemed, was the old-fashioned one. 'The bastard left someone else to clean up his mess.'

'Enough.' Mather was suddenly sick of the argument. 'He's dead. Leave him to God.'

'I'm happy to do that,' said George Munsel, 'but first I need a clean bill for my client.'

In the courtyard of Tor Merla, where once the pikemen had drilled and the cannoneers had lit their braziers, the first sun was warming the old stones and blackbirds were stirring in the chestnut tree. On the further hills the cypresses stood black against the dawn. Down in the valley the campaniles thrust themselves up through the mist and the Angelus rang, now clear, now muffled, in a counterpoint of chimes.

Max Mather stood at the window of the tower, breathed in the damp morning air and looked over the landscape – familiar in every peak and fold and farmhouse. It was a moment poignant with tenderness and regret, yet somehow luminous and healing.

Claudio Palombini had insisted that he come . . . Claudio, confident, restored in fortune, yet somehow changed, not half so arrogant as he used to be. On settling day in Zurich, with certified cheques changing hands and the bank official, sombre as an undertaker, presiding at the ceremony, Mather had felt ill at ease, vaguely ashamed. Claudio had seen his discomfort and said, 'No arguments, Max. We're quits. The documents say so, I say so. What you have, you earned. If you don't take it, the tax man gets it.'

Mather had shrugged and grinned uncomfortably. 'In that case, I'll buy the lunch.'

But for Claudio that had not been enough. Suddenly he had become the hard-head, the gonfalonier marshalling his minions into line.

'I refuse to leave it like this, Max. This isn't money any more; this is honour, family, *fratellanza*. But I am not going to stand here and argue with you. You must come back to Tor Merla. You must bring your girl. You will both need that.'

'We'll get round to it, Claudio, but I'm not sure I can face a sentimental journey just now. Matrimony alone is a scary project.'

'You have no choice. I shall invite Gisela myself – she will understand how important it is. No more discussions now. You buy me lunch.'

All that had been weeks ago in Zurich. Now Gisela was awake, standing barefoot beside him, waiting to be kissed.

When the kissing was done, she asked, 'What do you see out there, my love?'

'A lot of yesterdays. I'm not sure it was wise to come.'

'I'm glad we did. Claudio was right. It was a journey we both had to make.'

'I'm still not sure.'

'Why?'

'How can I say it?' The words were hard to find, harder still to say. 'The best of me is in this place, sitting down there in the courtyard with Pia – reading to her, listening to her music, brightening the small time she had left. . . . The worst of me is here too, driving out of that gate and down the road with the Raphaels in my luggage, a rogue – that's right, a rogue – scared of losing what I didn't own. Now I'm back; rich with money I haven't earned, gifted with a woman I don't deserve.'

'Are you too proud to accept them, Max?'

'Proud? My God, if only you knew. . . . '

'I do know. I know that unless you can forgive yourself and accept yourself, you're going to go on hating the man you see in the mirror. When that gets boring – as it will – you will start hating me; and then it will be Bayard and Madeleine all over again.'

'God forbid!'

'That's right, Max. God forbid!'

'But don't deceive yourself. It isn't as easy as it sounds to love Max Mather.'

'Whoever said loving was easy? Wait until you've been married to me for six months!'

Whereat the blackbirds broke out of the chestnut tree and flew off in a ragged black cloud towards the mountains, while the last nine strokes of the bells rose and fell and faded into the silence of the Tuscan dawn.